ANGÉLIQUE

Her first husband was supposedly burned at the stake for sorcery. Her second was killed in a siege. Now fleeing the king, she is swept up in the bloody Huguenot uprising.

ANGÉLIQUE

The most ravished and most ravishing heroine in fiction is caught up in the most exciting and perilous adventure of her tempestuous career.

"Her kaleidoscopic adventures will hold the reader enthralled."

—Denver Post

Angélique in Revolt

Sergeanne Golon

Translated from the French
by Marguerite Barnett

A NATIONAL GENERAL COMPANY

ANGÉLIQUE IN REVOLT

*A Bantam Book / published by arrangement with
G. P. Putnam's Sons*

PRINTING HISTORY

Originally published in France as Angélique se Révolte

Putnam's edition published May 1963

Bantam edition published August 1964

2nd printing ...... August 1964	6th printing .... June 1967
3rd printing .... June 1966	7th printing .... July 1968
4th printing .... June 1966	8th printing ... September 1969
5th printing ...... August 1966	9th printing .... April 1970

New Bantam edition published April 1971

Published simultaneously in the United States and Canada

Bantam Books are published by Bantam Books, Inc., a National
General company. Its trade-mark, consisting of the words "Bantam
Books" and the portrayal of a bantam, is registered in the United
States Patent Office and in other countries. Marca Registrada.
Bantam Books, Inc., 666 Fifth Avenue, New York, N.Y. 10019.

PRINTED IN THE UNITED STATES OF AMERICA

THE NOVEL is set in the France of the mid-1670s, when a new wave of persecution of the Protestant Huguenots was sweeping the country.

The following is a list of the principal characters, including those of any importance mentioned in retrospect. Those marked with an asterisk are known more or less prominently in history.

Angélique. Born Angélique de Sancé de Monteloup, of a family of the minor nobility in Poitou, she first married Comte Joffrey de Peyrac of Toulouse, Prince of Aquitaine, by whom she had two sons, Florimond and Cantor. Although lame and marked by scars, Joffrey was a man of remarkable force of character and brilliant gifts, and Angélique came to love him passionately. He was condemned by Louis XIV to be burnt at the stake on a trumped-up charge of sorcery and was supposedly executed in February 1661. Reduced to extreme poverty, Angélique became a member of the Paris underworld centred on the Court of Miracles. She later opened a chocolate shop, made a great deal of money and gradually re-entered society. Having been in love with her handsome cousin Philippe, Marquis de Plessis-Bellière, since they were both adolescents, she more or less blackmailed him into marrying her and regained a high position in Court circles. They had one son, Charles-Henri. Philippe was a brutal man and jealous of Angélique's success at Court and of Louis XIV's passion for her. He was killed at a siege in Franche-Comté. Angélique became convinced that Joffrey de Peyrac had not died at the stake and decided to set out in search of him in defiance of the King's command that she was to stay in Paris. She fled to the Mediterranean, where she was captured by d'Escrainville, a brutal pirate, and sold as a slave in Candia (Crete) to a masked buccaneer, who frightened but fascinated her. She escaped from him only to fall into the hands of Sultan Mulai Ismail. With the help of Colin Paturel, a fellow-captive, she succeeded in escaping from Mulai Ismail's harem but was arrested by the French authorities in Ceuta and shipped back to France, where the King's wrath awaited her.

Albert de Sancé. Angélique's younger brother. He became a favourite of Monsieur, the King's brother, and later a monk in the Abbey of Nieul.

Aunt Anna. One of the La Rochelle Protestants. She was Maître Gabriel Berne's aunt.

Barbe. Nurse to Angélique's children.

Bardagne, Nicholas de. The King's Lieutenant in La Rochelle.

Baumier. Nicholas de Bardagne's second-in-command in La Rochelle. A fanatical bigot and a member of the Company of the Blessed Sacrament.

Berne, Maître Gabriel. A Protestant merchant of La Rochelle. He had once met Angélique by chance on the outskirts of Paris in her Court of Miracles days. He had lost his wife some seven years before the present action.

Camisot, Anselm. A soldier who guarded the Lantern Tower of La Rochelle.

Cantor. Angélique's second son by Joffrey de Peyrac. He joined the Duc de Vivonne as a page at the age of nine and was presumed drowned when the Duc's fleet was sunk by Rescator in the Mediterranean.

Charles-Henri. Angélique's son by Philippe du Plessis-Bellière.

*Condé, Louis (II) de Bourbon, Prince de (1621-86). "The Great Condé." He fought against the Court during the Fronde, a minor civil war fought under Cardinal Mazarin's regency while Louis XIV was still a child. Defeated by Turenne, he was pardoned and became one of the King's most brilliant generals.

Denis de Sancé. Brother to Angélique. At first a soldier, he later retired to the family estate at Monteloup.

Desgrez, François. Lieutenant of the Paris police. He had been in love with Angélique during her days of poverty.

Escrainville, Marquis d'. A young noble whose diplomatic career was ruined by amorous intrigue. He turned pirate, captured Angélique and sold her to Rescator.

Flipot. Angélique's lackey, known to her from her Court of Miracles days.

Florimond. Angélique's elder son by Joffrey de Peyrac. The King had arranged for him to be placed in a Jesuit College during Angélique's absence from France.

*Fouquet (1615-80), *Comptroller of France to* 1661. His extravagance aroused the King's envy and suspicion, and he was sentenced to life-imprisonment in the fortress of Pignerol for peculation.

Gontran de Sancé. Angélique's elder brother who became a painter and was disinherited by his father.

Laurier. Gabriel Berne's seven-year-old son whose birth caused his mother's death.

*Lauzun (1632-1723). A favourite of Louis XIV. Angélique had had a passing weakness for him. His romance with Louis XIV's cousin, La Grande Mademoiselle,

caused a great flurry in Court circles. He subsequently incurred the King's displeasure and was imprisoned for five years at Pignerol.

La Violette. Steward and valet to Philippe du Plessis-Bellière. He became a member of Angélique's household after Philippe's death.

Lesdiguiére Father de. A young priest who had been Florimond's tutor.

Louvois (1641-91). Minister of War under Louis XIV.

Malbrant. An old man who taught Angélique's sons fencing and horsemanship. He was nicknamed "Swordthrust."

Martial. Gabriel Berne's fifteen-year-old son.

Marillac, Monsieur de. Governor of Poitou. He tried to stamp out Protestantism in the province.

Mélusine. A witch living in a cave in the forest of Nieul.

Mezzo-Morte (d. 1698). A pirate who became Lord High Admiral of Algiers.

Molines. The Huguenot steward of the Plessis estates.

Monsieur (Philippe, Duc d'Orléans) (1640-1701). Brother of Louis XIV, notorious for his effeminacy and profligate life.

Montadour, Captain. A fat, red-headed army captain billeted at Plessis to guard Angélique.

Morinière, Samuel de La. A powerful and intransigent Huguenot lord, who with his brother Hugh and Lancelot led the Protestant faction in the Poitou revolt.

Mulai Ismail (1647-1727), *Sultan of Morocco.* A cruel

though brilliant ruler who held Angélique prisoner in his harem.

Nicholas. A shepherd boy in Nieul Forest when Angélique was a child. Later he became a beggar and Angélique's lover at the Court of Miracles.

Osman Faraji. Grand Eunuch of Mulai Ismail, Sultan of Morocco. He was reputed to be a seer.

Paturel, Colin. A Norman sailor and sometime pirate who, after being captured by the Moors, became the leader of the Christian slaves in Morocco. He helped Angélique to escape from Mulai Ismail's harem and became her lover.

Raymond de Sancé. Angélique's eldest brother. Rector of a Jesuit College at Morens.

Rebecca. Old servant-woman in the Berne household.

Rescator. A pirate on the Mediterranean. He bought Angélique as a slave in Candia for 35,000 piastres. He always wore a mask.

Reynie, Monsieur de La. Head of the State Police Force.

Rochat. A French civil servant in Crete.

*Rochefort, Pastor. A Huguenot traveller who wrote about the new World.

Rodogone, the Egyptian. One of the vagabonds at the Court of Miracles.

Savary. A little old apothecary and alchemist whom Angélique had known at Versailles. He helped to save her from Rescator in Candia by setting the latter's ship on fire.

Séverine. Gabriel Berne's twelve-year-old daughter.

Valentine. The Miller of the Ablettes. As a boy he had been one of Angélique's playmates. Later he fell in love with her.

*Vivonne, Victor de Rochechouart, Duc de (1636-88). Brother of Madame de Montespan, Admiral of the French fleet and associate of Monsieur.

The Smouldering Fire

ON ARRIVAL at Marseilles Monsieur de Breteuil, the King of France's envoy, who had arrested Angélique at Ceuta, locked her up in the Admiralty prison. As long as they remained in the town where, not long since, the Marquise du Plessis-Bellière had so thoroughly fooled the royal police, the noble lord would never feel quite safe.

So it was a dark and gloomy dungeon that Angélique, erstwhile prisoner of the men of Barbary, fugitive from Mulai Ismail's harem, from which it had cost her so much suffering to escape, became convinced that she was going to have a baby.

The idea occurred to her the day after her imprisonment in the citadel when she woke up and realized that she was once again strapped like an animal.

The Admiralty prison lacked the barest essentials for her comfort. In spite of the patch of blue sky peeping in between the bars of the high-set window Angélique had the desperate feeling that she was suffocating. All night long she had fought against the horrible sensation that she was buried alive. It had come over her as soon as she closed her eyelids, and at dawn her nerves, which had held out tolerably well so far, gave way entirely.

She flung herself against the door in a fit of panic and beat her hands against the hard wood without uttering a cry but with frenzied strength.

The sky! The sky! Fresh air! They had shut her up in this tomb, a woman who for days and nights on end had known nothing but the vast enchanted circle of the desert.

The sense of constraint was a cruel torment to her.

3

Like a distracted bird trapped in its cage she bruised her limbs against the inexorable barrier of wood and iron, beating silently against it ever and again; for her frail hands, which still bore the marks of her privations in the desert, made no more noise against the massive door than the rustle of a bird's wing. When she felt the sting of her raw palms, she stopped hammering and drew back to lean on the wall.

Her eyes went back and forth from the door to the barred window. The blue of the sky was like fresh water after which she thirsted. But no Osman Faraji would come to fetch her and take her up on to the flat roof so that she could enjoy at least the illusion of space. The men about her were strangers with sullen eyes and hearts full of suspicion. From Paris the Duc de Vivonne, anxious to make up for his own past offences, had issued most severe orders against her. The Marseilles Admiralty was to give Monsieur de Breteuil every possible assistance. It would have been fruitless to try to win anyone over to her cause, and in any case she felt in no condition to make use of her weapons. An appalling weariness weighed upon her, and she thought she had never experienced anything like it, even on the paths of the Riff mountains.

The sea voyage from Ceuta to Marseilles with a call at Cadiz had been one long torment during which a little more of her courage had evaporated each day. It was almost as if Monsieur de Breteuil had destroyed her capacity to pick up the threads of her life again when he had arrested her in the King's name.

She dragged herself to her bed, which consisted of a very hard mattress on some boards, although that did not worry Angélique. She slept more soundly on it than in a feather bed, and the only resting place she could have wished for her aching limbs was a plot of turf somewhere yonder under the cedars.

Her gaze returned to the door. How many doors had closed behind her in the course of her life! she thought, and each one heavier and blanker than the last. Was it a game that fate delighted in playing with her, to punish her for what she had once been, a barefoooted child at

Monteloup, who had raced down the paths through the groves and the forest, so wildly in love with freedom that the peasants thought her half-bewitched?

"Thou shalt not pass," said the doors, and every time she succeeded in escaping another door rose up hastily, more inexorable than the last. After the door of poverty had come the King of France's door, then the gates of Mulai Ismail's harem, then again, today, the King of France. Would he prove the strongest?

She thought of Fouquet, of the Marquis de Vardes and even that Will-o'-the-wisp Lauzun, who were all prisoners too, not far away in the Pignerol fortress, and of all who behind prison bars were paying the price of unruly behaviour which had been less serious than hers.

A realization of her isolation and weakness overwhelmed her. When she had set foot on the soil of France once more she had entered a world in which men had only two standards of action: fear of the King or love of the King. Whichever way it was, the master's law took precedence over all else.

On these shores the physical and moral strength of a man like Colin Paturel, his infinite kindness, his subtle intellect, had no currency. Any dull lout wearing cuffs and a wig could look down on him.

On these shores Colin Paturel was powerless. He was only a simple sailor. Even his memory could not help Angélique. He had passed out of her life more completely than if he were dead.

She called him softly: "Colin, Colin, my sweet!"

Her distress was so great that she broke out in a cold sweat and felt faint. At that moment the idea occurred to her that perhaps she was pregnant by him.

At Ceuta she had put down the absence of certain physical phenomena to her shattered state of health resulting from her superhuman hardships, but now, with the passage of time, another explanation suggested itself to her and there could be no further doubt.

She was going to have a baby.

Colin Paturel's child! A child of the desert! She remained quite still, curled up on her mattress, while she

5

allowed doubt to turn into certainty, make its way into her and fill her being.

At first there was surprise, then a strange peace, and finally joy. It might have been distress, shame, a final overwhelming discouragement. Instead it was joy.

She was still too close to the desert and the burnous she had worn as an escaped prisoner to have entirely resumed the attitudes of a great French lady along with her costume. One whole part of herself still remained pressed to the Norman's heart, in the depths of those tinted, gold-studded nights when the force of love impelled them towards one another and had the savour of death and eternity.

Beneath the corseted French dresses, beneath the embroidered cloak and the jewels she had taken to wearing again at Ceuta, her skin was still rough, and she still bore the deep scar on her burned leg, and the other scars from the whiplashes on her back, although little by little they were fading. Inside her elegant shoes her feet had not lost the calluses they had acquired climbing the stone paths of the Riff.

She thought with a great surge of excitement that the traces of her fantastic Odyssey would remain indelibly with her through the child which would be born of her.

He would be fair-haired, broad-shouldered and strongly built. What did it matter that he was illegitimate? The sterling qualities of the man who had been the "king" of the captives made him the equal in point of nobility of the crusaders whose blood flowed in the veins of Angélique de Sancé de Monteloup. His son would have his eyes and his strength. A little god-Hercules brandishing his club, strangling the snakes, his head set in a halo of Mediterranean sunshine!

He would be as handsome as the first male child born on earth.

It was as if she could see him, and she marvelled at his life. For him and through him she would find strength and win him his liberty.

She remained a long time thus, giving herself up to her almost delirious reverie, forgetting the fortress walls, and sometimes nearly speaking aloud:

6

"No matter that you have fled from me, Colin," she said; "no matter that you have despised and rejected me. You will be with me all the same, Colin, my sweetheart, my darling. . . ."

A few days later a coach with windows barred and black curtains drawn left Marseilles and set out on the road to Avignon. It was escorted by a strong guard of ten musketeers. Monsieur de Breteuil, who was travelling inside with Angélique, was forcing the pace.

He had heard so much about the incredible cleverness and cunning of Madame du Plessis-Bellière that he was constantly expecting her to slip between his fingers; the one subject he could think of was the completion of his mission.

The fact that the young woman had appeared to overcome her fatigue made him anxious. That she sat upright and was occasionally rude to him made him fear the worst. She must be expecting help from her accomplices.

It is scarcely an exaggeration to say that he slept stretched out in front of her door, when they stopped for the night, and slept with one eye open at that.

Before passing through a forest where there was a risk of attack by armed bands bent on rescuing the prisoner, he moved heaven and earth to persuade the governor of the nearest town to grant him an extra contingent of soldiers. The travelling party began to look like a military expedition. Crowds gathered in the squares of the towns along the route and tried to catch a glimpse of the personage whose transport required such numbers of men. Monsieur de Breteuil paid men-at-arms to disperse the crowds with their halberds, but that only added to the curiosity and made the crowds bigger than ever.

Short of sleep and consumed by anxiety, Monsieur de Breteuil saw only one way out of his torments—speed. He would put up for a few hours only each night at inns from which the regular guests had been ejected and whose innkeepers had been kept under close surveillance. During the day the horses were given no respite, being constantly replaced by fresh animals, which a

7

courier riding on ahead ordered in advance so that there should be no delay when the carriage reached a posting stage.

Shaken by the bumps in the road and worn out by this mad race across the country, Angélique protested:

"Do you wish to kill me, sir? Let us stop for a few hours to rest. I'm completely exhausted."

Monsieur de Breteuil sniggered.

"You've got very delicate all of a sudden, Madame. Were not the hardships you underwent in the Kingdom of Morocco even more severe?"

Angélique did not dare tell him that she was pregnant.

Clinging to the seat or the door, nauseated by the dust, she prayed for one thing and one thing only—that they would at last reach the end of this nightmare journey.

One evening, after a particularly trying day, as the coach was galloping into a bend near the top of a hill, the vehicle tilted over on two wheels, then capsized. The postilion, who had seen the accident coming, had had time to rein in the horses. The jolt was less violent than might have been feared, but Angélique was hurled towards the near side and was pinned under the seat, which had come loose. She realized at once what was happening to her, quickly they removed her from the carriage and laid her on the grass slope by the roadside. Monsieur de Breteuil leaned over her with ashen face. If Madame du Plessis were to die, the King would never forgive him. In a flash of intuition he realized that his life was at stake, and he imagined that he could feel the chilly steel of the executioner's axe on the back of his neck.

"Madame," he implored, "are you hurt? It's not serious, is it? It was only a slight jolt."

Despairing, wild-eyed, she shrieked at him in a strange voice:

"It's all your fault! Driving like a madman! . . . You've deprived me of all I had. I've lost everything now through you!"

8

She threw out her hands and tore at his cheeks with her nails.

The soldiers carried her into the neighbouring town on an improvised stretcher. They were dismayed to see bloodstains on her dress and thought she must be seriously injured. But when the surgeon they had called in had done examining her, he declared that the case was not one for him, and that they should send for a midwife.

Lying in the Mayor's residence, Angélique could feel her own life ebbing away with that other life.

The huge burgher's house was pervaded by the smell of cabbage soup, which added to her nausea and her disgust with everything. The midwife's face, red and perspiring under her peasant's coif, kept on bobbing into her field of vision. Angélique's eyes ached as if she were staring into the setting sun. All night long the good woman struggled valiantly to save the strange, almost insubstantial creature with the honey-coloured hair spread around her on the pillow like moonbeams, and the oddly tanned face. The tan stood out in brown patches on her waxen skin, while her eyelids were of a leaden hue, and a purple ring marked the edges of her lips. The midwife recognized the death signs

"You mustna, my sugar," she breathed, bending over Angélique, who was only half-conscious, "you mustna . . ."

Angélique watched with supreme detachment while the shadowy shapes bustled about her. Now they were lifting her up and slipping clean sheets under her; then she was aware of the copper disk of the warming-pan as it traced its ceremonious patterns.

She felt better, and the cold which had chilled her limbs began to disappear. They rubbed her down and made her drink a cup of hot, spiced wine.

"Now you drink that, my dear, you must make new blood, you've lost too much."

She began to be aware of the sharp tang of the wine, and the taste of cinnamon and ginger.

Oh! The smell of spices, the smell of happy voy-

9

ages! ... Old Savary had died with those words on his lips.

Angélique opened her eyes. Before her was a big window with heavy curtains on either side. Against the panes crept a thick smoky fog.

"When will it be daybreak?" she murmured.

The rosy-cheeked woman who was standing at her bedside, gave her a pleased look.

"It's been day long since, bless you," she said cheerfully. "It's not the night you can see at the window, it's fog from the river down in the valley. A sharp morning it is this morning. The sort of weather when you're much better tucked up in your bed and not chasing about the countryside. You picked a good day for it and no mistake.

"Now that you're going to be all right, I'm bound to say that you had some luck with your accident. You got rid of that one all right, you did."

Taken aback by the wild glance thrown at her by her patient, the midwife persisted:

"Well, isn't that the way of it? For a great lady like you a baby is never welcome. I know what I'm talking about. I have enough of them coming to me to help them get rid of their brats. It's been done for you, and without much bother either, although I must say you did have me frightened for a while."

Perplexed by Angélique's continuing silence, she went on:

"Now believe you me, my good lady, you mustn't fret. Children are no good except to complicate your life for you. If you don't love them they're only in the way, and if you do they sap your strength."

She concluded with a shrug of the shoulders:

"And in any case, if you mind it as much as all that, you won't have any difficulty getting yourself another one, a beautiful creature like you!"

Angélique bit her tongue till it hurt. Colin Paturel's child could never be born again.

Now she felt utterly deprived. Everything was gone, everything! A violent emotion akin to hate began to stir within her and saved her from despair. It was like a raging torrent, that did not yet know which way it was to go, but it gave her the desire to fight on. It was a desperate longing to go on living so that she could take vengeance, vengeance for everything.

For, in spite of what she had already endured, she was clear-headed enough to realize that she was in considerable danger. Before long the journey which the Master of the Kingdom had decreed would continue; the armed guards would once again be about her and she would be treated like the basest of the King's subjects. But what was the punishment, what the prison to which she was journeying?

CHAPTER 2

A QUAVERING cry rose in the night, hung an instant upon the air, then faded, away, like a light going out. "A screech-owl," thought Angélique, "out on the hunt...."

Once again came the owl's thin hoot, soon dying away, muffled by the mists, rainbow-tinted under the moon.

Angélique propped herself up on one elbow. Lying on her mattress, which was spread on the floor, she looked at the gleaming black and white marble paving near her head and at the reflections of the furniture in its polished surface. At the far end of the room a soft milky radiance was streaming in through the open window, spreading and swelling through the gloom, bringing with it the enchantment of the spring night. Drawn by the light, Angélique rose to her feet, succeeded in keeping her balance, and advanced towards the silvery brightness with the faltering step of a lost soul. Standing rapt in the beams of the great round moon, which had just risen, she felt a sudden onset of faintness and had to support herself on the window-frame.

Before her rose the dark undulating lines of the forest profiled against the night sky, a crowded mass of trees rearing their leafy crests and stretching out their boughs like the arms of so many huge candelabra, while the

11

moonlight, streaming into the glades and clearings beyond, made their massy trunks stand out like the pillars of some dim temple.

"It's you! You!" she breathed.

From a near-by oak the hoot of the owl arose once more, sudden, sharp and piercing. It was like the voice of Nieul welcoming her home.

"You," she repeated, "you! My own forest! My own dear forest!'

That soft, warm stirring, so faint that at times it could be detected only a stronger waft of hawthorn blossom, was the gentle breath of the forest coming and going.

Angélique drew it in gratefully. Her parched lungs joyously greeted the familiar moist balm borne to her on the forest's breath and charged with the damp coolness of a thousand woodland springs and the perfume of fresh sap.

Her faintness fell from her, and she was able to abandon the support of the window and gaze about her. In a wooden frame above the alcove a young god of Olympus was disporting himself among the goddesses. She was at Plessis. It was the very same room in which long ago, as an inquisitive tomboy of sixteen, she had spied on the amorous sport of the Prince de Condé with the Duchesse de Beaufort.

It was on this same floor with the stately furniture reflected in its gleaming black and white surface that she had lain wracked with pain, weak and distraught, just as she was today, while her second husband, the handsome Philippe, staggered away down the corridors of the château after the cruel celebration of his wedding night. It was here too that she had taken refuge during the boredom of her second widowhood before yielding to the fascinations of Versailles.

Angélique got down and stretched out on her bed again, finding a restful pleasure in the very hardness of the floor. She wrapped herself in the blanket, curling up like an animal just as she had learnt to do in her burnous in the desert. A deep calm took the place of the torment of mind from which she had suffered all the time she had lain half-conscious throughout her illness.

"I'm home again, home again!" she murmured blissfully. "Nothing is impossible now...."

When she woke again, the sun had taken the moon's place, and her maidservant Barbe's whining voice was retailing its customary lamentations:

"There, just look, the poor lady. . . . It's always the same! Oh dear, oh dear! . . . Lying on the ground like a dog! It's a sheer waste of time me tucking her up in her bed every night. She manages somehow to drag her mattress down, as soon as I've turned my back, and she lies down on it like a sick animal. 'If you only knew how good the ground is to sleep on, Barbe,' she says, 'if you only knew how good it is!' What a shame! And she used to be such a one for her comfort too, and never could get enough blankets to suit her, she felt the cold so much. What those Barbary folk have managed to do in less than a year, you just wouldn't believe. You just tell the King, gentlemen . . . and my lady so beautiful and so refined too! It's not so long since you saw her at Versailles, and look at her now. It's enough to make you weep. I wouldn't believe it was her, if she still hadn't got the same old habit of acting to suit herself and nobody else, whatever you try to say to her! Savages like them don't deserve to be alive. The King should punish them, gentlemen!"

Around Angélique's low bed three pairs of lace-up boots and one pair of knee-boots took up their station. She knew that the pair with the red heels and the gilt buckles belong to Monsieur de Breteuil, but the others were strange to her.

She looked up. The knee-boots supported a fat-bellied personage, squeezed into a blue officer's coat and topped by a ruddy, moustachioed face with ginger hair.

The beaver-skin boots with the silver buckles but just the right touch of austerity, in which were planted a pair of skinny shanks, would have been sufficient identification for a pious courtier, even if Angélique had not immediately recognized their owner as the Marquis de Solignac.

The fourth personage, also with red heels and dia-

13

mond buckles, wore a large upstanding lace collar, a trifle old-fashioned. He had the stiff aristocratic face of a military lord, the severity of which was accentuated by a tuft of grey hairs on his chin. It was the latter, who, after bowing to the young woman lying at his feet, began to speak.

"May I introduce myself, Madame? I am the Marquis de Marillac, Governor of Poitou, whom His Majesty has commissioned to convey to you his orders and the decisions he has taken in respect of your case."

"Would you mind speaking a little louder, sir?" said Angélique, exaggerating her weakness. "I cannot hear what you are saying."

So Monsieur de Marillac had to go down on his knees so as to make himself heard, and his minions could not but do likewise. Angélique took in the spectacle through half-closed eyes, relishing the discomfiture of the four solemn boobies. She felt particularly pleased to notice that Monsieur de Brateuil's cheeks still bore the angry red weals left by her nails.

Meanwhile the Governor broke the seals and unrolled a parchment scroll. He cleared his throat:

"To Madame du Plessis-Bellière, Our subject, who has incurred Our displeasure by a grave act of rebellion. We, the King of France, find it necessary to make known to her Our sentiments in this regard, that she may never claim ignorance of them, and further to indicate to her the forms and conditions of her submission.

"Madame,

Great was Our sorrow when, a few months ago, you saw fit to repay by ingratitude and disobedience the favours and benefits We have deigned to shower upon you and yours. You flouted the orders We have given that you were not to leave Paris, although those orders were dictated only by the desire—knowing your impulsive nature—to save you from yourself and the ill-considered acts to which you might have been tempted. You did yield to these temptations, you did throw yourself in the way of the dangers and disillusions from which We hoped to save you, and you have been severely pun-

14

ished therefor. Your desperate appeal transmitted to Us by the Superior of the Redemptorists, Father de Valombreuze, upon his return from Morocco informed us of the deplorable situation into which your follies had brought you. Held captive by the men of Barbary, you were beginning to realize to the full the error of your ways, and with the inconsistency typical of your sex you turned to the Sovereign you had flouted to ask His succour.

Out of consideration for the great name you bear, the ties of friendship which bound Us to the Marshal du Plessis, and out of pity for you, who in spite of all remained not the least well loved of Our subjects, We did not wish you to bear the full burden of your punishment by abandoning you to those cruel barbarians, and We saw fit to respond to your appeal.

Now you are back once more safe and sound on French soil. We are well pleased.

It is, however, only just that you should tender your full and humble apologies.

We might have provided you with the necessary leisure for reflection by locking you up in a nunnery. The thought of the sufferings you have borne led Us to reject that idea. We preferred to send you to your estates, knowing that the soil of one's native place is the wisest of counsellors. You should not regard yourself as exiled there. You need remain there only until the day when you freely decide to set out for Versailles to make your submission. In expectation of that day—which We hope will not be far distant—an officer appointed by Monsieur de Marillac will be entrusted with your surveillance..."

Monsieur de Marillac broke off, looked up and pointed to the fat soldier:

"Allow me to present to you, Madame, Captain Montadour, whom I thought it right to entrust with the honour of guarding you."

At that precise moment the Captain was engaged in transferring his weight from one knee to the other, for he had suffered severe discomfort from the kneeling

15

posture to which his stout person was not accustomed. He almost fell, just managed to save himself, and declared in stentorian tones that he was at the Marquise du Plessis's service.

He was wasting his time. Angélique, who was still curled up in her blanket, with her eyes closed, seemed to be asleep.

Monsieur de Marillac went on gamely with his reading:

"We set forth hereinafter the terms under which Madame du Plessis is to make her submission. The unruly behaviour of the members of her family, one of whom has gone even to the point of rendering himself guilty of high treason, is too well known for his submission to assume any but the most public character, that those who might be tempted to follow such deplorable examples to their own perdition may be deflected from such rebellious courses.

She shall travel to Versailles in a carriage with black trappings. The carriage shall remain outside the gates and shall be refused entry to the Court of Honour.

Madame du Plessis shall be dressed in modest attire of sober colour.

In the presence of the entire Court she shall advance to meet the King, kneel before him, kiss His hand and renew her oath of allegiance and vassalage.

Moreover, she shall be called upon to make donation to the Crown of one of her fiefs in Touraine. The scrolls and deeds containing this cession shall be handed over to Our Lord Chamberlain during the aforementioned ceremony as a mark of homage and humble apology.

Henceforth Madame du Plessis shall devote every effort to serving her Sovereign with a fidelity which We insist shall be beyond reproach. She shall reside at Versailles, and accept such titles and honours as We see fit to grant her, which will be more irksome for her pride than not to be granted office at all; she shall discharge these offices scrupulously, and, in brief, she shall spare no effort to serve the King with devotion whether it be in His Kingdom, at His Court ..."

". . . or in His bed," concluded Angélique.

Monsieur de Marillac gave a start. For some moments he had been convinced that it was pointless to direct remarks of the type contained in the letter at an unfortunate creature lying half-conscious and desperately ill.

Angélique's interruption and the mocking glance of her half-closed eyes proved to him that she had been listening most attentively and that she was not in such a low state as she made out. The Governor's parchment-like cheeks reddened, and he said dryly:

"That is not stated in His Majesty's letter."

"No, but it is understood," rejoined Angélique sweetly.

Monsieur de Marillac scratched his throat and stammered a little before resuming:

. . . at His Court or in whatever place it may please His Majesty to send her in His service."

"Couldn't you stop there, sir? I'm tired."

"So are we," said the nobleman, losing his temper. "Are you not aware, Madame, of the posture in which you are compelling us to read to you. . . ."

"I am at death's door, sir."

An expression at once spiteful and fulsome appeared on the great lord's face.

"I should not advise you to spend too long there, Madame, for you must not think that His Majesty's patience is unlimited. And that brings up to the warning with which his letter concludes. The King, in his goodness, grants you several months to think things over before considering you for ever as an irreconcilable rebel. But once that time has passed, he will be implacable. It is now May, Madame; the King knows that you are ill and demoralized. He is resolved to be patient, but if by early October you have not made your submission as laid down in this document, he will consider your failure to do so as an act of rebellion."

"What will happen then?"

Monsieur de Marillac once more unfolded the King's letter.

17

"*Madame du Plessis will then be arrested and conducted to a fortress or a nunnery of Our choice. her residences will be placed under the Royal seal, and her town and country houses and her estates sold. Only the château of Plessis and the immediately surrounding lands will continue to be held in fief and in trust for Charles-Henri du Plessis, the Marshal's son and Our godson, of whom We shall assume custody.*"

"What of my son, Florimond?" asked Angélique, who had paled.

"There is no mention of him here."

There was a silence, and Angélique felt the smug gaze of these men she hardly knew fixed on her. She had done nothing to them, but they were rejoicing visibly in her defeat, so natural is it for degenerates to wish to see beauty brought low, and to humiliate those who refuse to crawl.

It would be a long time before Madame du Plessis raised her proud little head again and set up the barrier of her emerald eyes between the King and those who were vainly trying to influence him. She would only reappear at Versailles to submit to a humiliation which would tame her pride for good. She would then lose her indomitable strength, and be like the rest; she would became a compliant tool in hands made to guide and shape the destinies of men. Had they not done the right thing in advising the King to take a firm line?

Monsieur de Solignac was the first to break the silence with his low-pitched oily voice. This long spell on his knees meant nothing to him, for he was accustomed to interminable sessions of prayer in the privacy of his oratory in which he asked God for the strength to pursue the exhausting, secret work of imposing the divine law on a corrupt world. He said that he thought it was a suitable moment for Madame du Plessis to meditate on her past errors and to make good use of the time granted to her by the King's indulgence to prove abundantly a complete change of heart. Would not the King grant her eternal pardon if she could bring to him as her peace offering the conversion of her province, Poitou?

"You must be well aware, Madame, that the so-called reformed religion has but little time to run. Its adherents are being converted en masse and are returning into the fold of our Holy Mother the Catholic, Apostolic Church. A few hotheads are holding out, particularly in this remote and wild region where you were born and where you have your estates. Captain Montadour, who is one of our most zealous converters, was sent here a few months ago, but has had the utmost difficulty in persuading your Huguenot serfs to abandon their detestable heresies. Behold, Madame, what a noble task awaits you. Think how grateful the King whom you have offended will be for assistance in this holy work. You know the peasants of the region, you speak their language. You are their liege-lady. There are more ways than one in which you could compel your Huguenot serfs to give up their shameful beliefs."

What Monsieur de Marillac's reading had failed to do Monsieur de Solignac's speech achieved. Angélique was torn from her feigned torpor, and sitting up with a jerk she glared at them with her big eyes blazing in her emaciated face.

"Is it stipulated in His Majesty's letter that I am to undertake the conversion of my province?"

Monsieur de Marillac bared his yellow teeth in a sarcastic grin.

"No, Madame," he said, "but it is understood."

De Marillac, Solignac and Breteuil stooped down over her like one man. Montadour would have liked to do the same, but his fat belly got in the way. He bowed as far forward as he could. His mind was running on other matters than winning Angélique over to a holy work. The fact was that the half-dead creature who had arrived a few days before at the château almost ready to be sewn up in her shroud struck him as deuced attractive, deuced attractive!

The four faces crowded together reminded Angélique of the nightmares she had had on the Mediterranean, when her mind set free by sleep sometimes went back to the still fresh memories of her life at the French Court and conjured up the oppressive atmosphere of Versailles with its plots and threats, in which were strangely mingled the dread of prisoners celebrating their black masses in secret apartments, and the intrigues redolent of incense and holy water woven by fanatical propagators of the faith. All that she had fled and rejected for ever once more took concrete shape and recovered strength, and she felt its virulent, slimy clinging grip upon her.

"Madame," murmured de Marillac, "show us proof of your zeal, and we will see that you are spared the worst. We will find a way to move the King to clemency. We could suggest, for example, that he relax the severity of the penance imposed upon you. We must succeed in having the stipulation about your carriage remaining ouside the gates removed ... the dark clothes ... the oath of vassalage ..."

The man had a certain low cunning. He knew that for a woman like Angélique the hardest part to bear was these humiliating details rather than the cession to the Crown of her fiefs. They expected promises and undertakings, and were getting their instructions ready.

But she drew back haughtily.

"Have you done, gentlemen?"

The Governor pursed his lips.

"No, we have not done, Madame. I still have to deliver to you on His Majesty's behalf a personal message. Here it is."

Angélique broke the red seal and recognized the King's handwriting.

"Trifle, my impossible, my unforgettable child . . ."

The letters danced before her eyes; she let her hand drop, unwilling to read any further.

The King's envoys rose and withdrew. Monsieur de Marillac glanced at the outstretched form, then shrugged his shoulders. He would give His Majesty to understand that the woman's mind was deranged. Lying on the floor like that when she might have been Queen of Versailles! It was all most deplorable. He had been wrong to listen to Solignac and take a hand in this business. There was nothing to be gained for him, for the King or the Company of the Blessed Sacrament. It was quite obvious that she was going to die.

"Gentlemen!"

Angélique was calling them back. They stopped abruptly in the doorway. As she sat up again her loose hair formed a kind of dim halo about her face which accentuated the haggard brilliance of her eyes.

"Gentlemen, you are to tell the King that he has no right to show me indulgence."

"What does this mean, Madame?" asked de Marillac, taken aback. "Do you consider yourself unworthy of His Majesty's kindness?"

"No, I mean that there is no place for indulgence between us. His love is an insult to me. For, after all, are we not enemies? Between us there can only be war!"

The Governor's face went ashen. His felt dizzy at the very idea of having to repeat such words to the King.

The three noblemen went out considerably troubled.

"Oh, you must be mad, woman!" shrieked Barbe rushing to her mistress's bedside. "What madness has possessed you to destroy everything? To fling a thing like that in the faces of these great lords whom the King sent to you to patch things up. It's a strange way you go about purchasing your pardon!"

"So you were eavesdropping, were you, Barbe?"

But Barbe's righteous indignation had run away with her:

"Isn't it enough for you to be lying here like a wreck, a poor helpless creature without the strength of a mouse? It was a miracle you ever got away with your life, and now you've got it you play with it as if it were some worthless bauble!"

"Barbe, you've become very bossy while I've been away, and I won't have it."

"What do you expect when I've had to cope with our little Charles-Henri? You just leaving us like that, with the local police coming in all the time and asking questions and rummaging through the papers, and opening the cupboards and drawers. After that they left us alone. There wasn't any more they could get. Do you think it's a joke hanging around here saying one's rosary just so as we could see you turn up again one fine day, thinner then ever and in an awful mess and wilder than a stray cat? And now we've got soldiers in the grounds, and that fat Captain is laying down the law under your own roof and eating up the stores and making free with the maids. If you don't think I had to learn to stand up for myself, what *do* you think?"

Her faithful companion's outburst touched Angélique.

"Well, what do you think I should do?" she murmured faintly.

"Go to the King," whispered Barbe, taking heart again. "Then everything will be just like it used to be. You'll be the most powerful person in the Kingdom again. Your house and your sons will be honoured everywhere. Go to the King, Madame, return to Versailles."

Stooping over Angélique she scanned her face intently for signs of surrender. But under the bruised eyelids the glitter came back into the green eyes, and Angélique's expression was resolute.

"You don't know what you're talking about, Barbe. Go to the King? For you in your innocence nothing seems more desirable than life at Court. But I know what it's like. Haven't I lived there? Life at Court? What a joke! Death at Court, yes. Death from boredom and disgust and in the end from poison at a jealous woman's hands. Life at Court! You might as well try to dance on quicksands. I could never go back to that lot."

"The King loves you. You could do what you liked with him."

"He doesn't love me. He wants me. I shall never belong to the King. It's quite out of the question. Listen, Barbe, there's something you don't know. The King of France is all-powerful, but I succeeded in escaping from Mulai Ismail's harem. . . . You can't begin to imagine what that means. No woman had ever succeeded in doing that before. It was quite impossible, unthinkable. So why shouldn't I outwit the King of France?"

"Is that your plan?"

"Yes . . . I think so . . . I don't see what else I can do."

"Oh! You're mad, quite mad! God protect us," sobbed Barbe, rushing off, her face buried in her hands.

CHAPTER 3

CAPTAIN MONTADOUR was eating in the great dining-hall of the château. Angélique watched him from the doorway. Eating was not the word for it: he was stuffing himself. With his eyes starting from his ruddy face, whose colour was further heightened by a red moustache, he was entirely absorbed in the task of consuming a complete dish of ortolans set before him amidst a handsome array of pots. With a practised hand he grasped the ortolan, carefully stirred it round and round in the sauce-boat, then engulfed the entire bird in one mouthful. He crunched the bones, sucked them noisily, then wiped his hands on his napkin, which was spread over his chest and tucked into an open buttonhole.

"They call him Gargantua," whispered the little servant-girl who was also watching the scene, standing behind Angélique.

The Captain was ordering the servants about as if they belonged to him. One of them was not quick enough to suit his fancy, and the Captain called him a clumsy dolt and tipped the contents of the dish over his legs.

Angélique stole away.

It was incredible that the King should have imposed such a coarse brute on her under her own roof. The King probably knew nothing of Monsieur de Marillac's carefully calculated choice, but that did not absolve him from responsibility for the humiliation inflicted upon her. The King had left it to his toadies to bring the Marquise du Plessis to heel.

As she progressed towards recovery, Angélique had become aware of her double dilemma: she was at the mercy not only of the King but also of those who secretly aimed to rule the Kingdom. As long as she had

23

remained in the refuge of her chamber, she had had no clear realization of her situation. All she could do at that stage was to drag herself to the window to draw fresh strength from contemplation of the near-by forest. The luxuriance of its leafy fastness, its coolness and its shade filled her anew on each occasion with a mood of grateful exhilaration. She told herself that she was, after all, alive, that her bones were not whitening on some desert trail, and that it was an incredible miracle that she had ever been able to see her native land again. She had so often dreamed of the great shady trees of the forest of Nieul when, with parched lips and bleeding feet, she was struggling along behind Colin Paturel that everything seemed easy and simple to her now that she was back among them again.

Bit by bit she had yielded to Barbe's urgings and had agreed to take nourishment and to sleep in a bed. One day she had got dressed. Barbe had turned out for her from a chest one of her old dresses, for the newer ones were all too big for her.

As she ranged about her home Angélique had discovered that there was another side to her return. There were sentries posted at the doors and in the outhouses, and there were others camping by the gates.

She heard Montadour's loud, coarse voice. Convalescent as she was and still unsteady on her legs. Angélique was not quite sure that she was not falling back into another nightmare. Her servants' familiar faces seemed to belong to a world which had ceased to exist, which was shattered, and to bring back to her the tattered remnants of a life that she could scarcely believe was real.

They had come one by one to her little drawing-room to greet her and express their joy at seeing her restored to health. There were Lin Poiroux, the cook, and his wife, a jolly couple from Touraine who had been in service at Plessis for fifteen years without ever ceasing to lament the fact that they had to live among the barbarians of Poitou; there was Philippe's former valet, La Violette—she could have sworn that she had dismissed him; there was Joseph, the master of hounds, Janicou, the head footman, Hadrien, the coachman, and Malbrant-Swordthrust, Philippe's white-haired groom, whom country life seemed to have agreed with. He smoked his pipe, patted the horses and justified his presence by teaching young Charles-Henri the elements of fencing and horsemanship. But the boy was not so gifted as his elder brother, he used to say. Why was Florimond shut up in that old college, while good swords were rusting away for want of use? Malbrant, the right-hand man and ex-musketeer, who had seen it all, was the only one who seemed entirely at ease. All the others had something anxious and reproachful about them. During her absence they had felt cruelly abandoned. They had complaints. The soldiers were always tormenting them, made fun of them, treated them as if they were in conquered territory. The entire staff were deeply conscious of the shame inflicted on a noble's estate by having to billet troops just like peasants or townsfolk. Angélique listened without speaking, watching them with her green eyes, and a faint smile played around her still pale lips.

"Why don't you stand up for yourselves? Are you not men of Poitou? Have you not your knives, your axes, your whips, your good knobby sticks, and you, Lin Poiroux, your roasting-spits?"

The servants exchanged astonished glances. Malbrant-Swordthrust bared his teeth in a broad grin. Janicou, the coachman, stammered out: "That we have, my lady, but we didn't dare.... They're the King's soldiers."

"Anyone can make a mistake in the dark. A soldier of the King might get a drubbing just as easily as a peasant."

They nodded silently and their shrewd eyes narrowed. These domestics were still close enough to their peasant origins to understand that sort of talk.

"Well now, my lady," growled Janicou, "if that's all right by my lady, it's all right by us." They exchanged knowing glances. They had been right to have faith in their mistress. She would not be too easy to get the better of. They did not give the fat Captain long before he would be clearing out. Life in the country was going to be tough from now on for the King's soldiers. The

25

servants were childish, simple folk accustomed to following the fortunes of a single master, and the Marquise du Plessis's return seemed to them to mark the end of an anxious period when their fate had been at stake.

For Angélique things were not so simple. Beneath her surface calm she was trying to get her bearings before acting, and the more she took in the implications of her position the less she could see what she should do.

She took refuge in one of the downstairs drawing-rooms of which she was particularly fond, and allowed the past gradually to build a rickety bridge into the present.

The drawing-room was the one in which, long ago, when she was sixteen, she had stood up to the Prince de Condé in his angry mood.

At that time the great lord had come to Poitou to levy troops against Mazarin and the Queen Mother, and to plot to poison the boy King and his brother. She could still see him holding up to the light the green phial given him by the monk Exili and gloating over the opportunities the elimination of young Louis XIV would provide for his ambitions.

Princes' sport! Now Condé limped goutily night by night to the Queen's card-tables in the panelled halls of Versailles. The boy King had proved the stronger.

But did not the stench of plots and rebellion still linger on in this white château reflected in its pond at the fringe of the forest in the depths of a remote province?

Angélique looked out of the window. She could see a corner of the neglected grounds. The great chestnut trees bearing high their blossoms like pale red flames could not, for all their magnificence, make one forget the untidy state of the lawns where Montadour's men had pastured their horses. On the right shone the pond; two swans were hurrying to the bank. They had no doubt seen Charles-Henri out for a walk with Barbe, making ready to throw them bread. Angélique could not help thinking that in this nightmare atmosphere little Charles-Henri's beauty did not seem quite real.

Barbe brought him to her. He was now nearly five.

The devoted governess still dressed him in silk and satin, as if he were about to be presented at Court. He never dirtied his clothes. He stood before Angélique without speaking, and although she spoke to him in her gentlest voice she did not succeed in getting even a few words out of him.

"He's a little mischief when he feels like it, all the same," said Barbe, put out by her charge's silence. "You should hear him when I'm putting him to bed at night, when I put the locket with your portrait round his neck. He talks to it, and what he doesn't come out with! But perhaps he doesn't recognize you because you've become so different from your picture."

"Do you think I've changed much?" asked Angélique, anxiously in spite of herself.

"You're even more beautiful than you used to be," said Barbe somewhat peevishly. "When you come to think of it, it seems rather odd—I mean it just doesn't seem to work out. Your hair is in an awful mess, and the state of your skin is enough to make one weep. But that's how it is. There are times when you look twenty. At other times it's your eyes that strike one. It's almost as if you were a ghost returned from the other world."

"It is rather like that."

"More beautiful? I don't know," repeated the servant nodding her white bonnet, "but what I do know is . . . what I feel is that you're more dangerous than ever to men."

"Oh, leave men out of it," shrugged Angélique.

She looked at her hands.

"My nails are splitting again," she said, "I don't know what to put on them to strengthen them."

She sighed and stroked the child's silky locks. With his enormous blue eyes, his thick lashes, his pink and white complexion and his firm chubby cheeks he would have been a tempting subject for the brush of a Flemish painter. His beauty made her heart tighten. As she looked at him she could not help thinking of Philippe, her second husband, and remembering the dreadful blunder of fate that had sent her Joffrey de Peyrac's messenger when she had just remarried.

27

At that time she had done everything in her power to get Philippe, who had been as cold as ice, to marry her, and had thus dug with her own hands the gulf which had separated her from her first love. "Oh! Why dost thou ever force the hand of destiny?" as Osman Faraji used to say.

She sighed, averted her gaze and sank into a deep reverie. After a few moments the child crept away. For him at least she would not need to fear. Charles-Henri du Plessis, the Marshal's son, the King's godson, would not be stripped of his inheritance because of his mother's misdeeds, but the elder, the proud Florimond, who had been born rightful heir to the Counts of Toulouse, of higher lineage and of greater wealth than all the Plessis put together, was not his fate as uncertain and as obscure as a bastard's?

No sooner had she reached Plessis than she had attempted to get in touch with him, and with immense difficulty, her voice quavering with exhaustion, she had dictated a letter to Maître Molines for her brother, Father de Sancé, of the Society of Jesus. She did not know that her missive had aroused Captain Montadour's suspicions. As the latter was a man of somewhat sketchy culture, he had had the letter read out to him by the Lord Lieutenant, then, having weighed his responsibilities, had sent it first of all to Monsieur de Marillac. It had nevertheless reached its destination, for Angélique had now received her Jesuit brother's reply.

From it she learnt that Father de Sancé had been ordered by the King to keep young Florimond de Morens at his college until His Majesty saw fit to restore him to his mother. Father de Sancé was in full agreement with his sovereign's desire to protect the smallest of his subjects. Indeed, Florimond had nothing to gain by finding himself once again under the influence of a woman whose conduct had proved as ungrateful as it was ill-considered. Let her but show proof of repentance and return to the King's favour and she could see her son, to whom she would have ceased to offer a deplorable example of rebelliousness and irresponsibility. In any event it was much better for a boy of twelve to be in a college than to be trailed around by a mother who had always shown herself strangely unstable and fickle. He was on the threshold of adolescence. His uncle admitted that he was quite an able boy as far as his studies were concerned, but he was lazy, and it was difficult to know what was really going on in his mind in spite of his superficially open manner. Given perseverance, a good officer might be made of him.

Raymond de Sancé concluded with some oracular remarks, which betrayed the bitterness of his feeling. He was tired, he said, of bearing on his shoulders the weight of his brothers' and sisters' misdeeds, and consequently of being the only one to save the name of Sancé de Monteloup from royal disfavour. But how could one fail to bring down upon oneself His Majesty's displeasure when one was obliged, year in and year out, to intercede on behalf of offenders whose persistence in wrong-doing was equalled only by their incredible irresponsibility. A number of severe lessons had not sufficed to bring Angélique to heel. Had he ever ceased warning her and Gontran, Denis and Albert? But alas! Of what use were expostulations and warnings? Their wild untamed blood had always spoken with a louder voice. One day he would give up championing their cause. . . .

This reply disgusted Angélique more than anything else. So Florimond was being withheld from her. How shameful! Florimond, the orphan, belonged to her and her alone. She needed his friendship and his company.

It was the one living proof of her lost love that Florimond and Cantor, her first two sons, had grown very close to her since her Mediterranean journey. She felt she had regained Cantor's love by following him in her mad quest, by sharing the little page's secret dream. The dead child and his mother, lured by the same bait, had become accomplices, and since then she felt that he was less remote from her, that the gulf of death separating them was somehow less real.

But she needed Florimond, the elder, whose features were beginning to remind her of that other face which had been increasingly veiled by the mists of time. She

29

re-read the letter with impotent fury. Then her brother's protestations set her thinking. Why was his hostility now directed against the entire family, and why did he not blame Angélique alone for their troubles as was his wont? When they were children it had always been Angélique's fault if anything went wrong. But this time he was speaking in the plural.

She thought things over. One of Monsieur de Marillac's phrases came back to her: "insubordination of a family, several members of which have gravely offended me" or something of the sort. She no longer remembered the exact words, for at the time she had not paid particular attention. It was only when she set the phrase side by side with what Raymond said in his letter that she began to wonder if it did not refer to some occurrence unknown to her. She was absorbed in these reflections when a servant came to say that the Baron de Sancé de Monteloup wished to see her.

CHAPTER 4

ANGELIQUE'S FATHER, the baron de Sancé, had died the year before, during the winter which preceded her departure for Marseilles. So when they announced a visitor bearing his name, she sat upon the sofa, hardly able to believe her ears. The man who crossed the threshold looked just like her father, in his brown clothes and his heavy muddy shoes. She watched him coming towards her along the gallery and recognized the taciturn and sulky expression of the Sancé boys. Was it one of her brothers, Gontran perhaps? No, Denis.

"Is that you, Denis?"

"Hello," he answered.

When she had left, he had been a soldier with quite a good position in a garrison near Paris. All of a sudden here he was, the country squire, with the heavy gait and worried look of the Baron Armand. He was twisting a fold of his cloak somewhat nervously between his fingers.

"It's like this. I got an order from Monsieur de Marillac, the Governor of the province, to come and see you. And so I came."

"It's obvious that no one in this family does anything any more except under orders. How delightful!"

"Well, the situation is a trifle awkward."

"What's happening?"

"And you're asking, you who have had the country's entire police force after you and have been brought back home under guard like a criminal! The whole country's talking about it!"

"Oh, yes, I know that. But what *else* is going on?"

Denis sat down, quite overcome.

"Yes," its true, you don't know, and I'll tell you since that's why Monsieur de Marillac sent me to see you, 'to help to put some sense into you.' The words are his. So there you are."

"But what about?"

"Don't be impatient. You'll know soon enough. It's ghastly enough. Our family is dishonoured. O, Angélique, why did you go away?"

"Surely they haven't dared to attack my family because I chose to go abroad without asking the King's permission?"

"No ... It's not simply because of that. But if only you'd been here! ... It all happened a few months after you'd gone. No one knew quite why you'd gone, but the King was in a frightful mood. Oh, I didn't worry overmuch about that. I said to myself, 'Angélique's wriggled out of plenty of awkward situations before. If she's done something silly, she's quite beautiful enough to know how to put matters right.' The thing that was really worrying me, I'll admit, was that I didn't know where I could reach you to borrow some money from you. I'd just decided to buy a commission that was vacant in the regiment of Guards at Versailles. I was relying on you to help with your influence ... and with your money. As the negotiations were already well under way I went to Albert, for I knew he had influence in Monsieur's court. It turned out to be a bright idea, for I found our brother rolling in the stuff. He told me that Monsieur was crazy about him and was showering him with gifts

31

of one sort and another: money, offices, and even just recently the revenues of our great abbey at Nieul. That was something he had had in mind for a long while, the old schemer. And so he now felt free of the spectre of poverty till his dying day, the shrewd old thing. He could well afford to pass on a few hundred *livres* to me: I was only a poor soldier with neither the looks nor the brains to get on. He didn't need overmuch urging, and I was able to buy the commission. I moved into quarters at Versailles. It was more glamorous there for us officers, but tougher: constant parades for the King's pleasure. But all the same we did have the parties and the Court and the gambling. There were other things too, that I found less pleasant and that we were all too often mixed up in: we had to put down any sign of revolt amongst the stonemasons and the builders . . . you remember, they were doing a lot of work at Versailles at the time?"

"I remember."

The young man's monotonous voice conjured up a forgotten scene: the brilliance of the great piles of cut stone, grating under the huge saws, the web of scaffolding around the two wings of the palace that were being enlarged, the permanent hum of men at work that even reached the strolling gallants at the far end of the park: shouts, hammer blows, the creaking of carts, the scraping of shovels—a swarming army of workmen.

"They were wrong to conscript a lot of the workmen by force, as if it had been for the army. They had to live on the site, and they were not allowed to see their families for fear they might not come back if they were allowed away. And so there were a large number of malcontents. Things got worse in the summer when the King began the construction of an artificial lake down towards the forest, just in front of the great flight of steps that overlooks the Orangery. It was appallingly hot. The mosquitoes from the marshlands joined in, and then the men got fever. They were dying like flies. We were co-opted to help bury them, then one day . . ."

Denis described the sudden uproar amongst the slaves. Foremen had been thrown from the scaffolding. Hordes of men, awls and hammers in their hands, had
32

swarmed over the flowerbeds and brutally murdered the palace guards. Luckily a regiment was parading in the Place d'Armes. Immediately the soldiers took up battle order and marched up to the château. It took two hours to quell the riot; two hours of musket fire in the heat, amongst the shrieks of hatred and the groans of the dying. The poor wretches, pushed back until they were once more barricaded in their own scaffolding, tipped great blocks of stone down from a height of four floors on to the soldiers below, who died crushed like bedbugs. But the muskets were well aimed, and soon the white gravel was strewn with bodies. Madame de Montespan and her ladies were looking on, half swooning, from the south balconies.

Finally the workmen gave themselves up. The following day at dawn their leaders were taken to the edge of the woods, right opposite the château near the newly-started lake, to be hanged. It was at the very moment when the rope was being put round his neck that Denis recognized Gontran, their brother! It was Gontran de Sancé de Monteloup, their craftsman brother, his forehead covered in blood, a wild glint in his eye, his poor clothes torn and spattered with paint, his hands horny and corroded by contact with acids. Gontran!

The young officer had shrieked: "Not him." He had thrown himself in front of his elder brother, covering his body with his own. They could not commit the sacrilege of hanging a Sancé de Monteloup!

The men thought he had gone mad. A strangely mocking and weary smile played about Gontran's lips.

They had gone to fetch the Colonel. With great difficulty Denis had tried breathlessly to explain to him that this rebel with his hands tied behind his back bore his own name, was of his lineage, was in fact his brother, born of the same father and mother, and was also brother to the Marquise du Plessis-Bellière. The Colonel, persuaded by the famous name, the obvious resemblance between the brothers, and perhaps by the arrogant and haughty bearing—a nobleman's bearing—of the condemned man, postponed the execution. They could not, however, defy for too long the orders that before sun-

33

down all the mutineers should have paid the debt of their folly. Denis therefore had until sundown to obtain the King's pardon.

But how could he, an obscure officer, go to the King himself? He knew no one.

"If only you'd been there, Angélique! A couple of months before, you had been at Court, the King saw everything through your eyes, you would only have had to say one word. Why, oh why, did you vanish, at the height of your success, at the peak of your fame? Oh, if only you had been there!"

Once again Denis had thought of Albert, who of all the brothers at the time had seemed the most secure in his good fortune. To have gone to the Jesuit Raymond would have taken too long and, in any case, the Jesuits, powerful as they are, are averse to improvisations. Moreover, the Colonel had said sundown. Denis had galloped at full speed to Saint-Cloud. Monsieur was out hunting and of course his favourite was with him. Denis galloped after the hunt. It was noon before he had reached Albert. Then Monsieur had had to be persuaded to do without his companion for a few hours, and that had taken some time too.

"Albert is a past master when it comes to smiles and winsome ways. He's worse than a woman. I watched them making passes with their eyes, with their lace cuffs, and I thought about Gontran at the foot of his tree. You know, Albert disgusts me, but you must admit that he didn't back out of it. He did everything he could have done. At Versailles, which we reached early in the evening, he knocked on every door. He approached everyone. He was frightened of nothing; neither of importuning, nor of begging, nor of flattering, nor of being rebuffed. But he had to hang around here, there, and everywhere. I watched the sun sink in the sky. . . . Finally, Monsieur de Brienne deigned to listen to us. He left us for a moment. Then he came back and said that we might possibly have the opportunity to approach the King when he left his study, where he was receiving the principal aldermen of Paris in audience that day. We

34

waited amongst the courtiers, in the War Room, at the end of the Great Gallery . . . you know."

"I know."

The door opened, the King appeared, grave, majestic, and as the courtiers caught sight of him the murmurs were hushed, heads were bowed, and the ladies curtsied low with a rustle of silk.

Young Albert threw himself on his knees, pale and dramatic:

"Have pity, Sire, on my brother Gontran de Sancé," he implored. The King's expression was grim. He already knew who the two young men were, and why they were there as suppliants. He nevertheless asked them:

"What has he done?"

They bowed their heads.

"Sire, he was one of the men who rebelled yesterday and who threw the palace into a state of confusion for some hours."

The King's face wrinkled in an ironical pout:

"A Sancé de Monteloup, a nobleman of ancient lineage, amongst the stonemasons! What on earth are you talking about?"

"Alas, Your Majesty, it's true. Our brother always did have queer ideas. He wanted to paint, and so he became an artisan in spite of our father who, in his rage, disinherited him."

"A queer idea, indeed."

"Our family had lost trace of him. It was at the very moment that they were going to hang him that my brother Denis recognized him."

"And so you countermanded the orders for his execution?" asked the King, turning towards the officer.

"Sire, he was my brother!"

The King's expression was stony. Everyone knew whose ghost was flitting back and forth between the actors in this drama. An unspoken name, the light and haughty silhouette of a triumphant woman in all the finery of Versailles; she had disappeared, had run away and left the King stunned and hurt. He could not forgive. When at last he spoke, it was with a hollow voice.

"Gentlemen, you are members of a troublesome and

haughty family whose presence amongst us does not give us cause to rejoice. In your veins you carry the blood of those great vassals whose pride has so often rocked the foundations of our realm. You are one of the families that all too often has tended to ask itself whether or not to obey the King's orders, and all too often has decided not to. We know the man whose pardon you are seeking. He is a dangerous man, a blasphemous and violent man, who has stooped to mix with the common people in order to lead them the more easily into wickedness and rioting. We made inquiries about him, and, when we heard his name and family, how dumbfounded we were! You say he is a Sancé de Monteloup? And in what manner has he proved it? Has he paid the blood-tax to the realm that is due from all men of noble birth? No, he regarded the sword with contempt, and in its place took up the artist's brush and the craftsman's chisel. He preferred to demean himself, to cast aside the responsibilities he had towards his name, to abjure his ancestry by mixing with coarser beings and by preferring their company to that of his own class. For that is what he said: that he would rather talk to a stonemason than to a prince. If we had formed the opinion that this man's strange way of life was due to illness, weak intellect, or that he suffered from some abnormality that caused him to lead the outrageous life of a vagabond ... these things happen in the very best families. But not at all. We heard him. . . . We wanted to hear him. He struck us as intelligent, wilful, and fired by a strange hatred. We recognized the haughty tone, the bitter note, standing up to the King . . ."

Louis XIV broke off. For all his self-control there was something indescribable in his expression that frightening—a sort of deep hurt. Albert de Sancé's eyes, which shone with greenish lights when he opened them wide, reminded the King of those other eyes. In a hollow voice he said:

"He has behaved like a madman, and he must pay for his madness. Let him die the shameful death of a common criminal. Let him be hanged! Wasn't he planning to carry his insolence to the point of applying to Parliament for a hearing in the hope of persuading them to with-draw all labour from us, as Étienne Marcel did once, when he made the guilds by violence and rioting force their will on our ancestor Chares V? . . ."

The last remark was aimed at the aldermen of Paris, who had come that very day to submit certain claims on the people's behalf which the King was not prepared to entertain.

The King walked on, his hand resting on the gold knob of his ebony stick.

Young Albert de Sancé had a supreme inspiration.

"Sire," he cried, "raise your eyes to the ceiling. There you will see my artisan brother's masterpiece, painted to your greater glory. . . ."

A red ray from the setting sun shone through the windows and lit up the god Mars in his chariot drawn by wolves.

The King stood quite still and reflected. This expression of the beauty he so much loved must have established a momentary link between him and the rebel with callused hands who had stood up to him, must have given him a fleeting glimpse of a world where human nobility assumed other forms. Then again his practical mind was loath to get rid of a craftsman who could create such wonders. Real artists, those who could transcend what they had been taught, were rare. Why had Monsieur Perraut, who was in charge of the work going on at Versailles, not told him what a talented fellow this was that they had just condemned without a trial? Alarmed as they were by the riot, and fright-ened by the King's anger, no one had dared to inter-cede on behalf of this hothead. The King said quickly:

"There must be a stay of execution. We would like to look more closely into this man's case . . ."

He turned towards Monsieur de Brienne and dictated the pardon. The two brothers, still kneeling, heard him remark:

"He ought to work in Monsieur Le Brun's studio."

The two brothers ran across the darkened gardens as far as the lake from which the fatal miasmas rose, and on to the edge of the woods where the hanged men

37

were dangling. They were too late. Gontran de Sancé de Monteloup was dead, hanging from the bough of an oak, facing the palace of Versailles, a blank white cliff in the evening dusk.

You could hear the toads croaking.

The two brothers had taken down the body. Albert had gone to fetch a coach, his valet and his coachman. At dawn they had set off for Poitou. They had galloped without pausing through the burning summer sunshine, through the clear blue nights, in a frenzied hurry to reach the land of their forefathers and there to bury the great stricken body, whose hands were now still and impotent, as if only their own earth could heal his wounds and calm the bitter grief that showed in the lines of his swollen face.

Gontran the artist! Gontran the painter! Who saw goblins in the copper preserving-pans at Monteloup, who used to crush cochineal beetles and crumble the yellow earth to decorate the walls, and who became drunk with the beauty of green foliage as with a heady elixir.

Gontran of the untamed soul, a man with an inner life of unsuspected richness and magnificence!

Weeping like two children, Albert and Denis had buried him in the family vault near the village church of Monteloup.

"And then I came to the château," said Denis; "everything was dead: not a single sound in the house, not a child to be seen. Only Fantine, the wet-nurse in the kitchen, with her blazing eyes, and Aunt Marthe, the same as ever, fat, hunchbacked, working at her everlasting tapestry: two old bewitched creatures, muttering as they shelled peas.

"And so I stayed on. You know what our father wrote in his will: 'The son who comes back to the land will inherit it.' Why not me? I took back the mules, I went to see the farmers; then I got married ... to Thérèse de La Mailleraie. She's got no dowry, but she's well thought of, and she's got a nice nature. We're going to have a child at apple-picking time.

"There you are. That's what Monsieur de Marillac

38

wanted me to tell you about. I don't mean about my marriage, but about Gontran. So that you might think about it and understand better what you owe to the King after the way you and our family have insulted him. But I think ..."

He scanned his sister's face. She also was older than he, and he had always been a trifle afraid of her beauty, her daring, and the mystery that surrounded her repeated disappearances. Now she had come back again, and this time too she was different and a stranger. The fine bone-structure of her jaw showed beneath the more mature line of her cheeks. She was deathly pale and erect, struck to the heart by the tale she had just been told. Denis was both glad and fearful.

"Angélique will always be the same," he thought, but the days to come were not going to be days of peace.

"Monsieur de Marillac doesn't know you very well," he murmured. "In my opinion, if he wanted to get you to submit to the King, he's made a mistake in letting you know that a Monteloup has been hanged on the King's orders."

CHAPTER 5

MOLINES, the steward of the Plessis estates, had been calling on her daily since her return. The old man, with his account books under his arm, would walk slowly up the long avenue that led from his slate-roofed brick house to the château.

Independent, virtually his own master as he always had been, a well-to-do bourgeois with his own personal business affairs to dea with, Maître Molines was none the less a faithful servant of the Plessis-Bellières. They provided him with the trading title under cover of which he had, throughout his industrious life, carried on his own business. Angélique, and still more Philippe the Marquis, had always been unaware of the exact nature of Maître Molines's business. They knew but one thing, and that was that whenever he was needed he was always available on the spot, either in Paris when the lord and lady of the château were at Court, or at Plessis when either chance or disfavour had brought them back to their estates.

So it was Steward Molines's countenance, dour but gradually acquiring with advancing years an expression of age-old wisdom, that had been among the first to bend over the wan figure when it was lifted from the coach by two musketeers, while Monsieur de Breteuil called briskly to the assembled servants:

"I've brought Madame du Plessis home to you. She is dying. She only has a few more days to live . . ."

Molines's face showed not a trace of emotion. He had greeted Angélique as impassively as if she had just arrived on a brief visit from Versailles when the rents were due in order to sell some timber or land to pay her gambling debts. And it was when she heard him announce in his dignified manner that this year's harvest would be a disastrous one, that she began to realize where she was, began to feel her exhausted limbs transfused with a sense of security, a sense of being back on her native soil and in contact with her past.

He had neither reproached her, nor asked her a single question.

He might well have felt entitled to make some comment, for his relationship with the family was long-standing and he had not long since had a considerable share in the up-bringing of the Monteloup children.

He said nothing. He never referred to the worries and anxieties her departure had caused him, nor to the measures he had had to take in his energetic, determined way in order to rescue even the soundest of her business interests from the threat of collapse. For the report of a fall from favour is like a chill wind heralding ruin. The rats, the rooks and the wriggling worms that feed upon shaky fortunes were already making ready. Molines had seen to all that, he had given assurances and assumed commitments. Madame du Plessis was travelling, he said. She would be back. There were no plans to wind up the estate.

But what about the King? What about his anger ? . . .

Everyone knew about that. Wouldn't Madame du Plessis be arrested and thrown into prison?

Molines would shrug his shoulders and hint that he would not forget those who stood by him and, since he had often shown himself to be a dangerous man to cross, and a wily one too, the clamour was stilled. People resigned themselves to waiting. And so, throughout the whole year in which Angélique's fate had been a subject for anxious conjecture, the Steward had held together in his iron fist the social and financial structure of the runaway Marquise's fortune and that of her heir young Charles-Henri. Thanks to his efforts all the servants stayed put, both in the château and in her Paris houses in the Rue du Beautreillis and the Saint-Antoine district.

Molines now announced to all concerned the return of the lady of the manor. He did not mention the fact that she was under house arrest, reminding people only of the fact that the King was her friend and that she would shortly be looking into her affairs with the authoritative and competent eye that had drawn praise from Monsieur Colbert. This was aimed at the Paris merchants and the Le Havre shipowners, with whom Angélique had investments.

On the estate Molines continued his rounds. With his customary punctuality he visited the farms and inspected the crops and the work in hand. Protestants were visited on the same basis as Catholics. The tenants pointed out the soldiers in the house who were eating up the cheeses and the hams, and who put their horses in to graze on the sprouting barley. There were Monsieur de Marillac's converters. Maître Molines made no comment. He merely reminded the farmers of their liabilities to their overlord, and wrote down figures in his books.

"Maître Molines, what are we to do? Aren't you a follower of Calvin, like us?" the Huguenot peasants would say, standing before him with their great black hats held over their stomachs. Their eyes were dark and fanatical. "Must we give up our religion to keep

41

our possessions, or accept ruin?" "Be patient," he would say.

He had had the dragoons in his own house. They pillaged his comfortable home, burnt a hundred pounds of candles and beat upon his saucepans for two days and nights without stopping, to prevent him from getting any rest, calling out: "Recant, you old fox, recant."

This episode had taken place before Angélique returned. As Montadour had taken up his residence and was acting as guard to one of the most beautiful women in the Kingdom, and since Madame du Plessis was not a member of the Reformed Church, Marillac thought it politic to give orders that her retainers should be left alone.

Molines, free once more, began his regular visits to the château and Montadour, who regarded him as one of the worst Huguenots in the district because of his influence over the peasants, would shout at him:

"When are you going to recite the Creed, you old heretic?"

The first time he saw Angélique with healthy colour in her cheeks at last, as she sat in the Prince de Condé's room, the Steward breathed a sigh. His pale eyelids closed, and Angélique could have sworn that for a second he was thanking God. This was so out of keeping with his outward manner, that, instead of being touched, she felt vaguely uneasy.

It was on that occasion that Molines first spoke of the disturbances and the threat of famine that had hung over the region since Monsieur de Marillac had launched his attempt to convert Poitou.

"The propagators of the faith regard our province as an experiment. If the methods they use here to overcome the Protestants prove to be swift and effective, they will be applied all over the Kingdom. In spite of the Edict of Nantes Protestantism will be wiped out in France."

"What's that to me" said Angélique, looking out of the open window.

"I'll show you," replied Molines curtly.

Opening his books yet again, he had no difficulty in showing her that her lands, for the most part in competent Protestant hands, had already suffered heavy losses. The men were being prevented from going to work in their fields, or from tending their cattle. His figures succeeded in rousing her.

"We must lodge a complaint. Cannot your church councils remind those in authority of the terms of the Edict?"

"But whom are we to approach? The Governor of the province is himself the instigator of these abuses. And as for the King! ... The King listens to those who give him advice, those who persuade him. ... I was awaiting your return, Madame, for you could do much to stop the trouble. Go to the King, Madame. It's the only solution for you personally, for the provinces and, who knows, perhaps for the Kingdom."

So that was what he was after.

Angélique fastened her tragic gaze upon Molines. There were so many things she wanted to say that she could not utter a single one, and her closed lips trembled. He hastened to answer before she had spoken, for during the past days when he had bent over her sick face he had thought out in the agony of his heart all he would like to say to her.

Although he knew this strange girl from Poitou so well—he remembered her delicate, girlish grace as she walked along the lanes in the neighbourhood, and when they met she used to look at him boldly and yet shyly—still he had never felt her to be so strange and remote as now. He was not sure that she understood him. So he spoke abruptly and briefly, as he had done that day when she had come to his house to ask whether she must marry the Comte de Peyrac.

Today he was saying: "Go to the King."

But no matter what arguments he put forward, Angélique had been over them time and time again, and she shook her head.

"I know how proud you are," the Steward went on, "but I also know you are a sensible person. Forget your grievances. Did you not appeal to the King when you

43

were a prisoner of the Berbers, and did he not heed your call? You could do anything, if you went the right way about it. You could even regain the influence you once had over the man you have defied, and it would be all the stronger because he has been kept waiting so long."

Angélique still said no. In her mind's eye she saw Mezzo-Morte, the Admiral of Algiers, in his golden damask coat; she heard his laugh, the oily laugh of a pervert, as he said: "The man known as Jaff-el-Khaldoum died of plague three years ago," and she realized that it had been from that moment that she had begun to lose hope. She also saw a hanging body, turning this way and that in the dusk at Versailles. And she saw her second husband Philippe du Plessis-Bellière turned towards her with the look he had had on his face that last night, before setting out of his own free will to meet death in the cannon's mouth.

> Adieu my heart, adieu my love
> For we fain must serve the King,
> So let us part . . .

The King had taken everything she had.

She shook her head, and her unruly hair, that was so hard to dress, made her look, in spite of her regal, finely chiselled face, like the child in the lanes who once had haughtily refused to answer Molines's questions.

At last she spoke. She spoke of her voyage, her departure. She still made no attempt to explain it, but her remarks returned again and again to "him."

"I never found him, you see, Molines. And perhaps he's really dead now . . . of the plague or something else. Death comes so easily in the Mediterranean countries. . . ."

She seemed to think for a bit, then tossed her head and went on, more quietly:

". . . and resurrection too! . . . But what does it matter? I have failed. I'm a prisoner."

She drew her frail hand, that she would not adorn

with rings which had become too large over her eyes, as if to exorcise a persistent vision.

"I shall never be able to forget Islam. Everything I've been through is constantly before my eyes. It's like one of those huge multicoloured oriental wool carpets that are so wonderful to walk on with bare feet. Can I possibly agree to what the King is asking of me? No. Can I go back to Versailles? No. It makes me sick even to think of it. The idea of going back to all that barnyard cackle, those intrigues, those plots! You do not know what are you asking me to do, Molines. There is no point of contact between what I am, what I feel, and the life you want me to return to."

"But you have no alternative other than submission or revolt, have you?"

"I will not submit."

"So you will revolt?" he asked, ironically. "Where are your troops? Where are your arms? . . ."

His sarcasm did not seem to have any effect on Angélique.

"There are some things the King fears, you know, all powerful as he is. He fears rivalry between the great nobles, and he fears the hostility of his provinces."

"Those things only have their effect on kings after there has been much blood spilt. I do not know what you intend to do, but during your stay amongst the Berbers you seem to have learnt to hold human life very cheaply."

"On the contrary, I think I learnt its true value." She began to laugh as a thought crossed her mind.

". . . Mulai Ismail used to chop off two or three heads every morning just to whet his appetite. Life and death were so closely intertwined that you had to ask yourself each day which was really more important: to live or to die. That's how you come to know yourself."

The old Steward nodded his head several times. Yes, now she did know herself, and that was what made him despair. As long as a woman had doubts about herself, you could make her see sense. It was when she reached maturity and full self-possession that you could fear the

45

worst. Because then she would follow only her own code.

He had always had the feeling that there were innumerable facets in Angélique's personality which would come to the fore one by one like successive waves after each new blow that befell her. He would have liked to stem the course of destiny, to arrest the inexorable sweep of events that bore her further and further away. He was exasperated to see her give in to fate in the yielding way that women have, making no particular effort to create a consistent personality, but accepting themselves as different from day to day.

Why couldn't she have stayed at Versailles, since there she had everything she had wanted? At that time she had been accessible, whole, grasping, biting into the fruits of power, wealth and pleasure. Now the wave that had carried her on her mysterious odyssey had carried her beyond the world of appearances. She would no longer be satisfied with illusions. Her strength stemmed from her detachment, but her weakness lay in the fact that she could no longer be a part of the harsh, materialistic society that the King of France was building around him.

"How well you know me, Molines!" she said, guessing his thoughts with such accuracy that it made him start. "God knows what occult powers she has acquired in those wild and mysterious lands," he thought, more and more disquieted.

"... It's true, I should never have gone away. Then everything would have been simple, and I'd have gone on living at Court with my blinkers on. Court life! You can do anything you like there, except live. Perhaps I'm getting old but I could never be satisfied with those bright toys that keep all those puppets dancing. Huh! A stool at the King's feet.... What an achievement! What a delight to be allowed to sit at the Queen's card-table to shuffle for her! What profitless and pointless passions, and yet they overwhelm you and crush you like serpents: gambling, wine, clothes, honours.... Dancing was the only thing I enjoyed, and those lovely gardens, but the price was too high: craven compromises, the lust

of imbeciles to whom, in the end, you give your body
. . . from sheer boredom; smiles you have to bestow upon
revolting cankers, the more repulsive because you read
it in the depths of their eyes rather than see it on their
bodies, as I saw it on the bodies of the lepers in the
East. Do you really think, Monsieur Molines, that after
winning back my life at the cost of so much suffering,
after finding, by some miracle, that I am still alive, that
I should then stoop again to such servitude? No, no!
Otherwise the desert would have taught me nothing. . . ."

Seeing her there with the marks of her martyrdom
lying like a veil over her beauty, but showing up all the
more clearly the cleansed and purified details, Molines,
for all his hardness, felt overcome by respect and at the
same time discouragement. Angélique's powers of reasoning, in spite of her trials, were unshaken, but he
could only deplore the fact that she now cast so uncompromising an eye upon the baseness of her age. Molines
could not help sighing. In his struggle with her he was
trying less to convince her than to save her.

An unprecedented disaster was threatening, which
would wreck everything that had made his life a success. And it was not only his money that was at stake; his
investments were so various and so complicated that he
felt justified in hoping that some might weather the
storm. But there were other things that meant a great
deal more to him: the opulence and social distinction of
the Plessis-Bellière family, the prosperity of his native
province, the constantly increasing numbers of the
Protestants, from whom the ablest and most hard-work-
ing section of the peasantry was drawn.

Because of the influence she had over the all-powerful
King, Angélique represented the delicate pivot of the
balance of forces which had been so painstakingly established, and which could be tipped towards ruin by rebelliousness on her part.

"And what about your sons?" he asked.

The young woman stiffened, then looked, as he had so
often seen her do, towards the window, as if she were
asking the forest for help and comfort in her distress. Her

47

darkened eyelids fluttered nervously, while her mind was busy refuting Moline's arguments.

"I know ... my sons. They pull me in the direction of submission. My responsibility for their young lives tends to paralyse my initiative."

She threw an ironic, cutting glance at him.

"What a paradox, Molines, to think that virtue is using my children as a weapon to drive me into the King's bed! But that's how things are nowadays."

The Huguenot Steward said nothing. He had to admit that there was considerable perspicacity in her cynicism.

"God knows, I fought for my sons when they were young and helpless," she went on, "but things aren't the same now. The Mediterranean has taken Cantor from me, the King and the Jesuits have got Florimond, and, in any case, he's twelve now, and that's the age when a boy of good family can start to lead his own life. Charles-Henri is provided for by the Plessis-Bellière fortune. The King would never dispossess him. So am I not free to live as I please?"

The Steward's parchment-coloured face grew pink with anger. He brought both his hands down with a smash on his skinny knees. If she used her familiar implacable logic to justify her folly, he would never succeed in getting the better of her.

"You are shrugging off your responsibilities towards your sons so that you can be free to wreck your own life," he cried.

"So that I can be free above all not to sacrifice it to a lot of sickening hanky-panky."

He tried a different approach.

"But, Madame, you seem to regard it as a foregone conclusion that you will have to sacrifice your virtue to the King. In fact what are you being asked to do? You are only being asked to make a public act of submission in the presence of the Court so that it will not appear weak of the King to take you back into favour again. Having saved his face for him in that way. I would have thought that a woman like you, Madame, would be shrewd and clever enough—"

"Do you think that would work with the King?" she

said with a sudden shudder. "It's out of the question! With things as they are between us he would never let me get away with it, and I myself . . ."

She clasped and unclasped her hands restlessly. He thought she was more highly-strung than ever. And yet, in another way, she was more serene: more vulnerable and at the same time less assailable.

Angélique tried to visualize the long gallery as she walked the full length of it dressed in black, under the sharp, sneering eyes of the courtiers, and the King standing at the end, with that air of overwhelming majesty that came so naturally to his stony face and heavy eyes. Then the genuflexion, the oath of allegiance the kiss of bondage. . . . And then, when at last she was alone with him, and he came towards her, his enemy, to join in a combat he was determined to win, how would she be able to stand up to him?

Hers was no longer the thoughtless arrogance of youth, that veritable armour of ignorance that is so often an effective barrier to the temptations of the flesh.

By now she had lived through too many sensual experiences not to be aware of the manifold hidden influences at work in the sphere of love, and she knew that she would inevitably succumb to the subtle bond that draws a woman, with her inner longing for subjugation, into the arms of the man who has vanquished her.

She was a woman now to the very marrow of her bones, made so by so many male caresses, by so much desire and so many battles fought over her lovely body. So much so that she knew she would be quite capable of enjoying this delectable humiliation.

And Louis XIV, who knew more about psychology than most, could hardly be unaware of it.

He would bind her to him by branding her with his burning seal, as outlaws were branded with the fleur-de-lis.

She was too modest to tell Molines of the visions that filled her mind.

"The King is no fool," she said with a disillusioned laugh. "It's hard for me to explain what I mean, Molines, but I couldn't find myself face to face with the King

49

without it happening ... and it mustn't happen. You know why, Molines. I could have spent the rest of my days with the man I loved, with the man who had chosen me as his lady.... My life would not have been this succession of days spent in sorrow and useless waiting, with my happiness cut off at the root, a life full of anguish, then, after a period of childish and dangerous illusion, the worst blow of all: the realization that there are things in life you can never put right. Whether he is alive or dead, he had trodden a different road from mine. He has loved other women, just as I have loved other men. We have betrayed one another. Our life together was just beginning to take shape—our life together was choked to death, and it was the King who directed the operation. I cannot forgive that, neither can I forget it ... I *must* not forget it, that would be the worst betrayal of all. If I did, all my hopes would be dashed to the ground for ever."

"What hopes?" he interrupted.

She drew a distracted hand across her forehead.

"I don't know ... there's still a glimmer of hope that won't die. And besides," she went on briskly, "and besides, you talk of my interests.... Should I go and hand my cup to the Montespan for her to put poison in? I suppose you are aware of the fact that she tried to poison me, and Florimond as well."

"You are quite strong and clever enough to hold your own against her, Madame. People are beginning to say that she hasn't the influence she once had. The King is getting tired of her spitefulness. They say that he is spending a lot of time with another dangerous intriguer, Madame Scarron, who, most unfortunately, was once a member of the Reformed Church. She is encouraging him, with all the zeal of a convert, to embark on a campaign against the members of her old faith."

"Madame Scarron?" exclaimed Angélique, thunderstruck. "But she is her children's governess."

"Indeed she is, but the King is no less interested by her conversation for that; it has a certain appeal."

Angélique shrugged her shoulders. Then she remembered that poor Françoise was a member of the great

Aubigné family, and that all the Court nobles who had vainly tried to take advantage of her poverty as a means to seduce her, used, half in admiration, half in bitterness, to call her "the lovely Indian." She also remembered that she had rarely caught Maître Molines out talking for the sake of talking.

He went on:

"I say this to make you realize that Madame de Montespan is no longer as much to be feared as you might think. You managed to curb her even when she was at the height of her power. Now it would be child's play to get rid of her. . . ."

"Sell oneself," muttered Angélique, "buy, carry on that fierce underground war I already know too much about? Ugh! I'd rather fight a different sort of battle," she said, her eyes glinting. "And if it's got to come to a battle, let it be in broad daylight, on my native soil. . . . The only thing that seems real to me in all this chaos is being here. It does me good and hurts me at one and the same time. It hurts because here I can see to what extent I have failed. But it does me good because I had a terrible need to see the place where I was born again. It's strange. . . . It seems as if it was all preordained, that from the day I tore myself away from Monteloup—do you remember, Molines, when I was seventeen and the Comte de Peyrac's wagons bore me away towards the south—after much wandering I was to come back to the place where I had spent my childhood to play my last card. . . ."

The words she had just uttered made her stop and she became perplexed and anxious once more. She left Molines and climbed slowly up the steps to the turret from which she could see the horizon. Did pot-bellied Montadour, whose coarse silhouette she occasionally glimpsed against the gravel of the drive, imagine that she would remain there the whole spring and summer between the four walls of her château, waiting for autumn to bring the King's men to arrest her and take her off to another prison?

If she did not now venture out even into her own garden, it was because she knew that, when the time came, she could run into the forest just as she wanted, and her fat jailer with his fiery moustache would never know a thing about it, and would continue, full of self-importance, watching over the bewitched domains whose princess had fled.

Idiot he was, knowing nothing as he did about life in the fields, oblivious of the fact that every burrow has two exits. If it came to that, she would take refuge in the Bocage.

But before she became an outlaw, clothed in greenery to be better hidden from the eyes of the huntsmen, she must throw all she had into the scales.

"My last card ..."

To regain her liberty this time was proving more difficult, nay, even more impossible than escaping from Mulai Ismail's harem. Her femininity had helped her in that undertaking. The ruses she had made use of before would not help her in her present dilemma. She could not slide out into the darkness, trusting to the night and to silence. She could not adopt the methods of defence used by the weaker animals who mingled their colours with those of the earth; she could not claim nature as her ally. Such means would be entirely inadequate in her circumstances.

In order to smash the mighty, solid power of the King of France, what was needed was something bold, incisive and blatant, a challenge, something strong and virile and ferocious. All the trumpets of Jericho would not suffice. In this land where all were subject to the one master, where would one find anyone to brandish the sword of revolt?

Now she was back in her own world, amongst her equals, Madame du Plessis-Bellière could see she had no friends. It would be useless to hope for the complicity that friendship or passion, or, at very least, a common ambition might have provided. How cleverly the young King had managed to swing every defence in his direction. There was not a single proud courtier who did not bow to him. Their names came back to her like ghosts: Brienne, Cavois, Louvois, Sant-Aignan ... Lauzun was in prison. He would be there for years, and would come out an old man, his gaiety killed for ever. . . .

As she stood on the narrow platform with the white stone merlons. Angélique called to the horizon:

"Oh my province, will you keep me?"

The slates on the pointed turrets blazed beneath the sun with a metallic lustre. But the moist breeze that blew from the marshes made the weathercocks creak. A falcon with outstretched wings was circling overhead in the clear sky.

Behind Plessis was the forest. In front stood the grounds with their foliage, then that of the countryside. On the left, far, far away, suspended as it were between sky and earth, lay the edge of the Poitou marshes, half cloud, half dream.

From her turret Angélique could not see a single sign of life. For the Bocage, with its fields watched over by the shadow of a tree, looks to the eye of an observer exactly like the forest with its dappled leafy domes all golden with sunshine. The farmsteads are so well concealed beneath the arching chestnuts that whole villages are hidden away and the sound of their bells never penetrates beyond the curtain of trees. Even where country life was at its most active and bustling, you could see nothing save a green desert, scored with the black furrows of the great rock faults where the cold waters of the Vienne, the Vendée and the Sèvres ran.

Pink cliffs, gaping wounds in the earth's flesh, were riddled with caves where torchlight showed up yellow or black silhouettes beneath the saltpetre, painted by hobgoblins, so people said. Gontran had known about them as a child; his sister Angélique, who was the fairy reigning over these magical places, had shown them to him; but he had wanted to be alone to examine them and had sent the little girl away. She had felt very bitter about this and had kept her other discoveries to herself.

From the unseen plain, the home of the corn, the open path of invasion, ran the old Roman road. Its broad chipped blocks wound their way like a grey snake up towards the rustic fort that had once barred the entry

53

to the Gaulish lands from the Picts and had for a long time held up the legions of the Caesars.

To the north the forests of Fontevrault, of Scevolle, of Lancloître and of Châtellerault formed a continuation of Nieul forest; between the Vienne and the Creuse to the east lay the forests of La Guerche and Chantemerle, and on the southern side were the marshlands of Brume and Charente, with their lonely heaths forming an impenetrable tree-strewn barrier of damp and muddy land.

To be a stake in what game of fate had they brought her back to this familiar setting of trees and water which had shaped her soul? What lesson was she to be taught here that she refused to learn? What truths was she to discover lying in wait for her here since her childhood, buried in the folds of this ancient land, this blue bay, on whose shores the waves of successive civilizations had beaten?

Dolmens rose up, deep in the forests, ancient stone tables erected for some purpose as yet unknown, and menhirs stretched across the moors. At every crossroad stood an obscure shrine elaborately carved like a reliquary, in honour of some local saint, side by side with Roman temples whose gods the saints had come to destroy. Forest and marshland: these were the two impenetrable barriers that had risen against the billowing banners of the Arab hordes in 732 and had withstood the forays of the half-starved English during the Hundred Years War.

This was a land that bristled with dark castles built by witches or knights, and abbeys that had had to be exorcised like Ligugé, Airvault, Nieul and Maillezais.

This was the land of the wars of religion. The accursed field near La Châtaigneraie was not far off, in which in 1562 Catholic soldiers had butchered more than a hundred men, women and children gathered for worship. And around Parthenay people could still remember the old Protestant thug Puyvault who used to fricassee monks' ears.

This was also the land of rebellion and highway robbery, the land of Bruscambille, and under Richelieu of the "Vanu-pieds" who had massacred the tax-collectors, while in Mazarin's time the King's troops had tried in vain to hunt down the people of the marshlands who used to slip away like a lot of eels along the waterways. As a child Angélique had been quite sure that anyone who came from outside this area was a foreigner, virtually an enemy. She regarded them with suspicion and distrust. She feared any innovations they might bring with them to this land of her childhood to disturb the secret and delightful orders of things, which only she and her loved ones understood. Today she felt the same. The landscape stretching before her could not betray her to the point of allowing the King's messengers to get through and arrest her.

The soldiers who stood guard outside the château, idly shredding plugs of tobacco to fill their pipes, were few in number. The inhabitants of Poitou would soon deal with them when the signal was given. They'd see to those other squads that were plaguing the Protestants, too. Even now soldiers were found stabbed in ditches, and the women of Morvay and Melles, rather than be dragged to Mass, had greeted some with ashes and dust. They had had to beat a retreat, blinded, and slink back to their quarters at Plessis with their tails between their legs.

Samuel, Duc de La Morinière, and his two brothers Hugh and Lancelot, all high-ranking Huguenot noblemen, had taken refuge in the caves near Sansis ford, after they had killed the lieutenant of dragoons who had tried to take over their home.

The invariable conclusion to all their nurse Fantine's stories was beginning to come true again. "Men-at-arms laid waste the countryside, and the local people took refuge in the woods." Or else it would be. "The unhappy knight fled from the King's vengeance into the woods, where he lived for two years on eels and teal. . . ."

At eventide you could hear the sound of a hunting horn across the Bocage, but it was not to signify the end of a day's hunting. It was passing on secret messages between the hunted Huguenots and other members of their faith. One of them, Isaac, Baron de Rambourg, lived in an old tumble-down château on a hill not far from Plessis, and his black fortress was silhouetted against the red sky. A distant blast would answer him, far off, and she could sometimes hear Montadour swearing nervously below. Since La Morinière, that blasted heretical Patriarch, had taken to the woods, fewer people were being converted. The odds were that, in spite of their temples being closed down and sealed, these miserable moths were slipping off at night through the trees to some inaccessible spot to sing their hymns.

Montadour wanted to take his men into the forest to catch them red-handed. But his men were afraid of the dark labyrinth. All their attempts to bribe a Catholic poacher to be their guide were unsuccessful.

One vision haunted Angélique: she saw a man galloping up and knocking at the château door. It was the King. He took her in his arms and whispered the words he had written to one woman alone: "My unforgettable one . . ."

God be praised, the time was past when the King of France could have jumped on a horse and galloped nonstop to his sweetheart, as once he had been able to do when he was in love with Marie Mancini.

He too was imprisoned by his own magnificence, and he had to wait for her submission. He tried in vain to cull some hope from Monsieur de Breteuil.

"Do you think she will come, Monsieur?"

The courtier bowed, hiding a sly smile.

"Sire, Madame du Plessis is still worn out after the terrible trials she endured on her journey."

"Couldn't she have given you a message for me? Is she still full of blind bitterness towards us?"

"Alas, Sire, I fear she is."

The King stifled a sigh and his glance was lost in the distant shimmerings of the Great Gallery.

Would he see her come towards him one day, broken and repentant?

He doubted it. A foreboding mirrored back the picture of a beautiful woman in chains, standing at the top of a turret, watched over by black trees and still waters.

CHAPTER 6

ANGÉLIQUE was running along under the trees. She had taken off her shoes and stockings, and the moss felt good beneath her bare feet. She would sometimes stop and listen with rapt attention. In a flash she knew which way to go and dashed on again. She thrilled to the sense of freedom. She laughed softly. It had been so easy to go down into the cellar and find the little door behind the casks that led to that underground passage that every self-respecting baronial hall must needs have tucked away beneath it.

The underground passage at Plessis had nothing whatever in common with the extraordinary passage from her house in the Rue du Beautrellis in Paris, which started in a well, ran all the way under the ancient city of Lutetia through a series of vaulted tunnels linked with the sewers, as far as the outskirts of Vincennes. At Plessis it was nothing more than a damp, smelly hole which she had had to crawl through. As she came out into the coppice, she had looked through the branches and had seen the soldiers in their red cloaks going their rounds. She was, however, hidden from their sight, and the sentries could have had no idea that the woman they were supposed to be guarding was there, only a few steps from where they stood, watching them. Then she had pushed aside the intertwining branches of the thicket and slipped quietly away.

Once beyond this tangled mass of small trees and bushes, of raspberry canes and dogroses that grew along the edge of the wood, the true forest began, a vast green cathedral pillared with oak and chestnut.

Gradually Angélique's heart began to beat less quickly and, delighted with her success, she began to leap and run. Her strength was coming back to her. She had learnt to walk the hard way along Moroccan trails, so scrambling up mossy rock faces or clambering down steep paths to streams full of blackened leaves was mere child's play to her. Sometimes the forest would fall to

57

form a hollow where it joined a valley and sometimes it would rise to a plateau where nothing but low ferns grew. Angélique moved with sure steps through the alternating patches of light and shade, of dry and damp, past the musty stale smell that rose from the depths of ravines and the vibrant, almost southern perfumes, that wafted over the higher ground, where the thin covering of earth, red with flowers, was pierced here and there by the sharp rocks that formed the bony understructure of the land.

Angélique stopped again. There was the Fairy Stone in its clearing, surrounded by Druid oaks, a colossal dolmen with its immensely long table suported by four uprights that the centuries had driven deep into the earth.

She walked round it in order to get her bearings. Now she was sure she would not get lost. This bit of the forest had been the scene of her childish adventures, with its Fairy Stone, its Wolves' Coomb, the Trousepoil Fountain and the Three Owls crossroad with its Lantern of the Dead. If she listened hard she could just make out the dull thudding of woodcutters' long axes borne on the wind. The men, who came from the hamlet of Gerbier, regularly spent the summer months amongst the trees. Towards the east there were also charcoal-burners in their blackened huts, where she used to go and eat cheese and to fetch long sticks of charcoal for Gontran.

But she had gone there along the paths that led from Monteloup. She was less familiar with the way from Plessis, although she had often prowled around near that property of her dreams and tried to catch a glimpse of the white château and its pool which now belonged to her.

She shook her fustian skirt to remove the bits of grass that clung to it in exactly the same way that she had always done, standing in the very same spot, and she smoothed her hair that the wind had loosened as she ran, and let it fall over her shoulders. She smiled to discover that she still attached so much importance to these rites that nothing on earth would have made her miss in the past, then with a cautious and somewhat

58

slower gait she left the clearing and began to climb down a stairway carved out of the rock which was now covered over with humus and clay. The visit she was about to make called for a certain degree of solemnity. Never had Angélique been able to set her wild, bare feet on this path without being seized by a feeling of nervousness that was quite foreign to her nature. Her aunt Pulchérie would never had recognized her at that moment. It was only to the obscure sylvan sprites that she had ever showed this image of the quiet well-behaved little girl.

The path fell away steeply into the blue-green depths. Springs ran down the hillside, their banks bright with tall crimson foxgloves. Then the foxgloves gave way to toadstools which alone could pierce the thick carpet of leaf-mould turned to mud; their slimy domes, orange or rich purple, glowed in the undergrowth like baleful lanterns set in a dark place. It was all there—dread, mystic excitement mingled with distaste, curiosity, and the certainty of contacting that other world, the world of evil spells that give power and authority. The path was now so steep that Angélique had to cling to the trees. Her hair was getting in her eyes and she thrust it aside impatiently. She had forgotten that this place was so remote and inaccessible; then she breathed a sigh of relief as she realized it was growing brighter again. It was the sun shining on the other side of the cliff through the transparent green of the leaves. She fumbled with one hand, trying to feel the solid rock through the moss, and slipped, scratching herself a little on a narrow ledge that overhung the river, whose waters she could hear babbling below.

Still holding on, she bent forward and lifted up a curtain of ivy that hung over the mouth of the cave. She could no longer remember the word you had to say at that moment; try as she might she could not call it to mind. Someone moved within the rock. She heard feet dragging, then a skinny hand came round the wall, and she could just make out the face of a very old crone in the dim half-light.

She looked like a shrivelled medlar, with her brown

59

wrinkled skin, but a thick thatch of dead hair trailed down in snow-white wisps around her.

She blinked as she considered her visitor.

Angélique asked in the local dialect:

"Are you Mélusine the witch?"

"That I am. What do you want, lassie?"

"I've brought this for you."

She handed the crone a packet containing some snuff, a cut of ham, small packets of salt and sugar, a piece of lard and a purse full of gold coins.

The old hag examined everything carefully, then, turning her back which had hunched like that of an emaciated cat, she went back into the depths of the cave. Angélique followed her. Eventually they came to a round room with a sand-strewn floor, dimly lighted from a thorn-covered aperture above, through which the smoke that rose from a small fire was escaping; a cast-iron cauldron was standing on the hot embers.

The young woman sat down on a flat stone and waited as she had been accustomed to do in the old days when she came to consult the other Mélusine. It was not the same witch any more. The other one had been even older and blacker, and she had been hanged from an oak bough by the peasants, who had accused her of offering up their children as sacrifices. When people heard that a new sorceress had quietly installed herself in the Hauts-de-Mère caves, they had called her Mélusine from sheer habit.

Where do these forest witches come from? What paths of misfortune and malediction lead them to these same spots, there to become allies of the moon, the screech-owl and growing things? The present witch was said to be the most learned and the most dangerous that the region had ever known. It was alleged that she treated fevers with vipers' broth, gout with salts distilled from the blood of lice, and deafness with ants' oil, and that she also knew the art of imprisoning demons from Satan's chosen legions in a nutshell. If you then gave your enemy the nut to eat he was overcome by the most appalling convulsions—to your great delight—and the only way he could free himself from such a spell was to go on a pilgrimage to the sanctuary of Our Lady of Mercy at Gâtines, whose reliquary contains a hair and a nail of the Virgin.

Girls who were in the family way well knew the path to her lair as did also men tired of waiting for the natural death of some old uncle of whom they had expectations.

Angélique, who had heard all this tittle-tattle, scrutinized the weird creature with considerable interest.

"What wouldst thou of me, my daughter?" asked the witch after a time, in a deep, cracked voice. "Dost thou wish to know what the future holds in store for thee? Dost thou seek to bind someone to thee by the chains of love? Dost thou wish me to prepare thee infusions for the restoration of thy health which has been harmed by thy long journeyings?"

"What do you know of my long journeys?" questioned Angélique.

"I see a great space about thee and a scorching sun. Give me thy hand that I may read thy future."

Angélique declined.

"I have come to ask something simpler. You know the ways of all the forest dwellers. Can you tell me the hiding-place of the men who sometimes meet here to pray and sing hymns with peasants from the hamlets? They are in peril. I want to warn them, but I do not know their meeting-place."

The witch was seized with agitation. She half rose to her feet and waved her deformed arms.

"Why dost thou wish to save those men of darkness from peril, thou who art a daughter of light? Leave the crows to hover over the polecats."

"Do you know where they live?"

"Oh, I know! How should I fail to know when they are always breaking my branches, springing my snares and trampling my herbs. If things go on the way they are, I shan't have a petal left to dry for my potions. There are more and more of them coming; they creep in like wolves, and, when they are all met, they begin to sing. The animals are afeard, the birds cease their song, the rocks are shaken and I am compelled to flee far away,

61

for their singing does me great hurt, dost thou understand, my daughter? . . . Why do these men come to the
forest?"

"They are persecuted. The King's soldiers are tracking
them down."

"They have three leaders, three hunters. The oldest of
them is the darkest, and he is as hard as iron. He is their
great leader. He speaks little, but, when he speaks, it's as
if he was cutting a doe's throat with his dagger. He's
always speaking of blood and eternity. Hearken to me
. . ."

She drew close to Angélique until the latter could feel
her breath on her face.

"Hearken to me, my little one. One evening I was
watching them all assembled from between the trees. I
was trying to understand what they were doing. The
leader spoke standing under an oak tree. He turned his
eyes in my direction. I do not know whether he saw me,
but I found that he had eyes of fire, for my own eyes
began to burn, and I had to flee, I, who can stare out the
wild boar and the wolf. Such is his power. That is why
the others come at his call and are ready to obey him.
He wears a big beard. He is like the bristling bear who
comes to wash his bloodstained coat in the spring when
he has been devouring young girls."

"That's the Duc de La Morinière," said Angélique,
repressing a smile, "one of the great Protestant lords."

That meant nothing to Mélusine. She preferred to
think of him as her bristling bear. But gradually her
mood changed, and she even smiled, drawing back her
ashen lips over her toothless gums. Her remaining teeth
were broad and strong, and very white as if she looked
after them with special care. The result was weird in the
extreme.

"Why should I not take thee to him?" she said suddenly. "He will not make thee lower thy eyes. Thou art
passing fair and he . . ."

She gave a prolonged snigger.

"Male he is, male he remains," she said sententiously.

Angélique could not see herself tempting the austere
Duc de La Morinière—also known as the Patriarch—

into paths of perdition. She had very different matters on her mind and she had to act quickly.

"I will go, I will go," muttered Mélusine, in high good humour, "I will guide thee, lassie! Thy destiny is so terrible, so violent, and wondrous beautiful. Give me thy hand."

What was it that she read in it? . . . She pushed Angélique's hand away again as if she were rapt in a strange dream, her grey eyes glittering with a trace of burning malice.

"Thou hast come. Thou hast brought me salt and tobacco. Thou art my sister, my daughter. Great are thy powers!"

The first witch she had known had spoken to Angélique, when she was a child, in very much the same way, as she had sat somewhat timidly in the same place; the other witch had used the same words to express her stupefaction at all that was inscribed about that young head. The fear and interest the witches had shown had always filled Angélique with naïve pride. When she was a little girl, she had seen therein the assurance that one day she would possess all she might desire: happiness, beauty, wealth. But what of the present? She now knew that one can possess everything and yet know no satisfaction, so why did these promises of power still stir something within her? She looked at her hand.

"Tell me, tell me again, Mélusine. Will I triumph over the King? . . . Will I escape his pursuits? . . . Will I find love again?"

But this time it was the witch who declined.

"What can I tell thee that thou dost not already know in the depths of thine own heart?"

"Are you refusing to tell me what you have seen so as not to make me lose heart?"

"Away, away! The man with the black beard must be waiting," tittered the witch.

Before leaving the cave she went and fetched a little bag and gave it to Angélique.

"Here are some herbs. Soak them each evening in very hot water, leave them in the moonlight and drink the potion at sunrise. Thou wilt recover the strength of thy limbs and thy flesh, and thy breasts will swell as if gorged with milk. But it will not be milk, it will be the blood of thy youth."

They walked one behind the other after emerging from the ravine. The witch followed no path. She knew the trails by invisible signs.

The sky was darkening behind the branches. Angélique thought of her guard, Montadour. Would he notice her absence? It was unlikely. He requested to be allowed to greet her each morning. That was an obligation imposed by Messieurs de Marillac and de Solignac, not to bother the prisoner, but to make sure she was seen once a day. To all appearances the fat Captain would have been delighted to discharge his obligation more frequently, but Angélique's distant manner embarrassed him. Her icy expression cut short any attempt at conversation or gallantry. She saw him swallowing back his ponderous compliments and gnawing his ginger moustache. He would take his leave with the remark that he was off to hunt down the heretics, which was the other mission entrusted to him. Every afternoon he would jump on to his sturdy, dapple-grey horse and set off, accompanied by a detachment of horsemen to attend a few conversions in the neighbouring villages. Sometimes he brought back a particularly obstinate Protestant to deal with him himself, and the outbuildings of the château would then echo with the sound of blows and coarse shouts of "Abjure! abjure!"

If he hoped to compel the Marquise du Plessis's admiration for his zeal in the cause of God, Captain Montadour was making a big mistake. She came to detest him, and all his attempts to interest her in his good works were fruitless. But when she had heard him speak that moning of a certain pastor from Geneva whom he hoped to arrest that evening, thanks to his spies, at Grandhier château, where the pastor had been staying, she pricked up her ears.

"A pastor from Geneva? What's he doing here?"

"He's here to stir up riots amongst these blasphemers. Luckily I've been forewarned. Tonight he'll be leaving the forest, where he's been meeting that damned La Morinière! I'm going to ambush him near the château of Grandhier, and if the Duc is with him, which he may well be, I shall arrest him too. Monsieur de Marillac knew what he was about when he put me in charge of this bit of work. Believe me, Madame, by next year there won't be a Protestant left in Poitou."

She sent for La Violette who had once been Philippe's valet.

"Now you're a member of the Reformed Church; do you know where the Duc de La Morinière and his brother are hiding? We must warn them that they are about to fall into a trap."

The valet knew nothing. After some hesitation he said that the Duc sometimes sent him messages by means of a falcon that had been trained to carry notes. He himself obtained what information he could from the soldiers in order to help the Protestants. But there was not much to report. Montadour was not such a fool as he seemed, and, although he liked the sound of his own voice, he did not give much away.

"I don't think even the soldiers themselves know about this Protestant pastor you mentioned; in fact I'd be prepared to swear they don't. They'll only be told about it at the last moment. He's a suspicious one he is, and cunning too."

Angélique had sent La Violette over to Grandhier to warn the Seigneur and his lady. But they did not know where the meeting in the forest was to take place. The outlaws often changed their hideout. Monsieur de Grandhier had tried to enter the forest but had been stopped by a company of dragoons who "just happened" to be on patrol near his house.

It was then that Angélique remembered the witch Mélusine.

"I'll go to her and then I shall find them all right."

She had been planning to run off like this from under Montadour's very nose for a long time now; just to stretch the rope that held her tied to her stake. . . . Now it looked as if her venture would be successful.

65

The witch stopped, and raised a bony forefinger.
"Listen!"

Rising up over the dark cliffside, through the leaves, came a sound that could have been the soughing of the wind, but as they drew nearer they were able to pick out the rise and fall of a sombre melody and a recurring long-drawn-out invocation: it was the sound of psalm-singing.

The Protestants were gathered together by the river Vendée, deep in the gorge known as the Giant's Gorge, because Gargantua was said to have tipped the colossal round boulders that strewed the ground over the edge with one shove of his shoulder.

The red glow of a fire shone through the dusk that filled the gorge. You could only just see the white coifs of the women praying there, mingled with the big black felt hats of the Huguenot peasants.

Then a man stepped forward into the firelight. From the witch's description of him, Angélique had no difficulty in recognizing Duc Samuel. This huge bearded figure of a huntsman was impressive.

Louis XIV had not liked the look of him when the Duc had come to Versailles, bent on playing the same part in Court intrigues that Admiral de Coligny had played in the previous century. He had retired in disfavour to his estates where he had lived ever since.

With his high boots that reached half-way up his thighs, his black cloth doublet, girt with a broad belt that held a dagger and a crossbelt for his sword, and wearing one of those flat old-fashioned hats with a feather that Huguenots in the provinces wore, and that made them look like either Calvin or Luther according to how much they measured round the waist, Duc Samuel de La Morinière was a formidable figure of a man. He seemed to belong to another age, an age when men were rougher and more violent in their manner and despised delicacy. He was in his true element here, in this wild landscape of boulders and darkness, and, when he lifted up his voice, the walls of rock sent it echoing back even deeper, a voice as strong as brass, harsh and heavy, that made Angélique tremble.

"My brethren, my sons, the day has come when after our long silence we must lift up our heads and realize that to serve God we have to take action. Open the Good Book. What do you find?

"The Lord shall go forth as a mighty man. He shall stir up jealousy like a man of war; He shall cry, yea, roar; He shall prevail against His enemies. I have long time holden my peace; I have been still and refrained myself . . . I will make waste mountains and hills and dry up all their herbs . . . They shall be turned back, they shall be greatly ashamed that trust in graven images, that say to the molten images . . . Ye are our gods."

His voice rang out. Angélique felt a cold shiver run down her spine. She turned towards the witch but saw that she had slipped silently away.

The sky still shone silvery white through the treetops, but in the darkness of the Giant's Gorge a heavy cloud of anger hung over everything.

A voice shouted:

"But what can we do against the King's troops?"

"Everything. There are more of us than there are King's men, and God is on our side."

"But the King is all-powerful!"

"The King is far away and what can he do when a whole province rises up in its own defence?"

"The Catholics will betray us."

"The Catholics are just as afraid of the dragoons as we are. They too are overburdened with taxes and, besides, there are fewer of them. We have the best land . . ."

A screech-owl hooted twice, very close.

Angélique jumped. A silence seemed to have fallen on the Giant's Gorge. When she looked again she saw that the Huguenot lord had turned towards her. The flames made his deep-set eyes beneath their black brows glow red. "Eyes of fire," the witch had said, "but *you* could meet their gaze."

The owl's hoot rose again, velvety and sombre. Was it a signal? Was it a warning of some danger that lurked around the worshippers? Angélique bit her lip.

"I must," she said to herself. "It's my last card!"

She came forward, clinging to the thorny branches as she climbed down towards the group of Huguenots.

Angélique realized that by going to the Giant's Gorge to save the Genevese pastor's life she had chosen the way she was to go, and that it would not be easy to go back.

Samuel de La Morinière, the Patriarch, was the only man capable of shattering the faith in the Monarch that filled the hearts of loyal Protestant subjects.

La Morinière was almost fifty. He was a widower and father to three daughters—a great grief to him—and he lived on his estate with his two brothers Hugh and Lancelot, both of whom were married and had numerous offspring. The whole tribe lived under the grim rule of their Patriarch, and spent their days either praying or hunting. Gone was the time when La Morinière had provided the sumptuous setting for many a festivity. Now the La Morinière women spoke in low voices and had forgotten how to smile. The children, overburdened by a multitude of tutors, were brought up from their earliest childhood on Greek, Latin and the Holy Scriptures. The boys were taught how to handle hunting spears and daggers. When La Morinière met Angélique for the first time, when she appeared out of the dusk, her golden hair tucked into a shepherdess's hood with her feet bare and the polished speech of a lady, did he feel that here was someone who felt as passionately as he did, although as yet in an ill-defined way? Did he sense in her a feeling of bitterness that was seeking an outlet, and that would make her receptive to his suggestions?

CHAPTER 7

THE MAN who blew the hunting horn of an evening was spared from Montadour's persecution for the moment, perhaps because the manor house at Rambourg was close to Plessis, and the Captain felt sure he could lay his heavy hands, whenever he chose to do so, on this poor trembling wretch of a Huguenot, who looked as if he was entirely reconciled to the idea of being on the receiving end of the persecution.

When they were young, Angélique and her sisters had often made fun of the tall gangling lad with the prominent Adam's apple whom they met at village meetings and fêtes in the neighbouring towns. With the years the Baron de Rambourg had acquired a long drooping moustache, and a constantly pregnant wife with a flock of pasty-faced little Huguenots clinging to her skirts. Unlike the majority of his faith he was very poor. The local people said that the family had been unlucky since the ninth generation because of a knight of the house who had attempted to make love to a fairy sleeping in a château on the banks of the Sèvre. The curse had become even more disastrous, as was only to be expected, from the time the family embraced Calvin's religion. Isaac, the last-born of that name, lived in the shadow of his ivy-mantled tower, and all he could do or was asked to do was blow the horn. It was astonishing the amount of breath there was in that puny frame. All and sundry invited him to their meets, for he rendered the different calls so gorgeously and sumptuously that he thrilled hunters, hounds and game alike.

But over the last year the meets had become rare events. The Catholic and Protestant squires kept away from one another on their own estates and awaited the end of the disturbances created by the military. The Baron de Rambourg must have given in to the Duc de La Morinière's persuasions. The Duc was not an easy man to disagree with.

Angélique realized this more fully when she saw the Huguenot leader striding over the heath towards her with his black cloak floating in the wind. He was even more impressive standing out against the blue of the sky than in the darkness of the Giant's Gorge. His brothers were with him.

Their meeting-place at the edge of the forest was set on a cliff looking out over the landscape. On this strip of land overgrown with broom a Roman camp had once stood. A little half-ruined temple dedicated to Venus, with asphodels growing inside it, was still standing.

69

Had the Romans, finding themselves on the brink of the haunted abyss and at the edge of the dreaded Gaulish forest, prayed to the goddess to protect their virility against the threats of the ferocious Picts who did not hesitate to offer unspeakable trophies to their own gods? Only the ruins remained, a stone porch with twin columns and a pediment covered with Latin inscriptions. Angélique sat down in its shadow.

The Duc seated himself opposite her on a square block. His two brothers stayed to one side. The Roman camp was one of their regular rallying-points. Huguenot peasants hid arms and supplies for the outlaws in the temple. From up here they could survey the entire region and they could not be taken by surprise.

The Duc began by thanking her once more for what she had done for the Genevese pastor. Her act proved that barriers of belief could be overcome when people outraged by injustice made common cause against the abuses of their tyrannical rulers. He was well aware that she had had to suffer much from the King. Moreover, was she not kept under guard like a prisoner? How did Madame du Plessis manage to join them? She explained that she used an underground passage. Montadour suspected nothing.

It was difficult not to answer the Duc de La Morinière when he asked you a question. His imperious tone compelled you to give an immediate account of yourself. His eyes, very deep-set under his bushy brows, had an unwavering stare. They were like two gold specks, and their piercing brightness eventually tired you. Angélique averted her gaze. She thought of the witch, who was afraid of the grim servant of the Lord.

For her meeting with him today she had put on a dress suitable to her rank, dark in colour but of rich satin, and it had been no easy task to slip down the narrow passage leading to the forest, with her corset squeezing her waist and encumbered by the heavy folds of her three petticoats. La Violette, the valet, had accompanied her carrying her cloak. He was standing motionless a few yards away as a faithful servant should.

Angélique wanted the interview to be fairly formal so that she could speak to the Duc on a basis of equality.

She was sitting in a Roman porch, its stones darkened by the passage of centuries, her red leather shoes showing under the hem of her plum-coloured dress, while her hair, which had been put up in a rather severe style, gradually came loose in the wind. She listened to the heavy voice. She listened with a tight heart, attracted and yet fearful. An abyss yawned at her feet, or so it seemed to her. She would have to jump resolutely in.

"What is it that you wish of me, sir?"

"I want us to be allies. You are a Catholic; I belong to the Reformed Church. But we can be allies, allies in persecution, allies in our freedom of mind. Montadour is living under your roof. Spy on him, and report to us. And then there are your Catholic peasants."

He leant forward to make his imperious will felt even more strongly.

"Make them understand that they are on the same side as our peasants, that they are men of Poitou like them, that the real enemy is the soldier who comes and robs them of their crops. Remind them of the tax-collector, the property tax, the poll tax. Wouldn't they be better off living under the direct rule of their own lords, as they used to, than working for a far-off King whose only reward to them is to send them armies of foreigners to feed."

His leather-gauntleted hands—hawking gauntlets they were—were resting on his massive thighs while he thus spoke, leaning towards her, and she could no longer avoid his gaze. He instilled into her his profound faith in a desperate venture, which was like a bound giant's last convulsive writhings to burst his bonds. She saw this great peasant nation raising itself up and stretching itself in a superhuman effort to tear itself free of the clogging quicksands into which the man who had once been no more than the Lord of the Ile-de-France had plunged it. She saw the money hard won in the furrows of the provinces swallowed up in the festivities of Versailles or in the interminable wars on the borders of Lorraine and Picardy, the great names of Poitou holding the shirt or

71

the candle at the King's levees, while their domains were left in the hands of dishonest stewards; she saw others living impoverished on their estates which the Treasury was gradually taxing away from them while despising them for failing to find favour at Court; and now ruin and famine crawling like vipers over the countryside because of an army dispatched in defiance of justice and common sense to reduce to final despair those who grew the grain, guarded the pastures and harvested the fruit, peasants with work-worn hands and big dark hats, whether Huguenots or Catholics ...

She knew all that. She listened intently. The wind was growing sharper. She shivered and brushed aside a wisp of hair that persisted in blowing across her face. La Violette came up with her cloak. She wrapped it about her with a passionate gesture. All at once she wrung her hands and lifted a heart-rending gaze to Samuel de La Morinière.

"Yes, I will help you," she cried, "but your war must be forthright and bloody. What do you expect to gain from hymn-singing in a ravine? You must capture towns, control roads; you must turn the whole province into a fortress before they have time to send reinforcements; you must range from north to south closing all the gates, you must infect other provinces, Normandy, Britanny, Saintonge and Berry. The King must be compelled to negotiate with you as if you were another King, and be reduced to accepting your terms. . . ."

The Duc was shaken by the passion of her outburst. He straightened up, his face turned a reddish brown and his eyes flashed. He was not accustomed to having a woman speak to him like this. But he restrained himself. He sat silent for a moment, twirling the ends of his long pointed beard. He had realized that he could rely on the wild strength of this woman whom he had thought but a moment before to be only an insignificant creature like all women. All sorts of maxims that an uncle of his who had served with Richelieu used to repeat came back to him. The latter had been much given to using women's services in matters of espionage or politics. "A woman is twice as strong as a man when it comes to undermining the foundations of a town. . . . Even if they are prepared to proclaim it quite openly women never really admit themselves beaten. It takes a strong pair of gloves to handle that sharp instrument—a woman's cunning—but I know of nothing that cuts half so well. . . ." That was what Richelieu had said.

He took a deep breath.

"Madame, you speak truly. You are right in saying that that is the only goal to aim at. And, if we are not resolved to attain it, we might as well lay down our arms at once. Have patience. Help us. And one day it shall be as you have said, I promise you that!"

CHAPTER 8

AND THEN a new wave of crime and skirmishing swept over the land, and hatred of the red dragoons spread like the thousand tiny rivulets of a stream through the grass. It all began when four dragoons were found hanged at the Three Owls crossroad. Each corpse bore a placard on which was inscribed the words: "Fire-raiser—Plunderer—Famine—Ruin." Their comrades did not dare to remove the bodies, because they were on the edge of the forest, and it was now known that the Protestants were in hiding there. So the sinister scarlet-coated spectres hung there, slowly gyrating, to remind those who passed by of the threats that hung over the province: the threats of fire, of plunder, of famine and of ruin. . . . The dense summer foliage formed an emerald temple about them, a gorgeous chapel, and hanging in the midst of this beauty they seemed even more dead and hideous.

Montadour, frothing with rage, wanted to strike a telling blow. He had a Protestant tortured to make him tell where La Morinière was hidden, then, taking his most resolute men with him, he entered the forest. After several hours of tramping, their courage was drained from them by the silence, the darkness, the incredible thickness of the foliage, the colossal size of the tree-trunks, the knotty branches hanging low over them, and

73

the spreading roots over which they stumbled in their high boots. An owl hooted, suddenly wakened, and that finished them.

"It's their call, Captain, they are there among the trees. They are going to go for us. . . ."

The dragoons beat a retreat, looking frantically for a clearing, for a patch of open sky, for a well-trodden path. They got stuck in the thickets and lost their way. When dusk came and they saw the edge of the woods and the tilled fields before them, such was their relief that some of them fell down on their knees and vowed to burn a candle in the nearest chapel of Our Lady.

Had they reached their goal, they would have come back empty-handed. The Huguenot leaders had been warned.

Montadour could hardly have thought that his prisoner's new friendliness towards him had anything to do with his military setbacks. She, who had been so haughty and never to be seen, would now come up and speak to him. He had even been bold enough to ask her if she would care to eat at "his" table. He thought she must be bored, and that his well-known charms, along with the gallant way he had always treated her, were beginning to pay off. He redoubled his attentions. You couldn't dragoon these aristocratic ladies. You had to take pains with them. Montadour discovered the delights of a protracted conquest and became aware of the poet within him.

If only these blasted heretics weren't there to wreck so delightful a stay. He wrote to Monsieur de Marillac asking for reinforcements. He couldn't both guard the Marquise du Plessis-Bellière and cope with the growing task of conversion. Another regiment was sent to help him and was ordered to set up its headquarters near Saint-Maixent. Monsieur de Ronce, the lieutenant in charge, sent a message to say that he had been unable to take up quarters in the town because there were armed Huguenots in an old château overlooking both the road and the river Sèvre. Should he capture it?

Montadour swore yet again. What was he to think? That the Protestants were not going to be terrorized any more? This man Ronce didn't know what he was talking about. It would only need a visit from Montadour himself...

"What, would you leave me so soon?" asked Angélique in her most winsome way.

She was sitting facing him. She had just been brought a basket of the earliest ripe cherries, and she was eating them greedily. The glistening enamel of her healthy teeth shone white against the red lustre of the fruit.

Montadour made up his mind that Monsieur de Ronce would have to get on as best he could, and move a bit higher up, towards Parthenay. He had enough to do here himself, considering the general hostility amongst the people. They were already scattering nails on the ground for the horses to tread on. These wretches were all the same, whether they were Huguenots or Catholics. They had jars full of gold pieces in their cellars, but that didn't make them any easier in their minds. Whichever way they turned, they saw the glistening eyes of their three age-old enemies: the wolf, the soldier and the tax-collector.

They were becoming more and more panic-stricken, because often, when a Protestant's crops were fired, the blaze would spread to Catholic fields. Not a single one of these boorish peasants would give up three ears of corn for his religion. They all came from the same litter, these Poitou men with their Arab eyes, who shook their fists at you when your back was turned.

"Send the awkward customers to me," said Angélique. "I'll give them a good talking-to."

And so there was quite a lot of coming and going at the château. Some of Angélique's Catholic neighbours also called on her. One of them was Monsieur de Croissec, fatter than ever, who was not long in coming round to her ideas and gladly took orders from a mouth he had worshipped secretly for years. Monsieur and Madame de Faymoron, the Mermenaults, the Saint-Aubins and the Maziéres also called. A kind of society life started up between the outcast and the recluses of the Bocage. Montadour thought how charming it all was. He wrote and told Monsieur de Marillac that Madame du Plessis was helping him most assiduously in his weighty undertaking, and these gentlemen of the Company of the Blessed Sacrament must have rejoiced in their hearts.

The Captain found it more and more difficult to tear himself away from the fascinations of this woman who became more attractive to him every day. Angélique, fully restored to beauty, once again delighting in wearing elegant dresses, had begun to rule her own household.

Was the witch's potion responsible for the new glow in her cheeks, the new lustre of her hair? Her body was transfused with a lucid strength, her soul flooded with the intensity of her passion. Once again she felt that heady sensation of invincibility which had often taken hold of her when she was about to undertake a difficult task. Of course, on occasion the feeling had misled her. Beneath her feet the earth moved, the fever rose, the storm clouds were massing as they did in July, dazzling mounds in the scorching blue of the sky.

Summer hung over them. It was haymaking time. All too often the work had to be stopped. Dragoons were busy, dragging the women to Mass by their hair, and, if they would not take part, the soldiers would burn the soles of their feet, then take their pleasure of them. But over and over again the looters and converters would be met by peasants with flails in their hands.

The ferment of unrest was growing.

CHAPTER 9

THE DUC DE LA MORINIÈRE communicated with Angélique by means of a falcon that La Violette caught on his closed fist.

The bird bore a message. The meeting-place that night was to be in the Roman encampment or at the Fairy stone, at a crossroad, by a wayside cross, by a spring, in a cave . . . Angélique would go alone. These nocturnal forays did not frighten her; she enjoyed them. Would Montadour have recognized his elegant prisoner, if he had glimpsed the woman dressed in a short fustian skirt, creeping from the end of the underground passage off into the thicket at moonrise?

For a brief space as she covered the ground to the meeting place, Angélique would revel in the joy of walking in the half-light. Diamonds sparkled on the myriad beech-leaves and cascaded from the chestnuts, and the oaks were studded with silver.

Never for one moment did she fear running into any of the wild beasts that still had their lairs in the forest: there were boars, wolves and, rumour had it, sometimes even bears. The forest frightened her less than human society, which wounds one to the heart when it strikes, and as she walked on she seemed to be at one again with the innocence that had been hers in the desert and that she still yearned after.

Once at the meeting-place, her joy left her. She began to look around, impatient and apprehensive, for the Huguenots. She could hear their footsteps, the sound carried from afar through the leafy silence. She could make out the sound of low voices and could see their red torches shining through the trees.

At first the Duc de La Morinière came with his brothers, then more and more often he took to coming unaccompanied. This made her uneasy.

When he was alone he did not carry a torch. He too seemed to be able to see in the dark and to be familiar with the faintest of forest tracks. And when he appeared in all his blackness, his heavy boots snapping the dry twigs underfoot, and came out into a pale moonlit clearing, she had to suppress a shudder that she herself did not fully understand. The Patriarch's voice was rough and very deep, almost sepulchral, and his blazing eyes seemed to be trying to probe the depths of her soul. She could see contempt and arrogance in them. There was something about the man that repelled her. Even Mulai Ismail had seemed less fearsome. He had been a terrible master in his own way, but, as a woman, she had not feared him.

Mulai Ismail loved women and he delighted in taming them. He was responsive to their charms, to their beauty, their wiles and their seductiveness. A tiny hand could, with a little cleverness, keep the desert lion at bay.

For the Duc de La Morinière, women were all either good or bad. He was still famous at Versailles for his diatribes against the fair seductresses, and he must never have noticed that his own wife was ugly and cantankerous. He was a widower and had never remarried. Perhaps the austere life he led, hunting and mortification of the flesh, helped him to keep his hot-blooded temperament under control. He despised woman as something impure and must have deplored the fact that the Creator had found a place for her in His universe.

Angélique was quick to sense such sentiments, and they exasperated her. But she needed this man's strength if she was to pit herself against the King. Nothing would deflect him from his path. She could not, however, help feeling guilty before God and the Virgin for having entered into an alliance with the Huguenot.

Their latent antagonism led to an outburst one night when they were creeping along a hilltop path on their way to the marshes. A pastor from Niort travelling through the waterways was waiting for the Duc, and Angélique had offered to guide the Duc to the rendezvous. The forest seemed to be thinning out, the moonlight shone brightly through the gap, and they caught a glimpse of amethyst roofs and translucent belfries down below them.

They were looking down on a shrine carved out of pure silver, a vast edifice of light and shade in which the velvety black festoon of a cloister stood out against the brilliant white patch of a courtyard with the black dot of an ornamental well in the centre: Nieul Abbey.

Angélique held her breath. How marvellously beautiful it was! There lay the Abbey, serene and enclosed, enshrining the murmuring prayers of the monks. Angélique felt herself swept by a flood of memories; of a night that she had spent at the Abby when she was a girl, and of the monk, Brother John, who had rescued her from the doubtful attentions of fat Brother Thomas. He had taken her to his cell so that she would be safe. He had looked at her, his eyes full of a luminous tenderness:

"Your name is Angélique. Angélique, Daughter of the Angels," and he had shown her the bruises on his body, lamenting: "Look! ... Look at what Satan has done to me!"

The enchantment of that mystic night came back to her heart.

The Duc de La Morinière spoke, and his voice was full of hate.

"A curse upon these lewd idolatrous monks! One day the Fire of Heaven will strike these walls and there shall not remain a stone upon a stone. And the earth will be purified."

Angélique rounded upon him, beside herself with indignation.

"Silence, heretic! Heretic! How I hate your infamous sect."

Her cry came echoing back, and suddenly she was seized with horror, her nerves straining with impotent rage and anxiety. The Duc had stepped close to her. She could hear his low breathing. He seized her roughly by the shoulder, and his grip was like a vice. Her throat tightened. She would have liked to shake off this yoke but could not. He was dangerously close, his face cut off the light, and she could only remain motionless, breathing in the smell of this man, a smell of war and hunting.

"What is this you say?" he breathed, "you hate us? What matter! You will continue to help us all the same," he insisted, "you will not betray us?"

"I have never betrayed anyone," she said proudly, choking back her tears. Her legs were trembling. She was afraid that she was going to faint, and to collapse against him. She stiffened herself to escape from the hand which was bruising her shoulder.

"Leave me alone," she said faintly, "you frighten me." The vice of his fingers relaxed, and he slowly removed his hand.

Angélique walked on again, her heart pounding. She had been afraid, of him, yes, but of herself as well; afraid of sliding into the nameless darkness which the forest boughs hold open to desire. With the dawn, which showed grey at first and then russet among the trees, they reached the charcoal-burners' camp. Angélique was cold and drew her cloak tightly about her.

"Ho there, peasants!" shouted the Duc, "have you broth, bread and cheese?"

They sat down on wobbly stools at a table in one of the smoke-blackened huts and their host's wife set a jug of milk before them. She added a dish of burning hot beans garnished with bacon and onions. The children, half-naked and black to the eyes, stared open-mouthed at the two people silently eating, the black-bearded man and the woman with the golden hair lying loose and wet with dew upon her shoulders, whom they had seen looming up like phantoms out of the night through the morning mists across the ash-bed.

Angélique cast furtive glances at the Duc de La Morinière. It was probably something reminiscent of Colin Paturel in his broad shoulders that attracted her to him. But Colin Paturel was Adam, the splendid man of Paradise Lost; this man was a man of Sin, a man of Darkness.

"He came right to your bedroom door," her little maid, Bertille, whispered to Angélique when she got back to Plessis.

"Who do you mean?"

"Gargantua. He scratched and knocked and called. . . . But you didn't answer . . ."

"There was good reason for that," she thought to herself.

Captain Montadour returned the following night. He called:

"Marquise, Marquise!"

His hands wandered over the locked door and she could hear his uniform buttons on his fat belly scratching against the wood.

She listened, half propping herself up on one elbow. Montadour's panting lust at her door in the night frightened her even less than it tempted her.

Indeed it was he who was beginning to be afraid. There was no denying that there was a strange silence behind that door at night, and he was almost prepared to believe the stories told by the servants about their mistresss changing into a hind at night and ranging the forests.

The apples reddened on the trees, and all at once La Morinière's three brothers galloped through the province. From Tiffauges in the north to Moncontour in the east the Protestants' defensive movements assumed unexpected proportions.

"Stay where you are," Marillac wrote to Captain Montadour. "The region in which you are stationed is the focal point of the rebellion. Try to get your hands on the leaders."

He added a postscript:

"Keep a close watch on the person you are guarding. I note that unrest is constantly growing and she may have a hand in it!"

Thereupon the Governor placed himself at the head of his pikemen in northern Poitou. Four Protestant villages which had withstood a full-dress siege by the soldiers ordered to occupy them were burnt to the ground. The men they could catch were hanged. The rest had gone to swell the forces recruited by La Morinière. The women and children were gathered together and driven out on to the roads after publication of an edict concerning them: "It is strictly forbidden to offer counsel, comfort or aid to the heretical women of the villages of Noireterre, Pierrefitte, Quingé and Arbec, or take them in, feed them, give them fire or water, or offer than any humane service."

Whereupon the Governor's troops rushed off to central Poitou in order to hunt down the Protestant bands. As they had been warned that La Morinière's three brothers had succeeded in mobilizing considerable forces, they requested the assistance of the Bressuire militia.

The town in question, which had a Protestant majority, supplied but few men. Monsieur de Marillac learnt almost immediately afterwards that La Morinière's little army had entered Bressuire, thus stripped of its defenders, and had spread through the deserted streets shouting: "The town is captured! The town is captured!", and that they had plundered the arms stores.

Monsieur de Marillac did not deign to recapture the town. He was still unwilling to admit to himself that these skirmishes were assuming the proportions of a religious war, if not a civil one. He called at Plessis to consult Montadour.

From the ramparts of the forest of Nieul the Huguenots watched the long gray column of the army with its bristling pikes winding along the Roman road.

The following day the troops withdrew, leaving only a few reinforcements with Montadour's dragoons. The hostility of the local people, even the Catholics, who had denied the soldiers bread and wine, and had greeted them with showers of stones, disturbed the Governor. He could not leave all these troops in position without running the risk of a more extensive uprising. He marched his soldiers back to beyond Poitiers and set out for Paris to discuss with the Minister, Louvois, what measures should be taken.

CHAPTER 10

ANGÉLIQUE raced along like a mad woman, tugging at the bushes, drawing her cloak around her to free it when it got caught up in them, not paying the slightest attention to the branches which lashed her face.

"You've smashed the statues," she cried to Samuel de La Morinière as soon as she caught sight of him.

He had risen to his feet beside the Fairy Stone, and stood there as black as primeval obsidian, hateful, the very image of evil. The more terrified he made her feel, the more violent she became.

"You are the one who's the traitor. You have deceived me. You wanted to make an alliance with the Catholics so that you could destroy them more effectively afterwards. You are a man without honour."

She broke off, choking; there was a buzzing in her head, and the full round moon sailing above the tops of the oaks which stood about the clearing danced before her eyes and appeared to jerk about in all directions. She had to lean on one of the dolmens to save herself

82

from falling. The feel of the stone brought her round.

"You struck me!"

A cruel leer lit up the Patriarch's black beard.

"That is how I treat weak, impudent women. Never before has woman dared to take that tone with me."

Angélique's feeling of humiliation made her lose her head. She succeeded in finding the only barbed shaft capable of penetrating the fanatic's thick skin.

"Women! I can't imagine any woman who wouldn't prefer to be made love to by the devil rather than by you."

She could have bitten her tongue out as soon as she saw his reaction. He seized her by both arms and began to shake her roughly, growling:

"Made love to! Made love to! Who's talking about lovemaking? Vile, sinful creature! Pernicious wretch!" He was pressing her to him with the strength of madness, and his breath was hot on her face. She now understood why she had feared him. She must have felt subconsciously that he would kill her, that she was to die by his hand. He would strangle her or cut her throat. It would be easy for him in this remote corner of the woods, and the sacrificial stone stood ready to hand.

Nevertheless, she struggled furiously, bruising herself on his belt buckles and against the rough material of his doublet in her efforts to tear herself free. Her opponent's strength was gradually overcoming her. Her fear was giving way to another feeling, a feeling tinctured with primitive desire, blind, avid, carnal desire. The erotic frenzy which seemed to have taken possession of the man was paralysing her in her struggle and was undermining her resistance in spite of herself.

She was lying on the ground, her throat hoarse with her rending breath, her eyes dazzled by the brightness of the moonlight striking full on her face.

Her movements were becoming aimless.

She had forgotten what he was ... who he was. Her head lolled back, and she felt the coolness of the ground on her naked back.

But just as she was about to abandon herself, her brain, haunted by insane visions, suddenly projected

83

into her consciousness an hallucination in which the evil spells hanging over the Druids' glade were mingled with the witch's prophecies.

She gave a wild cry.

In one demented bound she wrested herself from his grasp, rolled over, sprang to her feet and rushed off through the trees.

She ran for a long time, borne along by her terror. Instinct guided her over the dark paths which she had so often followed in recent months. She did not lose her way. Now and then she stopped to weep with nervous exhaustion, her head pressed against a tree. She wanted to turn her hate against the forest, the sublimely indifferent monarch that sheltered equally in its fastnesses the prayers of monks, the psalm-singing of the hunted Huguenots, the crimes of poachers, the coupling of wolves and the pagan rites of sorceresses.

She felt the hurt of a child who has no further refuge in this world, who has been hurt by the pain of living. The night was even darker when she reached the outskirts of the Plessis château.

Twice she gave the call of the owl, raising her hands to her lips quite mechanically, so natural had this gesture become to her. Her servants were on the look-out, and an answering call came from the top of the tower.

Malbrant-Swordthrust was standing in the cellar at the entrance to the passage with a stub of candle in his hand.

"This sort of life can't go on, Madame," he said. "All this wandering about the woods at night . . . it's madness. Next time I'll go with you."

The old groom must have noticed the disorder of her clothes and her hair, and the marks of tears on her cheeks, which she had not wiped properly. She drew herself up straight, resumed her normal expression and groped after a handkerchief in her cloak pocket.

"Yes, you come with me next time, or rather La Violette, for the forest is too damp for your rheumatism. And I haven't got much faith in that fellow either. But who can I have faith in?" she muttered.

They were emerging from the cellars into the silent house. She forced herself to smile indifferently:

"Is the other ogre asleep?" she questioned, pointing in the direction of the Captain's apartment.

Once back in her room she took off her torn clothes and washed herself in the neighbouring dressing-room. She could still feel the grip of the Huguenot leader's arms scorching her backbone, and the feel of his rough hot hands on her skin.

She took the jug of cool water and poured it over her naked body. Then she wrapped herself in a bathrobe and combed the twigs out of her hair.

She still felt horribly sore. The thought of what had happened that night in the forest would never leave her. It reminded her of the bitter experience she had had with that hysterical madman, Escrainville. "And I thought I'd been through the worst," she said to herself. She went back into her bedroom and put down the candle beside the mirror.

Stooping forward she scrutinized her face and read in it the transformation that it had undergone in the space of a few weeks. Her cheeks had regained their smooth oval line, her eyes were less hollow, and her lips were bright and soft and red again like the flesh of wild strawberries.

All that remained of the past was the new, rather tragic shadow beneath her cheekbones, moulded by the hand of suffering which gave her face, that for so long had stayed like a young girl's, the proud mark of maturity.

A favourite no longer, a queen now.

"And what if the worst is still to come? . . ."

She tried to tone down the touch of wildness in her expression. How would her new face look under Versailles make-up?

She opened the doors of her dressing-cabinet and drew out the creams and powders she kept in onyx-jars. She also took out a small sandalwood box inlaid with mother-of-pearl and opened it mechanically.

There she could gaze upon the different phases of her

85

adventurous life summed up in a few trinkets: a quill
that had belonged to the Gutter Poet, Rodogone the
Egyptian's dagger, little Cantor's wooden egg, the neck-
lace of the Plessis-Bellière women, the one they could
not wear "without their thoughts at once running on war
and rebellion." There were two turquoises side by side,
Prince Bakhtiari Bey's and Osman Faraji's: "Have no
fear, Firousi, for the stars are telling the most beautiful
story in all the world . . ." Her first wedding ring, lost
when she was at the Court of Miracles, stolen, she
suspected, by Nicholas the beggar while she was asleep,
was missing.

It had been a hard road with sunlight and shadows
alternating ever since the King's will had made her a
widow without name, rights or resort. She had been
only twenty at the time. Later, after her marriage to
Philippe and up to the time of her departure for Candia, the years she had spent amid the pomp of the
Court could be regarded as years of peace. Yes, if one
considered her triumphant existence as a great lady
heaped with favours, with her great private house in
Paris, her own apartment at Versailles, hurrying from
one party to another. No, if she remembered the intrigues in which she had been involved, the traps laid
for her at every step. But there she was at least conform-
ing to the established order, and ranked among the
mighty of this world.

Her break with the King had flung her into the chaos
of the outer darkness. What was it that the great seer,
Osman Faraji, had said:

"The power which the Creator has put in thee will not
let thee stop until thou hast come to the place which
thy destiny has decreed."

"Where is that, Osman Bey "

"I know not. But until thou hast reached it, thou wilt
trample to ruin all that lies in thy path, even thy own
life . . ."

She would see Samuel de La Morinière again. She
would have to! She began to curse him in her heart,
irritated by the morbid temptation which still lodged in
her breast, and which would overcome her again when

she stood once more in his presence. The man was at least twenty years older than she. He was a heretic, with no sense of humour, sombre and cruel. But the thought of him obsessed her, and she looked into her heart in an attempt to discover whether he really possessed the superhuman power that had frightened her so badly When she thought of certain things that had happened during their struggle, her throat grew tight.

She took some cream on her fingertips from one of the jars and began to massage her temples lightly with it. The looking-glass, which was as clear as the water of a forest pool, reflected back the light on her hair. In it she saw, dimly at first but becoming increasingly clear like a nightmare shape, wavering back and forth and gingery red in the middle, the reflection of Captain Montadour's moustache.

He had crept silently to her door, turned the handle, and to his surprise found that it opened without difficulty. His initial feeling of triumph giving way to fear, he had peered into the darkness lit by a single candle. He had seen Angélique standing in front of her mirror.

Was she going to turn into a hind?

Her long transparent dressing-gown revealed her perfect figure. Her hair hanging loose on her shoulders was like a warm-tinted cape. She bent her head slightly forward, and her fingers brought delicate roses to her cheeks.

Then he had crept nearer.

Angélique turned round, stunned with surprise.

"You?"

"Were you not good enough to leave your door unlocked, my beauty?"

He was sweating profusely, and his eyes were almost out of sight behind his red swelling cheekbones, so anxious was he to put on his most ingratiating smile. He reeked of wine, and his outstretched hands were trembling.

"Come now, my beauty, haven't you kept me on a string long enough? You must be quite keen by now yourself, pretty young thing that you are. We could have a jolly good time together, don't you think?"

He was not making a very good job of it, and he knew it. But he could not get his tongue round the pretty speeches he had meant to make, and here he was trotting out his ghastly vulgarities. He thought it better to get on with the serious business, where he would have a better chance to shine, and grabbed her with both arms. She was almost sick when she felt the flabby mass of his great belly against her and threw herself back, knocking over one of the onyx-jars, which broke on the stone floor.

Men's arms, everywhere men's arms groping after her: the King, the hired soldier, the Huguenot, and a lot more, always men's arms and men's bodies against hers. . . .

She snatched up Rodogone the Egyptian's dagger from the box and held it on guard before her in one rapid movement as Polak had taught her to do.

"Stand back or I'll bleed you like a pig."

The Captain drew back a couple of paces, his eyes round with astonishment.

"What . . . how?" he stammered. "And she'd do it too!"

His incredulous gaze went from the glittering blade to the no less glittering eyes of the woman who held it.

"Oh! come now. . . . There's some misunderstanding. . . .

Then he turned round and saw the servants, who had massed in the shadows of the room and were blocking the door, Malbrant with his sword drawn, the flunkeys, the valets, one with a stick, another with a knife, and even Lin Poiroux, the cook, with his white cap and his scullions at his back, all of them armed with their roasting-spits and their best larding-needles.

"Would there be anything you require, Captain, sir?" asked the groom in a tone heavy with menace.

Montadour threw a glance at the open window and then at the door. What the devil were they all doing here with their wild looks?

"Clear out!" he growled.

"We only take orders from our mistress," retorted Malbrant ironically.

La Violette slipped quietly across to the window and closed it. It was now no good Montadour trying to call.

He realized that there was nothing to stop them murdering him there and then with a few thrusts of their swords or larding-needles. His men were in their quarters outside and there were only four of them at that, as the others had been sent to a village where there had been a report of Protestant bands.

His forehead broke out in a cold sweat which flowed down the fatty rolls of his neck. Out of military habit he put his hand on his sword, resolved to sell his life dearly.

"Let him go," said Angélique to her servants.

She added with an icy smile:

"Captain Montadour is my guest.... If he behaves himself as a gentleman, nothing will happen to him *under my roof.*"

He went out shaken and suspicious. He brought his men into the château. He no longer felt safe in this God-forsaken hole. A nest of bandits under the orders of a dangerous female, that was the mess he had got himself in!

The silence of the grounds broken only by the hoot of an owl froze his heart with terror. He posted a sentry at his door for the night.

CHAPTER 11

TWO SLIM young silhouettes stood out black in the sunlit doorway.

"Florimond!" exclaimed Angélique.

She repeated, unbelievingly: "Florimond! Father de Lesdiguièrel ..."

They walked towards her, smiling. Forimond dropped on one knee and kissed his mother's hand. The priest did likewise.

"But why? ... Who? ... How on earth? ... Your uncle said ..."

Questions crowded to her lips. After her initial surprise she felt quite overwhelmed.

The priest explained that when he had heard of Madame du Plessis's return he was still committed for some

89

time to Marshal de la Force in whose household he had obtained the post of assistant chaplain after Angélique's departure. As soon as he was free, he had set off for Poitou, and on his way had called to see how Florimond was getting on in the College at Clermont. There, Father Raymond de Sancé had been only too pleased to hand over his old pupil to him, so that they could travel together, for his nephew had been about to set off alone to Poitou.

"But why? . . . Why? . . . Angélique repeated. "My brother said that . . ."

Father de Lesdiguière lowered his long eyelashes in confusion.

"I gathered that Florimond wasn't satisfying them and that he was being expelled."

Angélique's gaze wandered from the pleasant-faced young priest to her son. She hardly recognized him. And yet it was undoubtedly he. He had grown so, and beneath his black school jacket he was as thin as a rake. His waist, girt with a belt on which hung an ink-horn and a pen-holder, was as slender as a woman's. He was twelve! He would soon be up to her shoulder. It was when he threw back a troublesome lock of his long hair—with an off-hand uncontrite gesture—that she realized why she had been so overcome when she saw him. He looked more and more like his father. That clean-cut profile, those slightly hollow cheeks, those full and mocking lips were beginning to emerge from his childish features. It was the face of Joffrey de Peyrac if you allowed for the disfigurement of his scars. Florimond's hair seemed to be twice as thick as before, and it was jet-black.

There was a gay, mocking twinkle in his eyes that belied his quiet, well-behaved schoolboy bearing.

What had happened? She had not kissed him, she had not clutched him to her breast. But neither had he rushed at her with outstretched arms as he used to do.

"You're both covered in dust," she remarked, "you must be worn out."

"Yes, we are indeed," replied the priest. "We got lost and went at least twenty leagues out of our way. Near

Champdeniers we were stopped by a band of Huguenots who didn't like the look of my clerical garb. Florimond calmed them down by mentioning your name, and they allowed us to pass. And after that we were set on by some beggars who just wanted to relieve us of our purses. Luckily, I had my sword with me. . . . The province seems to be in a dreadfully disturbed state . . ."

"Come and have something to eat," she said, feeling somewhat recovered from her shock.

The servants bustled around. They were delighted that the young master who, with his brother Cantor, had lived for so long at Plessis, was home again. They quickly prepared fruit and cheese.

"No doubt you are surprised to see me wearing a sword," went on the priest whose soft-mannered voice struck her as being not quite real, "but Monsieur de la Force cannot bear to see any nobleman without a sword, even if he is a priest. He obtained permission from the Archbishop of Paris for his chaplains of noble birth to wear one."

He went on to explain, while delicately plying his gilt spoon, that, when the Marshal was in the field, he always insisted that his daily Mass be celebrated with as much pomp as if they were in the chapel of his château. This had led to some quaint situations with the chaplain saying Mass beneath the walls of a besieged town, and wreaths of incense mingling with the smoke from the first cannonade. "The Ark of the Covenant beneath the walls of Jericho," the delighted Marshal would comment. This was the man that Father de Lesdiguière had worked for while she was away. He had thought he would never set eyes on her again, and his heart was brimming with unspeakable joy now that he had found her once more.

While the two travellers were finishing their meal, Angélique walked over to the window to read the letter that Father de Sancé had given to her son's tutor. It was about Florimond. The child was not responding in spite of all their efforts, he said. He was not keen on intellectual studies, and this might well be because he lacked the necessary intelligence. He would repeatedly hide himself away and pore over a globe or astronomical instruments when he was supposed to be having a fencing lesson, or he would go off on horseback just as the mathematics master was about to begin a lesson. In short, his standard of discipline was abysmal, and, worst of all, he appeared to be quite unmoved by it all. The letter finished on this gloomy note, and no further explanation was offered. Angélique thought: "I know what this means," and, as she raised her eyes, she saw that the edges of the forest foliage were turning gold, and that a thicket of wild cherry had, in the past few days, taken on a blood-red hue.

Autumn had come.

All these words were only a pretext. Florimond could never have left the Jesuit College without the King's permission. Feverishly she hurried back to the young men.

"You must leave here right away," she said to the priest. "You should never have come back, nor brought Florimond with you."

Malbrant-Swordthrust entered the room and cut short the young churchman's dismayed protests.

"Well, my boy, what's become of your good sword? You've rusted up like her, learning all that rubbish. But we'll get into training again. Here! Here are three blades as fine as you'll see anywhere. I sharpened them myself for you. I was sure you'd be back soon."

"Madame," whispered the priest, "what did you say just then? Surely you can find some use for me. Couldn't I go on teaching Florimond Latin and teach your youngest son his letters. I've been ordained and I could say Mass each day in your chapel. I could hear your servants' confessions. . . ."

It was frightening how little he understood. The tenderness in his eyes betrayed his adoration; she read in them the tears he had shed in secret when he thought her gone for ever and the overwhelming joy at finding her still alive.

Could he not see how changed she was—that she was

a marked woman, that the brand of royal disfavour was upon her?

Could he not sense the dangers of revolt around them, not feel the tension? Even here in the château, could he not feel the atmosphere, heavy with sensuality, with hatred and with blood?

"Say Mass! You must be out of your mind. My house is defiled by the military. I am a prisoner here, I am humiliated and ... and ... I am a woman accursed. ..."

She had spoken, without realizing it, in a low voice, her face drawn, and she stared fixedly at the young man's eyes, the young man with the child's face, as if she wanted to find refuge in his innocence. A grave intensity came over Father de Lesdiguière's features.

"All the more reason why I should say Mass," he said gently.

He took one of Angélique's hands in his and clasped it earnestly, and his fine eyes were filled with infinte forbearance.

She glanced away, suddenly weak, and shook her head several times, as if to shake off a veil that was suffocating her. Then she yielded:

"Very well, then! You stay ... and say your Mass, my little priest. After all, it may do everybody good."

It was the season of homecomings. Two days later Flipot, having taught the rudiments of his slangy vernacular to the son of the Italian nobleman who had hired him at Leghorn, arrived back from Italy. It had taken him six months by mule, up hill and down dale, to make the journey. He had acquired the exuberant mannerisms and the volubility of a comic stage valet from working in the ornate palaces of the Adriatic coast. His tanned skin and broader shoulders were a legacy of his wanderings through the snow of Alpine passes and along the dusty roads of the French countryside. He had a mocking, sly look about him, the good looks and glib tongue that would have been just right amongst the Pont-Neuf beggars.

"Weren't you ever tempted to go back to Paris instead?" Angélique asked him.

"I did go there to inquire after you, but when they

told me you were back on your estates, I took to the road again."

"But why didn't you stay in Paris?" she persisted. "A smart lad like you would have had no difficulty in finding a good job."

"I prefer to be in your service, Madame la Marquise."

"But I can promise you no security here. I am in the King's bad books; you have always belonged in Paris, you'd feel more at home there."

He had after all been brought up in the Court of Miracles.

"But where would I go, Madame la Marquise?" he asked, pulling a wry face. "You are all the family I ever had. You've just about been a mother to me since you saved me from being beaten at the Tour de Nesle. I know myself too well: if I went back to the Pont-Neuf, I'd be back cutting purses again in no time. . . ."

"I hope you've got out of that bad habit."

"Oh, that's a different story," said Flipot. "A chap like me's got to keep his hand in. After all, I did pass my trade exams with full honours, and in any case, how would I have kept myself alive on my travels? . . . But it's when it's your only source of income that it soon gets too risky. When we were all kids at the Court of Miracles, there was an old man, I think it was old Father Hurlurot, who used to say to us every morning: 'Children, remember that you were all born to swing.' I didn't like the idea, and I still don't. I don't mind doing the occasional job, but I'd prefer to remain in your service."

"Well, if that's how it is, you can stay, and you're welcome, Flipot. You and I have been through a lot together."

The very same evening a pedlar climber up the hill to the château gates. A servant girl came to tell Angélique that a man was asking to see her "from her brother Gontran." She felt the colour drain from her cheeks and asked again and again for the name. The man was in the kitchen, standing before his open bundle, tempting the servants with ribbons, needles, gaudy pictures and patent medicines. He also had a full artist's outfit.

94

"Am I right in thinking that you claim to come from my brother Gontran?" asked Angélique.

"Yes, Madame la Marquise, I do. His lordship your brother, our workmate, gave me something for you when I set off on my trip around France. He said: 'When you're passing through Poitou, go to the château of Plessis-Bellière, near Fontenay. Ask to speak to the lady of the château and give her this from her brother Gontran.'"

"How long is it since you saw my brother?"

"More than a year."

That explained it all. While he was telling of his wanderings through Burgundy, Provence and Roussillon, of his long stops in the Pyrenees and on the shores of the blue-green ocean, he fumbled in a leather bag and took out a canvas, carefully rolled in oilskin.

Angélique took it. She told the servants to look after the craftsman, and she assured him that he would be welcome to stay beneath her roof for as long as he wished.

As soon as she was in her room, she drew the canvas from its covering and unrolled it. It was a remarkably life-like portrait of her three sons. Cantor stood in the foreground with his guitar, dressed in the green that matched his eyes. The painter had captured that special expression of his, both dreamy and amused. This was her dead child; such vitality radiated from him that it was hard to believe that he could be gone. "I shall live for ever," he seemed to be saying.

Florimond was dressed in red. Gontran—how could he have guessed!—had portrayed him with the adolescent's face he now had, with all its delicacy, its intelligence and it fire. His black hair formed a dark splash amongst all the brilliant colours in the delightful painting, and highlighted the greens, the reds, the children's pink faces, and the silky gold of little Charles-Henri's curls. He stood between his two older brothers, still a baby in his long white robes, just like an angel. He was holding out his two dimpled hands to touch Cantor's and Florimond's arms, but they did not seem to be aware of his touch. The conventional stiffness of their pose had something symbolic about it that wrung Angélique's heart. It was as if the painter—and who could ever know the depths of foreboding that filled his artist's soul!—had wanted to underline the differences between the two stocks: here were the two older boys, sons of the Comte de Peyrac, standing boldly in the foreground, as if the light of life played upon them, while the youngest, Marshal Philippe de Plessis's son, stood back a little, wondrously beautiful, but alone.

Because her heart was wrung by this feeling, she pored longest over the baby's face. "I know who he's like," she suddenly realized. "He's like my sister Madelon!" and yet it was still Charles-Henri's portrait. What subtleties there were in this inspired brush that could give to a lifeless image all the moving shades of life. The hand that had once held this brush had fallen lifeless. Death. Life. Destruction and immortality. Oblivion and yet resurrection. . . .

As she looked at the painting Angélique thought she could glimpse, as in a turning prism, or as in the shadows of clouds passing over the countryside, the interplay of gloom and brilliance that made up her life, and she sensed that there was more to come that she could not yet foresee.

Florimond had never asked her any questions. He had accepted without comment the fact that soldiers filled the grounds and that their Captain was living in his mother's house.

Since the night when the Plessis servants had threatened him, Montadour's feelings had become a mixture of impotent rage, storming arrogance and black forebodings. He would disappear for days on end, leaving the château in the hands of his lieutenant, to give chase to the Huguenots. But they would scatter in the Bocage and the corpses of dragoons sprawled across the paths. Then Montadour would hang the first peasant he came upon, and sometimes it was a Catholic. He had only to show his face for the people to start cursing him.

He was often drunk. At such times his dark fears mingled with the throbbing lust that haunted him and found an outlet in fits of uncontrolled storming anger. He would stagger through the entrance-hall slashing to right and left with his sword at the marble stairway or at the gilded frames that hung around the portraits of Plessis-Bellière's ancestors, while they looked down at this pot-bellied drunkard in haughty consternation.

His own men would creep away when he was in this sort of condition. He felt the servants' eyes glittering as they peered through cracks in the doors; sometimes through his delirium he would hear little Charles-Henri's rippling laugh, for Barbe would bring him along to see the fun. Then he would call down curses upon them all. He had been abandoned. He was at the mercy of demons and a witch. He would weep maudlin tears at the thought of his fate, then his wrath would get the upper hand again.

"You damn slut!" he would bellow, looking towards the top of the stairs, but completely unable to negotiate even the first few steps. "I know you, you run off into the forest at night, after a mate, that's what ..."

Angélique was not altogether happy about it. How could he know that she went off into the forest? The Captain's speech would end in obscure accusations, something about a hind and witchcraft.

One day when he was carrying on in this manner, he felt a violent stab in his backside, and turning round, saw Florimond who without warning had stuck his sword into the Captain's fleshy parts.

"Are your remarks intended for my mother, Captain?" he asked. "Because if they are, I shall have to ask you to give an account of yourself."

Montadour swore and tried to defend himself against the nimble sword. All his swimming eyes could distinguish was a thick black furry mass turning round and round him. The she-wolf's cub! His hand was gashed and he dropped his sword and called his men to his rescue. They ran in, and Florimond fled, cocking a snook at them.

When his hand had been dressed and he had sobered up, Montadour swore to exterminate the lot of them. But he had to wait for reinforcements. He was in a critical situation, cut off from Monsieur de Gormat, and the letters he had sent to Monsieur de Marillac must have been intercepted.

Apart from this particular intervention, it seemed as if Florimond was not fully aware of the situation.

He would spend hours duelling with the groom and his tutor, would hunt squirrels and go off goodness knows where for hours at a time. He would take Charles-Henri on his shoulders and race along the corridors. It was odd to hear their high-pitched laughter. He would harness his horse and put Charles-Henri in the saddle with him, and go off into the countryside, completely ignoring the sentry, who tried to stop him but eventually let him go on because he did not really know what he was supposed to do about this young Catholic nobleman.

One day Angélique came upon Florimond sitting in a corner of the drawing-room with Charles-Henri facing him like a pupil answering his master's questions. The elder boy was placing various powders that he had taken from some carefully labelled little bags into plates that lay before him.

"What is this yellow substance called?"

"It's sulphur."

"And the grey one?"

"Those are crystals of caliche or Chile saltpetre."

"Very good, my boy. I see you've been paying attention. And this black powder?"

"That's wood charcoal that you've sifted through silk."

"Very good, but you should say 'sir' when speaking to your teacher!"

One night, quite late, there was an explosion near the steps leading to the main doorway and a shining object flashed up into the sky, and fell in a shower of sparks on to the lawn. The soldiers grabbed their arms and shouted: "To arms, quick!" Montadour was away. Windows were flung open. They found Florimond, his hands and face black with soot, standing before a weird contraption he had made, and Charles-Henri in his long nightshirt shouting with delight at the success of his "teacher's" ingenious rocket.

Everyone began to laugh, including the soldiers themselves. Angélique laughed as she had not done for a long time, and the laughter lightened her heart and brought tears to her eyes.

"Oh, you little whippersnappers," sighed Barbe, "there's no peace when you're around."

The curse that hung over the château seemed to be lifting. Perhaps Father de Lesdiguière's Masses had something to do with it.

The following day a falcon hovered over the turrets and Florimond caught it like an expert falconer. He and Father de Lesdiguière took the note they found tied to the bird's foot to Angélique. She flushed and seized the little container. With one sharp thrust of her little pocket-knife she prised the letter from its casing. Samuel de La Morinière's angular scrawl summoned her to the Fairy Stone for the following night. She clenched her teeth. At the Fairy Stone, what insolence! How he must despise her to dare to give her such an order! Did he think she was his slave? She would not go! She wouldn't help them any more.... She could only have done so if she could have kept out of the Patriarch's way. But she could not agree to meet him alone in the forest where everything was an incitement to sensuality—the smell of autumn in the undergrowth, the mist rising from the rivers. No, it would never do. If he dared to lay a finger on her once more, what might she not do? Would her fear of him prove stronger than the strange attraction to him she had felt in her flesh ever since the episode that other night? She tried in vain to think of other things. His dark presence bent over her in her sleep, and she would waken with a moan.

She was torn between the forest, with its power lying hidden beneath the trees, calling to her like the belling of a stag, and the temptation to arrest all action, to do nothing.

Autumn had come, and she had not bowed low in submission to the King. But the emissaries he would send to arrest her would never be able to pass through the ring of fire and steel that the Patriarch had already drawn round the borders of the province. Beyond the confines of the gardens where her sons played, they were beating women, burning crops, and the peasants were on the prowl, ready for anything.

Florimond and Father de Lesdiguière were watching her; wherever she went she felt those pure, questioning eyes upon her. The King had known what he was about when he had sent Florimond back to her. "Children," the midwife had said, "children only complicate your life. If you don't love them, they're in the way, and, if you do, they sap your strength."

Her heart, struck by too many blows, wavered. The Mediterranean had penetrated her defences. At the very moment when she thought she had been toughened, her ability to suffer had been increased tenfold by her greater subtlety of thought. Everything hurt her now. But the forces which had been unleashed drew her on in spite of herself. Isaac de Rambourg's hunting horn called to her through the copper-coloured evening sky, rising up out of the tawny leaves. They had agreed upon a code graded according to the urgency of the message. He was blowing the mort, that meant: "Help! Emergency!" The mort! ...

"Madame, you must come," entreated La Violette, all breathless after his race to the neighbouring domain. "It's the women, the women from the Protestant villages of the Gâtine . . . those who were turned on to the highway a few days ago with nothing. . . . They have taken refuge in Monsieur de Rambourg's château. If Montadour gets word of this, they'll be done for. The Baron is asking for your advice. . . ."

Angélique crept down the underground tunnel. She slid through the woods to the grassy gardens surrounding the Rambourg château set on its hilltop. In the courtyard, beneath the keep, exhausted women were sitting on the bare ground, clutching their skinny children to them. They looked dejected and their white coifs were thick with dust and crumpled. They were telling the Baroness about their aimless wanderings through hostile Catholic villages where the priests had enjoined their parishioners to obey the edict and not to afford them an sustenance or office of humanity; not

100

even a crust of bread. They had been feeding on turnips they tore from the fields at night and for a long time they had lived on the outskirts of the forest. They were hounded out by dogs. Squads of soldiers would appear from nowhere and harry them. There were always some posted at the approaches to Protestant villages, to make sure the edict was obeyed. The women had walked with their children under the merciless summer sun, and through the lashing rain of thunderstorms. In the end they had decided to make for La Rochelle, that ancient Protestant metropolis, where there were still enough of their faith to dare to defy the edict and take them in. For several days they had been passing through territory held by Samuel de La Morinière's bands, and they had been able to rest awhile in the farms of their Protestant brethren. But the farmers were impoverished, and food was scarce, so they had been forced to go on. When they had reached the bed of the river Vendée, they had met Montadour's red dragoons. In a panic, they had left the roads and taken to the regions remote from the main highways. They had found themselves in this dead-end on the fringe of the impenetrable forest and then had learnt that one of the Protestants' worse persecutors had his headquarters there. By a supreme effort they had managed to drag themselves up to the Rambourgs', which someone had pointed out to them.

The snotty-nosed Rambourg children stared open-mouthed at the visitors. Angélique caught sight of Florimond, standing by Nathaniel, their eldest. In her anxiety she spoke curtly: "What are you doing here? Why are you mixed up in this Protestant business?"

Florimond smiled. Since he had been at college he had taken to never answering back when rebuked. It was maddening. Baroness de Rambourg, who was in the seventh month of her ninth pregnancy, was handing out pieces of bread to the women. It was stale and black. One of her daughters was helping her by carrying the basket.

"What are we to do, Madame?" she asked Angélique. "We cannot keep these women here, let alone feed them all."

101

Baron de Rambourg came up with his hunting horn slung over his shoulder.

"If we put them back on to the road, that will be the end of them. Montadour will go round the forest and catch them up before they reach Secondigny."

"No!" said Angélique, who had already come to a decision. "They must get to the Ablettes Mill, in the marshes. From there they can go by boat to Monsieur d'Aubigné's estate where they will be safe. If they gradually make their way across the waters guided by the marsh folk, they will come out right near the outskirts of La Rochelle. They will then have only two or three leagues to go and will have covered the whole way right off the beaten track."

"But how will they get to the Ablettes Mill?"

"They'll cut straight across the forest. It's only a two or three hours walk.'"

The Protestants' faces fell.

"Who will guide them?"

Angélique looked down at the weary faces and saw the dark glow of her countrywomen's eyes.

"I will."

As they came out from under the trees, their feet sank into the spongy moss. This was the beginning of the marshes. They looked just like green fields, and you might well have tried to walk on through the alder and the aspen if you had not noticed the punts chained to the bank that betrayed the presence of water. Angélique had taken three young footmen with her to help work the boats. True to local form, they were pessimistic.

"We shan't get away as easily as all that, Madame la Marquise. At the Ablettes Mill the miller controls the river and everyone who wants to go out on to the marshes has to pay a toll to him, and he is for ever hurling abuse at Protestants, because he can't abide them. He's got all the keys to the boats. There are people in the near-by villages who will go miles out of their way to avoid having to pass the mill."

"We haven't time to do that. It's our only way. I shall take care of the miller," said Angélique.

102

They had set out well before nightfall, carrying lamps to be lighted when darkness fell in the woods. The children were tired. The way seemed long. When they reached the mill, the sun had already set. The dusk was full of the croaking of frogs and the piercing cries of waterfowl. A chill unseen mist rose from the ground and gripped them by the throat, while little by little the trees with the submerged roots became blurred in the blue darkness.

They could still make out the squat mass of the mill on the left and the paddles of the wheel standing out of the still waters studded with water-lilies.

"Stay here," Angélique said to the women who were huddled together trying to keep warm.

Some of the children coughed and stared with anxious eyes through the mists.

Angélique managed to reach the mill, wading part of the way. She found the rickety bridge and immediately beyond it the familiar foot-bridge over the mill-race. Her hand touched the rough wall hung with bindweed.

The door was open. The miller was counting over his money by the light of a candle. He was a man with a low forehead, and his hair, which hung in a thick fringe over his eyebrows, made him look even more stubborn and narrow-minded. Dressed as he was all in grey, like all memebers of his trade, with a beaver hat pulled down about his ears, he looked quite well-to-do. He was wearing red stockings and steel-buckled shoes. People said that this miller was rich, avaricious and intolerant.

Angélique let her gaze wander over the rustic furniture over which hung an impalpable velvety layer of flour. There were sacks piled up in one corner and everything smelt of wheat. She smiled to find it all just as it had been. Then, stepping forward, she said:

"Valentine, it's me ... Hello ..."

CHAPTER 12

THE BOATS went on through the long dark tunnel. The yellow circles cast by their lamps could scarcely pierce the darkness, hemmed in by the great arching trees. Maître Valentine's height forced him to stoop at times. He called warnings to the other guides in the local dialect. The women were no longer afraid. You could sense their feeling of relief and occasionally a stifled laugh came from the children. Peace, such as they had not known for many a long day, was creeping into the fugitives' hearts: the peace of the inviolate marshlands. Had not good King Henry IV written to his sweetheart: "You can be happy here in peacetime, and safe in war." For what enemy would pursue his adversary into this area? Even if he had attempted such a thing, even if a few soldiers had set off in those punts, Montadour would have seen them return chilled to the bone and covered in mud. They would have turned this way and that amongst the channels and creeks would have stepped out on to a bank only to feel it give under their jackboots, would have gone round and round in this labyrinth whose walls were green or gold according to the time of the year, where in winter the way was barred by a network of branches. And they would have finished up exactly where they had started. In fact they would have been lucky to get back at all; these vast expanses could have drawn them for ever into their silent depths. Many a nameless corpse sleeps beneath these dead waters, beneath the green velvet of the watercress beds. . . .

Maître Valentine the miller had stood up when Angélique spoke. He had shown no surprise at seeing her there. She could distinguish, beneath his heavy features, those of the stubborn, taciturn boy who used to punt the young lady of Sancé out into his marshy kingdom and keep her jealously from the brassy calls of Nicholas the shepherd: "Angélique! . . . Angélique!" The shepherd would run through the meadows, crook in hand, his dog and his sheep behind him.

Angélique and Valentine, hiding in the reeds, would hold their sides in silent laguhter, then would go off still farther until the shouts died down, muffled by the trees: alder, elm, ash, willow and tall poplar.

Valentine used to pick sprays of wild angelica, and

they would alternately suck it and breathe in its perfume. "So that I have your soul," he would say.

He was no prattler, like Nicholas. He frequently went red in the face and was subject to terrible fits of anger. Goodness knows why, but the Protestants seemed to provoke his hatred. He and Angélique would lie in wait for the Huguenot children as they came out of school and wave their rosaries in their faces, to hear them shout: "Save us from Satan!" All these memories came back to Angélique, as the bow pushed its way through the carpet of duckweeds with a sound like the pattering of a light shower of rain.

Valentine still disliked Protestants, but he had not been able to resist the gold coins that the Marquise du Plessis gave him. He had taken his bunch of keys and told the women and children to embark in the punts.

A stronger breeze sprang up, suggesting a widening of the waterway. The first boat touched dry land. The moon was rising over the trees in an iridescent halo, which revealed the dwelling of the lords of Aubigné lying asleep among the willow-trees and grassy lawns. The château had been built on one of the innumerable islands in what had once been the Poitou Bay, where the low, flat rocks had been battered by the waves. Even now in winter-time, the water came right up to the big flight of stone steps. A Renaissance château, whose builder had been lured by the reflection of white stones in the fathomless depths, and perhaps also by the splendid isolation of the place. A home just made for conspirators if ever there was one!

Dogs barked. People came towards them. Mademoiselle de Coesmes, the old Marquis's cousin, came forward holding up a candlestick. She listened dourly to Angélique's tale of these unfortunate women, most of them widows, whom she had escorted this far in the hope that they would be taken charge of and helped to reach La Rochelle. She disapproved of a Catholic as suspect as Madame du Plessis meddling in Protestant affairs. Was not her licentious conduct at Court all too well known? Nevertheless she asked her in and while the peasant women were being taken to the kitchens, she cast a glance at the fustian dress Angélique wore beneath her cloak when she went on her nocturnal expeditions, at her flat, muddy shoes and at the black satin headsquare she wore over her hair to hold it back.

Once again the old maid pursed her lips, and with a martyred look of resignation she informed her visitor that the Duc de La Morinière was in the house.

"Do you wish to see him?"

This piece of information upset Angélique's composure. She felt herself blushing, and she said that she did not wish to trouble the Duc.

"When he got here he was covered in blood," whispered Mademoiselle de Coesmes, who is spite of herself was quite excited with so many things going on. "He had a brush with some of that unspeakable Montadour's dragoons. He couldn't get clear of them so he made off into the marshes. His brother Hugh has captured Pouzauges, so they say. Monsieur de La Morinière is sorry not to have been able to get in touch with you."

"Well, if he's wounded . . ."

"Let me tell him."

She waited, all atremble, but when she heard the Patriarch's tread on the flagstones of the landing, she braced herself and watched him walk downstairs, eyeing him with a bold, hard look.

He came up to her. A deep gash ran across his forehead, and the swollen flesh was not yet healed. The gaping wound certainly did not soften his appearance. He seemed to her bigger, heavier and blacker than ever.

"Madame, my greetings." He made as if to offer her his gloveless hand. "Are you keeping our alliance?"

It was Angélique who looked away. She nodded towards the servants' quarters. Through the open doors came the glow of a fire and the sound of the Protestant women's voices, now calm and confident.

"You see."

She would never have thought that what had occurred at the Fairy Stone could take such a grip on her and paralyse her with embarrassment and desire. Was she falling under the spell of this man who, it was said by some of his contemporaries, had a personality that people found fascinating in spite of its unpleasantness? No one could disobey him—neither his brothers nor his wife, his brothers' wives, his daughters, his nephews, his servants nor his soldiers. He merely had to appear. It was written of this great Protestant lord, who rose in this hour in a brief but ferocious struggle against Louis XIV, that "with so much of the god in him there was also more than a touch of the devil."

He did not apologize to her. Had she perhaps wounded his inordinate pride by not answering his two summonses?

At last he said: "Pouzauges, Bressuire: we have the townspeople on our side. We have stripped the garrisons of their arms and handed them out to bands levied in the countryside. The troops that Monsieur de Marillac had left in the north have retreated eastwards, and we have occupied their positions in Gâtine. Messieurs Gormat and Montadour and their forces are now quite cut off, and the are as yet unaware of the fact."

She looked keenly at him, her face lit up.

"Is that so? I didn't know."

"How could you have known? You were silent."

"In that case . . ." muttered Angélique as if she were speaking to herself, "the King . . . the King cannot reach me any more. . . ."

"In a few days' time I shall leave the marshes and hound Montadour off your lands."

"May you be thanked, Monsieur de La Morinière."

"And forgiven?"

These words must have cost him an almost superhuman effort, for the veins in his forehead swelled and drops of blood pearled on the edges of his wound.

"I don't know," she said, looking away. And she walked to the door saying softly:

"And now I must get back to Plessis."

He followed her to the doorway and went down the steps with her.

As she turned into the path that led to the landing stage, he seized her about the waist in a convulsive, irresistible movement.

"I beg you, Madame, look at me."

"Be careful," she whispered, pointing towards the shadows where Maître Valentine was waiting with his boat.

He pushed her behind a willow-tree and, standing beneath its drooping tendrils, clasped her in his rugged arms.

Repugnance and desire together made her stiffen against him. Yes making love with the Patriarch would be a terrible and unusual experience. Her whole body was betraying her. She clasped the Huguenot's shoulders in her clenched fists, not knowing whether she was pushing him from her or clinging to him like the indestructible rock of which her precarious existence stood in need.

"Why?" she panted, "why upset the alliance?"

"Because I must have you!"

"But what sort of a man are you?" she moaned. "I don't understand anything any more. Don't people make you out to be a man of prayer, an ascetic? They say you despise women!"

"Women? Yes, I do. But you . . . In the Roman porch, you were Venus. . . . I understood then . . . Oh! what a veil was rent asunder. . . . To have waited so long, a whole lifetime, to understand what a woman's beauty is."

"But what did I say? What did I do that day? Didn't we talk together about your struggle for your faith. . . ."

"That day . . . the sun shone on you, on your skin and on your hair . . . I did not know. Then suddenly I realized. A woman's beauty." He drew away a little. "Do I frighten you too? Women have always feared me. I'm going to tell you something, Madame, something shameful that rankles deep inside me. When I used to go into my wife's room she sometimes used to beg me with clasped hands not to touch her. She was nevertheless a dutiful wife to me and gave me three daughters, but I am quite aware that I was repugnant and horrible to her in that way. Why? . . ."

She knew. It was one of the ironies of fate or of heredity that this descendant of a race of men that perhaps had some Moorish blood in their veins, this

108

strict Protestant, should have been so redoubtable a lover.

He had been thunderstruck by his discovery of Angélique. So there was another facet to life, perhaps accessible to him. And because she had seemed weak and defenceless, in spite of the power of her beauty, all the demons of lust had been loosed within him. He relied on the fact that he dominated her, and, although he feared her glance, he gave her orders. It was an exhausting battle because of the violence of the emotions that gripped them both. They were thrown together in the complicity of rebellion, and found themselves forced into acknowledging their disturbing passion as they were forced to acknowledge that they must exterminate the King's soldiers and defy the King.

"You *shall* be mine," he repeated in a hollow voice, "I *will* have you. . . ."

This was the very way the King had pressed his suit, his imperious bargaining.

"Perhaps some day . . ." she stammered; "don't be brutal."

"I am not brutal"—his voice was almost trembling—"don't you talk like the other women who are afraid of me. I know you, you won't be afraid. I shall bide my time. I shall do whatever you ask. But don't continue to ignore my summons to the Fairy Stone."

As she sat in the bottom of the straw-strewn punt, she felt a sensation of emptiness and of languor, as if she had in fact just been possessed by this frenzied giant. What would it be like when she did agree to it? Angélique shook her head to chase away unbearable visions.

One night in the forest the black huntsman would come and she would be his quarry. He would pin her down on the mossy ground and crush her beneath his huge clumsy body. And she would struggle beneath his hands, his bushy beard, until that magical moment when her flesh, awakened by desire, forgot the anguish to revel in delight. Oblivious of everything she would gasp, she would cry out. . . .

She threw back her head, exhausted. A fine drizzle wet

her hair, and yet it was not raining. That boat left a black mottled furrow in its wake, which slowly disappeared into the milky thickness of the tiny close-growing plants.

The moon, like a huge opalescent pearl, cast only a dim light beneath the trees, and Maître Valentine's silhouette, as he stood at the back of the punt with the pole in his hands, was hardly less weird than those of the aspens that bent over the water.

A strong smell of mint betrayed the closeness of the bank. Sometimes they brushed against it, and the wooden punt was scraped by the overhanging branches, but the miller needed no lamp to find his way through this maze. Angélique spoke to throw off the temptations that assailed her.

"Do you remember, Maître Valentine? You were already master of the marshes when you used to take me eel-fishing."

"Yes, that I was."

"Have you still got the hut where we used to get out and cook our eel stew and have a feast?"

"Yes, it's still there."

Angélique went on talking to break the silence.

"Once I fell into the water. You fished me out, all covered in waterweed and, when I got back to Monteloup, I was severely punished. They forbade me ever to go into the marshes again, and soon after they sent me away to the convent. We never met again."

"Oh yes, we did. At old Saulier's daughter's wedding."

"Oh yes."

She remembered.

"You had a fine broadcloth suit on," she laughed, "and an embroidered waistcoat. You stood stiff as a poker and didn't dare to join in the dancing."

In her mind's eye she saw the barn where she had gone to sleep, worn out from dancing farandoles. Valentine had crept up there after her and touched her budding breasts with his hand. This heavy, somewhat simple-minded boy had been the first to show desire for the Marquise of the Angels. The unwelcome memory disturbed her.

"And afterwards," the miller's slow voice droned on as

if he had followed her thoughts, "I was ill. My father said: 'That'll teach you to go fondling fairies.' He took me to the sanctuary of Our Lady of Mercy to have the spells exorcized."

"All because of me?" said Angélique with a start.

"He were right, weren't he? You are a fairy."

Angélique answered neither yes nor no. She was amused, but Maître Valentine's voice kept its solemnity.

"I did get better, but it took a long time. Later on I never married. I just had a servant girl to look after me. Never again. When you're bewitched by the fairies, you don't get over it that easily. It's not so much your body that suffers as your heart. You pine away. P'raps it's your soul that's sick. . . ."

He fell silent, and the silky whisper of the waterweed as it drew apart to let them pass filled the silent air. Suddenly a frog croaked.

"Not far now, we're nearly there," said the man.

The boat hit the bank. The smell of woodland and earth wafted down to them. Farther back, the other punts were being tied by the young footmen.

"Would you care to come and have a glass of something at the mill, Madame la Marquise?"

"No, thank you, Valentine. I've still a long way to go."

He walked as far as the edge of the forest with them, holding his hat in his hand.

"You see that old oak? That's where Nicholas the shepherd used to wait for you with a leaf full of wild strawberries."

It was surprising how the echo of a voice could restore her child's heart to her woman's breast, which had known so many ups and downs of fortune, and how it could conjure up before her eyes the picture of a small boy with black curls and sparkling eyes holding a stick in one hand and some fragrant strawberries in the other and waiting for her at the entrance to *her* domain: the fields and woods.

She thrust aside this vision, besmirched by the passage of time, and said:

"And do you know what happened to Nicholas? . . . He became a bandit, and was sent to be a galley-slave on one of the King's ships. Do you know how he died? He led a mutiny and an officer pushed him overboard. ..."

Maître Valentine said nothing, so she went on:

"Aren't you surprised, Maître Valentine, that I should know so much about Nicholas Merlot when it's so long since he was seen around here?"

He shrugged:

"Oh no, because you can see into both the past and the future, can't you? Go on, we all know who you are, we know where you come from! ..."

CHAPTER 13

AT PLESSIS Montadour's voice was making the walls shake. Angélique could hear him from the cellar.

"I wonder whether he's noticed my absence?" she thought, standing absolutely still.

She crept cautiously up to the hall.

"Abjure! Abjure!"

A wretched creature bent double, with hands held before his face, burst out of the drawing-room and collapsed at Angélique's feet. It was a poor half-stunned peasant with his face swollen and covered with blood.

"Gentle lady," he moaned, "you have always been good to the Protestants. . . . . Mercy! Mercy!"

She laid her hand on his shaggy head, and he began to sob into her dress like a child.

"I'll kill the lot of them," roared Montadour, appearing at the door. "I'll crush them like so many lice, and I'll exterminate any Catholic who helps them."

"How can such things go on in our country?" exclaimed Angélique, seething with indignation. " 'Abjure! Abjure!' Anyone would think they were at Meknès. You're no better than the fanatical Moors who torture their Christian captives in Barbary."

The Captain shrugged his shoulders. He could not have cared less about the fate of the Christian prisoners in Barbary. He scarcely knew of their existence.

Angélique lowered her voice and spoke to the kneeling man in the local dialect:

112

"Take your scythe, peasant, and go and join La Mornière's forces. Every able-bodied man available is to follow you. March to the Three Owls crossroad. There the Duc will send you orders and weapons. In two days, perhaps even sooner, Montadour will be driven off the estate. Preparations are being made, I know."

"Since you say so, Madame la Marquise," he said, taking heart, his eyes shining with hope.

Then his peasant cunning came to the fore, and he went on:

"All right then, I'll sign their abjuration for them, so that they'll give me a bit of peace, and I'll be able to get away. . . . It's only for two days, and it's in the Lord's service, so He can hardly hold that against me. I'll make them pay for their *Credo*! . . .

Two days later, when Montadour and his men were out on patrol, leaving only a few soldiers on guard at the château, a horseman might have been seen coming up the drive, slumped over his saddle-bow. It was a wounded dragoon who swayed from his horse, collapsed on the gravel of the courtyard and had only time to shout to his comrades, "Ambush! The bands are coming!" before he died.

A confused clamour arose beneath the oaks. The Duc de La Morinière and his brother Lancelot were the next to appear, sword in hand and followed by the compact mass of his armed peasants. The soldiers ran to the outbuildings to seize their muskets, and as he ran one of them fired his pistol, just missing the Duc. The Protestants overtook them and savagely stabbed them to death. They were dragged over the stone to the esplanade fronting the dwelling of this noble Poitou family that they had profaned, and the Duc de La Morinière had their bodies thrown at Angélique's feet.

Molines was holding her two wrists in his hands.

"You must go to the King and carry out your mission. *You alone* can stop this carnage."

"Let me go, Maître Molines," said Angélique quietly.

She rubbed her bruised wrists. The new silence which had fallen on the château and its grounds, where the

113

snorting of horses or the coarse voices of the dragoons were no longer heard, was strangely unaccustomed, but it brought no solace to the heart.

"I have been informed," resumed the Steward, "that troops despatched by Louvois, the Minister of War, are on their way to Poitou. The repression of the revolt will be terrible. When the Duc de La Morinière is taken prisoner or executed, the signs of insurrection will be made a pretext for the extermination of the Protestants. As for you ..."

Angélique remained silent. She was sitting at her inlaid table, acutely aware of the passing of time, hour after hour falling heavily into this bright autumn day smelling of dead leaves, a day which hung upon the brink of the abyss, poised between two destinies, two irretrievable disasters.

"La Morinière's bands will be decimated," Molines went on. "There's no use thinking the whole of Poitou will rise. The Catholics will allow the armies to pass because they will be frightened, and because they don't like the Protestants and covet their land. And we'll see the horrors of the Wars of Religion back again—we've had a sample of it already. Crops will be burned, children thrown on to the pikestaffs. . . . The province will be bled white for many years to come and placed beyond the protection of the law. . . . That is what you have willed, you proud foolish woman."

She threw him a dark, impenetrable glance but did not deign to reply.

"Yes, you have willed it," insisted the old man mercilessly. "The choice was open to you, but you preferred to follow the dictates of your own nature which has reverted to the primitive. You have deliberately drawn close to the forces of the earth of which you have always been to some extent the incarnation. It was easy for you to canalize the aspirations of the La Morinières, those fanatical brutes, or of superstitious peasants. You have only to show yourself to fill them with ardour."

"Is it my fault if men cannot see a woman pass without lusting after her? You are exaggerating, Molines. I have long administered these domains and indeed have

114

lived on them, particularly after the Marshal's death, without causing the least disturbance to the peace."

"You were a lady of the Court at that time, a woman no different from all the rest. You do not realize what you are doing today, what effect a single glance of your eyes may have. You have brought a kind of fascination back with you from the East, a kind of mystery, I don't know ... but I hear the stories that are going the rounds of the cottages, where they remember you when you were regarded as a sort of good fairy. They say you used to be seen in several different places at once, that where you had passed the crops were richer, and all that because you used to lead the idle little wretches of peasant children on the prowl and had them absolutely worshipping you. And they say, now that you're roving the woods by night, that you have come back to deliver Poitou from its tribulations and restore its prosperity by means of your magic powers."

"You talk just like Valentine, the miller."

"It's the miller now, is it?" growled Molines. "That simple-minded old skinflint. Another of the credulous folk you used to take off with you to your witches' sabbaths at the Fairy Stone when you were ten! The charm works just as well today, I'll wager. After the miller whom will you sink to next in your quest for lovers, Madame du Plessis?"

"Monsieur Molines, you're going too far," said Angé-lique, drawing herself up with dignity.

But instead of bursting out in anger as he expected, her face softened and a smile played around her lips.

"No, don't try to awaken my scruples of conscience by reminding me of my wild youth. I was a pure child, Molines, and you know it very well. You sold me to the Comte de Peyrac as a virgin, and you never doubted it otherwise you would never have made the deal. Oh! Molines, I wish I had never lived! If only I could go back to the simple pleasures of those happy times, when my body was at peace and my mind was delightfully alive. But one can't return to childhood as one returns to the fold. It is the only land to which one can never return. The posies of forget-me-nots that Valentine used

115

to pick for me. Nicholas's wild strawberries, our dances around the Fairy Stone, while the moon was coming up behind the trees—it was all perfectly innocent and incomparably beautiful. There was never a jot of harm in it all. But later my feet have never been able to tread the same ways without being stained with blood, death and lust. Have I been out of my mind? I thought that my own soil would defend me."

"The soil is a female. She serves those who protect her and render her fruitful, not those who give her over to disorder. Listen, my child ..."

"I am not your child."

"Yes, you are, in a way. ... You must go to the King, and then peace will return."

"You, a Protestant, you are asking me to betray the folk of your own sect to whom I have promised my support?"

"It's not a question of betraying them, but of saving them. Here you are on your domain, and yet you cannot count the bodies of the hanged swaying from the branches of the oak-trees all over the region. Women are weeping with shame after being assaulted by sadistic brutes. Children are abandoned to their cruel sport and hurled into the fire. In many places the year's crops are being lost. The frenzy is mounting because the soldiers are afraid. When reinforcements arrive, their atrocities will redouble to avenge themselves for having been scared. The persecution will be all the more terrible because the rest of the Kingdom will know nothing of it, and that includes the King himself. It will be conducted quietly by the shrewd members of the Company of the Blessed Sacrament whom the King has in his entourage, and the only signs of all this blood-letting that he will ever see will be the names of the converts on ever-lengthening lists. You alone can save them. You alone can speak to the King and warn him what is being plotted against his subjects. He will listen to you. He will believe you, you and you alone. Because in spite of your faults and rebellious behaviour, he has boundless confidence in you. He wants you for that reason as well. You

116

will be all-powerful. You will be able to get whatever you want from him."

He leaned forward:

"You will have Montadour hanged and Marillac disgraced. You will rescue the King from the bigots, and peace will return to the countryside, justice and industry will reign."

"Molines," she moaned, "it is a terrible temptation you are subjecting me to, the worst possible . . ."

She looked at him as she had done long ago when he had persuaded her to marry an unknown nobleman who was said to be crippled and addicted to black magic, in order to save her family.

"You will be all-powerful," he repeated. "Think of the hour that will follow your submission. The King's words. . . . You know full well that they will not be severe."

"Trifle, my impossible, my unforgettable child . . ."

In the half-light of dawn at Versailles, after a night in which the pressure of his lips had stifled her cries of revolt—and perhaps she had shrieked them out like those of a criminal under the branding iron—the King would bend over her.

She would still be asleep, her bodily appetites glutted—Oh! how well she knew that supine, marvellous feeling of relaxation, that infinite relief—still enjoying perhaps in the depths of her sleep the luxury and splendour to which she had been restored. Under his caress she would half wake up, turning over amid the lace, unconsciously sensual, and suddenly opening wide her forest-tinted eyes. She would see him and cease to struggle, and she would hearken to his words, captive and captivated, while he repeated to her in an undertone, like a command, like a triumphant call, "Angélique . . . you and I together . . . are invincible. . . ."

She shook her head in despair.

"It's awful," she moaned. "It's like asking me to die, to give up all hope."

She felt she had already lived through this scene with

117

Molines, and she saw Osman Faraji once again trying to persuade her to give herself to Mulai Ismail. But she had not yielded to Mulai Ismail, and they had massacred all the Jews of the *mellah* and impaled the slaves. . . .

Thus everywhere, on all sides, there were tyrannical masters and enslaved peoples, who were made the sport of their caprices; it was the inescapable law. . . .

Outside a light drizzle began to fall, pattering down on the forest, and suddenly she heard the shouts of Florimond and Charles-Henri running in the rain.

The Steward went over to her bureau, picked up a sheet of paper and a quill and laid them before Angélique.

"Write. . . . Write to the King. I'm leaving tonight and I shall take the letter with me."

"What shall I tell him?"

"The truth. That you are going to come and make your submission to him. That it is neither out of regret for what you have done, nor out of remorse, but because his most faithful subjects are being put to intolerable tortures around you. That you cannot believe that it is on his orders. That you will not go to Versailles until Monsieur de Marillac's dragoons have been withdrawn from the region and those sent by the Minister, Louvois, have been recalled. But that you will make your submission humbly and in accordance with terms laid down by His Majesty because you recognize his justice, his goodness and his patience. . . ."

She began to write feverishly, and was soon absorbed in her indictment of the torturers of Poitou. She told of all the cruel baiting measures that had been taken, of how a drunken thug of an officer had tortured people under her roof. She mentioned Montadour, de Marillac, de Solignac and Louvois by name, gave details of the present positions of the royal regiments, spoke of the growing, inevitable disaffection of the peasants, begged mercy for them, and, while she was writing, the young King's face was constantly before her eyes, grave and attentive, in the silence of his study at night.

"He cannot have wanted this," she said to Molines.

118

"He may have wanted it without knowing. The conversion of the Protestants is very dear to his heart as a means of making up for his own sins. He closes his eyes and ears. You will force him to open them. Yours is a blessed role."

When she had finished, she felt exhausted but quite calm. Molines sprinkled sand on the missive and sealed it.

Angélique saw him back to his house. She no longer knew where she was. There was something sinister in the silence of the fields. Every now and then a smell of burning was borne on the wind.

"More crops burning or smouldering," said Molines settling on his horse. "Montadour's men have fallen back on Secondigny, and have been setting fire to everything in their path. Lancelot de La Morinière is holding them, but if his men give way . . . The Patriarch must have gone up into Gâtine to face Louvois's troops when they arrive."

"Will you be able to get through safely, Molines?"

"I'm taking a weapon with me," he said, drawing back his cloak to show the butt of a pistol.

His old servant was accompanying him, mounted on a mule. They rode off.

Florimond was hopping on one leg in front of the château and kicking stones with the other. He came up to Angélique and announced to her with the excited face of one who has good news to tell:

"Mother, we must leave now."

"Leave? Where for?"

"Far, far away," said the lad pointing towards the horizon, "for another country. We can't stay here. The soldiers may come back, and we have nothing to defend ourselves with. I've been looking at the old culverins up on the ramparts, but they're only toys, and rusty at that. You couldn't get them to fire the smallest sort of cannon ball. I did have a shot at getting them into working order, but I almost blew myself up. So you see we just have to leave. . . ."

"Have you gone out of your mind? Where ever did you get such ideas from?"

119

"Oh! I just use my eyes, that's all," said the child with a shrug. "This is war and it's only just starting, I think."

"Would you be frightened of a war?"

He blushed, and she read in his dark eyes surprise and contempt.

"I'm not afraid of fighting, if that's what you mean, Mother, but I just cannot work out who we're supposed to be fighting: against the Protestants because they won't obey the King by changing their religion, or against the King's soldiers because they come and insult us in our own home? I just don't know. It's not a good war. That's why I want to go away."

He had never had so much to say to her since he had come home. She had thought that nothing ever bothered him.

"Don't worry, Florimond," she said. "I think that things are going to turn out all right. Listen, how would you, she found it hard to say, "how would you like to go back to Court?"

"Oh no! Not that!" said the child spontaneously. "There were too many people there trying to make up to me and hating me because the King liked you. And now they hate me because he doesn't like you any more. I'm fed up with it. I'd rather go away somewhere else. And in any case I'm bored in this place. I don't like it here. The only one I like is Charles-Henri."

"And what about me?" she said, barely succeeding in controlling her voice, and minding it terribly.

Here he was getting his own back because she had offended him a moment ago.

"God knows that I have fought for my sons, and have sacrificed myself to them. Today again I have sacrificed myself."

Without saying a word she walked to the steps leading up to the entrance. The act she had performed in writing the letter to the King had left her nerves raw. She had not got the heart to put on a calm exterior to reassure her son. "It's amazing how children slip between your fingers," she thought. "You think you know them, and that you've won their friendship. All it takes is an absence. . . ."

120

Before Angélique's departure for the Mediterranean he would never have behaved in that way, but he was reaching the age when children began to wonder about their future. Since her encounter with Islam had left such a deep impression on Angélique, why should the year he had spent with the Jesuits not have transformed Florimond too? A soul at the parting of the ways. . . . It can never be brought back again.

She heard Florimond come running. He laid his hand on her arm and repeated urgently:

"Mother, we must go!"

"But where do you want us to go to, child?"

"There are lots of places we could go. I've arranged everything with Nathaniel. I'll take Charles-Henri."

"Nathaniel de Rambourg?"

"Yes, he's my friend. We used to spend all our time with one another when I lived at Plessis, before we went to serve at Court."

"You never told me that."

He raised his eyebrows in an ambiguous expression. There were a lot of other things too that he had never told her.

"If you don't want to come, too bad. But I'm taking Charles-Henri."

"Don't talk such nonsense, Florimond. Charles-Henri cannot desert this estate; he's the heir to it. The château, the grounds, the woods and the land belong to him and will revert to him when he comes of age."

"And what about me? What shall I get?"

She looked at him, her heart tight in her breast: "You have nothing, my son, my proud boy! . . .

"I have nothing?"

His tone was imploring. He was hoping against hope. Every second of his mother's silence caused the weight of the verdict he had already suspected to sink more heavily upon him.

"You will have the money I have invested in commerce. . . ."

"But my name, my estates, my own heritage, where are they?"

"You know very well . . ." she began.

He turned brusquely away with a far-off look in his eyes.

"That's really the reason why I want to go away."

She put her arm around his shoulders and they went into the château together. "I'll go to the King," she thought; "I'll walk up the Grand Gallery dressed in black under the mocking, delighted gaze of the courtiers, I'll kneel . . . I'll give myself to the King. But afterwards I'll have your titles and your inheritance restored to you. I have wronged you, my son, in trying to preserve my freedom as a woman. There was no other way out." She pressed him closer to her. He gave her a puzzled look, and then, for the first time since her return, they smiled lovingly at one another.

"Come on, let's have a game of chess!"

It was one of the boy's chief delights. They sat down by the window at the big chessboard with the black and white pieces that King Henry II had presented to one of the lords of Plessis. The pieces were made of ivory and bone. Florimond set them up, his lips drawn tight in concentration.

Angélique looked out of the window at the trampled lawn and the exotic trees that the dragoons had felled for firewood, out of sheer vandalism, for the woods were only a stone's-throw away.

Her life was like the ruined park. She had not succeeded in bringing order into it. Strange passions had ravaged it, and now at length she was falling under their yoke. Sitting there beside her still frail son, with nothing to protect him, she realized the full extent of a lonely woman's weakness with no one to defend her. In the past she had felt herself capable of anything in order to have her way. Now the word "anything" tasted like gall in her mouth. She had taken the measure of human vanities. Islam had taught her that only the fulfilment of one's being puts it in harmony with one's soul.

Now she was going to give herself to the King—an act worse than treachery to herself, to her past, to the man she had not been able to forget. . . .

"Your move, Mother," said Florimond, "and if you take my advice you'll play the queen."

122

Angélique smiled wanly and played the queen. Florimond worked out a complicated combination, played and raised his eyes.

"I know very well that it's not your fault," he said in the soft voice he had brought back from the College. "It's not easy to find yourself back among people who wish you ill because you are beautiful. But I think we ought to go before it's too late."

"It's not as simple as that, darling, as you've just said yourself. Where can we go? I'm just back from a very long journey, Florimond. I've run terrible dangers, and I still had to come back without finding what I was looking for. . . ."

"But I'll find him," said Florimond with great positiveness.

"Don't be presumptuous! It's an expensive fault."

"I just don't recognize you any more," said he severely. "Are you the same person that I guided through the tunnel when you decided to go and search for my father?"

Angélique burst out laughing.

"Oh, Florimond, I like your spirit! You're right to scold me, really, but you see . . ."

"If I had known all this, I would have gone with you instead of staying behind locked up in that old college of theirs. With the pair of us together we might have succeeded."

"Presumptuous lad!" she repeated tenderly.

All at once she saw in her mind's eye the cruel Mediterranean, the slave boys bought and sold, castrated, the storms, the battles, the endless buying and selling of human flesh. Thank God she had not taken Flormiond with her on her expedition. How often she had reproachéd herself with her imprudence in trusting Cantor to the Duc de Vivonne to go and fight the Turks.

"You have no idea of the difficulties and dangers of such a journey. You're still too young. One has to find something to eat every day, a roof to sleep under, fresh horses, and lord knows what else. It takes a lot of money to pay for all that."

"My purse is pretty well lined with my savings."

"Is it now? And what about when it's empty? Men are hard, Florimond. They never give away anything for nothing, remember that."

"Right," said Florimond, obviously offended, "I understand. I won't take Charles-Henri, because he's too small, he is, to face all those difficulties, and in any case he has his inheritance. I hadn't thought of that. But I'll go and find my father and Cantor. I know where they are."

Angélique froze in amazement, a piece poised in her hand.

"What did you say?"

"Yes, I know because I saw them in a dream last night. They are in a country full of rainbows. It is a weird country. Everywhere there are clouds floating into one another, and as they come together they form all the colours of the prism. In the middle of these coloured mists I saw my father. I couldn't see him properly. He was like a phantom, but I knew that it was he. I tried to go to him, but the fog closed in on me, and suddenly I saw that my feet were in the water. It was the sea. I've never seen the sea, but I recognized it by its movement and by the foam which kept on coming and going and splashing my feet. The waves got higher and higher. In the end I saw an enormous wave and riding on top of it was Cantor, who was laughing and shouting to me: 'Come and join me, Florimond; you've no idea what fun it is.'"

Angélique pushed back her chair and stood up. An icy chill ran down her back. It was as if Florimond's words had turned to certainty the thought she had always suppressed—DEATH! The death of the two beings she had loved, and who were now wandering in the land of shadows.

"Stop," she murmured, "you're making me feel faint."

She fled to her room and sat at her writing-desk with her head in her hands.

Shortly afterwards the door-handle turned softly and Florimond slipped into the room.

"I've been thinking, Mother. I think I'll have to embark on that other sea, you know. . . . There is another sea than the Mediterranean. I learnt that from the Jesuits.

It's the western ocean, which is called the Atlantic because it stretches over what used to be the continent of Atlantis, which sank one day allowing the northern and southern waters to join. The Arabs called it the Sea of Darkness, but now it is known to lead to the West Indies. Perhaps there ..."

"Florimond," she said, her patience exhausted, "I beg you, we'll talk about it again later, but now leave me alone, or . . . or I think I'll have to box your ears for you."

The boy went away sulkily, banging the door behind him.

For a few moments Angélique didn't know what to do to avoid bursting into sobs. At length she pulled open a drawer and drew out the King's letter, the letter she had not wanted to read.

". . . *My unforgettable child, listen no longer to the foolishness of your heart. Come back to me, Angélique. In your utmost distress you asked my pardon through Father Valombreuze. To test your sincerity I want to hear you ask for it with your own lips. You are a formidable woman, my beautiful Angélique. There are so many forces slumbering in you that are at variance with mine. Will you come and place your two hands in mine? It is a lonely King who awaits you. All your prerogatives will be restored to you, and I will not suffer anyone to slight you. You have nothing to fear. For I know that you can be an honest friend as well as an honest enemy. . . ."*

He continued in the same vein, and she was grateful to him for not trying to lure her into a trap by false pretences. He said: "*You will be my mistress, and I am now in a position to realize all that means in your particular case. I have confidence in your sense of fair play, trust mine too. . . . Speak to me, and I will listen to you. Obey me, and I will obey you. . . ."*

She closed her eyes, worn out and defeated. She had been right to give way. Tomorrow injustice would be opposed. She would bend every ounce of her strength to see that it was.

Florimond was wandering about on the main drive,

125

sling in hand, trying to hit squirrels. Angélique felt
sorry for him and went down to comfort him. She would
speak to him of the King and dazzle him with the titles
that would be his again, and the high appointments she
would obtain for him.

But when she reached the gardens, Florimond had
disappeared. All she could see was Charles-Henri, who
was standing beside the pool watching the swans. His
satin coat was as white as their plumage, and his hair as
bright and fair as the willow leaves dropping above his
head.

Something in the attitude of the three swans patrol-
ling up and down the bank awakened her anxiety. It is
well known that these birds are very spiteful, and that
they are capable of dragging a child into the water to
drown it. Angélique hurried over to him and took him
by the hand.

"Don't stand so near the water, darling. The swans are
bad-tempered."

"Are they really bad-tempered?" he asked raising his
azure-blue eyes. "And yet they're so beautiful, so
white. . . .

His plump little hand in hers was gentle and trusting.
He trotted along at her side without taking his eyes off
her. She had always thought that all his looks came from
Philippe, but Gontran was right. In the rosy little face
raised towards her she recognized something reminiscent of Cantor, a pout, a curve of the chin which had
been the characteristic of some of the de Sancé children:
Josselin, Gontran, Denis, Madelon, Jean-Marie . . .

"Yes, you're a son of mine too," she thought, "you too,
dear little boy."

He answered her: "Yes, Mother. Yes, Mother," in a
shrill little voice, full of feeling.

Was he simple-minded? Probably not. The look of his
thick-lashed eyes had his father's inscrutable and
vaguely melancholic expression. Was he not as Philippe
had been: a lonely little aristocrat in the house he was
one day to inherit? She pressed him to her heart. She
thought of Cantor whom she had fondled so little and
who was now dead. Life was spent in violent adult

intrigues, and she no longer had time even to be a good mother! She used to play with Florimond and Cantor when they were still poor in the little house at Francs-Bourgeois. But since then she had often sent Charles-Henri away, and that was bad, for she could not disown the love she had felt for Philippe. A different love from the love she had given to her first husband, but still love and the flowering of an adolescent dream, the intoxication of a difficult conquest, and a kind of fraternal bond deriving from their common childhood and their native province.

She took the round cheek in the hollow of her palm and kissed it gently several times.

"I'm very fond of you, darling, you know. . . ."

He stirred no more than a captive bird. His lips half opened over his white teeth in a smile of wonder.

Florimond reappeared from among the trees and hopped up to them on one leg.

"Know what we'll do tomorrow, boys?" said Angélique. "We'll put on our oldest poaching clothes and go off all three of us to the woods to catch crayfish."

"Bravo! Bravissimo! Evviva la mamma!" shouted Florimond, to whom Flipot was teaching Italian.

CHAPTER 14

IT WAS a wonderful day in which present bitterness and threats for the future all seemed swept away. The forest encompassed them with its gentle golden boughs. Everywhere there was sunlight, reflected in the russet oaks, the purple beeches, the early bronzing of the chestnuts. The chestnuts were dropping on to the mossy ground below, their shells bursting open to reveal the deep perfect sheen of the fruit. Charles-Henri whooped for joy to see so many, and stuffed the pockets of his pink linen trousers full of them. What would Barbe have to say? In spite of Angélique's instructions, she had dressed him as if he were going for a walk in the Tuileries gardens. At first he looked anxiously at his lovely clothes, that already bore greenish stains. Then, seeing that Angélique

127

didn't seem to mind, he grew bolder and tried to climb some of the tree-stumps: paradise lay open before him, and it was his mother's doing! He had always known that she was the sum of all bliss, and that was why he used to gaze at her portrait so long every night.

Flipot and Father de Lesdiguière had come with them. Angélique felt a certain pride in the fact that Florimond and the young men were watching her, and were more and more lost in respectful admiration as she led them along seemingly invisible tracks and unveiled the secrets of the streams. This side of her was so new to these men who had known her at Court, that they found it hard to know what to think. They were soon caught up in the general excitement and joined in the fishing as keen as mustard. They splashed about in the water-holes, or lay stretched out on the mossy bank watching the crayfish crawling towards the submerged basket-traps baited with carrion. Florimond was a trifle put out to find he could not catch the crayfish in his hand as Angélique had done several times. She laughed to see his crestfallen expression, and her heart swelled with pleasure at the thought that she was winning back his esteem.

As they crossed a clearing, they met Mélusine the witch. The old woman was picking mushrooms, groping about on the ground with her gnarled fingers. Copper-beech leaves were twirling down around her, and as the wind set them dancing they almost seemed to be going through some weird ritual in honour of the sinister spirit of the forest personified by this black hunched figure with the halo of hair that shimmered like snow.

Angélique called out:

"Mélusine! Ho there!"

The crone straightened up to watch them come towards her, but instead of being calmed by the presence of the woman in whom she recognized powers similar to her own, her face was convulsed with horror, and she threw out her arms to stop them coming any closer.

"Go away, go away! Your motherhood is accursed!"

Then she fled into the bushes. Meanwhile it suddenly

began to rain and they all went and took cover beneath the great crosspiece of the Fairy Stone. Inside the megalithic tomb the ground was strewn with pine-needles, and they were able to sit out of the rain. Carved by some ancient chisel in the block that supported the pointed end of the flatstone were ears of wheat, symbols of plenty.

As they sat in the shadows fragrant with resin and heather Florimond said that he was reminded of his underground expeditions, except that they hadn't usually smelt as nice.

"I like being underground," he said. "I like to get to know the earth's secrets. All those rocks that form down there and move into position where we can't see them. Once at school, I went into the cellars and dug a tunnel with a pick. You could see the rock face. I got some derful samples. . . ."

He embarked on a fantastic story, full of Latin names and chemical formulae, all about the samples of rock he had wanted for making explosive mixtures.

"Goodness knows how many retorts I blew up in the college laboratories. I got into awful trouble. And you know, Mother, I assure you I had just about perfected an extraordinary gadget that could have revolutionized the whole of science. I'll explain it to you. I think you're the only person who would understand it."

"And to think that the Jesuits are quite convinced he isn't intelligent!" said Angélique, calling Father de Lesdiguière to witness. "He makes you wonder why they have such a reputation as teachers."

"Florimond's intelligence doesn't fit into the classic mould, that's what puts them off."

"If they are unable to help it to blossom, is that a good reason for stifling it? I shall send you to Italy to study," she said to Florimond. "On the Mediterranean coast you can learn the latest about all the sciences. Arab science, especially, may give you what you are after. The word 'al-chemy' is an Arabic word. And you might find a great deal to interest you in the secrets of the Chinese.

And for the first time she told them something about her voyage to the Levant.

Charles-Henri was resting, leaning against her, his cup of happiness running over. The rain drumming on the leaves and the gusts of wind were like the sound of the sea.

Angélique went on to talk about her disobedience to the King.

"His Majesty had forbidden me to leave Paris, and you yourself know how I escaped. Now everything is going to be all right again. The King is going to forgive me. He is asking me to go back to Court. I've sent Molines with a message from me. Soon now the soldiers who have insulted and tormented us will be punished, and we shall have some peace again."

Florimond was listening to her very intently.

"So you're no longer in danger? Nor Charles-Henri?"

"No, I assure you we aren't," she replied, trying to shake off the sadness that weighed on her heart, in spite of everything.

But she was going to give her sons back the security they had a right to.

"I'm so glad," he said with a sigh of relief.

"You don't want to go away any more?"

"Oh no, since you've said everything is going to be all right."

They got back very late. Barbe was already getting anxious. This wasn't the time of year to be wandering about the forest; there were wolves on the prowl. Her heart was in her mouth. And look at Charles-Henri's clothes! The poor pet was asleep on his two feet. He wasn't used to going to bed at all hours of the night.

"There," said Angélique, "calm down. Your little cherub has been stuffing himself with blackberries and he's had a simply wonderful time. There's plenty of time for sleep. The night's not over yet. . . ."

No, the night was not yet over, that terrible night at Plessis.

CHAPTER 15

AS ANGÉLIQUE was about to undress she thought she heard a solitary horse galloping somewhere near the château. She stood still and listened. Then, fastening her bodice once more she went out onto the landing, opened one of the casements and leant out. The galloping hoofs beat a tattoo, faster and faster, and the horseman, whose silhouette she could not recognize, after riding round the pond plunged into the darkness of the main avenue.

"Who could it be?" she wondered.

She shut the window, thought for a moment, then started down the stairs to go to the servants' quarters where she might find someone still up. Then on second thoughts she turned and went back up the few stairs to Florimond's room. She pushed the door gently ajar:

"Are you asleep?"

Earlier, before going up, he had said good-night to her and had hugged her, his eyes shining.

"Oh, Mother, Mother mine, what a glorious day! How I love you!"

And he had let his thick tousled head fall on her shoulder in the sweet trusting way he had once had with her. His hair was full of tiny twigs and smelt of the autumn woods, and she had laughed and kissed his thorn-scratched cheek.

"Sleep well, my boy. You'll see, everything will be all right."

She went in and walked over to the bed. It had not been disturbed. The lace pillow revealed no sleeping boy, weary after his day in the forest. Angélique looked around. She could see no clothes, no sword, no coat. She rushed into the next room where Father de Lesdiguière was asleep.

"Where's Florimond?"

The young man stared at her in stupefaction, only half awake.

"But . . . he's in his room! . . ."

"No, he isn't. Quick, get up, we must find him!"

131

They woke up Lin Poiroux and his wife who were snoring in their little nook by the kitchens. They had seen nothing, heard nothing, and in any case, wasn't it past midnight anyway?

Angélique threw a coat over her shoulders, and followed by some of the hastily dressed servants she ran to the stables. A little mop-headed stable-boy was sitting humming by a lamp, munching at a bagful of burnt almonds on a stool in front of him.

"Who gave you those?" shouted Angélique, guessing what had happened.

"Master Florimond."

"Did you help him to saddle his horse? Has he gone?"

"Yes, m'lady."

"You idiot!" she yelled at him slapping him across the face. "Quick, Father, get your horse and catch up with him."

The priest had neither boots nor coat on. He rushed back to the château, while Angélique hustled the little stable-boy to saddle the other horse.

While he was getting on with that, she ran out towards the broad walk, trying to hear the distant hoofbeats. But the wind was rustling in the dead leaves, and she could hear nothing else. She called;

"Florimond! Florimond!"

Her cry died away in the damp night. The woods were deaf to her calls.

"Go as quickly as you can," she begged the priest as soon as he got back. "As soon as you are out of the gardens, put your ear to the ground to find out which way he went."

She stood there alone, unable to make up her mind whether she should not also saddle her horse and go looking for Florimond in another direction.

At that instant the sound of Isaac de Rambourg's horn rose, deep and mournful, into the air. The brassy notes rose one by one, floating over the night air, like bubbles rising through dark waters. It was the MORT!

Again it rang out, piercing the stillness, and again, and again! Each echo was swallowed up in the next blast. The forest rang with the tragic calls.

Angélique's blood ran cold. She thought of Florimond. Perhaps he had gone up there to meet his friend Nathaniel.

A horseman, whose approach she had not heard, rode up into the circle of light cast by the large wrought-iron lamp that stood on the porch. It was the priest.

"The dragoons are coming," he panted.

"Did you find Florimond?"

"No, the soldiers wouldn't let me through, and I had to turn back. There are lots of them, in close order. Montadour is in command and they are on their way up to the Rambourgs'."

The mort still rang out, despairing and deafening, as if the man who was blowing the horn was going to burst a blood vessel.

Angélique realized what was happening. The King's dragoons must have broken through the thin lines of Protestant troops hemming them in. They were surging back into the area they knew best, but were furious because they knew they would come up against the barrier of the forest or the marshes.

"We've got to get up there," she said. "The Rambourgs need help."

She was still thinking of Florimond whose wild fancies had led him into this hornets' nest.

Accompanied by the young priest, she climbed the hill to the Protestants' home. Light could be seen among the trees, and they could make out a confused hubbub of sound. Half-way up they ran into a wailing throng: Madame de Rambourg, her children and her servant-girls.

"Madame du Plessis, we are coming to take refuge in your house. The dragoons are up there with lighted firebrands. They seem to be mad with drink. They've set our outhouses on fire and I think they are out to sack the house."

"Isn't Florimond with Nathaniel?"

"Florimond? How would I know? I don't know where Nathaniel is."

She turned to the children and wailed:

"Where's Nathaniel? Where's Rebecca? Joseph, I thought you were holding her hand...."

"I'm holding Sarah's hand."

"Then she must still be up there, poor little thing. We'll have to go back. And your father?"

The unfortunate woman was staggering, her hands clasped over her belly. The baby was due in a few days time.

"Go down to my house," Angélique said. "Father de Lesdiguiére will show you the way. I'm going up there to see what is happening."

She reached the top of the headland, behind the old keep and stood quite still, hidden from sight by the wall. Above the uproar created by the dragoons who were now inside the manor, there rose the blood-curdling shrieks of men under torture, and the shriller cries of women being overpowered by the brutes. The horn was silent.

Angélique crept carefully along the left wing, keeping in the shadows. She suddenly stumbled on a body strangely paralysed in the coils of a golden serpent. It was Baron de Rambourg with his hunting horn across his shoulders. She bent over him and saw that he had a hunting spear stuck through his body—a wounded beast butchered by the huntsman.

There was a sound of running feet. Angélique ran for the cover of the trees. Dragoons sprang up all round like red devils dancing the looting dance, that intoxicating reward held out to all soldiers since man first went to war.

As they placed their tall halberds against the wall they uttered wild shrieks of anticipation of the pleasures to come.

"On to the pikes, on to the pikes!"

From a window above them a little creature was hurled, a whirling doll. It was Rebecca!

Angélique buried her face in her hands.

Horror-stricken she crept through the thicket and went back to Plessis.

134

The servants were gathered together watching the flames licking around the neighbouring keep.

"Did you find Rebecca?" asked Madame de Rambourg. "And the Baron?"

Angélique took a firm grip on herself.

"They have taken refuge in the forest. We must, too. Quick, lads, get coats and some food. Where's Barbe? Someone go and wake her up and tell her to dress Charles-Henri."

"Madame," said La Violette, "look over there."

He pointed out the multitude of bright dots moving down through the trees towards them: dragoon firebrands.

"They're coming here ... through the Rambourgs' gardens!"

"Here they are!" called a young servant-lad.

At the end of the long carriage drive, more torches appeared like a bunch of flowers. The dragoons were coming towards the château, showing no great haste. You could only hear their voices, far off, calling to one another.

"Get into the house and shut every door and window," said Angélique, "everyone, do you understand."

She herself tested the bars across the main door, and the bolts and the great wooden shutters they drew across the ground-floor windows. Many of these windows had metal bars over them. Only the two casements on either side of the front door were unprotected.

"Fetch all your weapons and stand by those windows." Father de Lesdiguière calmly drew his sword, Malbrant came back laden with muskets and pistols.

"Where on earth did all those come from?"

"I decided to build up the armoury a bit in view of the disorder in the region."

"Oh thank you, Malbrant, thank you!"

The coachman began to hand out the muskets to the lads. He even gave the servant-girls pistols and they took hold of the heavy butts timorously.

"If you can't cope with gunpowder, you can always hold your gun by the barrel and whack 'em over the heads, duckies."

135

Madame de Rambourg, who had taken refuge with her brood in the drawing-room, watched Angélique with an agonized expression in her dark-ringed eyes.

"What has happened to my little Rebecca? And my husband? You do know something, don't you, Madame?"

"Please, Madame, I beg you, keep calm. Would you like me to help to lay the children down so that they can rest a bit? We must see they don't panic."

The Baroness de Rambourg slid to her knees, with clasped hands.

"Children, we must pray. I know now. This is the day the Lord spoke of when he said, 'I will forsake the remnant of mine inheritance, and deliver them into the hand of their enemies.'"

"Madame. The dragoons!"

The servants were looking anxiously out through a half-open casement. They could see Montadour on the terrace lit up by the red torchglow, his huge dappled horse scarcely able to support his great backside. The Captain seemed even bigger and more massive than she had remembered him. He had a week's growth of red beard, which made his face look even more coarse. It looked as if it had been fashioned out of some red clay, like a half-dry brick.

Behind him stood a group of cavalry and foot-soldiers, some armed with muskets, others with halberds. They seemed to be in some doubt as to what course of action to take.

They were shut out! But behind the tinted panes of the headlights, they sensed the shadows watching them.

"Open up there!" yelled Montadour, "or I'll break the door down."

Not a soul stirred. More soldiers arrived from the Rambourgs' hill. They had come through the woods to join their comrades. They were egging one another on, and reminding everyone that this was the house they had been driven out of, and that it had been on this very doorstep, less than a week ago, that La Morinière had hurled the corpses of four of their comrades.

The Captain motioned to two men who came forward carrying enormous hatchets. The first blows they struck on the carved wooden door shook the house. One of the Rambourg children began to cry, then was quiet again. Their mother was leading them in prayer.

"Malbrant," whispered Angélique.

The coachman slowly raised his gun and slid the barrel through the open window. There was a shot, and one of the axemen rolled down the steps. A second shot! The other soldier fell likewise.

The dragoons howled with rage. Three men with muskets rushed forward and began to beat on the door with their gun-butts.

Malbrant was reloading. La Violette, from the other window, fired twice with cool precision. Two men fell. Malbrant dealt with the third.

"Get back, you idiots!" yelled Montadour. "Do you want to get picked off one by one?"

The soldiers backed like ravening wolves. When they were far enough away, Montadour placed his musketeers in a row. There was a crackling burst of fire. The broken window-panes shattered in a thousand coloured fragments over the tiled floor. La Violette, who had not ducked in time, collapsed. Father de Lesdiquière picked up the gun that had fallen from the valet's hands and took up his position at the broken window. Through the tangled mass of twisted lead could be seen the leering faces of the advancing dragoons. Nevertheless their officers had to decide on a less dangerous means of attack than battering the door down, which had already cost them the lives of five men.

Angélique crawled to La Violette on her hands and knees and dragged him by the shoulders into a corner of the entrance hall. He had been hit in the chest, and his pale yellow and blue livery—the Plessis-Bellière colours— was stained by a spreading patch of red.

The young woman dashed to the kitchens to find brandy and lint. She was surprised to see Dame Aurélie, the cook's wife, sitting in front of the fire carefully watching the contents of a large cauldron. She said:

"What have you got there? Soup?"

"Madame la Marquise, I'm boiling oil to pour over them, the way they used to in the good old days."

Alas! The château of Plessis had hardly been built to resist storming the way its predecessors had in the Middle Ages.

Dame Aurélie suddenly pricked up her ears.

"They're at the shutters! I can hear them scratching at them, darn them."

She was right. The soldiers had gone round the house and were trying to tear down the heavy wooden kitchen shutters. Soon after they heard the first hatchet-blows. One of the servants climbed on to the sink to see whether they could be got at through the fanlight. But it would have been difficult.

"Go upstairs to the first floor," Angélique told the three lads who had pistols, "and fire down on them from the windows."

"I've only got a crossbow," said old Antoine, "but believe me, Madame la Marquise, it can do a good job of work. I'm going to make pincushions of those sly rats."

Angélique went back to La Violette, carrying a cloth. The hall was dim with wreaths of smoke that stung her eyes. As she knelt down, she could see straight away that nothing she could do would be of any help. The valet was dying.

"Madame la Marquise," stammered La Violette, his voice thick with blood, "I wanted to tell you ... The most beautiful memory I have was holding you in my arms."

"What are you talking about, my poor boy?" ... "He's delirious," she thought.

"But I did, when the Marshall sent me to kidnap you. I had to hold you in my arms, I even had to squeeze your throat a bit hard to do what I had to. ... Afterwards I carried you and looked at you ... and that's why it's the most beautiful memory of my whole life, because a woman ... as lovely ... as you ..."

His voice began to fade. The last words came in a whisper, giving them the semblance of a secret confided.

"... There just aren't any such."

He was only just breathing. She took his hand:

"I forgive you for what you did that night. Shall I call Father de Lesdiguière to give you his blessing."

138

The man started, rallying his last defences:

"No, no, I want to die in my own faith, I do."

"Of course, he's a Protestant, I was forgetting."

She stroked his wrinkled forehead.

"The poor man! The poor tormented man. Oh well, go, go now. . . . May God rest you."

La Violette was dead. A little servant-wench was wounded and lay in a corner moaning. Malbrant-Swordthrust's face was black with gunpowder. The young valets were carrying ammunition from one floor to the other.

"We must do something to stop this," thought Angélique. She went upstairs and resolutely opened a window.

"Captain Montadour!"

Her clear voice rang out through the night thick with acrid smoke.

The Captain of the dragoons made his horse back up so that he could see better. He recognized her with a mixture of fear and triumph. She was there! Caught in the trap! He was going to have his vengeance.

"Captain, what right have you to attack a Catholic household? I shall appeal to the King."

"Your Catholic household is a den of Huguenots! You give us that heretical she-wolf and her brood and we'll leave you and your sons alone."

"What do you need to bother with women and children for? Your time would be better spent chasing after La Morinière's men."

"Your accomplice!" shrieked Montadour. "Do you think I've not seen through it all? You have betrayed us, you have sworn allegiance to the devil, you witch! And all the time I was fighting for our religion, you were running around the woods to sell us to these bandits. I've made one of your fancy boys talk. . . ."

"I shall appeal to the King," Angélique shouted back as loud as Montadour. "And Monsieur de Marillac will also be informed of your behaviour. In these intrigues between the mighty, it's the over-zealous underlings who are always the first to be punished . . . remember that!"

Montadour hesitated an instant. There was some truth

in what she said. Already, struggling as he was from one ambush to another, cut off from all orders, with his men either downcast or sullen, he did not imagine he'd get much credit for the way he had handled the conversion of Poitou. But his troops needed to do some killing and looting to give them back their self-confidence. And he would never get another opportunity to possess this woman, the sight of whom had tormented him for months and who had led him a dance like a common cur, him, Montadour! After that he'd see! But first he was going to have her, to make her yell, to humiliate her.

"Smoke out this bitch's lair," he growled, waving his arms. He stood up in his stirrups and a harsh peal of coarse laughter came from him in which Angélique could sense both his hatred and his lust.

She stepped back. She would gain nothing by bargaining. There was a new smell in the air, a smell of smoke, but not from the guns. Dame Aurélie's shrill voice shrieked from below:

"They've set fire to the shutters."

Barbe's still sleepy head looked round a half-open door:

"What on earth's all the racket, Madame? You'll wake my baby!"

"The dragoons are after our skins. Quick, fetch Charles-Henri, roll him in a blanket and go down into the cellar. I shall see if the coast is clear. . . ."

The underground passage! It was their last hope. They must send all the children and the womenfolk out that way, and they must just pray to God that there were no dragoons left in the little copse where they came up above ground.

She flew to the cellar, but, as she slipped between the wine casks, she became aware of the horrible truth. There were dull thuds and sound of voices coming from the door to the passageway. They had found the way in; probably the man they had tortured had told them.

Angélique stood transfixed, candle in hand, and watched the half-rotten wooden panel already bulging under the blows, as if a whole army were leaning on it.

She went back up the steps and drew the bolts.

"Stay there," she said to Lin Poiroux, whom she caught sight of standing with his spit in his hand, "and stab any of those stinking beasts who climbs out of that hole."

"Fire, fire! shouted Dame Aurélie running back.

The soldiers had piled logs against the walls, the heavy wooden shutters were crackling and smoke was coming in through every crack. The boys came down from the first floor. They could not see their assailants any more, and in any case they had run out of ammunition.

They looked at Angélique, and, as they looked, fear took hold of them bit by bit.

"M'lady! M'lady! What shall we do? . . ."

A voice said:

"We must go for help."

"What help?" she cried.

They heard voices singing, poignant and sad:

> Welcome us in heaven, Lord,
> We have served you this long day. . . .

It was the Huguenot servants who were singing with the Rambourg children, clustered around their mother, and strangely the fear that had twisted their poor little faces was vanishing to make way for a look of hopeful serenity.

Angélique's hair stood on end.

"No, no, no . . ." she repeated.

Once more she climbed the stairs like a mad creature, right to the top, to the turret. She came out on the narrow ledge and looked this way and that, seeing nothing but the blackness of night reeking with the ghastly smell of the funeral pyre.

"What help? What help?" she cried again.

She did not even know where Samuel de la Morinière's troops were.

Inside the château there was a kind of dull explosion. She thought one wall had collapsed, but it was only the

141

demented roar that rose from the throats of the unhappy
people in the house, as the first dragoons appeared.

Angélique came down again and looked over the banisters. The ground floor was a scene of utter and terrible
confusion. Shrieks everywhere, the shrieks of servants
fighting for their lives, the shrieks of molested women,
the shrieks of children torn from one another by brutal
hands; the howls of soldiers whom Dame Aurélie was
sprinkling point-blank with her boiling oil. And the
pleading voice of Baroness de Rambourg, on her knees
in the middle of the drawing-room, her clasped hands
stretched out in supplication.

Malbrant-Swordthrust had seized a heavy-backed
chair by the legs and was knocking out everyone who
came within reach. Cries of women being raped, cries of
pain, cries of the dying . . . and the cry of the pack at the
kill: "On to the pikes!" Angélique saw one of the
dragoons rushing upstairs holding one of the little Rambourg boys at arm's length. She ran towards him and
stumbled over an abandoned musket. Its charge of gunpowder lay beside it alongside the flint. She grabbed the
gun and prepared it in a kind of trance. She did not
know how to load a musket. And yet when she lifted the
heavy weapon and pulled the trigger, the soldier she
had aimed at spun round like a puppet and toppled
over backwards, a gaping black hole where his face had
been.

She leant on the banisters for support and went on
shooting at the red coats that were trying to get up the
stairs, until someone's arms seized her from behind and
paralysed her.

Her eyes registered three more images. She saw Barbe
run past, clutching Charles-Henri to her bosom. She saw
Bertille, her own servant, her face streaming with tears,
in the clutches of three obscenely unbuttoned soldiers.
She saw windows, open to the night, through which
bodies were being hurled. Then she lost all awareness of
what was going on around her, in her primitive preoccu-
pation with her own fate. She had never known such
animal panic, even when she had been chained to the
pillar to be tortured. On these occasions her mind had

142

kept the upper hand, it had stood above other creatures, above life and death.

But this night she felt nothing but the despairing blind will to escape what was about to happen to her. The more she struggled, the more her panic grew as she realized how helpless she was. She remembered the occasion when the gentlemen of the Tavern of the Red Mask had thrown her down on a table to rape her. Sorbonne the dog had come to her rescue.

But tonight, no one would come! The devils would wreak vengeance on this invincible woman, who all too often had spoilt the traps they had laid. They came at her from all sides, with their devils' masks, their red coats—Hell's livery—and their hairy hands. Tonight they would destroy her and her magic potion that preserved her from defilement. She had often passed through the flames of sin without being burned. They would dishonour her and she would be like the others. Nevermore would she flaunt her amorous charms before their eyes.

Stinking breaths on her proud mouth, hideous faces against her lips, whose cries were stifled beneath the sickening ravishment. Fingers like loathsome slugs moved over her body, and her dress was ripped to pieces.

Her body was stretched out, while someone with hands like iron bands held her ankles on the ground. Her flesh was theirs. Obscene shouts rang in her ears and she felt suffocated, like a drowning woman deep in black waters, as they brutally had their will of her.

This to her was worse than a murderer's dagger. Her body was no longer her own, but had become an object of shame. Unbearable pain stabbed through her, engulfing her in sombre excruciating torment until the merciful moment when she sank into unconsciousess.

CHAPTER 16

ANGÉLIQUE half raised herself from the ground. She was lying on the stone floor and her cheek was still chilled from contact with it. The dawn mists mingled with the stale smell of smoke lay heavily all about her. She stared uncomprehendingly at the scorch marks on her hands. It had happened when she was priming the musket, but she had not even noticed. Her memory came back, and she tried to get up, giving a groan. She stayed on her knees, leaning on her two hands, panting with grief. Her hair hung down over her bruised face and her posture was strangely reminiscent of the one she had assumed after falling on the stony paths of the Riff, when all her strength had deserted her.

Ah! You thought you had escaped from the demons, invincible, too beautiful woman! But the demons have caught up with you where you thought you were most secure, on your own childhood estate amid your own people. It was there that the worst awaited you. You could not hope always to keep that look full of life which scorned obstacles and mocked the bitter-hearted. Now you have lived through the worst. But you will never rise again! You still do not know all. All you know is the incurable wound inflicted on you last night, Angélique, proud Angélique. Mean and envious hearts may now rejoice.

This woman struggling to her feet in the wan light, leaning against the wall, casting haunted looks about her, will never again be the woman who fought, who hoped, who burgeoned over and over again to face new tasks, new loves, with the insolent vigour of a splendid flower blooming at the sun's faintest ray.

Her hand groped about, seeking mechanically to draw her torn clothes around her. At the recollection of what had happened to her she uttered a low moan. Smells and touches haunted her. Her own body disgusted her.

There were forms lying on the floor around her, including some red-uniformed dragoons. She did not see that they were dead. The dread that one of them might wake sent her scurrying towards the stair case. She began to go down it with stiff, aching limbs. She saw Barbe lying across the steps with the child in her arms.

Charles-Henri was asleep in the dead woman's arms. A wave of frantic joy made Angélique tremble. She bent down over him, unable to believe her eyes. It was a miracle. He was sleeping as only a child can in the midst of a devastated world, his long lashes shading his cheek, his lips parted in a half-smile

"Wake up," she said softly, "wake up, little Charles-Henri!"

But he did not wake. she shook him gently to make him open his eyes. Then his head lolled back like a pigeon's with a cut throat, and she saw on his neck the gaping wound through which his life had ebbed away.

Angélique unclasped the dead servant's arms with some difficulty and pressed her child to her bosom. Feeling him heavy and limp against her shoulder seemed to do her some good.

Downstairs she passed through the scene of slaughter with unseeing eyes stepping over the bodies as she would have over any obstacle in her way, and went out into the gardens.

The sun was beginning to sparkle on the surface of the lake. Angélique walked on, feeling nothing, neither the pain of her body nor the child's weight. She looked at him.

"The fairest of the sons of men . . ."

She no longer knew where she had heard that phrase. "The fairest . . ."

With unspeakable anguish she began to notice his immobility, his absence, the waxen pallor of his round cheek, as lily-white as the long nightgown he was wearing.

"My angel . . . come . . . I'm going to take you far away . . . we'll go together . . . you will be pleased, won't you? I'll play with you."

The sunshine was glistening on the silky golden locks on her shoulder, and the hair was alive, stirring in the breeze.

"Poor little boy! Poor little lord!"

Some peasants creeping timidly up the main drive saw her coming towards them.

They took her burden from her hands, and led her to Molines, the Steward's house. It had been plundered, but the dragoons had not set fire to it. She refused to go into the house, but they succeeded in getting her to drink some brandy, and she stayed there never saying a word, her hands on her knees.

The whole district, that is to say all the peasants left in the neighbouring farms and hamlets, were coming up to Plessis. Their eyes were raised with stupefaction towards the sluggish pall of smoke that hung over the trees. The entire right wing, the kitchen-wing, had gone up in flames. The fire had died out, no one quite knew why, and that had saved the survivors from roasting alive. Malbrant-Swordthrust was resuscitated. He had been miraculously protected by the furniture behind which he had entrenched himself, and there were three women servants who had suffered no harm beyond the bestial assaults of the soldiery. They were crying, their faces buried in their arms.

"Come on, come on, get over it," said the old women chivvying them out of it, "it don't do to make a great song and dance about it. What woman hasn't been through the mill once in her life? You're not dead, that's the main thing. As far as the rest is concerned, it's soon over and soon forgotten. That's the only sensible way to look at it. . . ."

Towards mid-morning Flipot showed his sharp, shrewd face. He had succeeded in escaping out of a window with one of the lads and had hidden in the forest.

A wounded head leaned on Angélique's knees, and frail shoulders were shaken with sobs. It was Father de Lesdiguière, his forehead encircled by a bloody bandage.

"Oh, Madame, Madame, it's terrible. They struck me down. I wasn't able to defend you to the last, you and this poor child. . . ."

They must have spared him because of his cloth.

Angélique thrust him aside with a shudder of horror not on his account but on hers.

"Don't touch me, whatever you do, don't touch me."

Then, suddenly:

"Where is Florimond?"

"I don't know. Over at Rambourg they haven't found him or young Nathaniel either. . . ."

146

She appeared not to hear him, falling back into her stunned condition. She saw Florimond in her mind's eye larking with Charles-Henri while Gontran was painting their portraits.

"Little angel with the cherub's smile, you are so sweet
Little Will-o'-the-wisp full of mischief, you are so sweet."

"The poor lady is going out of her mind," whispered one of the women watching beside her.

"No, she's praying, she's saying the litany of the saints."

What's that noise coming from the direction of the park?" asked Angelique emerging from her stupor.

"It's the sound of the grave-diggers' spades, Madame. They're getting on with the burying."

"I will go there."

She stood up laboriously. Father de Lesdiguière supported her. At the edge of the woods, near the gates, they had already dug several graves and lowered bodies into them. All that were left slumped in the grass were the cook Lin Poiroux and his wife, Aurélie, whom they had left till last because of their corpulence.

"We've laid the young master over there," said one of the peasants pointing to a mossy mound a little apart from the others. The grave was already covered with wild flowers.

The man added in an undertone as if to excuse himself to Angélique:

"We had to do what we could as quickly as possible. Later we'll take him to Plessis chapel with full honours. but the chapel has been burnt down. . . ."

"Listen," said Angélique, "listen to me."

Her voice, which had become faint, grew strong again all at once, and rose till it was vibrant with emotion:

"Listen to me, peasants," she cried, "listen. The soldiers have killed the last of the Plessis-Bellières, the heir to the estate. The family is extinct. The succession is broken. They have killed him. They have killed your master. You have no master any more. It's all over, all

over for good. There will be no more lords of Plessis.
The lineage is extinct."

The peasants gave vent to a mournful, grief-stricken
cry, and the women's sobs redoubled.

"It was the King's soldiers who committed this crime.
The troops who are paid to lay waste your crops and
ill-treat the people of the provinces. Pilferers, good for
nothings, who can only hang and desecrate. Foreigners
who devour our bread and kill our children. . . . Will you
let their crimes go unpunished? We've had enough of
the brigands who hold us at their mercy in the name of
the King. The King himself would have them hanged.
But we'll see to it by ourselves. Peasants, you won't
allow them to leave the district, will you? You must take
up arms . . . they must be sought out . . . and avenge
your young lord."

All next day they followed Montadour's dragoons.
The traces of the troops passing were easy to pick up,
and towards the close of the day they felt a kind of grim
joy when they realized that the mercenaries had been
unable to cross the river and had fallen back into the
interior again. Did they know that they were being
followed? Probably not. But they had encountered deserted villages, and the now silent country wrapped in
the mystery of its trees was beginning to get on their
nerves.

Night fell and the moon rose. The peasants crept
forward low down out of sight along the sunken road.
They were not tired. An instinct told them that the end
of the hunt was near. The carpet of dead leaves muffled
the sound of their heavy clogs, and the lumbering fellows moved with a wariness that betrayed their poacher
ancestry.

Angélique's ear was the first to catch the chink of
curb-chains on the bridles of the grazing horses.

She signalled to the men to stop and, hoisting herself
up the side of the ditch, she peered between the branches. On a sloping field white beneath the moonlight the
dragoons were sleeping huddled against one another,
worn out both by the orgy of the previous night and by

148

their anxious and indecisive march. A sentry was drows-
ing beside the embers of a fire from which a trail of
smoke was mounting sluggishly towards the starry sky.

Martin Genet, one of the tenant farmers, who had
assumed leadership of the peasants, took in the situation
at a glance. Orders were whispered in the local dialect,
and with no more noise than a rustling in the leaves part
of the group dispersed. Shortly afterwards the quavering
call of a screech-owl rose from the direction of the vale,
to be answered by another call.

The sentry stirred anxiously, waited, then returned to
his musing.

From the four corners of the field rushed swift, flitting
shadows. There was not even a shout, only a few low
grunts such as men might make who wake for a moment
then go back to sleep.

The following day Lieutenant Gromat, attempting to
join up with Montadour, arrived in the region with a
contingent of sixty men. He was looking for the dragoons. He found them in the middle of a field with their
throats cut, lying as if asleep. The job had been done
with scythes and billhooks. Montadour was recognized
only by his fat paunch. His head had disappeared.

The field was afterwards known as the Dragoons'
Field. Nothing but brambles and bindweed ever grew
there again. . . .

That was how the great Poitou revolt began.

PART TWO

Honorine

I T W A S all in vain that the King disowned Monsieur de Marillac as Governor of the province and replaced him by Baville.

Angélique's letter of intercession carried by the aged Molines—who had been received in person by the King as soon as he had reached Versailles—had come too late.

While the King was sending for Louvois, Marillac's hypocritical and bored accomplice, to find out from him exactly what was happening, and was giving orders, Poitou was catching fire.

From a distance no one suspected that what had triggered off this violent explosion was the vile murder of a little boy with golden curls. From the outset the situation was very confused, and for a long time Protestant outlaws were blamed for burning the château of Plessis and for the disappearance of the Marquise and her sons. It would have been easy to call for a heretic-hunt. But the first troops who tried to enter Gâtine found themselves, to their considerable astonishment, pitted against Catholics led by a man called Gordon de la Lande, whose ancient name was out of favour at Court like all those who at that time lived on their estates.

Meanwhile, south of the Bocage, Samuel de la Morinière the Huguenot was on the offensive again.

The royal regiments withdrew along a line running from Loudun to Niort via Parthenay while the mists of winter slid through the bare trees, and guerrilla warfare began, terrible in its savagery, its mystery, and the implacable determination of the forces of resistance. They were like shadows. Everywhere you had an impression

153

of a land swarming with people you never saw, of closed doors; it was like a desert. Who was there to parley with? Why this sudden wave of hatred? Against whom was the bitterness directed? Was it the King, or the troops, or the tax-collectors? Why were they fighting? Was it over religion, was it local patriotism, was it narrow regionalism? What had the peasants and provincial gentry suddenly gone mad about? What were they trying to achieve?

In the King's Council it became fashionable for the courtiers to raise their hands to the heavens and indulge in every possible type of conjecture. But no one would have dared voice what they all knew, what they all felt. No one would admit even to himself, that all this snarling and growling, reminiscent of the last desperate stand of a wounded beast in the forest, was neither more nor less than the dying throes of a people that refused to be enslaved.

The winter began with famine in Poitou. Monsieur de Marillac's experiment in conversion had tipped the scales on the side of disaster as a result of the destruction of the Protestant farmer's crops. For the economy of the area had already been undermined by the crushing burden of taxation and the poor harvest of the previous year. While Montadour had been busy setting fire to wheat-fields round the Protestant churches, the revenue men had been busy among the Catholic spires and had even had houses pulled down to realize cash on the sale of the beams. The tax-collectors had seized beds, clothing, plough-oxen and horses, and even the bread, that stood piled high on the shelves to last the six months of winter, in great round sweet-smelling discs as big as cartwheels. What did it matter if one man was ruined! But when there are many such, they leave a village deserted and wander along the autumn roads, miserable hollow-cheeked creatures fearful of hunger and more than ready to steal from those who have stolen from them.

Whole convoys of supplies on their way to Nantes for the army were completely plundered by the peasants.

While the sky had been cloudless and the sun hot, and

154

the summer had held out every hope of a good crop, the disturbances had destroyed everything and now there was famine.

It was only little by little that people realized the part one woman had played in setting alight these fires of hatred, and how she had succeeded in unifying the aims of the Protestants, the Catholics, the nobility, the peasants and the bourgeoisie of the small towns.

Some people at Court smiled at the legends that grew round this woman.

Others believed them! The days of the Fronde, when beautiful women had played such a prominent part, were not so far back, and no one in France would easily forget that once a woman called Joan, born of the land, had led the common soldiers into battle. This woman was no peasant because the nobles listened to her. Gradually the little-known rural nobility, whose ancient names and lineage were treated as a great joke at Versailles because they were as poor as church mice, were getting their men together and, by some miracle, finding arms for them.

The weapons were taken down from the walls over the chimney-piece. There were muskets, lances and halberds, old wheel-lock guns, guns with wicks, lansquenets, those short swords with a double cutting edge like the ones the Germans used in the wars of religion, when they came in their tawdry finery, bearded and plumed, to terrorize the people. Their warlike spirits would pass into whoever picked up their swords from the battlefield. There were even huntsmen's bows and arrows, deadly weapons in the hands of a man standing hidden amongst the oak leaves above a sunken road. The King's soldiers soon wished they still wore breast-plates as in the old days.

This woman was also said to be young and beautiful, hence her power over the leaders of the war. She travelled on horseback, wearing a riding habit and wrapped in a dark coat whose huge hood covered her blonde hair.

Angélique visited every château, every manor house in the region. She went to the proudest of them, stand-

155

ing on their hilltops, within their moats full of stagnant water, to those perched strategically on the escarpment overlooking the river. She found tall keeps with nothing to guard any more and inside she saw families shivering round a low fire. There were châteaux of the Renaissance period, built for festivities, where whole suites of vast rooms were boarded up and given over to the mice. They were too cold. The noblemen who lived there were either too poor, or they had a son at Court in Versailles who was playing ducks and drakes with the family fortune. There were the manor houses, built from great blocks of stone, more comfortable in their bourgeois simplicity, where the owners lived modestly in hopes of one day rising in the world although they never seemed to manage to bring it off.

Angélique found it easy to talk to these people in language they could understand. She would mention names to them, reminding them of the renown of their ancestors and of their present humiliation.

They would gather all the peasants together in the courtyard of a château or on a piece of open land. Then when she appeared before them, a proud silhouette in her dark coat, sitting astride her horse or standing at the top of a flight of grey stone steps, she would begin to speak in a calm, clear voice that carried far through the frozen air, and these primitive creatures were shaken by a trembling awareness of themselves that suddenly compelled their attention.

She was denouncing just the things that for many a long year had rankled silently with them. She reminded them of the terrible years of 1662 and 1663 when they had had to eat hay and grass, when they had eaten the bark off the trees, cabbage stalks and roots, when they had even been obliged to grind nutshells and acorns to eke out their last handfuls of rye or oats. She reminded them of their children who had died, of their treks into the towns; it was in that year that Nicholas and other starving peasants had made their way into París like wolves. It was also in that year that the great carnival of Paris had taken place and the King, his brother and the princes had appeared covered with jewels.

The following year, as they were binding up their wounds. Colbert had brought back the salt-tax in its two forms: the one known as "the saucepan and salt-pot tax," the other as "the curing and cattle tax." This meant that everyone had to buy this essential commodity from the granary and at an exorbitant price.

She was touching on matters that were a sore spot with every French peasant when she reminded them about these things. Faced with the impending avalanche of disaster, the peasants, made idle by the winter months, saw first and foremost in her appeal the possibility of a respite from taxation. Since they were rebels, they could fling the bailiffs down the well-shafts or chase them off with their forks. And what a relief to be able to keep the little they had for themselves!

She would tell them:

"The local lords are your true overlords. When you go hungry, so do they. How often have they not paid the 'tenths,' the poll-tax, the tithes and the tolls on common-ers lands that lie in their fief? They do this to protect you from too grasping hands."

"That's true . . . she's right . . ." the peasants would mutter.

"Follow them. They will create a new order for you where you will prosper. The time had come to put an end to this poverty."

She reeled off more figures: the wastage that she had seen at Court, the sale of offices, the big financiers juggling with money, all the things that conspired yearly to force the State to seek more and more money at source, in other words, from the peasants' earthenware pots.

They all took up arms: the Masson de la Guyonni-ères, the Goilard d'Amboises, the Chesbron de La Foulières, the Aubery d'Aspremonts, the Grosbois, the Guinefols, and many others of lesser name.

Towns like Parthenay, Monterray and La Roche, that tried to sit on the fence, were either forced into partici-pating by the Protestant troops or were eventually talked round. There were plenty of middle-class folk who had grudges against the King. Angélique knew how to move them with talk of money and business. The town stocks were distributed amongst the people against a famine year. And yet this organization and the looting of military convoys would not have sufficed to save these people who had been proclaimed outlaws by the King, if the people on the Atlantic coast had not joined forces with their brothers from the Bocage.

This was a predominantly Protestant region, and it was also the salt country, the scene of a bitter and virtually age-old battle between the people and the Crown. A dealer in contraband salt persuaded the other members of his guild to join in. Thereafter food was brought into Poitou, landed at heaven knows what beaches, transported down little rivers well away from the eyes of the authorities. Good money was paid for it. A merchant from Fontenay-le-Comte impressed upon his guild the fact that the gold would be useless to them if they all died of hunger.

The Kingdom of France was watching Poitou. Winter sealed it off as effectively as its rebellion. The outside world was waiting for the end of the cold and foggy weather with its snow and ice to enter the stronghold and count the dead. But the people of Poitou were not dying.

During all these frozen months, Angélique hardly ever stayed put in the same place. She lived where the peasants lived. She went to see those she needed to, and would sit by a château fireplace above which hung a coat of arms or before a farmer's pot, or in the back-shop of some wealthy influential town merchant. She did not mind having to talk to so many different sorts of people, and the ready hearing she received comfirmed her convictions that the ferment was ready to bubble over. You could feel that something was about to happen!

But where she felt really at home was on the hollow paths echoing with the hoofs of her horse and of those of her escort.

The Baron du Croissec was one of her constant companions. It was to him that she had first turned to ask for shelter after that tragic night. Since then the big fat man went everywhere with her, followed by a few of his servants.

All the Protestants on Angélique's estate had gone to join La Morinière's troops. The rest, under the command of Martin Genêt, had formed themselves into a sort of free corps, each man living in his own home but ready to gather together, armed, at the slightest summons.

The survivors from Plessis remained permanently with Angélique: Alain the groom, Camille the chef's assistant, old Antoine with his crossbow, Flipot from Paris, who would not have known what to do with himself in those woods, and Malbrant-Swordthrust, growling away but pleased to be involved once again in the hardships of a military campaign.

Father de Lesdiguière had never left her side from the start. Every time he lost sight of her, he would hasten to look for her. He was afraid of what lay behind that smooth, cold face with its fixed stare. He was haunted by the terrifying thought that she might try and take her own life.

After a day's ride she would sometimes fall into a deep silence in which all those about her seemed to have vanished. She would be sitting before the fire in a great hall with arms and tapestries hanging on the walls. This was the sort of environment she had known as a child. Outside, the wind howled, tearing at the dilapidated shutters, and the weathercocks creaked on the tops of the pointed turrets. And often another sound could be heard above the crackling of the burning wood: the measured beat of the Duc de La Morinière's boots on the flagstones. He was there, pacing up and down, and his huge shadow jumped about as the flames leapt up. From time to time he would stop and cast a hawthorn log into the hearth. This woman was cold and needed to be kept warm. He resumed his pacing up and down again, like a caged beast. He would look at Angélique's face as she sat there, her mind far away, and at the thin figure of Father de Lesdiguière sitting a little behind her on a stool, his head sometimes nodding with weariness. He would mutter into his beard with impotent

159

fury. It was not so much the presence of the young priest that exasperated him.

The barrier that stood between him and this woman, whom he desired every day with growing passion, was of a different kind, and much more insuperable than the mere presence of a slender page with the eyes of a young girl. He could have brushed him aside with the back of one hand, had there not been this other thing about which his implacable will and the force of his love could do nothing.

For now she was slipping away from him for ever.

When he had heard of the attack on the château of Plessis, he had returned to the region by forced marches. For several days he sought the vanished lady and he had found her. Samuel de La Morinière's wrath at what Montadour's soldiers had done was mixed with another feeling, hitherto unknown to him—grief. The thought that this woman had been sullied drove him mad. While he was searching for her, he had several times been tempted to throw himself on to his sword to escape the torments which were devouring him body and soul. He was even unable to utter the name of the Lord any more, to cry out to Him.

One evening, as he sat on the steps of a wayside cross that stood at a windy crossroad, beneath a sky traversed by scudding clouds, this cruel man had felt his heart bleed and tears trickle down his cheeks. He was in love. Angélique's face took on the aura of a breath-taking discovery: love.

When he had found her, he had almost fallen on his knees before her and kissed the hem of her dress. She looked calm and the dark rings under her eyes heightened their mystery. He was bowled over by her distant, wounded beauty, and the passion that his dreams had fanned burned brighter still.

As soon as he found himself alone with her, he wanted to take her in his arms. She went white and drew back, horror written all over her face.

"Don't come near me, whatever you do, don't come near me. ..."

Her fear drove him mad. He wanted to kiss the lips

that others had besmirched, he wanted to blot out all trace of them and make her his so as to cleanse her.

A nameless frenzy, composed of despair, mingled with jealous love and the wish to possess her filled his being., and, ignoring her plea, he drew her passionately to him. When he saw her convulsed, whiter than marble, with closed eyes, his frenzy was calmed. She had fainted. Trembling and petrified he had laid her down on the tiled floor.

Father de Lesdiguière rushed in, transformed from a seraph into an avenging archangel.

"You wretch! How could you have dared to touch her?"

He pulled the huge hairy hands off Angélique, battling with this great Goliath.

"How could you have dared? . . . Don't you understand? She can't stand anything like that. She can't stand a man touching her . . . You wretch!"

It had taken nearly an hour to bring her round.

Angélique and the Duc de La Morinière still used to meet by chance in their followers' houses during this time of guerrilla warfare. Then there would follow long evenings when their hosts, vaguely terrified, would leave the Huguenot alone with the Catholic girl. Silence would reign, and the sound of footfalls, while the flames leapt in the hearth. And so the hours ticked by in the heart of an ill-defined and agonizing drama.

Some time towards February Angélique found herself near Plessis. She did not wish to go and see the ruins of her old home so she stayed at Guéménée du Croissec's place. The fat Baron seemed keen to justify his vegetative existence as a bachelor *seigneur* by his unshakeable devotion to Angélique's cause. He had been more active during the past four months than in the whole of the rest of his life. He felt himself to be Angélique's trusted friend on whom she could depend no matter what happened, and it was true that she never felt disturbed by his presence. The three La Morinière brothers and other leaders of the rebellion used to meet there to discuss the situation. They could foresee

161

that in the spring the King's soldiers would start a general offensive on all fronts. The north was short of men, Could they count on the Bretons, who in any case were only half-Breton since they lived on this side of the Loire?

Soon afterwards there was some fierce fighting in the neighbourhood. It was still the focal point for attacks by the royal army because it was there that everything had started. They must have known that the Rebel of Poitou was in the region. There was a price on her head, although no one knew who she was. The Dragoons' Field was near by, and the memory of it was an incitement to the military to take up the hunt. Angélique almost fell into an ambush. She was saved by Valentine the miller with whom she and Father de Lesdiguière, who had been wounded, took refuge. To get her out of reach of any possible search parties, Valentine took her right into the marshes where no one could follow her.

CHAPTER 18

ANGÉLIQUE spent several weeks in Valentine's hut, which, in spite of its situation at water level, and its blackened thatched roof looking like a fur cap, was quite comfortable. A special kind of distemper, made of blue clay, straw and manure, a secret of the "hutmen," covered the inside walls like thick felt and absorbed the moisture as well as keeping out the cold. It was warm and dry inside, and, when the peat fire was burning with its short, violet flames, the atmosphere was cosy enough to make you forget the marshy waterlogged landscape that lay heavily all around.

There was only one low-ceilinged room, with a sort of penthouse to one side, half-stable, half-storehouse, from which could be heard the tinkling bell worn by the goat that Valentine had brought in his punt to keep them supplied with milk and cheese. There were also a stone pond with eels swimming about in it, which went into Valentine's stew, a stock of beans and onions, some loaves of bread on a low shelf and a barrel of red wine.

162

The furniture was a strange mixture. The bed was extremely primitive, consisting only of a layer of heather spread over a truckle frame, but Valentine had not failed to install in his marshland fastness the "Virgin Mary's box" so dear to the hearts of the men of Vendée. The miller's was said to be the finest specimen of the lot. It was a weird curio consisting of a glass bell under which were heaped up in incongruous array, around a portrait of the Virgin, shell and pearl flowers, laces and ribbons, coloured stones and genuine gold crown-pieces arranged in a pattern representing the sun. Angélique, who was familiar with it from of old, could not look at it without having the strange feeling that she was transported back into the past. For a brief moment it was as if time were standing still and she was back again gazing at it in open-mouthed wonder as she had done when she was a child. Then, suddenly, she was herself again with all her physical and spiritual hurt, with her grown-up distresses seething inside her like the eels in the pond. A bleak, hellish, revolting hurdy-gurdy, that was what her thoughts were like, and sometimes they made her feel almost physically dizzy.

Here she did not feel the need to flee aimlessly on, as when she had been on the firm ground outside the marshes, driven on by the thought that she must erect barriers between herself and the King's ostracism, the abiding horror of which had become an obsession with her. She would emerge from the marshes in the spring when the offensive began. Her presence would then be required to rally the faint-hearted and to remind all concerned of what was at stake.

Valentine kept her supplied with news. The country was calm: on a war footing, but calm. Troops were still being levied, and the fight against famine was still going on. But, thanks to the rebellion, the meagre resources were no longer being swallowed up in the bottomless pit of taxation and requisitions, and the country managed to live. The people were thankful for it. "Everything goes better when you're left to manage for yourselves." But would they have it in them to defend their basic liberties? They were all getting ready for that too.

Valentine came almost every day. What did he do the rest of the time? Did he return to his mill? Did he go hunting or fishing among the reeds? He sometimes came with full nets, or with brightly plumaged birds hanging, head down, from a pole.

The occupants of the hut spoke little. The priest was ill and slept in the hay-loft. The wound in his side had been healed by herb poultices, but he was often feverish. He was like a sad, gentle shadow between two other shadows also absorbed by their thoughts. The three were strangely assorted: a beautiful, tragic woman, a slow-thinking, laconic miller, a bit odd in the head, and a little priest bred to Court life, pale and trembling, all of them shut in amidst the silence of the stagnant waters.

Angélique slept on the heather bed covered with a thick sheepskin. Her sleep was deep and dreamless—something quite new to her. The experiences she had been through seemed to have left no physical trace on her. When she did wake up, she listened to the rain pattering on the flat surface of the marshes outside, the low sound spreading out in concentric rings as far as the remotest horizons. Or again it might be the croaking of frogs, the sharp squeal of water-rats, the cries of night-birds, the myriad whisperings of the water jungle. It brought her a kind of peace.

When Valentine was there, she saw him too at night, sitting in the rush and polished-wood armchair. He had his eyes open, and the bluish firelight played over his rough, sombre, stolid features. At times a gleam would come into his deep-set eyes. She had the impression that he was staring at her. Then she would close her eyes and go back to sleep.

Valentine was no more to her than a familiar figure from the past who waited on her. He cut the peat for the fire, milked the goat, put the milk in the pot under the hearthstone to curdle, cooked the soup and fish and mulled the wine so that the sauce for the stew should not taste too bitter. He would have made a cook fit to serve under the great Vatel. He sometimes brought her baskets of buns and cheese cakes made from the finest flour, which were eaten locally at Eastertime, black in

164

the crust and golden inside. On several occasions Angélique found herself pouncing on them with sudden greed. She was constantly hungry. Something vaguely resembling a smile came into the man's bold eyes as he watched her sinking her white teeth into the cakes. She would feel queer, stop eating and go outside to avoid his stare.

When she had come to the little island in the marshes, it was still midwinter and the sodden earth recalled primeval times when the saline mud had been full of sea-urchins, molluscs and fossil shells. Some seabirds still occasionally came to nest in the reeds. The tall poplars brought by the Dutch in Henry IV's time transformed the marine landscape, as did the alders, the aspens and the ash-trees, whose outlines stood silhouetted against the shimmering waters or the mist as thin and transparent as porcelain, as if drawn in black ink with a fine pen. Rooks cawed loudly gliding above the desolate countryside. Standing in the reeds Angélique gazed far away across the maze of boughs and twigs and slim trunks standing over their reflections which made up the tangled architecture of the marshes. The black-and-white etched picture cast a spell over her despairing heart, and all at once she thought she saw Florimond, Charles-Henri and Cantor passing by in the fog, three lost little silhouettes holding one another's hands. She cried out, wringing her hands:

"My sons . . . my sons!"

She called again and again, and her voice died away into the immense distance until Father de Lesdiguière came stumbling through the mud to take her arm and lead her gently back to the house.

"You have sacrificed your sons," he said in a low voice, "wicked, foolish woman! You should never have left Versailles, never have gone to those eastern countries, which have corrupted you. You should have made your submission to the King. You should have gone to bed with the King . . ." And she began to sob bitterly again, calling softly to them and begging them to forgive her.

It was an early boisterous spring, which clothed the

165

vast expanses in emerald, decked the desolate landscape in a sumptuous garment that transformed it and restored their bluey-green mystery to the cress-beds. The water-lilies bloomed again with their honied, waxy perfume. Frail dragonflies were beginning to skim the surface, discovering as they went tufts of forget-me-nots and mint on which to settle. From the pools came the splash of wild ducks, crested grebes, great grey geese and wary herons. Behind the hanging branches boats could be seen gliding silently by. Like the woods the marshes offer an apparently deserted spectacle but are in fact swarming with intense life. The "hutters," descendants of the Colliberts, form a numerous and independent nation. "In the marshes live bad men who pay taxes neither to King nor Bishop," her nurse had told her when she was a child.

It was March, but the weather was exceptionally mild.

"It looks as if it won't have been too hard a winter," Angélique said to Valentine one evening, "The good spirits are on our side. I'll soon have to be thinking of going back to dry land."

The miller was putting a pitcher of steaming red wine and some mugs on the table. The meal was over. Father de Lesdiguiére had gone up to the loft to sleep on his hay-bale. It was the time when Angélique and Valentine drank mulled wine spiced with herbs and cinnamon sitting in front of the fire. Valentine filled her mug, settled down on his stool and quaffed his portion rather noisily. She looked at him as if she were seeing him for the first time and noticed with surprise his powerful rounded back under his grey flannel jerkin and his clumsy shoes with their metal buckles. Neither a merchant nor yet a peasant was Maître Valentine, miller of the Ablettes, a stranger who had always been there.

He looked at her over the edge of his mug. He had grey eyes.

"You're thinking of leaving?"

He spoke in local dialect and she answered him likewise.

166

"Yes, I must find out what our people are doing. Come summer we'll be at war."

He drank a second mugful, and then a third, breathing heavily.

Then he put his mug down on the table and stood in front of Angélique with his arms swinging, staring at her.

Irritated by his stare she held out her mug to him.

"Put that on the table."

He obeyed then returned to stare at her again. His face was ruddy and pockmarked, and behind his half-opened lips she caught a glimpse of his decayed teeth.

The loneliness which Angélique had so far not minded in the least began to weigh on her heavily that evening. She gripped the arms of her chair and murmured:

"I think I'll go to bed."

He took a pace towards her.

"I've put down fresh heather, fresh gathered from the undergrowth, so as to make the bed softer."

He bent forward, took her hand in his and looked at her with supplication in his eyes.

"Come down on the heather with me."

Angélique pulled back her hand as if it had been burnt.

"What's come over you? Are you mad?"

She stood up and scrutinized him anxiously. The aversion she felt for him—that she felt for all men now—was preventing her from defending herself as she ought to have done. Her heart was pounding wildly in her breast. If he laid a finger on her, she would faint, as she had done with the Duc de La Morinière. She shuddered to remember the horrible spasm that had choked her that day, while the memory of the night at Plessis made her want to vomit. There was a glint in the miller's eyes that frightened her. They were misty and yet blazing.

"Don't touch me, Valentine."

He stood head and shoulders above her, his back slightly stooping, his lower lip hanging, with the same stupid look that he used to have when he stood before her, and at which she had laughed.

"Why not me?" he said with an effort. "I love you . . .

167

I've had all my life taken from me with the love you laid upon me. I've waited long enough for this hour. I thought it would be impossible, but now I know that you're going to be mine."

"Just like Nicholas!" she thought with dismay. "Just like Nicholas!"

"I've had my eye on you since you've been here. I've been watching you fattening up like a pregnant ewe. Then I felt mighty glad because I realized that you weren't a fairy, and that I could have you without you casting a spell on me."

She listened to these ravings without understanding what he meant as he babbled on in his hoarse but soft dialect.

"Come on, my pretty, my dear ... come down on the heather."

He drew close to her and pressed her to him. His hand stroked her shoulder lingeringly.

She succeeded in regaining her self-possession and struck him in the face with all her might with her clenched fists.

"Take your hands off me, peasant!"

Valentine quivered and drew back at the insult. He was the miller of the Ablettes again, a man dreaded throughout the countryside for his harsh hot-tempered character.

"Like the other time," he growled, "like the other time in the barn on Chaudut night. You haven't changed, but that doesn't make any difference. Tonight I'm not frightened. You're no fairy. You'll pay. Tonight you'll be mine."

He said the last words with terrifying determination. Then turning away he stumped heavily to the table and poured himself a drink.

"I've got plenty of time, but remember that no one insults Maître Valentine and gets away with it. You've wounded me to the heart and you're going to pay for it."

She thought she must try to calm this madman.

"Don't misunderstand me, Maître Valentine," she said in a broken voice. "I don't despise you. But even if

168

you were the King himself, I wouldn't have anything to do with you. I can't bear a man to touch me. That's how it is. It's like a sickness. Try to understand my situation. . . ."

"It's not true." You're lying. There are lots of others you let rock you in their arms and you like it. He must have touched you, the fellow that put the lambkin in your belly."

It was an expression from the south-east of France, but it was occasionally used in the north. Angélique knew it. A "lambkin" meant a baby.

"What lambkin?" she asked, looking at him so blankly that for a moment he weakened, completely taken aback.

"What one do you think? The one you're carrying. In fact that was what convinced me that you weren't a fairy. They say that fairies can't bear children to human beings. It was a wizard told me that. Real fairies don't have babies."

"What baby?" she shrieked hoarsely.

The abyss was yawning at her feet. The menace was mounting from the limbo of the subconscious; it grew and took possession of her, while in the giddiness that she had so often taken for a passing indisposition she detected the slow movements of a living being within her.

"You can't say you didn't know," commented the miller, his muffled voice seeming to come from a great distance. "It's a good five or six months that you've been carrying him."

Five or six months! But it was impossible. Since Colin Paturel she had not made love with anyone. She had not given herself to any man.

Five or six months! . . . The autumn! . . . The red night at Plessis, the shots, the blood, the fire, the sobbing of children, the screams of women, the hideous spectacle of the dragoons with their breeches unbuttoned. . . . Struggle and pain, maddening humiliation, and now, five months later, the ghastly truth.

She gave a great, heart-rending shriek like a wounded animal:

"No, NO! Not that!"

During the months she had been riding about Poitou, her whole mind concentrated on one purpose, entirely forgetful of herself, she had not noticed anything. She had not wanted to think of her body, and had not wondered at irregularities which she thought must be due to her terrible shock and the exertions of her travels.

Now she remembered, and it was all quite obvious. The monstrous progeniture had developed. It was distending her dress under her corset. Her figure had lost its slimness. Valentine seemed disconcerted by her demented demeanour. There was a deep silence broken only by the splash of a fish leaping out of the calm water.

"What difference does that make?" resumed the miller. "You're all the more attractive for it."

He came at her again. She evaded his outstretched hands and cowered in the dark corners of the room, petrified and unable to utter a cry. He succeeded in catching her and taking her in his arms.

At that moment there came a violent banging on the door, the wooden latch burst and the tall figure of Samuel de La Morinière stooped to enter the hut. He looked about him and gave a growl as he descried the couple.

Since Angélique's disappearance he had been consumed with fear. He had been told that she was being held prisoner by the accursed miller, who had thrown a spell on her to keep her in the marshes. A fig for such gross superstitions! It was none the less true that the Papist miller was a shifty, dangerous customer. Why had the nobly born lady followed him? Why did she not return? Unable to bear waiting any longer he had gone off without telling anyone and had found a guide to lead him to her.

He arrived and found her in this idiot brute's arms.

"I'll cut your throat, base peasant," he roared, drawing his dagger.

Valentine only just succeeded in avoiding the blow. He bent double and rushed for shelter to the other end of the room. Fury and frustration gave his face an expression as frightful as the Huguenot's.

"You shan't have her," he panted in his gruff voice. "She's mine."

"You filthy pig, I'll spill your guts for you."

The miller was just as tall and strongly built as the Protestant lord, but he was unarmed. He began to edge behind the table, his eyes fixed on the newcomer, who was trembling with insensate jealousy and watching for his chance to cut his throat. The fire had died down and the corners of the room were plunged in darkness.

Valentine was trying to reach the long woodman's axe hidden behind the floor-bin.

Angélique rushed to the ladder leading up to the loft, tripped in the hay and, bending over young Lesdiguière, shook him with all her might.

"Father! They're fighting. . . . They're fighting over me."

Half-awake, the young man looked at her in amazement, in the light of the old lantern hanging from the rafters, this woman with her teeth chattering and her dilated pupils.

"Fear nothing, Madame. I'm here."

Down below there was an inhuman bellow and the heavy thud of a falling body.

"Listen. . . ."

"Fear nothing," he repeated.

He picked up his sword, which was lying beside him and slipped down the ladder behind Angélique. They saw the Huguenot Patriarch lying face down, where he had been struck. His skull had burst open leaving a gaping red wound in his hairy scalp.

Standing at the table Valentine was drinking out of the pitcher of wine, the bloody axe beside him. His grey clothes had been splashed. His eyes were those of a madman.

CHAPTER 19

H E C A U G H T sight of Angélique and put the jug down with a grunt of satisfaction.

"You always have to fight the dragon to win the princess," he said in a fuddled voice. "The dragon came, and I killed him. That's over and done with. Now I've earned you, eh? You won't get away from me now."

He came staggering towards her, drunk not only with wine but with violence and frustrated lust. In one smooth movement the young priest slipped to Angélique's side and took up his stand in front of her with raised sword.

"Back, miller," he commanded calmly.

"Get out of the way, Father," growled the other; "these things are no business of yours. You're an innocent. Stand aside."

"Leave this woman in peace."

"She belongs to me."

"She belongs to no one but God. Get back, leave this house. Do not risk losing your soul for eternity."

"That'll be enough sermons out of you, Father. Let me pass."

"In the name of Christ and the Virgin, I command you to go back."

"I'll crush you like a louse."

The dying firelight struck a glint from the point of the outstretched sword.

"Do not attempt to come forward, miller," murmured the priest. "Do not attempt it, I beseech you."

Valentine rushed at him.

Angélique hid her face in her hands.

The miller staggered back, his hands clasped to his side. He collapsed on the hearthstone.

All at once he began to scream:

"Give me absolution, Father! Give me absolution. I'm going to die! I don't want to go in a state of mortal sin. Save me. . . . Save me from hell. I'm going to die. . . ."

172

His inhuman shrieks filled the hut. Then the cries grew fainter, and were broken by lamentations and dying gasps mingled with the priest's murmured prayers as he knelt by the dying man.

At length there was nothing but silence.

Angélique was incapable of movement. The priest had to drag the two bodies out unaided, hoist them into the punt, take them some little way off and tip them into the dark waters.

When he got back, the young woman had not moved. He closed the door carefully and went over to the fire-place to pile on peat and wood and get the fire blazing again. He came across to Angélique and grasped her arm to support her.

"Sit down and get warm, Madame," he said in a low voice.

And when she appeared somewhat recovered, he added:

"The man who led the Duc here has run away. I heard the sound of his boat. He was a Collibert. He won't talk."

She was seized by a violent shudder.

"It's horrible, horrible!"

"Yes, so it is ... these two men dead ..."

"No, that's not what's horrible, it's what he told me first."

She looked at him intently.

"He told me that I was going to have a baby!"

The young man bowed his head and blushed.

Angélique shook him furiously by the shoulder.

"You knew and yet you said nothing to me."

"But, Madame," he stammered, "I thought ..."

"Fool, fool that I've been! How could I let so much time go by without realizing!"

She really felt as if she were going out of her mind. Father de Lesdiguière tried to take her hand, but she eluded him, because she could feel the unmentionable thing moving in her. It was worse than feeling oneself eaten alive by an unclean beast.

She flailed her arms, tore her hair, wanted to throw herself in the marsh, while he begged and implored her

173

and held her back, and she thrust him away, gripped by a terrible delirium in which the gentle voice speaking to her of God, of life, of prayer, speaking to her words of love through his tears, tried in vain to reach her.

At last she regained her calm, and her features became composed as they had been in recent days. The priest watched her anxiously for he sensed that she had come to some irrevocable decision, but she forced herself to smile at him.

"Go to bed, young fellow," she said, "you're worn out."

Her hand ran lightly over his dark hair framing his delicate adolescent features and his fine eyes, in which she could read an ardent expression of sorrow and adoration.

"Every wrong you suffer is torment to me, Madame."

"I know, my dear."

She pressed him to her breast, comforted to feel him there, because he was pure and loved her, and that was all the sweetness left her in the world.

"My poor guardian angel . . . go to bed."

He kissed her hand and went off regretfully and anxiously, but he was so exhausted that she heard him stumbling on the rungs of the ladder before falling heavily on to his bed.

She stayed quite motionless, like a statue, for several hours, and then at first light she wrapped herself in her cloak and stole noiselessly from the hut. The miller's boat was there, at the door, chained to a ring set in the daub wall. She untied it and taking the wooden paddle, which she would manage better than the punt pole, she pushed off into the green waters of the channel. The light was still uncertain. The boat passed through the midst of the wild birds chattering as they woke.

Angélique thought of the youthful priest. He would wake and call despairingly after her. But he would not be able to catch her up and stop her doing what she intended to do. There was a yawl in the storehouse. He could, if necessary, use it to get across to the hutmen in the marshes.

The sun came up on the horizon and turned the thin wraiths of mist to gilded violet. It was getting warmer.

174

Angélique went slightly off course in the absinthe-and-pearly-hued canals. But towards mid-morning she reached dry land.

CHAPTER 20

"You must, Mélusine, you must do it, or I'll curse you."

Angélique dug her fingers into the old woman's bony shoulders. The witch and she were facing one another, their eyes blazing. They were like two embattled harpies, and anyone catching sight of them in the half-light of the cave, with their flying hair and flashing eyes, would have fled in terror.

"My curse is stronger than yours," Mélusine hissed.

"No, it isn't, because if I were dead I would be stronger than you. I shall certainly die if you refuse me the drug and then I shall see you stripped of your power. I shall stab myself through the stomach to kill it."

"Very well," said the hag, suddenly giving in, "let me go." She shook her old bruised back under its patches of torn sacking. One more winter spent in her damp den had carried still further the subtle transformation of this human being into some kind of animal or even plant life, and had given her body the appearance of an old gnarled tree-stump, her hair the semblance of woody plants or spiders' webs, and her eyes the look of a fox in a thicket.

She hobbled over to her cauldron, looked suspiciously at the boiling water, then, making up her mind, began to throw innumerable herbs, leaves and powders into it.

"What I said. ... I was thinking of you. It's too late. You're in your sixth month. If you drink this potion, you may well die."

"What do I care? I must get rid of this thing."

"You're as stubborn as a mule. ... Oh well, you'll die, but it won't be my fault. You won't come and haunt me from the next world."

"I promise."

175

"It would be a bad thing for me to cause your death," muttered the old woman, "because you are destined to live to a great age. . . . You are strong and healthy. Perhaps you will stand up to it. I shall chant my incantations over you so that fate will be with you. When you have drunk the potion, go and lie down on the Fairy Stone. It's a special place of safety. The spirits will help you."

The potion was only ready as night was falling. Mélusine filled a wooden bowl with the black decoction and handed it to Angélique, who resolutely drank it to the last drop. It did not taste too horrible. She breathed a sigh of immense relief, in spite of the fear of the hour to come that held her in its grip. But afterwards she would be set free. This horror would be cast out. She must find the courage to face the ordeal. She got up to walk to the Fairy Stone clearing. The witch was muttering her incantations, and slipped some nut-like objects into her hand.

"If the pain gets too bad, nibble one or two of these. They will ease it. And when the child has been born, leave its body on the Druids' stone. Go and gather some mistletoe to cover it. . . ."

Angélique walked along a path where the new grass was growing up through the dead leaves. These delicate blades were nevertheless strong enough to overcome the weight of the humus. Everything was green and tremulous. She reached the hilltop, and there stood the dolmen, high and dry like a stranded shark in the evening shadows. Her feet made the dry leaves crackle and she recognized the familiar smell of the oak-trees, that stood like lords around the clearing, their powerful trunks covered in moss and their branches intertwined like candelabra. She lay down on the stone that had been warmed by the rays of the sun, which had been of summer strength. Her body had not yet reacted. She placed her arms in the form of a cross and drank in the beauty of the still bright sky in which hung one shimmering star.

It had been to this clearing that she had come, as a

child, to dance with the local girls and boys. They would sing weird forbidden refrains, in an attempt to make the fairies or goblins appear, just once. She imagined she could hear their thin sharp little voices and the sound of their little clogs on the acorns or dry ferns that strewed the ground.

> *Fille, filoches*
> *Ren ne voidoches. . . .*

Then they would shout in their excitement: "There, I saw a sprite! Climbing up that oak-tree." "It was a mouse!" "No, it was a sprite. . . ."

Night came and the last glimmers of light vanished. The moon rose behind the trees, first red, then golden, and finally came out in all its silver splendour above the clearing.

Angélique writhed on the grey stone. The pains racking her body gave her no respite.

She was panting and with each onslaught she wondered whether she could stand another.

"This must stop!" she said to herself.

But it did not stop. Her temples were bathed in sweat and the moonlight hurt her tear-filled eyes. The moon seemed to travel across the sky infinitely slowly, drawing out her seemingly endless torment. In the end she cried out in her agony and the branches above her took on the appearance of leaning spectres. That black trunk there, that was the bandit Nicholas, the other was Valentine with his hatchet, and the third, coming towards her snapping the branches as he came, was the black, bearded Huguenot, his eyes burning like two candles and his skull gaping like a split pomegranate.

This time she did see those Will-o'-the-wisps, travelling up and down the tree-trunks at dizzy speed. She saw, too, the black cats whose claws left a luminous trail, while the owls and bats, companions in their midnight revels, spun round above her head. She was shaking with fever. When a particularly unbearable pain gripped her, she remembered the nuts that she had slipped into her pocket when the witch had handed them to her. She ate one of them and shortly after the pain became less intense. It was still there, but seemed far away and stifled. She went on eating the nuts as fast as she could, terrified lest the pain return in all its former harshness and cruelty. Then she slowly sank into a sleep akin to death.

When she woke the forest had lost its terrors. A bird was singing, perched on the tip of a branch against a pearl-grey, pink-tinted sky.

"It's all over," thought Angélique, "and I have been spared."

Utterly prostrated, at first she did not move. At last she sat up, her body weighing on her like lead. She remained seated, supported on her outstretched arms, and looked about her at her surroundings, familiar and calm once again. Her thoughts were vague but happy. "You are free, You have been delivered."

But there was not a sign of the night's events. The spirits had removed every trace.

Angélique was slowly getting her bearings. There was something she failed to understand.

"What has happened?"

Her question was answered by the gentle flutter she felt within her, and she understood, horror-stricken and shattered, what had happened.

"Nothing has happened. I went through all that for nothing! Oh, how awful! How awful!"

So the blight had not left her. Madness seized her for an instant and she beat her own body with her fists and banged her head repeatedly on the stone. Then she jumped down from the dolmen and ran all the way to Mélusine's cave. She almost strangled her in her rage.

"Give me some more of the potion. . . ."

The witch had to use all her powers of diplomacy to save her wretched skin.

"Why do you want to get rid of the child since everyone can see what's happened to you? Wait another two or three months . . . wait till your time is up! The child will leave your body whether you like it or not. . . . And without killing you as it nearly did today. You can come

178

here, and I will help you. . . . After that, you can do what you please with it. You can cast it into the Vendée from the top of the Giants' Gorge, as a sacrifice, if you like, or you can leave it on someone's doorstep, in town. . . ."

Angélique eventually listened to her.

"I shall never have the strength to wait any longer," she wailed.

But she already knew that the witch was right.

She left the forest and went to join the Duc de La Morinière's two brothers. She found them at the château of Rouçay, near Bressuire. She told them that the Patriarch was dead but they must carry on with his work. It was difficult for them to question her about the circumstances of the great Protestant Lord's death. Angélique's manner was chilling to the boldest amongst them. It was now obvious that she was pregnant and she no longer attempted to conceal the fact. There was something about her that cut short all comment. La Morinière's two brothers continued to treat her with the greatest possible deference. They thought it was Samuel de La Morinière's child she bore.

She also found Father de Lesdiguière again. They never referred to past events, and the young priest took up his station again as one of the Poitou Rebel's itinerant escort.

With the advent of spring, nature and men alike seemed to tremble with the same power. The days of fighting were at hand. The skirmishes became more frequent, and the time of battle drew near.

A tireless woman galloped through the province, with her faithful followers.

They said that wherever she went the partisans would be sure of victory.

Towards July she wanted to come back to the Nieul area, and there she vanished for a few days.

Her companions and servants looked for her at first and asked one another what could have become of her, then they fell silent as the same thought suddenly crossed their minds and they realized why she had left them and gone off alone.

They waited anxiously for her return, sitting round the fire. She would come back, paler, no doubt, and different, but with the same enigmatic look in the depths of her green eyes. And no one would dare to look at her slim waist.

They never left the clearing where they had been when she had gone away. She must be able to find them without difficulty. Alas! They were powerless to help her. They could do nothing to ease the pain and torment she was undergoing deep in the forest. They were men and she was a woman. She was beautiful and proud and of noble birth, but she had suffered the curse of womankind. They did not dare to think of her, alone in the forest, and they felt ashamed that they were men.

CHAPTER 21

ANGÉLIQUE had galloped like a mad thing to the edge of the forest of Nieul. There she left her steed on a small farm where lived a woman who worshipped her. She was breathless and clung to the bushes to walk faster. Once under cover of the trees she felt better but she still had a long way to go. Fear gripped her. She thought she would never get down the path that led to Mélusine's hideout, and she stumbled into the sandy cave like a wounded beast.

The old witch picked her up and laid her on a bed of ferns, and stroked her hair, wet with perspiration, with her gnarled fingers, quite overcome, as if she had been Angélique's old mother.

She gave her a calming potion to drink and covered her with plasters that brought her some relief. The child was born very quickly. Angélique sat up to look in horror at this creature born of crime. She had always expected it to be disfigured, misshapen. No child conceived as it had been could have been healthy. She cried out in terror:

"Oh, Mélusine, look . . . it's a monster . . . it's got no genitals. . . ."

The witch took one frightened look at her from under her white wisps of hair.

"Well, no hardly! It's a wee girlie!"

Angélique lay back seized by uncontrollable giggling.

"Oh how stupid am, I never thought of that. A wee girlie! A daughter! I never thought of that. You see . . . I'm not used to the idea . . . never done it before . . . I've only had boys, yes, three boys . . . three sons . . . and now I've none. Not a single one! A daughter! Oh! That's too funny."

Her laughter turned to uncontrollable weeping that shook her like a storm of rain.

Almost immediately as she wept, she fell into a deep sleep, and her fair hair that lay loose about her head gave her a look of innocence.

When she woke up she was filled with the peace that sleep had brought her. It was a peace of the body but it nevertheless suffused her tormented mind.

Leaning on one elbow she looked towards the entrance to the cave and saw a wonderful sight: a doe with her fawn was feeding there, plainly delineated against the carpet of greenery. She must have been a familiar visitor to the mouth of the witch's cave, for she did not quiver anxiously as wild creatures do when they sense the nearness of humans.

Angélique held her breath and watched them for a long while, and, when the graceful animals had gone, she lay down again with a sigh. It was so quiet in Mélusine's home. She understood just how a woman, too often hurt, could come and take permanent refuge in the woods, finding her only salvation in their solitude. That was how you became a forest witch.

Towards evening she was wakened by a different noise and she sat up once again a prey to anxiety: it was a thin, strangled cry, not the cry of an animal.

"She's thirsty!" said the witch going to the back of the cave to fetch something. She came back holding a shape-

181

less bundle wrapped in a scrap of red cloth from which the wailing came.

Angélique looked at the witch in wild incredulity.

"What! She's alive! But I thought she never cried when she was born."

"You're right! But now she's crying. She's thirsty." And Mélusine made as if to place the child at the young mother's breast.

Angélique's whole being recoiled. Her eyes flashed. "No," she shrieked. "no, never. She's had my blood, but she'll not have my milk. My milk is for little lords, not for that drunken soldier's bastard. Take her away, Mélusine! Take her out of my sight. Give her some water, anything to keep her quiet, but don't bring her near me. Tomorrow, I shall take her to the town."

During the night, Angélique began to talk. She was not quite asleep. She spoke in a half-dream. She talked about all she had lived through at Plessis, the night the dragoons had held her to the ground and murdered her last-born son. She talked about what she had seen as she had walked through her devastated house, clasping the dead child to her breast. These were visions engraved for ever on her retina. She would never forget them.

"Yes, yes, I remember," muttered the witch, who sat crouched over the fire. "When I met you in the autumn in that clearing, I saw the sign of death hanging over the fair-haired child."

The following day she got up. She was anxious to complete the final stage of her deliverance. The child was driving her mad with its incessant crying.

She put on her shoes, tidied her hair under her black satin headsquare and threw her coat over her shoulders.

"Give her to me," she said in a firm voice.

Mélusine handed her the baby who was purple in the face with shrieking, all tied up in the red rag. Angélique took her and walked with determined steps towards the mouth of the cave.

Mélusine ran after her.

"Listen, my daughter, listen to my advice."

182

She held her back, her brown hand gripping Angélique's arm.

"Listen to me, daughter. You must not kill her."

"No," said Angélique not without effort, "I shall not
do that, have no fear."

"Because she has been born with a sign on her. Look."

She made Angélique look down at the tiny shoulder
where she saw a brown star-shaped mark.

"Children who have a mark like that on them are
under the protection of the heavenly bodies."

Angélique, tight-lipped, pushed past her. Mélusine
caught up with her once more.

"I can even tell you the name of this rare sign . . . it's
Neptune's mark."

"Neptune?"

"The sea!" said the witch, her eyes glowing with a
strange phosphorescence.

The young woman shrugged and freed herself from
the witch's grip.

In spite of her weak condition, she reached the top of
the hill without difficulty, sustained as she was by the
wish to have done with the whole thing. She crossed the
Fairy Stone clearing and turned right to get out of
the forest of Nieul past the death lantern, known also as
the dove lantern because of the white bird carved on its
summit. The road to Fontenay-le-Comte crossed the
path not far from there.

After two hours of walking, Angélique had to stop
for a rest in a cobbler's hut. She was exhausted and felt
the sweat on her brow that came from her state of
weakness. Perhaps the cobbler might recognize her, but
this would not matter, because he was a deaf-mute and
lived there from one year's end to the other, with his son
who was deaf and dumb like himself.

Angélique asked for a bowl of milk and a hunk of
bread.

She dipped a small piece of bread into the milk and
slipped it between the child's lips, and it stopped crying. She herself got a few mouthfuls of milk down with
great difficulty. After resting for a while she set off again
and soon found herself on the road. A light cart overtook

183

her and she asked the driver to give her a lift. He was not going to Fontenay-le-Comte but said he could drop her about a couple of miles from the town.

Towards the end of the journey the child began to cry.

"Put it to the breast," said the peasant, irritated by the noise.

"I've no milk," she replied curtly.

He set her down at the agreed spot and pointed out the far-off ramparts and steeples with his whip.

Fontenay-le-Comte was held by the partisans. But Angélique thought that no one would recognize this peasant-woman, come to town to abandon her child, as the woman known as the Poitou Rebel whose decisions had had the force of law with the leading citizens of Fontenay when she visited them at Christmas-tide. She would wait for night to fall before going into the town.

The child's round head weighed like lead in the crook of her arm. She could hardly go on. Her nerves were all on edge. She was filled with a desire to stop the piercing cries, to put an end to this life that tortured her. She wanted to suppress, to wipe out what had been. She had to halt, frightened by her own desires.

"I ought to pray," she told herself.

But she could not. God had deserted her, and she sometimes wondered in terror whether she did not hate Him, too.

She went on again towards the town that was growing blue in the dusk. Beneath the ramparts, she hesitated for a long time and walked up and down like a forest animal frightened by the bustle of the town.

When she saw the watchmen about to close the gates she slipped into the town by the Wheat Tower Gate. The townspeople were still going about their business in the narrow streets. It was good to breathe in the sweet balmy air that the spring had brought so suddenly, as a reward for so many sacrifices. People seemed in no hurry to go indoors and were calling cheerful greetings to one another from the front of their shops.

Angélique knew that the Board of Guardians had their headquarters in Pillory Square, near the Town Hall.

So many children were abandoned that the convents could not take them all in and, under Monsieur Vincent, they had started civic reception centres for them. The Fontenay Home had been a grain-store in the Middle Ages before being converted into a foundling hospital. The front of the building with its great beams was covered with carved wooden figures. Angélique did not dare to go up to it and walked away, embarrassed by the stares that the child's shrieks drew from local gossips. She prowled up and down the neighbouring back alleys waiting for the streets to be more empty as night came on darker. She also discovered what she had been looking for—the turntable.

The little turntable had been placed in a dark side-street where very few ever came, to hide the shame of the unfortunate girls who approached it. The only light came from a little oil-burning night-light that stood over the turntable by a statue of the infant Jesus. Inside, there was a little straw. She put the child down. Then she pulled a bell-chain on the right and there was a prolonged ringing sound.

She stepped back and stood on the other side of the street, hidden in the shadows. She was shaking like a leaf. It seemed to her as if the child's screams would rouse the whole neighbourhood.

At last something creaked behind the door. The "table" began to move and little by little the new-born child's wails grew fainter and died away. Angélique leant back against the wall. She was on the point of collapse. She felt above all a sensation of inexpressible relief, but also a terrible distress that took her back several years. This period of her life had reminded her most poignantly of the sordid atmosphere of the Court of Miracles which she had sworn to herself she would never taste again. Was life no more than an infernal roundabout that bore you from one horror to the next?

She left the street with halting steps. She forced herself to hold her head high. She must escape from this solitude felt by women wounded by their own sins, she must leave these streets, and escape from the anonymity that hung over her here.

She whipped up her pride in herself: "You are Angélique du Plessis-Bellière, you are the woman who is
leading the whole province in revolt against the King."

CHAPTER 22

THE CHAPEL of St Honoré, which had been built to
comfort and reassure travellers, was on a par with the
area it watched over—dark as a cave, stocky as an oak,
its façade swarming with statues like some sylvan ex-
travaganza, its belfries bristling like thorn bushes, under
which long-bearded figures with snails' eyes were engaged in strangling apocalyptic monsters.

It stood at the top of the long, lonely, sinister road
over the heath on the marches of the Gâtine and the
Bocage.

It was there that Angélique assembled the leading
conspirators in order to agree on plans for the summer
compaign. She once again succeeded in persuading
Catholics and Protestants to sink their doctrinal quarrels
in the interests of a higher cause. Victory could only be
won if there was concord.

They spent three days on the Gâtine Heights, lighting
fires in the evening around the chapel and sleeping
under the oak-trees in the heat heavy with the sound of
crickets. St Honoré, holding his head in his two hands,
seemed to bless them, and the Catholics regarded his
patronage as a good omen for the coming battles.

St Honoré had been an honest thirteenth-century cat-
tle-dealer who had been murdered by robbers. Berry,
where he had been born, and Poitou, where he had met
his death, had long quarrelled over his relics. Poitou had
succeeded in keeping the saintly dealer's head.

The men used to come and dip their weapons in the
holy water from a spring which flowed into a stone
trough.

Angélique too would come surreptitiously to dip her
veil in it and cool her burning forehead. Fever was
pounding at her temples, and it gave her eyes an unnatural brightness. In spite of the witch's medicines she
186

was making a poor recovery from her clandestine delivery.

As soon as she had got back from Fontenay-le-Comte, she had wanted to set out for the Gâtine. She wanted to deny what had happened, but nature were there to remind her of the curse with which God had branded Eve's body.

She suffered particularly at night. In the surrender of sleep the excitement of war and vengeance left her, and she found in the depths of her being a desperate anguish, and began to hear the first cries of a new-born baby.

One night St Honoré appeared to her, holding his head in his hands:

"What have you done with the child?" he asked. "Go and find her before she dies."

Angélique woke in the heather. St Honoré was still there above the chapel door. The dawn was breaking. It was cold, and yet she was streaming with sweat. Her whole body ached. She got up to go to the drinking well to refresh herself.

"When my milk has dried up, I'll stop thinking about the child," she told herself.

Towards mid-morning scouts announced the approach of a carriage up the winding road. Hitherto they had seen no one pass except one horseman, a merchant, no doubt, for he had seemed scared by the deserted place and had galloped off as soon as he saw suspicious shapes between the tree-trunks.

The partisans scattered and disappeared under the trees, but the traces of their camp were too obvious, and Angélique sent Martin Genêt and a few peasants to stop the carriage when it reached the top of the slope. They had to be on their guard against travellers going from one region to another who might not be over-scrupulous about reporting the rebels' movements to the royal troops stationed in the area in return for a cash consideration.

From the halted carriage she could hear the men roaring with laughter, and the parleys looked as if they

187

were never going to finish, so she went over to find out what was going on.

It was a shabby old shandrydan drawn by an equally pitiful old nag. The driver, a toothless old fellow, was trembling so much with fright that he could not utter a word.

Under the patched tilt in the midst of a fearful stench sat three fat sweating women and there were babies wriggling in the dirty straw like a litter of rabbits.

"Please don't hurt us, sir highwaymen," begged the women on their bended knees.

"Where are you making for?"

"Poitiers. We are going to go by way of Parthenay, because we're told that there were soldiers on the way by St-Maixant. We poor women were frightened of those lustful wretches, and we thought we'd go the long way round, like, on a quiet road. If we'd known . . ."

"Where are you from?"

"From Fontenay-le-Comte."

And reassured by the sight of a woman, the fattest one explained volubly: "We're wet-nurses from the home at Fontenay, and we've been told to take this lot to Poitiers, because there's more than our place can cope with. We're respectable folk, we are, ma'am, we've been sworn, we have, ma'am. . . ."

"Let them pass," said Malbrant-Swordthrust; "we won't get anything out of them except their milk, and they'll not have much to spare after they've dealt with that swarm of brats."

"Well you may say, kind sir," exclaimed the nurse with a noisy laugh. "They don't know what they're doing, and that's straight, putting twenty of the creatures on to three of us like this. We'll have to give half of them the bottle as it is."

She pointed to a jug containing bread soaking in a mixture of water and wine.

"Not to mention those who'll never see journeys end. That one over there looks as if it won't last long. We'll have to stop at the next village and give it to the parish priest to bury."

188

She held out a sort of skinned rabbit, quite inert and wrapped in a scrap of red rag.

"That's misery for you. Just have a look at that, good gentlemen."

They pulled disgusted faces.

"Right! You can go on. But keep your mouths shut when you get to the plain. Say nothing of what you've seen in the mountains."

They fell over themselves with their whining promises.

"Whip 'em up, driver," shouted Malbrant, slapping the wretched horse on its bony back.

"No, wait!"

Angélique's blood had drained from her face as soon as the woman had said: "We're from Fontenay-le-Comte." She had known why St Honoré had appeared to her that night. But it was as if she were paralysed, and her every movement was weighted down like in a nightmare.

Nevertheless she bent down and picked up the baby the nurse tossed to her wrapped up in its red rag.

"Now, drive on."

"What are you going to do with that, my beauty? Didn't I tell you it's practically dead?"

"Drive on," she repeated, looking at them so fiercely that the good souls recoiled and kept very quiet.

Drawn up very stiffly Angélique walked away. By the fountain her legs gave way, and she had to sit down on the stone edging.

A hand was laid on her shoulder. Two dark eyeballs, ardent and grave, sought to meet hers. Father de Lesdiguière had followed her. He was stooping towards her, sustaining her, enveloping her with his passionate sympathy. He was trying to read in her eyes.

"It's your child, isn't it?"

She gave an almost imperceptible nod.

"Are you sure?"

"I recognized her by the birthmark on the shoulder and by the red cloth in which she was wrapped."

"Before abandoning her, had you baptized her?"

"No."

"Did they baptize her at the foundling's home? There is much carelessness and impiety in human hearts these days, Madame."

"She's dead already."

"Not yet. What do you want to call her?"

"What do I care?"

He glanced about him.

"St Honoré has restored her to you. We'll call her Honorine."

He dipped his hand into the fountain, filled it and poured the water over the child's forehead while murmuring the words and prayers of the rite. And because these words were addressed to the wretched creature she had begotten in shame they struck her with stunning force and she was left petrified.

"Be a light, Honorine, in this dark world in which you are called upon to live. May your eyes be open to all that is good and beautiful. . . ."

"No, no," she cried, "I'm not her mother. You can't ask that of me. . . ."

She looked despairingly at Father de Lesdiguière leaning towards her. She read her condemnation in his pure gaze.

"Do not despise the life given by the Creator."

"Do not ask me that."

"You alone can save her. You are her mother."

"No, not that."

She saw her own sorrow reflected in the dark eyes appealing to her.

"Oh God!" he cried. "God! why did you create the world?"

He ran and threw himself down on the threshold of the chapel, and she heard him praying aloud, his forehead pressed against the door.

The baby had stirred ever so slightly in Angélique's arms. She drew her to her breast.

CHAPTER 23

As THEY came out of the gorge the horses snorted beneath the trees. The dead leaves, which filled the gorge like a frothy tide, crunched under their hoofs, and they pushed them to one side as they passed. The bright blue sky shone through the bare branches. The last leaves were twirling gently down.

Angélique picked up one of them shaped like a russet star from her cloak and dreamily examined the perfection of its delicate veins. Another autumn had come. Another winter was on the way. The heat had gone out of the sun; there was no mistaking it. You could sense the sharp north winds in the distant mists, whose gold and saffron hues were giving way to the mauves and greys of November.

She glanced at Father de Lesdiguiére, who was riding beside her, and gave a shrug.

"Did you ever see anything so ridiculous, Father? A military commander turned wet-nurse, and the army chaplain rocking the baby."

The young man laughed and looked at her with warm affection in his eyes.

"What difference does it make? It did not prevent you from leading your soldiers to victory, Madame. One might almost have thought the child was a lucky charm."

He looked proudly at Honorine who was sleeping in the crook of his arm, sheltered by his black priest's cloak. This had been the only cradle Honorine had ever known: the pommel of a saddle and the arms of the men who passed her from one to another until it was time for her mother to take her off to feed her. Angélique had given life back to her with her milk. Her conscience was at rest. It still remained a cruel sacrifice and bitter humiliation every time she did it.

So she let her retainers carry this cumbersome little animal that fate had not let her get rid of. Honorine had a taste of all the trots and gallops there were, from Father de Lesdiguière's horse to Malbrant-Swordthrust's,

191

via Flipot's steed and old Antoine's. Even the worthy, fat Baron du Croissec sometimes took her on his broad, comfortable lap. But on the other hand, no matter where she was when night fell, she would begin to cry and would only stop when Angélique took her in her arms. And so she was obliged to keep the child close to her.

"How ridiculous," she said again. "I wonder how I've managed to command obedience from the partisans under the circumstances."

"Your influence over everyone is so strong, Madame. And our successes can only strengthen their confidence in you."

Angélique's face grew sombre.

"Success? Victory? We must not congratulate ourselves too soon. Nothing is settled yet. The royal army has not been able to break into Poitou, but we are still in a state of siege. And now the winter is coming on. Most of our land is uncultivated, and the harvest will not be enough for us. Hunger will bring discouragement, and the King is counting on that."

"Make them realize that if we can only survive until next summer, we shall have won. The King is not in a position himself to have a whole province in a state of rebellion. The whole economy of the country is thrown topsy-turvy. He will have to come to terms with us or crush us. And we have the forests to protect us. The soldiers dare not enter them."

"You speak like a strategist, my little Abbé, and you quite impress me. What would your religious superiors say if they heard you?"

"They would remember that the blood of old Lesdiguière, that great Hugenot nobleman from the Dauphiné, who stood out for so long against the king of his day, flows in my veins. Although my family have since been converted, my name nevertheless aroused the suspicions of my teachers at the seminary. Perhaps they were not so far wrong!"

He laughed again, happily. The breeze made his curls dance on his sunburnt cheeks. His coat, his silver-buckled hat, his clerical dress with its bands were quite threadbare, worn out by dust and bad weather.

His horse shied, frightened by the root of a tree, and cantered on ahead. Angélique watched the priest for a moment, then caught up with him.

"Father," she said solemnly, "listen to me. You should not stay here with me. It is wrong of me to draw you into a venture that befits neither your cloth nor your rank. Go back to your own people. The Bishop of Condon was your patron and had great faith in you. He will find a higher position for you at Court. Or you could go back to Monsieur de la Force. No one must know you have been with me. . . . But you would not give anything away."

The young man lost countenance, so violent was his reaction.

"Are you sending me away, Madame?"

"No, my child. And you know it. But the life we are leading is culpable in the eyes of the law, and your place is not amongst outcasts."

"And why not?" he said in a low voice. "Madame, if you are worried because you think that only my devotion to you keeps me here, I must reassure you. Even if my life is yours, there is more to it than that. I feel . . . I know that you are right. I too have lived at Court. How could anyone who hungered and thirsted for justice not listen to you? I think back, and my heart tells me you are right."

Angélique gritted her teeth and her fingers clenched the horse's reins.

"Do not attempt to seek excuses for my actions," she said sharply. "There is nothing forgivable in me. I am a hate-ridden and wretched woman. And one who sees no end to her hatred. . . ."

He looked up at her, his eyes wide with alarm.

"Do you not fear damnation?"

"Those words mean nothing to me any more. I know only one thing: that is that unless my heart was fired by this great hatred, I could not bear to go on living. Thinking about battles and about the defeat of our enemies is the only thing that gives me the strength to carry on, and I even get some pleasure from it."

And, seeing the distress in his eyes, she went on:

"Why bewail my fate, Father? The fact is that the panelled halls and the honours of Versailles did not suit me. I have always been an unbiddable, country-bred creature, with a predilection for bare feet and brambles along the wayside. When I was a child my brother Gontran—the one the King hanged—painted me dressed as a robber chief. He always did have a sort of second sight. I have already spent some time amongst the thieves and brigands of Paris. Have you never heard our Flipot holding forth about the time I met the Great Coësre, the King of the Beggars? I've travelled on every road, every path, I've known every sort of privation, every kind of prison. I have crawled on hands and knees, my flesh torn, dressed in rags, along the roads of the Riff. That is my destiny, and I do not like having a roof over my head. Now I know, nothing will save me. Do not be sad, my little Abbé. And leave me. . . ."

She added almost inaudibly.

"I bring bad luck to those that love me. . . ."

He did not reply. She saw his long eyelashes suddenly fluttering on the curve of his delicate profile, and his lips trembled.

The horses picked their way down a stony path across a wild hillside.

The château of the Gordon de la Grange family, with its four corner-towers set in its reddish-brown parkland, had now come into view.

The travellers did not need to warn the inhabitants of their arrival by any special signal. An ambush would have been out of the question here, in this isolated house lost in the depths of the Bocage.

Here one could forget the war-ravaged countryside, the villages razed to the ground, the fierce fights across the moors, or the even more fearsome traps set deep within the confines of a narrow gorge, fights to the death. The villages that lay near the borders of the province were abandoned. In the interior the peasants had spent the summer with one hand on their ploughs, the other on their muskets. Towards the end of September one regiment of the royal army had penetrated right into the centre of the province, laying waste everything in its path. The local people seemed to evaporate as the soldiers approached. They found very few men to hang but burnt everything they saw: hamlets, townships and crops. Already rumour had it in Versailles that the surrender of the terrified revolutionaries was imminent, when, somewhere in the region of Pouzauges, the regiment seemed to vanish into thin air. No more was ever heard of them. The whole area had clamped down on the soldiers like a gigantic vice.

A few survivors, who, by slipping furtively from one coppice to the next had eventually managed to reach the Loire and to cross it, spoke with horror of the gleaming scythes, reaping death, of the clusters of forms that came swinging down from the trees when least expected and planted their razor-sharp knives between men's shoulder-blades before they could utter a single cry. They had all been slaughtered, in spite of their weapons and in spite of their officers. The Poitou countryside had swallowed them all up inexorably, one by one.

There was general consternation. After this disastrous campaign, both troops and high command adopted a policy of wait and see. Since winter was upon them, it was useless to encourage the soldiers to embark on further expeditions. So they all took up their winter quarters.

Angélique spent three months in the château de la Grange. There she saw some of the rebel leaders, and the mayors who came to tell her of their worries. They were all on short rations. With trade paralysed, people were beginning to grumble. Luckily the winter was not too hard.

About the month of March, Angélique set off again on her rides through the province. She had stopped feeding her child and wanted to leave it at the château. A kindly servant had taken it under her wing. But Father de Lesdiguière persuaded her not to leave it.

"Don't leave her, Madame. If she is separated from you she will die."

195

"I shall come back later on and fetch her, when things are—"

"No," he said, looking her straight in the eye. "You would not come back for her."

"What sort of a life is it for the child to be dragged up hill and down dale like this?"

"It suits her, because you are there, and you are her mother."

He himself wrapped Honorine in a warm blanket and mounted his horse, clutching her possessively to his bosom.

It was about this time that vague inklings began to stir in Angélique's mind when she looked at her daughter. The fear of an unspoken menace, a moment of wondering, the terror of suspicions that bit by bit became certainties.

They were in a dangerous region, where the King's men sometimes made raids. So as not to fall into any ambush, Angélique and her retinue would take refuge each night in the caves that riddled the cliffs of the Sèvres Valley. The peasant women from the near-by hamlets used to meet there each evening to spin and knit. They resorted there because it was always warm and they did not need to light a fire. After their evening meal, they would go there, distaff in hand, with their tow and hemp, and a good hot foot-warmer under their arms.

They showed Angélique the most spacious of these natural rooms and the little group rested there, protected from the sharp cold of the early spring nights.

A reassuring light glowed in the cave wall: it came from a little lamp bearing a primitive candle made of a stick of Aaron's rod soaked in nut oil.

Angélique watched the child rolling around on the ground and trying to crawl. She was ten months old and seemed strong. Was it the reddish torch-light that gave her short curls that coppery tinge? Her eyes, on the other hand, were narrow and black, and slanted towards her temples when she laughed. Then her fat little cheeks seemed to hide them altogether and her expression—her expression seemed to be one that Angélique knew; it reminded her of another face, an obscene caricature of it.

She drew back so violently that her head banged against the rocky wall of the cave and she stood there stunned.

"Montadour! His bloated carroty pig's face!"

Sweat broke out on her brow. It couldn't be. . . .

The hatred a mother feels towards her bastard child is often only the transferred hate she feels for its procreator. To Angélique it seemed worse to be able to put a name to the criminal than for his identity to remain unknown. She would have loved Colin Paturel's child. But the thought of her, Angélique de Sancé, sharing the responsiblity for this human being with a drunken soldier of the lowest sort, gave her a feeling of slimy and horrible complicity, a feeling of debasement forced upon her by fate. She could never accept it. Life was nothing but a monstrous, hateful comedy, directed by a blind and sadistic god.

Father de Lesdiguière ran towards her, hearing her cry.

"Take her away," said Angélique, panting for breath. "Take her out of my sight. I might kill her."

At midnight, the cave was still echoing with Honorine's howls. Angélique, stretched out on her bed of hay, tossed in exasperation.

"Naturally 'they' have forgotten to give her her bit of fern."

Honorine would never go to sleep without a fern-leaf in her hand. This was her favourite rattle and she seemed entranced by its filigree patterns.

In the end Angélique could stand it no more. She went into the main room where the priest, the groom, the valets and the Baron had exhausted their entire repertoire. With a look of crushing scorn she picked up the baby, who stopped crying by some miracle, and carried her back to her own den. Naturally the child was soaking wet, freezing cold, and ner nose was running. Angélique rubbed her down with an expert hand and roughly wrapped her in her woollen shawl and buried her in the hay up to her eyes. Then she left the cave to go to the edge of the woods for a fern-leaf which she plucked near the base of its stem. Honorine put out her hand and grabbed it, then watched the furry crook in ecstasy as it sent colossal prehistoric monsters' shadows dancing over the cave walls. Calm once more, she slipped her thumb into her mouth and looked at Angélique from out of the corner of her little slit eyes with a look of deep contentment.

"You know me," she seemed to be saying. "I know where I am with you."

"Yes, I know you," murmured Angélique. "Yes, we can neither of us do anything about it, can we?"

Propped up on one elbow, her cheek resting on her hand, she examined the child with keen attention. The look of utter bliss that suffused her features loosened the painful bands that constricted Angélique's heart.

No past and no future. The earth was silent. And images rose up in her mind, not words, and calmed her with their gentle fleeting shadows.

"You are nobody's child, little girl of the forest ... only a little girl of the forest. Red hair like the autumn leaves ... black eyes like the blackberries in the hedgerow ... white skin, pearly like the sand in the caves. You are the incarnation of the woods, a sprite, a pixie, nothing else. You are nobody's child. Go to sleep. Sleep in peace."

CHAPTER 24

FATHER DE LESDIGUIÈRE stepped out of the thicket, his hands full of mushrooms.

"Something nice for you to eat, Honorine."

She tottered over towards him. She had had her first birthday during the summer, while the King's soldiers were posted all round the small farm where Angélique and her followers had taken refuge.

They were caught like rats in a trap, and were about to surrender when Hugh de La Morinière and his Protestants had helped them to break through to freedom. Angélique had only been able to get out of the farmhouse by clambering over the dead bodies. Honorine had a cough from all the smoke she had breathed in. Her life was inseparably associated with the smell of gunpowder and fires, the sound of explosions, the sight of blood and sweat on hang-dog faces, escapes on galloping horses and black nights deep in the heart of the forest.

She had taken her first steps at Parthenay, one day when the alarm-bell was tolling over the besieged township. The assailants had been repulsed and had fallen back, but the little town, worn out by its many privations, remained lifeless. Angélique had not been able to find Honorine in the room where she had left her on a chair. She was in the street. This was how she learnt that the child could walk and even get down stairs.

She had uttered her first word on the day that Lancelot de La Morinière had been killed in the course of a violent battle on the heath near Machecoul. And Honorine's first word had struck Angélique a blow to the heart like a musketball.

She had found a poppy and had said: "Blood." And she had wrinkled up her funny little nose like a man in pain, as she had seen wounded men do.

She repeated proudly: "Blood ... blood," pointing to the flower. It had been the recurring theme of the evening, and Angélique had thought she would go out of her mind.

She was becoming weary of the fierce summer fighting, and fear began to prey on her. The King was not backing down, and Poitou was faltering. Hugh de La Morinière, without his two brothers, was like a body without a head. He had never been able to think for himself. It had been Lancelot that persuaded him to have faith in Angélique, and, now that he was gone, Hugh's puritanical mistrust of women got the upper hand. And Samuel was no longer there to bolster his pride in being a vassal standing up to the King. The end of the summer made it possible to stave off imminent disaster. The high command, taken in by the fierceness of the resistance, were at a loss to know what measures to take. The king was in favour of letting the rebels wear themselves out and break up under the pressure of famine, want and shortage of ammunition. His ministers wanted to overwhelm them by superior force, the King himself leading his men in a repression so bloody that it could be held up as an example to all the other provinces. They could not lose sight of the fact that Aquitaine, Provence and Brittany were in a state of ferment and that you could never be sure of the recently acquired provinces, Picardy, Roussillon, and so on.

Angélique had no knowledge of these hesitations and uncertainties. She could guess at what was happening, but without proof it was hard to convince her prostrate troops. Still she was alone in reminding them that they had no choice between fighting and serfdom. So, after the summer's upheavals, in the fevered, torrid days, she took refuge with de la Grange and his men in the Mervent gorges. They pitched their camp deep in the heart of the hundred-year-old forest that spread to the north of the forest of Nieul. They were gathering strength and licking their wounds.

Father de Lesdiguière was busy with his flints setting fire to the dead sticks he had gathered, so that he could cook the mushrooms he had found for Honorine. He put his gun, which now hardly ever left his side, down in the grass, and he warned the child not to touch it. She acted a kind of dumb-show which proved that she had learned to have a wholesome respect for this thing that let off smoke and bangs.

Angélique was sitting watching them, perched on a mossy stone a few yards off.

The priest was wearing a rough sheepskin jacket. He had replaced his silver-buckled round hat with the kind of huge faded object the local peasants wore. He no longer wore his clerical bands, and his tattered shirt-collar hung open, showing his young sunburnt chest. A gold crucifix hung round his neck on a piece of faded ribbon. She had transformed this well-bred young tutor, refined to the fingertips, into this man of the woods! There was no comparison with the young lad he had been in Versailles or Saint-Cloud, who had smiled with touching urbanity at the teasing and provocative looks of the

Court beauties and bowed so prettily to the powerful corrupt noblemen. His shoulders had grown broader and showed off his slim figure to greater advantage. He no longer looked delicate. The only thing that remained was the doe-like expression of his eyes in his weather-beaten face. How old would he be? Twenty? Twenty-two? ...

She called him suddenly, and he came to her with his customary deference and desire to please, that created about her a little oasis of luxury from the past, when she had been at home, surrounded by a large staff of servants.

"Madame?"

"Father, I have begged you many times to go, to leave us. Now you must do so. We are being hunted. I little know what disasters we are heading for. Go back to your own kind ... I beg you, do it for me. I could not bear to be responsible for your downfall."

As on every other occasion that she had broached this subject, he went pale and put his hand on his heart.

"That is quite impossible, Madame. I could not live far from you, if we were separated."

"But why not?"

He looked at her passionately. His expression told her more than any words. She on her side was not offended, only moved to tears. She looked away in distress.

"No, my dear child," she begged almost inaudibly. "No, you must not ... I am ..."

He cut her short.

"I know what you are. You are the woman I adore, the woman I love with such passion that I can now understand how a man could forget God for a woman's lips."

"You must not say these things!"

And as she stretched out her hand towards him, he grasped it in his. She did not dare to take hers away, so surprised was she by the freshness and masculinity of his grasp.

"Allow me ... just once ... to confess to you," he said in a strangled voice. "You have filled my life with worldly, life-giving sensations which I cannot bring myself to

201

regret. The sight of you has always filled me with delight and every word you utter . . ."

"But you know all my faults. . . ."

"They have only made you dearer to me, because they made you weaker and more human. Ah! I would have liked to take you in my arms and save you from your enemies and from yourself; to have protected you with all my strength. . . ."

This strength he claimed flowed from him with the imperious violence of his youth, as he stood yearning towards her in the evening shadows. And for the first time in many a long month, she became aware of the flow of life with all its permeating force, that seemed to want to draw her to it and snatch her from her engulfing despair.

She knew that he used to go off in the evenings into the woods, and fall on his knees in protracted prayer. But for how long could his love for God and the love he had sworn to an accursed woman share his heart between them?

Angélique could find no words. She took her hand away and drew her coat tight about her, shivering.

"You need have no fear of me," he said gently. "I would have worshipped you, if you had deigned to look my way. Had you given a single sign, I should have been lost in you—blissfully lost: please don't take offence. I am your very humble servant. I know that the barrier that lies between us is insurmountable."

"Your vocation?"

"No . . . you yourself. I mean the horror you feel for men and their desire since . . . I am not the one, unknowledgeable that I am, ever to overcome that. . . ."

"Stop. . . . You do not know what you are saying."

"Oh yes I do. . . ."

His grief made his face look hard.

"I do know. They have destroyed you with their horrors. And the sickness of your mind has infected your body. Had it not been so I would have gone on my knees to you and begged you to love me. Let me say my say. I beseech you. I have followed you along the highways and byways now for too many years to be able to do without your presence any more than I can do without the air I breath. . . . If you had not become so . . . invulnerable, things might have been different."

He fell silent.

"But things are *not* different," he continued softly. "It's better that way. Because of this barrier between us I have to stay on God's side. I shall never be your lover. That's an empty dream."

He seemed to be making a superhuman effort.

"At least, I shall save you."

His magnificent eyes shone with their familiar idealism.

"I shall save you. I shall do more for you than all the men who have held you in their arms. I shall give you back all you have lost—your soul, your heart, your femininity, all they have taken from you. At the moment I am powerless, but I shall die for you, and only then, on the day when I see the light of God, I shall have the power to save you. The day I die. . . . Oh death, come soon!"

He clasped his hands fervently above his heart.

"Oh, death! come soon. Then I shall be able to set her free!"

They had not heard the owl hoot. Suddenly a rider wearing a big lace collar entered the gorge, his plumes flying in the wind. Behind him rode red-coated men carrying lances.

Angélique leapt towards Honorine. The priest seized his musket and covered her retreat as she ran towards the trees and clambered up the cliff-side with the child on her back clinging to her neck. Falling stones revealed where the partisans were scattering, as high as they could get up the slope made slimy by the dead leaves.

The officer was the first to recover his wits.

"They're here," he shouted. "We've stumbled on the brigands' den! Hi! you men, after them!"

The soldiers dismounted and ran towards the mountainside in their turn.

Angélique and her breathless companions were watching them as they came nearer.

"They're coming up. . . ."

"Just a minute. Let's get up higher."

Just when the soldiers had reached the steepest point, where the cliff rose almost sheer, she shouted:

"The stones, the boulders!"

A dull rumbling filled the dark gorge. Huge stones, whole pieces of the rock face were rolling downwards, hurled down by the peasants. Down went the soldiers, hit full in the face or chest as they clutched, precariously balanced, at the cliff. They lost their hold, slipped and tumbled down pell-mell.

The peasants levered with their shoulders at the great round granite blocks that had lain, hanging over the edge of the precipice for centuries, set in their clay sockets. They broke away slowly, then gathered momentum and rolled faster and faster, making the tree-trunks ring out, as they struck them. They rebounded, then fell to the bottom of the gorge, crushing like flies the soldiers standing at the foot of the slope.

The officer sounded the assembly and the soldiers carefully retreated, carrying the wounded and leaving the dead.

The sun still cast a crimson light on the men's uniforms. Angélique stood watching them through the trees. She recognized their officer. It was Monsieur de Brienne, one of the men who long ago at Versailles had paid her such gallant court. To see him here made her realize how far she had travelled since those days of ephemeral glory at Versailles, and what a gulf—even deeper than this valley they stood in—now separated her for ever from that world.

She leant over and called out in a mocking voice that rang out in a long echo:

"Greetings, Monsieur de Brienne. Go to His Majesty and say that Trifle wishes to be remembered kindly to him!"

When they told the King what she had said, he went pale. He shut himself up alone in his study and stayed there for several hours, with his face in his hands.

204

Then he sent for the Minister of War and told him to do everything in his power to crush the Poitou rebellion before the following spring.

CHAPTER 25

AMONGST THE regiments the King sent to Poitou in 1673 was the 1st Auvergne regiment commanded by Monsieur de Riom, and five of the most famous companies of the Ardennes. The King had heard enough about the soldiers' superstitious fears of ambushes in the Poitou forests. The men he was sending there now were sons of Auvergne and the Ardennes, picked from among forest dwellers, and they had all been accustomed since their earliest youth to the haunted darkness of the woods, to wild boars, wolves and cliffs, and were used to finding their way through apparently trackless wastes. They were all the sons of cobblers, woodcutters or charcoal-burners. They came, no longer dressed in red like the dragoons, but all in black, reminiscent of the sinister Spaniards, with their steel helmets with tall sharp crests, and their tight boots coming right up to the top of their thighs. They brought dogs with them, powerful, savage hunting dogs.

The beat of their tall drums boomed out long and loud over the empty, petrified countryside.

Together with them came terror into Poitou.

Three thousand infantry, fifteen hundred cavalry, two thousand men to act as grooms, quartermasters and gun crews. They brought cannon to deal with the towns.

The King had said: "By the spring."

Winter would not call a halt to the war.

By the spring, there was only one last stronghold that had not capitulated. It was the area between the marshes and La Châtaigneraie where the revolt had first broken out, and where the last of the conspirators had drawn together.

It was a hard spring. The cold weather went on and

on, and even at the end of March the frozen ground showed no signs of relenting.

Angélique was peering through the narrow window of the farmhouse, watching for Flipot to come back. He came in, thin and cadaverous, like a wolf on the prowl. Neither hunger, cold, nor this life like a hunted animal had got the better of his habitual good humour.

"I managed to make contact with them," he said. "They thought you must be either dead or captured. I told them how you had succeeded in escaping at dead of night from the château of Fougeroux. Just think of them coming to look for you, even there! There's no doubt about it, we've been betrayed and sold. There are traitors everywhere now!"

He glanced out of the corner of his eye at the peasant-woman and her old father-in-law who sat before the fire, then drew his sleeve across under his reddened nose and went on, lowering his voice:

"I saw the priest, Malbrant-Swordthrust, Monsieur le Baron, and Martin Genêt. They all agree that we must leave the country. Now they say it's become a man-hunt, or rather, a woman-hunt. It's you, Madame la Marquise, they're after. There's a price on your head, and they are sure to find someone who will sell you for five hundred *livres*. People are so frightened and so hungry. So this is what they've decided. Tonight we are to meet at the Dove Lantern, and when we are all together we'll go into the marshes via the forest and then on to the coast. They haven't yet captured Ponce-le-Palud, and he will help us either to go into hiding ... or to take ship."

"Take ship," Angélique repeated.

The words seemed to set the seal on her defeat. Throughout this ghastly winter she had slowly lost all sense of purpose in the battle they were waging. Their only object in life—and even then it had consumed all their energies—had become to save themselves as they were hounded from place to place, to find themselves still alive as each night fell. There was nothing left but flight.

"I didn't tell them to meet us here," Flipot whispered,

"because I don't trust these here folk. They know who you are and, like all the others, they blame all their misfortunes on you."

The two peasants were muttering together, casting dark looks in their direction. Angélique had reached the stage where she did not dare to come up close to the meagre fire with her daughter, for she was acutely conscious of the hostility that these unfortunate folk felt towards her.

The woman's husband had been killed fighting against the King. The soldiers had stripped them of all they had as they passed by, their bread, their cattle, their grain, and had taken their eldest daughter off with them. No one knew what had become of her.

At the back of the room, where the big Vendée bed stood, four pale little faces peered out from under the torn covers. The children were made to stay in bed all day so that they would keep warmer and not feel so hungry.

A few moments later the old man signalled to his daughter-in-law, got up, put on his greatcoat and took his axe, saying that he was going out to the spinney to cut some wood.

"I shouldn't be surprised if he was going to tell the soldiers," Flipot said under his breath; "perhaps we'd better clear out right now."

Angélique was of the same opinion. For no obvious reason the woman tried to keep her from going. Angélique cut short her good-byes. Without asking she helped herself to a hunk of bread and some cheese for Honorine. The peasant woman showered abuse at her.

"Be off with you! Be off with you! And good riddance to you, too. You've done enough damage already making trouble between me and my goblins, you and that accursed child of yours. Since you've been here I haven't heard them nibbling inside the walls. If the goblins leave the place, what will become of us?"

The disappearance of her goblins seemed to have made more impression on her than all the horrors she had lived through.

Angélique set out on a mule so gaunt that it had

barely the strength to walk. Flipot led it by the bridle. They passed through burnt-out villages, with corpses swinging mournfully from the elm-trees in the village squares.

Night was falling when they reached the Dove Lantern. It was burning. These death lanterns were the lighthouses of the Bocage. They were great stone candlesticks standing on pedestals with steps running up to them, that had been built at crossroads to guide travellers at night who might get lost in the pitch-blackness of the sunken roads. They also served to draw wandering souls and to prevent them from haunting the dreams of sleeping mortals. In spite of the shortage of oil or fat towards the end of that winter, pious hands attempted to keep them alight. The cobbler who lived near the Dove Lantern used to come down every evening with his flint to light the hemp wick in its carved mantle.

Angélique dismounted and sat down on the mossy stone steps.

"There's nobody here," she said. "We may well freeze if we have to sit here with the child for several hours. Flipot, you take the mule and go and find the others. Tell them to hurry up or to find a barn where we can spend the night."

Flipot went off and the weary clop-clop of the mule's hoofs rang out for a long while through the crystal air. The trees, stiff with frost, crackled with a stealthy sound like broken glass. The gnawing cold had a bitter penetrating chill to it that cut her through and through. As she sat there without moving, Angélique felt the very marrow of her bones grow cold. Her breath condensed in a cold mist before her face. Although Honorine was huddled up in her cloak, her cheek did not even feel warm to her touch. By the faint light from the lantern she could make out the child's eyes, black and wide awake like a squirrel's, watching the night about them. Angélique's arms no longer were enough to keep her warm. Her tiny hands, clutching the hunk of bread and the bit or cheese, were red with cold. Angélique remembered the peasant-woman's words.

" 'The accursed child.' So that's what they called her!"
Her lips shook with anger.

"What business is it of theirs, the clodhoppers? It's for
me to say whether you are accursed or not."

Yet again she took the folds of the shawl in her stiff
fingers and rearranged them around the child. She
strained her ears, always hoping to catch the distant
sound of hoofs. But her attention was caught by a rustling and crackling of twigs.

"Who's that?" she called.

She tried to make out what was moving in the undergrowth. Suddenly there rose a long drawn-out howl, and
she stood up, her heart in her mouth. Wolves! She ought
to have guessed they might come!

They had all been discomfited several times during
the past months by the boldness of the wild animals,
whom the long winter had driven famished from their
woodlands. Bands of wolves had not even hesitated to
follow mounted troops. They prowled around the camp-
fires and the men had had to throw lighted brands at
them.

Here, the lamplight was not enough to scare them
away. Angélique carried a pistol in her belt. She might
frighten them, but not for long.

She remembered the cobbler's hut, a bit farther up.
She must reach that before the wolves got too close and
while there was still a faint glow in the blue sky that the
frost had made incredibly clear. She began to walk,
knowing she was being followed and aware of the dull
thuds made by the wolves jumping through the brushwood.

Now when she looked back, she could see the luminous glow of their eyeballs. Without slowing her step,
she bent down, picked up some stones and threw them
at them, as if they were vicious dogs. Above all, she
must not trip and fall. She breathed a sigh of relief
when she saw the red glow of the window, and knew
the hut was there, huddled beneath the trees. She had
to hammer on the door before the deaf-mute would
make up his mind to open it. Angélique made him
understand by sign-language that the wolves were after

her and that he must barricade his house against them. To reassure the poor devil and his disabled boy who both eyed her in terror, she placed a gold piece on the table, the last of the supply that Baron de Croissec had recently lent her. In this time of famine a ham would have been more welcome. All the same the cobbler, whose hands were blackened by the sap from the new wood he handled, took the coin and turned it round and round before slipping it into his belt.

Angélique went and sat down by the hearth. At least it was warm here. The deaf-and-dumb boy threw a handful of wood shavings on to the fire, and Angélique drew Honorine's little feet towards it, rubbing them gently to get the blood flowing again. The child, now warmer, looked a better colour and started eating her piece of cheese while she examined her new surroundings with her usual shrewd look. She was particularly interested in the clusters of wooden shoes that hung from the beams. Angélique kept an ear open, hoping to hear the musket-shots her companions would surely fire when they reached the meeting-place and realized that she had had to take refuge from the wolves. She would then step outside the door of the hut and fire a shot from her pistol. But she heard nothing. She eventually gave up and lay down with Honorine on the truckle-bed that the cobbler pointed to. Its mattress, filled with wood shavings, was comfortable. She refused a dubious-looking blanket, but accepted a rough sheepskin.

She felt strangely calm and even managed to sleep for several hours without dreaming. She had long since stopped fretting about her past, worrying about what might or might not have been, or about the dramatic ups and downs of her relative short life. She had certainly looked for trouble and strife! She had wanted to live outside the law and throw over all she had been taught. Had not her first husband paid dearly for just this crime? Instead of having learnt from that, she had continued to pit herself against established law and order. Her struggle for survival had become second nature to her and she had moved out of the tame world of privilege into

210

the realm of wild animals, who have to fight daily for their lives and ward off a thousand dangers.

Somewhere towards the middle of the night she woke up and saw the cobbler standing by the narrow window, on the look-out. She joined him there and saw the wolves prowling about the clearing. The biggest one sat down on his haunches and let out several howls. The goat in its stable tugged at its rope and bleated.

Angélique lay down once more beside Honorine. With delicate fingers she drew back the red curls from the baby's forehead and watched her peaceful sleeping face. The wolf's howl, that sinister omen, strengthened the feeling she had in her heart and she told herself: "This is the beginning of the end."

In the morning there was a light covering of powdered snow lying all around. It had come on velvet paw to steal away the first hopes of spring. The stricken land refused to come to life.

Angélique searched the hut in vain for a scrap of paper and a pen. In the end she took a piece of sheeting and wrote on it with charcoal. It took a great deal of patience to explain to the cobbler's son where the Fayet farm was and how he should get there.

At last the young lad went off in the snow, clutching to his breast Angélique's message telling Father de Lesdiguière where she was hiding.

He did not get back till the following day. By means of signs he succeeded in making her understand that he had seen one of her companions who had fixed a rendezvous at the Fairy Stone, of which the boy drew a surprisingly good sketch on the wooden table-top.

Why had they not come here themselves? Why had the priest not given a note to the little deaf-mute? Since she was unable to communicate any better with them, she decided to go to the clearing where the dolmen stood. She was very likely to find them there waiting for her.

So she went off, rather sorry she was not dressed in men's clothes, as her skirts hampered her in the snow. Luckily they were peasants' skirts that were worn short, just over the ankle.

211

On reaching the Wolves' Coomb she hesitated at the sight of the snowdrifts. The summit path would have taken too long so she decided to cross the ravine, although she realized that Honorine would encumber her movements. She put the child down under a tree where the close-growing branches had left a dry space and tied her to the tree-trunk with her scarf, telling her to wait there and be good. The priest and Flipot would soon come and fetch her. Honorine was used to this sort of thing. She had often waited in the rear-guard, while the others were fighting or out on a reconnaissance.

Angélique got across the ravine only with the greatest difficulty. She fell several times and found herself up to the waist in snow. As she reached the top she thought she saw human shapes on her left, and, thinking they were her companions, she was about to call to them when the sounds died on her lips.

Soldiers were leaving the woods. They had not spotted her and were moving along the edge of the forest on the right-hand side of the dell. They stood out, black and thin, with their shining helmets and their lances patterned against the grey sky, and walked with the cruel and furtive tread of wolves.

Angélique, terror-stricken, waited until they had disappeared before she moved again. Where had these soldiers come from? What were they doing in these remote parts of the forest? What were they looking for?

Slowly now she made her way towards the Fairy Stone. She could hardly breathe in her anxiety. On the edge of the clearing she realized she was too late. There were men hanging from the oak-trees all around the dolmen. The first one she recognized was Flipot. . . .

Poor Flipot! Only the day before he had been so full of life! She had not been able to alter his fate: he had been born to be hanged, and hanged he had been.

Then she recognized them all, one by one: Father de Lesdiguière, Malbrandt-Swordthrust, Martin Genêt, Alain the groom, Baron du Croissec. All the familiar faces hung there, filling the clearing with their seemingly living presence, and she could almost have said to them: "There you are at last . . . my friends . . ."

She had to lean against a tree.

"A curse upon you, King of France," she said, "a curse upon you!"

She stood there, stunned, unable to believe her eyes. What sort of trap had they fallen into? Who had sold them? And these soldiers she had seen just then? No doubt it was they who had carried out these gruesome executions. . . .

With the desperate hope that perhaps they were not yet dead and that she might be able to revive one of them, she clambered up on to the stone and tried to untie Father de Lesdiguière. She was successful and his body fell to the ground in a limp heap. In spite of the cold, he was not yet stiff. Angélique knelt beside him, trying to discern a heartbeat, a sign of life still there. But death had done its work. She clasped him to her heart and kissed his smooth brow.

"Oh, my dear guardian angel! My sweet child! You are dead . . . dead for me. What will happen to me now you are gone?"

She looked, heart-broken, at his fine eyes now fixed in a stare, seeing her no more. Gently she closed his eyelids and his swollen mouth.

A thin cry rose through the frozen air, and she got up, Honorine!

Angélique pulled herself out of the stupor that had engulfed her. She must save the child.

Honorine was still beneath the tree. She was not crying but her little nose was as red as a holly berry. She waved her hands about to show how pleased she was to see her mother.

Angélique untied her and picked her up. At that moment she became aware of someone watching her. She turned round and there, on the other side of the Wolves' Coomb, stood a soldier eyeing her. . . .

As Angélique turned to run, the man gave a guttural shout.

She reached the top of the embankment and threw herself under cover of the trees. She began to walk straight ahead, following the paths as they came, one after the other. Her heavy skirt was soaked, and held her back, but she went on as fast as she could, borne on by fear.

From far away she could hear the echo of baying hounds. Were the soldiers after her with their mastiffs? She was gasping for breath and her arms were benumbed by the child's weight.

She could no longer be in any doubt: they were after her. The barking drew nearer, and she heard the noisy shouting of the soldiers. They must have the dogs still on the leash. The woman's footsteps showed up in the wet snow. Try as she might to throw them off the track by twisting and turning like an animal at bay, it would be easy for them to find her, and they were closing up on her relentlessly.

Night fell. The leaden sky seemed to move nearer the earth with the darkness. Angélique felt the gentle touch of the first snowflakes. Then they began to fall faster and thicker, until soon she was running forward through the moving folds of an opaque suffocating curtain. But at least the snow was blotting out her footprints.

The pursuit did indeed seem to have lost momentum. She could no longer hear the barking of the dogs. Not a sound. She was moving on in a deathly hush, a world filled entirely by the hurried fall of snowflakes. Her sweating face was paralysed with cold. Several times she gave herself a nasty knock against the trees.

At last she stopped. It was pitch-dark. She had no idea where she was. The snow was gently covering her over. She was tempted to sit down, just for an instant. But she would never get up again.

The child stirred against her.

"Don't be frightened," said Angélique very softly; she could hardly move her lips. "Don't be afraid, I know the forest, you know. . . ."

There was the barking again! They had not given up. Angélique set off once more. She stumbled and only just got her foothold again. The earth had given under her foot. She must be on the edge of a cliff or a steep slope. She could sense the emptiness before her by an indefinable new feeling of space in which the night was freed from the choking trees.

As she stood quite still, she heard the muffled sound of a bell. Its rhythmical tolling spelled sanctuary to her.

Crazy with hope she began to climb carefully down the slope and soon made out the high walls of Nieul Abbey towering above her. She hung on the bell-chain at the doorway. She already felt somewhat safer in the porch, out of that oppressive and frozen nightmare.

A hand drew back the shutter to the spy-hole and a voice said:

"Blessed be God! What can I do for you?"

"I have lost my way in the forest with my child. Please grant me sanctuary."

"We do not allow women in the Abbey. Go on another fifty paces to your left and you will find an inn where they will look after you."

"No. The soldiers are after me. I must have the protection of your walls."

"Go to the inn," the voice repeated.

They were going to close the spy-hole. She shrieked wildly:

"I am the sister of your beneficiary, Albert de Sancé de Monteloup. For the love of God, let me in ... let me in. ..."

She sensed a moment's hesitation. Then the shutter banged to. A moment later she heard the rattle of keys and the sliding of bolts. She rushed in through the half-open door, looking the living image of the storm accompanied by a flurry of snow that swept in behind her.

Two little monks with white hair looked at her in perplexity.

"Close that door," she begged them. "Close it tight and above all don't open it if the soldiers come knocking at it."

They did as Angélique bade them, and she only breathed again when she saw the great wooden bar slide into position across the panels.

"Did we hear you say that you are the sister of the

215

beneficiary of this Abbey, Monsieur de Sancé?" one of the monks asked.

"Yes, I am indeed."

"Wait there," he said, showing her into a sort of parlour where a thick candle was burning in a copper candelabrum. It was hardly any warmer beneath these stone arches than it was outside.

Angélique's teeth were chattering and she was trembling all over. She could no longer feel her arms clasped around Honorine, who was shivering.

At last she saw two other monks walking towards her round the cloisters. One of them was carrying an oil lamp. They wore the white robes of Superiors of the order. They entered the parlour, and stood before her. The younger of the two moved closer still and held up his lamp so that he could see the visitor's pitiful face.

"Yes, that is her," he said at last, "that is really her, that is my sister, Angélique de Sancé. . . ."

"Albert," whispered Angélique.

CHAPTER 26

THERE WAS a violent ring on the gate-bell, and the porter came to report that a band of armed men were demanding admission to the Abbey.

"Don't let them in," implored Angélique, "or it will be all up with me. It's me they are after."

"The Rebel of Poitou," murmured Albert.

She glanced at him in dismay. She was so used to inhumanity that she could not regard these tight-lipped monks as anything but enemies. They would give up the outcast to the authorities.

She slid to her knees, her eyes raised to the Abbot's cold, stiff face, and her lips moved in the old impassioned appeal of the Middle Ages, which for so many centuries had brought cruel man-hunts to a halt at the threshhold of churches:

"Sanctuary! Sanctuary!"

He motioned to her to be calm and went off to the

arched gate-house looking like a phantom in his white habit.

Shortly afterwards he returned. He must have sent the soldiers away to the inn. They were too weary from their pursuit over the snow to be in any state to storm the strongly built Abbey, which had withstood the on-slaughts of many wars. They departed the more readily because the porter had called to them that the innkeeper had some barrels of good Charentes wine, which was not easily come by in these troublesome times.

Silence reigned once more within the monastery walls. Angélique was still on her knees, in a thoroughly exhausted condition. Albert stooped down and took up the shivering little creature with the dark eyes, as bright as a wild animal's, that she was clutching to her.

"Rise, Madame."

The Father Abbot held out his hand to her, a thin hand but uncommonly strong. She stood up.

"We have few amenities to receive you with, Ma-dame."

His voice was deep and flat, almost as if disembodied, the voice of one accustomed to intoning plain-chant.

"There are only two places of any comfort I can offer you: the kitchens to give you a meal and the cowshed to sleep in."

Angélique's face all mottled with the cold must have assumed an expression of bliss at the mention of these humble quarters, for something suspiciously like a smile played over the Superior's austere countenance.

"Go in peace," he said. "Your brother will show you the way."

By the great blazing kitchen fire, her heavy dress soaking wet and steaming, Angélique rubbed Honorine's little frozen feet and made her swallow a bowl of hot milk. Then she undressed her and wrapped her in a warm blanket. The lay brothers in their black habits served her in silence according to the rule. The only sound to be heard was the shuffling of their sandals and the crackling of the fire, on which they had thrown two big faggots of brushwood. Angélique's clothes were soon dry but she was too exhausted to want to eat.

She fell on to the hay, and was asleep immediately, just as if she had fainted. Albert de Sancé's hands laid little Honorine to sleep in a manger, a true rustic cradle, well supplied with straw and hay. Before going off he brought more hay and laid it on his sleeping sister.

Outside, the snow was still sifting down, forming a white cloak over the Abbey, over the still forest, a white shroud over the bodies of the men hanged at the Fairy Stone.

CHAPTER 27

ANGÉLIQUE WOKE in the night. A bell was ringing, and the cows lying in their stalls behind the partition occasionally stirred and made blowing noises. In the background, like a pure angel choir, rose and fell the slow cadences of plain-chant.

She put out her hand and gave a start: she had touched something burning hot. It took her a moment to realize that it was Honorine's forehead. She unhooked the storm lantern from beside the door, and by its yellow light she bent over the child, and saw that she was red in the face, and that her breathing was rapid and shallow.

For three days she never moved from the sick child's bedside. The nursing brother often looked in. He had white hair, and his eyes were the same faded mauve colour as the flowers he gathered in the forest to make his herb-teas.

"If she dies," said Angélique wildly, "I'll go out and kill the soldiers who pursued us with my own hands."

"Come, come, it would be better if you prayed to Our Lady, the Virgin; she was a mother like you," he answered gently.

One morning she woke to find Honorine sitting up and playing solemnly with an ear of corn. Beside herself with joy she called the lay brother who was milking the cows a few stalls off.

"Brother Anselm! Come and see! I believe she's over it."

Fat Brother Anselm and the two young monks who were with him grouped themselves around Honorine. The baby had lost weight, and there were dark rings under her eyes, but she seemed to be perfectly aware of what was going on. She took the milk she was offered together with the congratulations of the assembled company with all the condescension of a queen surrounded by over-excited page-boys.

"The little Christ-child will not be leaving us," said Brother Anselm beaming all over his face.

Then turning severely on Angélique he added:

"Give thanks to the Lord and praise Him, impious woman! I haven't seen you make the sign of the cross once since you've been here."

Albert de Sancé came to see his sister, carrying a little red leather chest with pokerwork arabesques outlined in gold. It was strange how much better the rough habit of a monk suited her brother than the soft satins he had worn in his courtier's days. She could now see that his pale, narrow face seemed to have been destined for the tonsure. The circle of hair around the shaven patch suited him much better than a wig. The folds of his habit and the wide sleeves emphasized his measured gestures which formerly had been irritating.

In those days he had given an impression of unhealthy slyness. The slyness had become serenity, forbearance. His sickly pallor, which had been conspicuous amid the well-fed courtiers, was here no more than an ascetic transparency.

"Do you remember what I always used to say, Angélique," he asked, "that one day I should have Nieul Abbey? And now I have achieved my aims."

Looking at his tall, frail figure, bearing the marks of flagellations, in which very few would have recognized the former favourite of the King's brother, she thought:

"I'm inclined to put it the other way round. Nieul Abbey has you."

They did not refer to the event which had worked such a transformation in the young man's life, his heartbreak and anguish when he had taken to the roads after his brother Gontran's burial, sobbing aloud and wiping his eyes on his lace cuffs, he, the favourite, the corrupted, while the scent of hawthorn brought back memories of his childhood to him, nor to the way in which his steps had led him unconsciously to the gate of Nieul Abbey. When Albert de Sancé was a boy, he had often come to the Abbey for Latin lessons. It was during those studious hours that the spell of the Abbey had settled into his heart, leaving a subtle nostalgia that the giddy round of the Palais Royal and Saint-Cloud had never succeeded in eradicating.

That day he had pulled the hanging chain and the gate had opened. . . .

"You make some extraordinary discoveries in the attics of abbeys," he told Angélique.

"Austerity has not held unbroken sway down the ages. Our Father Abbott thought that you might need certain things, and he's asked me to give you this."

The small leather chest proved to contain a toilet set of gold-embossed tortoise-shell.

When she was alone again, Angélique squatted down in the hay and gave her hair a long and thorough brushing, holding a round looking-glass as clear and bright as a sunlit pool in one hand, and a richly-worked brush, heavy to hold but soft to the touch, in the other. Honorine, leaning fascinated over the edge of her manger, demanded her share of the fun. Angélique gave her a small brush and a tortoise-shell-and-gold shoe-horn.

Who was the Madame de Richeville so sensual and mystical who had left these worldly objects within these walls?

The previous Superior of the Abbey, whose blue eyes had once led the Comtesse de Richeville astray, had been an epicurean equally enamoured of scriptural exegesis and less rarefied matters, and Angélique thought she had once glimpsed the remnants of a canopied fourposter stowed away in a store-room, that the monks

220

had set up whenever the fair dame had announced her intention of coming to make a retreat.

His successor had made a clean sweep of these free and easy ways. He had the reputation of being a hard, uncompromising man.

Angélique none the less asked to be received by him so as to thank him. She was now looking like a human being again, and she was not averse to giving the Superior an opportunity to see for himself that she was very different from the poor, afflicted wretch of a woman whom he had had to help to her feet.

Her clothes were not smart, although she had washed and ironed them, but she left her hair loose upon her shoulders, now that its condition had been restored, as her only adornment. Bending over her mirror she studied the bright mass of it with a touch of anxiety. Those long sun-tinted wisps among the warm lights of the curls could scarcely be anything but newly-appeared white hairs. She was only thirty-three, but she could see the time coming when her smooth face, still bearing all the grace of youth, would be framed in a halo of white. Age was laying its icy hand upon her, and yet she had never lived! For until a woman's heart has known fulfilment her life is nothing but waiting. . . .

She went round the cloister, then, after ascending a staircase worn by the passage of innumerable processions, she came to another open gallery reminiscent of the closed Arab houses built around a patio. Through one of the round arches supported on square columns she had a glimpse of the courtyard, where Brother Anselm was drawing water from the well with Honorine at his heels.

The corridors were deserted. The rustle of her footsteps reminded her of the time when, as a child, she had gaped at Madame de Richeville sweeping proudly by, wearing a black mantilla.

The Abbot was waiting for her in the vast library with its richly tapestried walls. Rare incunabula dating from the earliest days of printing, thousands upon thousands of bound books of every format and thickness shone

221

with the dull glint of gold in the shadows of the room, which was chilly but redolent of precious leather, of parchment, inks, and the ebony of lecterns on which huge illuminated missals lay open.

He was seated under a stained-glass window on a gothic throne, and the stiffness of his white, statue-like form made the intense life which shone in his eyes seem even more impressive: they appeared black at first, and then proved to be merely dark, as steel or bronze is dark, and ageless, as the eyes of ascetics so often are. His hair was still black, but his skin was as if it had been mummified and was stretched over his bones. The stern expression of his sensitive mouth struck a chill upon Angélique and put her on the defensive. She kneeled before him, then got up and sat down on a stool which had been placed ready for her. He gazed at her with fixed attention, with his hands concealed in the long sleeves of his rough habit, and she was compelled to speak first in order to break the unbearable silence.

"Father, I must thank you most sincerely for having received me here. If those soldiers had got hold of me, I should have been lost. The fate which was in store for me . . ."

He gave a brief nod.

"I know. There is a price upon your head. You are the Rebel of Poitou."

Something in the way he said it made Angélique's hackles rise, and the latent hostility she felt towards him blazed out:

"Do I take it that you condemn my conduct?" she asked proudly. "By what right? What can you know, shut away here in a monastery, of the upheavals that are taking place in the world, and of the reasons which may drive a woman to take up arms to defend her freedom?"

She was defying him. It would ill become this man of religion to remind her of women's duty of submissiveness. She would throw the King's demands in his face.

"I know enough," he said, "to recognize the sneering lineaments of Satan starting out from your eyes."

She gave a sarcastic laugh.

"That's the kind of superstitious nonsense I might have expected to hear in this place. You'll be telling me I'm possessed next."

"Is there one feeling in your heart that is not compounded of hate?"

She was silent, and he went on in a compelling monotone:

"Satan is hate. Satan is he who no longer understands love. He is the other face, the opposite face of love, without any admixture. Hate, the poisonous plant that delights to spread. Noble hearts are more prone to it than the rest. Do you not know that Satan feasts on blood, on sorrow and defeat?"

All at once his features were rent with an expression of almost physical suffering, and he exclaimed with infinite sadness:

"You have used the power of your beauty over men to lead them to hate, to crime and rebellion! And yet your name is Angélique, Daughter of the Angels!"

It was then that she recognized him.

"Brother John! Brother John! Was it not you who brought me to refuge in your cell long ago? Yes, it is you! It is you! I can tell you by the way your eyes shine. . . ."

He nodded without speaking. He was contemplating the image of the little girl with the bright hair forming a halo around her sweet face, as innocent as a child's, but already as refined as a woman's, whose spring-coloured eyes were scrutinizing him curiously.

"Pure child," he murmured, "whatever has become of you?"

Something gave way in Angélique's heart.

"I've been hurt," she stammered. "Oh! if only you knew how much life has hurt me, Brother John."

He turned back his gaze to the huge crucifix on the opposite wall.

"And what of Him? What hurt has been spared Him?"

That night she could not sleep. The peace of the Abbey had rent its veil of deceit as once before and revealed the presence of the Prince of Darkness. The thin ringing of the bell punctuating the dark hours and then the sound of matins were a reminder of the eternal struggle. Holding their lamps, the monks proceeded down the corridors on their way to chapel. "Pray, monks, pray," she thought. "Your prayers are needed as long as darkness reigns over the sleeping earth."

In this place the Spirit of Evil appeared in leering form. When she closed her eyes, she thought she caught the sound of dripping blood. She would stretch out her hand and touch Honorine's round little hand as the child lay fast asleep. The child offered her the only effective protection against the horrors of the endless night. It was not until the first cock crowed that she succeeded in getting to sleep.

Still she would not admit herself defeated. She asked to see the Father Abbot again.

"What would have become of me if it had not been for my hate?" she asked him. "If I had not had hate to sustain me, I should have died of despair, I should have destroyed myself, I should have given way to madness. The spirit of revenge which possesses me is like a brace which keeps me alive and sane. You must believe me."

"I do not doubt it. There are times in life when we can only go on living because of some spiritual sustenance, some strength greater than our own. The human spirit is a weakly thing. In happiness it is enough in itself, but in time of sorrow it must turn either to God or to the Devil."

"You don't underestimate the need for the feelings I have resorted to then?"

"I shall never underestimate the power and spiritual strength of Lucifer. I know him too well for that."

"Oh! you're always going off into this crude, visionary talk. You don't understand anything about what goes on on this earth."

She paced up and down in front of him, a splendid creature with her hair floating loose about her shoulders, her chin held high, her eyes flashing, quite impervious to the impression she was making, so intensely was she concentrating on her inner struggle.

The Abbot, as motionless and impassive as a statue,

followed her with his eyes, and as he watched her a mildly ironical smile played around his lips.

"You defend yourself vainly against being possessed by the Devil, my daughter. To less experienced eyes your very agitation might seem to call for a few drops of holy water."

"Oh! you exasperate me!" she cried. "I'm agitated because I want to exonerate myself, and because I've got out of the way of thinking about matters of this sort. This public contumely for which you blame me, but which forced me to take up arms against excessive tyranny, what proof have you that it does not come closer to the spirit of justice willed by Christ than to destructive evil?"

He appeared to be thinking over the argument.

"You are not an easy opponent," he conceded. "Speak then, and explain your motives."

It was painful to her to speak after such a long silence. The words all rushed to her lips at once, and her sentences were broken as if they came straight from her heart, and so disordered that they irritated her: the King, the stake, the pious hypocrites, Colin Paturel and Monsieur de Breteuil, the poor from the slums of Paris, her butchered child, the Protestants, bribery and corruption, the taxes. . . .

What could he make of her ramblings? Nothing! All he would be capable of was preaching at her. From time to time she tossed back her hair which kept falling forward over her cheeks in her vehemence. She could not stop pacing up and down and talking. Sometimes she leant both her hands on the arms of his throne and bent towards him to drive home the truth of what she was saying.

"You blame me for the blood shed on my orders, but is the blood shed in the name of God any less red, or any less criminal?"

He met her anger and rancour with a stony face, and his eyes had suddenly lost their fire and become impenetrable.

"Yes, I know what you're thinking," she went on feverishly. "The blood of Protestant children thrown on the

225

pikes is, of course, *tainted*; the King's lusts on the other hand are *sacred*, the peoples sufferings are just and justified, in fact *deserved*. They should have taken the precaution of not being born poor. Obey the mighty, crush the weak, such is the law."

She was literally exhausted from so much talking, her forehead was covered with perspiration, and she felt completely drained of strength.

He rose with the remark that it was time for compline. She watched him walking off down the cloister with his hands in his sleeves looking like a tall wax candle with his cowl thrown back. He had understood nothing. He was as wrapped in his serenity as ever.

Nevertheless Angélique slept better that night, and when she woke she felt as if a great weight had been lifted from her.

The Abbot sent for her. What did he have in store for her, a thorough dressing-down or a soothing sermon? She welcomed the opportunity of crossing swords with him. She went in with bowed head and was startled to hear him burst out laughing.

"You look as if you were preparing to charge, Madame. Am I such a formidable foe that the Rebel of Poitou is making ready her full armoury against me?"

"Don't call me that any more," she said somewhat embarrassed.

"I thought you were proud of the title."

"I regret nothing," she said, "and I never shall regret anything I have done."

"But you frighten yourself."

Angélique bit her lip.

"You can't understand anything I feel, Father."

"That may be so, but I feel your inner distress, and in particular I see the dark halo about you."

"The aura?" she asked thoughtfully. "The holy men of Islam speak of it. Is my aura so very dark, Father?"

"You shudder at the very idea of looking into your own heart. What are you so afraid you will see?"

She stared at him. His eyes as bright as quicksilver penetrated to her very soul, and she could not look away.

226

"Free yourself," he urged, "otherwise you will never be capable of living again."

"Living again? Living again? But why live again? I do not want to live again."

She was shouting pathetically, her two hands on her breast as if she were stifling.

"What do you expect me to do with life? I reject it and detest it. It had deprived me of everything. It has made me this woman who ... yes, it's quite true ... frightens me."

She collapsed on the stool.

"You'll never be able to understand, but I'd be glad to die."

"That is utterly false. You can have no appetite for death."

"Oh! I have, I have, I assure you."

"That's only a reflex of your tiredness. But an appetite for death, a relish for death, only comes to those who have made a success of their lives, whether long or short, who have lived to experience what they wanted to experience. Such is the song of old Simeon: 'Lord, now lettest thou thy servant depart in peace . . . for mine eyes have seen thy salvation.' But until a creature has known such fulfilment, so long as he has only wandered far from his goal, so long as he has known nothing but failure, he cannot wish for death. Forgetfulness, sleep, nothingness, yes. Weariness of life is not death, death, the treasure God commits to us together with our being, that ineffable promise. . . ."

Angélique thought of Father de Lesdiguière, of his radiant young face. "Make haste, oh death," he had said. She thought of Colin Paturel, who had so often been given over into the executioner's hands, and of what she had herself experienced when she was bound to the pillar under Mulai Ismail's cruel gaze. At that time she would have been able to die well; she had felt herself drifting towards the ultimate splendour. But not now.

"You're right," she said with sudden dismay, "I cannot die now, it would mean that my life had been a mess."

He laughed.

"I like these bursts of vitality. Yes, Madame, you must

live. What a mockery it would be to die a failure! The worst mockery of all."

She was still resisting. She was afraid to raise her eyes to him and to receive the shock of his sombre gaze.

"You're watching me like an animal watching its prey," she said.

"I should like to see you set free so that you could live again."

"But free from what?" she cried in exasperation.

"From the buried something that is stopping you from being on good terms with yourself and with life."

"I could never forgive."

"That is not what I'm asking of you."

Angélique was struggling. He could see her rapid breathing, and the anguish mirrored on her beautiful but distraught face was a torture to him.

"Listen to me, Brother John, listen to me. Have you heard of the Field of the Dragoons?"

He nodded.

"It was I who ordered the massacre."

"I know that."

"That is not all. They brought me Montadour's head, and the sight of it gave me a ... horrible pleasure. I felt like bathing my hands in the blood."

The monk closed his eyes.

"Ever since that night I've been afraid of myself," whispered Angélique, "and I've taken care not to look into my soul."

"You have been drawn towards the pit of hell. Do you want that memory to be blotted out for ever?"

"With all my heart."

She looked at him hopefully.

"Have you lost your childhood faith so completely that you doubt that it can be done?"

"God knows everything. What does it matter whether I confess it to you?"

"God knows everything, but without confession and repentance even He cannot blot out your sin. That is the meaning of human freedom."

He had overcome her.

After receiving absolution she felt as if she were entering upon her convalescence. She looked at her open hands spread before her.

"And will the blood on my hands be wiped out too?"

"It is not a question of going back on the past or escaping the consequences of your actions, but of a return to life. For years now you have been nothing but hatred, for the future be nothing but love. That is the price of your resurrection."

She gave a disillusioned laugh.

"That policy doesn't suit me at all. My fight is not yet over."

"What I have in mind is an inner attitude."

She mocked at her own upset feelings, shaking her long hair defiantly.

"What a lot of fuss about one head being cut off! Mulai Ismail used to sacrifice two or three a day in order to please God. You see how hard it is to tell what is good and what is bad when you travel."

The idea seemed to amuse Father Abbot hugely. His laugh was as bright as a ray of sunshine falling on snow. His face lost its severe stiffness of expression and became astonishingly young and affable.

When in repose he seemed to be carved from stone; his whole appearance was icy. One would have thought that nothing could soften such strictness, and yet when he spoke his features revealed a wealth of emotional response, gaiety, sorrow, anger, and warmth and human sympathy. When she thought of him, her image was of an austere, inscrutable man. In actual fact his face could not have been more expressive or responsive.

He had made her feel so shy with him at first that it took her a long time to notice this other side of him and to draw comfort from the warmth of his personality.

His answer to her quip about Mulai Ismail was:

"Evil is what you feel to be injurious to your moral health. Good is what satisfies your personal sense of justice."

"It's my turn to ask you, Father, whether your approach is not a trifle heretical too."

"I wouldn't say that to anyone I did not think was capable of taking it the right way."

"So you have got faith in me then?"

He gazed at her for a long time.

"Yes, for yours is no common destiny. You must work out your salvation along an unknown path."

He asked her a lot of questions about Islam. He was intensely interested in her impressions of the customs of the Moslems and their fervent faith, and she made no secret to him of her abiding admiration for them and her nostalgic memories of her experiences.

They looked through huge illuminated tomes containing the history of the Arab invasions and Mohammed's message as interpreted by the Fathers of the Church. Angélique was never to forget those hours spent by the lectern when time did not seem to exist, while the Abbot turned the pages with his long, thin hand which was so delicate that it was almost like a woman's. He had spent so long copying and studying the primitives that he seemed to have acquired something of their disembodied gracefulness.

One afternoon when she was waiting for him, Angélique discovered in an illumination a green-eyed angel's face that struck her as familiar. The same angel occurred several times in the missal. Its face was sometimes grave, sometimes smiling, and its eyelids were lowered under its halo of fair hair.

"Was it Brother John, formerly novice at Nieul Abbey, who decorated this volume?" she asked with a smile when the Abbot came in.

He looked at the pictures and smiled in his turn.

"How could I ever forget the child who came in the night and the strange poetry that emanated from her? Freshness, beauty, the zest for living—all these treasures were in her and shone out of her eyes. I think God must have sent her to the monastery to remind me of the beauty of His creation."

"And now I am old and blighted."

The Abbot laughed.

"Whatever put such nonsense into your head? How could such a beautiful mouth dare to utter such bittter words? You are young! Oh, how young you are!" he

230

repeated, his eyes shining. "You have kept your exuberance, and it's almost like a miracle. You have lived through a great deal, it is true, but your life lies *before* you, I assure you."

"My hair is going white."

"You will be all the more attractive for it," he said in a teasing voice.

For the first time for many months she became aware of herself as he fixed his eyes upon her. She felt the vigour of her body, her stamina increased by the open-air life and by her constant rides on horseback. Her figure was less slim, her shoulders were stronger, but she had recovered her Poitou complexion, pink and golden, and the rings under her eyes, the product of many a tear shed, lent a touch of pathos to her expression and made her eyes seem all the brighter.

She had grown so indifferent to her physical appearance that she felt somewhat embarrassed to discover herself again so suddenly, and she automatically drew her cloak across her breast.

"It's no good your trying to encourage me," she said, with a shake of the head. "You can't understand. I may seem lively enough, but inside I feel so blighted. . . ."

"It takes more than a day to get over a serious illness."

He strode slowly over to his throne and sat gazing at her thoughtfully.

"But the cure is progressing. What a difference there is already since the evening you sought refuge here with your child! Be patient. Turn to the light and not the darkness and you will get well in both body and soul."

She registered surprise.

"In body? I'm not ill."

"You fear and hate men, that is your malady, your abnormality, perhaps I should say. And that you must get over. It would stifle your soul because you are made for love."

For a moment Angélique was stupefied, then she burst out angrily:

"What are you talking about?" she shrieked; "what are you meddling with? What do you know about the tortures of a woman pursued by men's desire, the way she

231

can end up abominating herself, and them, the degradation involved in love? And aren't you churchmen the first to hold up the bogy of impurity and to cry penance?"

He did not appear to be disconcerted in the slightest by the vehemence of her outburst, and merely smiled.

"Why are you smiling?"

"Because the more I look at you the surer I am that you were made to sleep in a man's arms."

The image he had conjured up both disturbed and calmed her.

He went on quite unperturbed:

"I'm not using the plural. I said *a* man. You are too sensual to live without love. Seek your cure for the sake of the man who will come, the man . . ."

"Yes, the spouse awaited by the wise virgin with the lamp. That sounds just like me."

She thought with deep sorrow:

"The spouse! I knew him. He gave me everything I needed, but they tore him from my arms."

"You must turn your eyes towards the future. You must know how to recognize the man who will come, and be prepared to meet him. Are you resolved to keep the shame of your sins for ever on your soul? No! Then away with your pride in your body. It is less important. Do not foster the memory of its shame. Spring always returns after winter. Flesh and blood are renewed. Your health seems sound. . . ."

She was both embarrassed and comforted that he dared to speak to her so frankly of the hidden malady that was devouring her.

"That won't be easy," she said. "It's easy to see that it wasn't you who—"

"Foolish creature. You must learn to turn your mind from what hurts you. Look, the sun is shining for the first time for many days. Take your child by the hand and go for a walk with her in the garden and meditate on the theme of hope."

She was not at all sure that she wished for the future he was holding out to her. Was there a man alive capable of taming her again? Her wound was too deep.

Still, when she thought of the instinct which made her turn to the Abbot of Nieul longing for comfort and support, she had to admit that one whole part of her seemed ready to yield. He had drawn her on with all the patience of a bird-catcher, but the charm of his manly personality wasted by penances had had something to do with it too. Yes, he was right. She was still very much a woman!

"What on earth has happened to me here at the Abbey?" she asked. "I sometimes feel as if I'm lost, as if I'm suspended in mid-air."

"You have been thrown into what the mathematicians call the passage through the infinite."

"What do you mean?"

"When one studies mathematics, one learns that not all solutions to a problem are necessarily reducible to figures. In other words they do not all necessarily derive from one another and take a purely rational form. Take a few simple cases—we do not know whether the solution of an equation should be expressed positively or negatively, or, to put it differently, whether we have gained or lost. The mere extraction of a square-root raises a philosophical problem with considerable, indeed incalculable implications—what can the nature of the root of a negative number possible be? Finding ourselves thus on the brink of the inconceivable we reassure ourselves by stating that it is an 'unreal' number or a trigonometrical line. But that is tantamount to admitting that we do not know what is going on any more, for it means that we have passed over to a different plane of physical structure. We might try to make the point easier to grasp by saying that we have 'passed through a break in continuity' or that we have 'passed through the infinite.' Do you follow me?"

"Yes, I think I do. I have experienced something like that. There are times when the problem one is considering seems to vanish."

"How profound this abyss is, even in the realm of mathematics! But it is also omnipresent in our everyday life. And when our mind sees no 'plane' solution, a passage through the infinite, or the irrational, or the supranormal is inescapable. We emerge from it and resume our ordinary life, but the solution has by that time been discovered."

"Do you think I'll ever be able to get back into the run of life again? I seem to be drawn this way and that by so many contradictions."

"You are one of those women who need to fight in order to achieve self-awareness, and to stay young and beautiful—oh yes, I assure you that there are such cases. Do you imagine that you would ever be content with a humdrum existence, taken up with your needlework, or even with a life of pleasure?"

"I just don't know any more. I sometimes used to think that I was suited to a homely, rustic type of life—a husband to love, children around a table, for whom I baked cakes. Every woman keeps that vision tucked away somewhere in a corner of her heart, even those who have wandered furthest from the paths of respectability, even the most worldly of them. And like all other women I have also hankered after wealth for the sake of the enjoyment it can bring—jewels, and lovely clothes, the admiration of men. But it didn't take me long to see that, even if I succeeded in feeling at home in that sort of world, I certainly wasn't happy. It didn't really suit me. On the other hand, I did enjoy tremendously being a military leader. You may say that a woman was not made to shed blood, that it is against her nature, but personally I love war, and I would be a liar if I denied it. Adventure, battle, the expectation of victory, binding together scattered forces, giving them a goal and a purpose. And even the fear, the anxiety, the hope of saving a desperate situation—they all suited me. I have suffered during these last two years, but I have never been bored."

"Freedom from boredom is indeed said to be an essential prerequisite for happiness for men, and even more for women."

"Aren't you shocked by what I've told you? How do you explain these contradictions?"

"A human being is capable of so many things. The

web of life is made up of such varied threads—good and evil, rebellion and submission, gentleness and violence."

"There is a time for everything," he went on softly, "a time to every purpose under the heaven: a time to be born, and a time to die, a time to kill and a time to heal; a time to weep and a time to laugh; a time to mourn and a time to dance, a time to embrace and a time to refrain from embracing, a time to keep silence and a time to speak; a time to love and a time to hate. . . ."

"Who said that?"

"One of the great sages of the Bible, Ecclesiastes."

"Does that mean that in my rebellion there was something else besides the sordid and hateful things?"

"Yes, indeed."

Angélique's face lighted up.

"Your indulgence brings me greater comfort than your severity. You were so hard towards me at the beginning. . . ."

"I wanted to frighten you, to pull you up out of the slough of despond. I wanted to make you talk. I like to think I succeeded. It is the heart which is shut against the outside world that grows corrupt."

He meditated, leaning his jaw on his hand as if wrestling with a difficult problem.

"You must go to another place," he said at last.

"Do you mean that I am to die?" she exclaimed suddenly feeling very much afraid.

"No, no, not that at all, dear soul. You are the very essence of life. I meant that you ought to get away from this part of the country, the place where you were brought up, in fact get right away from this country altogether where there is a price on your head. Leave this tormented world where Christian culture is so recent that it has not yet succeeded in advancing beyond the initial conflict—God versus Satan. You are not suited for these mystic wrangles, you are too close to nature. Your straightforwardness, your essential balance cannot be satisfied with emotions which are extreme and to some extent unnatural. Your basic values lie on a quite different plane, and here you will always be at variance with those about you. You are rather like—I should

235

think—rather like the first woman created by God who took such delight in the fruits of Eden. You ought to go somewhere else."

"Yes, but where?"

"I do not know—where you can build a new world, something more earthy, more tolerant. . . ."

He raised his eyes towards the window.

"The snow has gone, the sun is bright. Spring has come. Have you noticed?"

The blue sky formed a curve in the Romanesque arch, and two pet turtledoves were cooing on the window-sill.

"I have made inquiries. The soldiers have left the district. The country is calm even if not properly pacified. You won't have any trouble in reaching Maillezais in the marshes and from there the coast. Have you any supporters to join up with?"

"Do you mean that I must leave?" she breathed.

"Yes, the time has come."

She imagined the hostile world awaiting her outside the Abbey gates and saw herself setting forth into it lonely and surrounded by spying eyes, with her bastard child in her arms.

She went down on her knees beside him.

"Do not drive me away. I feel so much at home here. This is God's sanctuary."

"The whole world is God's sanctuary to those who believe in His mercy."

She closed her eyes, and tears dropped from her long lashes and slid down her cheeks in shining furrows. He saw the black halo of misfortune around her head. She was not yet out of danger, but he knew that the certainty that victory would be hers was already growing in her. It was his duty to cast her out into the storms of the world.

He stretched out his hand and she felt the infinitely gentle weight of it on her hair.

"Courage, dear soul, and may God bless you."

The following day the porter came to fetch her. He had saddled a mule for her, as she had asked. She was to leave it with the monks of Maillezais to send back. He had loaded the mule with two baskets of provisions and a blanket. Angélique wrapped up her daughter's head very carefully in a shawl. Granted that she was unable to hide the colour of her own eyes, at least she could hide the colour of her daughter's hair; she was well aware that the description of her that had been issued said that people should be on the look-out for a green-eyed woman carrying a red-headed child. It was unfortunate that they both had distinguishing characteristics.

For a moment she hesitated with her hand already on the mule's neck. Could she not greet the Abbot once more, and her brother?

The porter shook his head. Holy Week was about to begin, and the monastery was already in retreat.

It was true that a more than usually heavy silence hung over the Abbey. These consecrated men were drawing together for the terrible pilgrimage of the days before Easter, and the woman had to withdraw.

Once again something was being torn from Angélique's heart, leaving it bleeding painfully. But this very suffering and the fact that she was capable of bearing it could be regarded as a sign of her resurrection.

She sat side-saddle on her mount, held Honorine to her and passed through the gates.

As she was climbing up the path leading to the forest the sound of the gate banging to behind her reached her ears, and almost at once there came three clear strokes on a bell.

So many doors had shut behind her before, each time closing lines of escape, like beaters around a hunted animal. Each time the chances of escaping her specific destiny had been narrowed down, and soon there would be only one path left open to her—her own path. What path was it? She still did not know; all she could do was to sense it. She was beginning to realize that both catastrophes and insurmountable obstacles had on each occasion turned her aside from following her own whims and had brought her harshly back to a single goal, one that she could not see but which was unquestionably hers by destiny.

Once more, and for the last time, she was crossing the

forest. She did not dare go near the main roads in broad daylight. Through the forest and then across the marshes she would reach the Abbey of Maillezais without being interfered with.

When she drew near the Wolves' Coomb, the sun was high in the sky. It was striking straight across the valley, and Angélique halted, overcome with a sense of the miraculous.

A bare two weeks before at this very place she had stumbled through the snow hardly able to breathe in the biting cold, and she had felt in her flesh all the harshness of the barren winter. Today the valley was carpeted with green velvet, the stream that she had crossed, then sleeping beneath the ice, was now bounding along with all the grace and vigour of a young goat, and there were violets along the fringe of the wood. The cuckoo was calling his promise of warm days to come, of budding blossoms, of the coming of spring.

Angélique's eyes grew dim with tears as she looked at these marvels. Nature and life have their pleasant surprise too. Out of an exceptionally long and hard winter, grass and flowers were springing ten times more abundant than usual; from an odious crime, from a horror without name had been born this flower of grace, plump, white, crowned with flames, wondrously serene, that she was holding asleep at her breast—Honorine.

Father de Lesdiguière, the Abbot of Nieul! It had taken two archangels to pull her out of the abyss into which she had fallen. It had taken these two pure men of religion to wipe out the evil memory of the monk Bécher.

She thought that it was just and necessary that she had lived to see this day.

CHAPTER 28

THE FOLLOWING day she reached Maillezais, the magnificent Abbey built on an island surrounded by stagnant waters and willow-trees. At night one still seemed to hear the sound of waves which, in the twelfth century, had battered at the foundations of the Abbey. The monks here led a sleepy bucolic life, fishing for frogs and eels, more concerned with their siestas than with their breviaries, bent on upholding the traditions of Rabelais who had written his *Gargantua* within these very walls. It was a far cry from the devout atmosphere of Nieul. The monks were frightened of the Protestants. For in these parts and as far as the coast the Protestants were in the majority.

The King's men were gradually getting life in the region back to normal. Angélique had a letter of introduction from the Abbot of Nieul—"A man too holy for this world," the Prior of Maillezais said with a sigh—and she was well received and given a guide to take her as far as Sables-d'Olonne.

She carried Honorine on her back and scrambled down a path part sand, part mud, beneath a vault of dwarf oaks and hazel-trees. It had rained, and the clean air had a strange taste to it. She stopped to pick some hazel-nuts for Honorine and to crack them between her teeth. The petals of a hawthorn blossom, damp with rain, fell to the ground as she touched them.

An unaccustomed sound was coming from behind the hedge.

It was the last lap.

The sound grew louder. Angélique went forward, treading warily, fascinated, and there was the sea.

It was not the Mediterranean. all blue and gold, but the Ocean, the sea of darkness, the briny deep of the Atlantic. . . .

It rose up, grey, blue and green, high on the horizon, which in its turn merged into a misty sky.

As she moved nearer, Angélique could see the mauve line of the shore along which stretched a silver network of pools. Then she saw the chequerboard of the salt-pans, and the salt, raked up into white cones, which the sudden advent of evening had coloured pale pink.

A hovel stood on her left. It was there that Angélique was to have met Ponce-le-Palud, the Protestant dealer in contraband salt, who had been one of the very first of the partisans. But Ponce-le-Palud had been taken the day before and executed, on a double charge of dealing in contraband salt and of rebellion against the King.

The last of his band still lived there, hiding amongst the sparse woodlands that lined the shore, living on roots. Angélique negotiated with them for a chance of embarking on a ship bound for Brittany. There perhaps she would be able to hide for a time. The most urgent thing was to get away from the patrols.

The seaside folk who had stayed faithful to the King or had come back to his side did not scruple to sell their erstwhile friends in order to impress the authorities with their zeal. Losers have no friends. Angélique grew anxious at the thought of finding herself amongst these bitter Protestants who knew the extent of her downfall and how helpless she was. Only one thing was possible and that must be done soon: she must take ship! Only the sea now welcomed her and held out a prospect of security.

On the third day some haggard-looking men dressed in rags came running into the woods shouting that a convoy of merchants was approaching. It was on its way from Marans and was carrying wheat and wine. It was months since they had seen anything like it. The others, urged on by the newcomers, got together their arms, rapiers, swords and sticks. They had neither gunpowder nor ammunition for their muskets.

"Please don't do that, I beg you," Angélique implored them. "You will have the whole of the constabulary after you. If they once start to search these woods . . ."

"We've got to live," growled their chief.

Through the sparse trees they could already hear the tinkle of mule bells and the creaking of cart-wheels. Then there were shouts and a clash of arms.

Angélique no longer knew which way to turn. But it was clear that she must stop these desperate men from embarking on acts of banditry which would bring the soldiery and customs men to their hiding place. Alas! She had known them for too short a time and had little influence over them. She could not even speak their

240

dialect. She tied Honorine to the foot of a tree and ran towards the fighting. If only men's lives could be spared, if only they could come to some agreement with the merchants. . . .

But the merchants, instead of losing their heads, had made up their minds from the start that they would defend themselves to the limits of their powers. They were carrying pistols and used them now from the cover of their carts. The road was already littered with the wounded.

Angélique crept up to the chief smuggler as he stood behind a bush.

"Retreat," she begged him.

"It's too late now. We've got to get their goods, and we shall have to get them too, to stop them talking. . . ."

He leapt towards one of the carts. A shot was fired and he fell to the ground. After that there was a moment of great confusion. The four merchants, realizing that the bandits' mainstay was gone, came out from their shelter and gave chase. Wielding sticks with a vigour that one would not have expected of peaceful merchants, they hit out wildly, smashing limbs and belabouring skulls. Angelique was struck violently on the back of the neck. With swimming eyes she still had time to see the man who had hit her. He was dressed in black—they were no doubt Protestants—and was fairly corpulent, with pale eyes, not full of hatred but determination. St. Honoré, the merchant saint, must have looked rather like him. Another blow fell on her temple and she lost consciousness.

As she came to, she had a distant and terrifying vision. Florimond had been caught by Grand Coësre and Cantor had been kidnapped by the gipsies. She and La Polak were running after them along the muddy road to Charenton, after escaping from the formidable Châtelet prison. She opened her eyes. She was in prison, all alone, stretched out on a bed of rotting straw.

She was too shocked to have any feeling left in her. She no longer even had the strength to curse the reckless salt-smugglers, to curse this disaster and her own bad luck. Within a few hours she would have been at sea, for she had just completed negotiations for her passage across to the Breton coast. She fell into a sort of stupor and did not even ask herself which township she had been dragged to. Was it Sables-d'Olonne, or was it Talmont? She did not ask herself whether she had been recognized, nor what the charges were against her. The back of her neck hurt her and she felt very tired and ill. She lay in a state of prostration until suddenly a shattering thought crossed her mind, and she half sat up on her pallet—Honorine!

A nightmare took hold of her.

What had happened to the child after the disastrous skirmish? Angélique had left her tied to a tree. Had the salt-smugglers seen her as they ran away? Had they taken care of her? And what if nobody had noticed her? What if the little girl was still there, alone in the forest? The clearing was well back from the road. Could she hope that someone might hear her cries?

Angélique broke out in a cold sweat. It was nearly night. Behind the bars of the tiny window a reddish glow showed that it was evening.

Angélique hammered on the cellar door, but nobody came, no one answered her call. She went back to the loophole and clutched at the bars. The opening was at ground level. A dull roar told her that she could not be very far from the sea. She called again, but in vain. Night was coming on, caring nothing for the prisoners walled up here alive, who could hope for nothing from their fellow men until the morning. Her mind became blank and empty for a while, and she must have rushed around and round shrieking like a soul in torment. A faint sound outside made her pull herself together. It was the sound of footsteps. Angélique went back to the cold rusty bars that covered the window. She clung there as the footsteps came nearer. Two shoes appeared at the other end of the little opening.

"For the love of heaven, please stop, whoever you are going by. Listen to me," shouted Angélique.

The shoes stopped.

242

"For the love of God," she repeated fervently. "Listen to my plea."

Nobody spoke, but the shoes remained motionless.

"My little girl is in the woods," she went on; "it will be the end of her if nobody goes to her rescue. She will die of cold and hunger. The foxes will eat her. Whoever you are going by, have pity on her."

She must say where Honorine was. She did not know all the local place-names.

"She is not far from the road where the merchants with the wheat were set upon by robbers."

"Was it yesterday or today?" she asked herself, her head suddenly swimming.

"As you turn off the road on to the path, there is a milestone"—she had just remembered this detail—"yes, that's it, if you go down that path you will find a clearing. . . . She is there tied to a tree. . . . My little girl, she is not quite two. . . ."

The feet walked on. The passer-by went on his way. Had he even listened to the wild cries that came out of that hole in the ground? "Some madwoman they have locked up," he would say to himself. "They've got all sorts of women in their prisons! . . ."

She woke, sickened, from a sleep in which she had heard her child weeping incessantly, and found herself faced by a jailer and two armed guards who roughly ordered her to get up and follow them.

She had to climb a spiral stone staircase before coming to a vaulted room whose walls dripped water and were being eaten away by salt. There was a brazier that took the chill off the room. Its purpose was not only to warm this medieval crypt. Angélique realized that when she caught sight of a burly man with bare arms wearing a scarlet singlet. He was leaning over the brazier and carefully twisting a long thin iron rod round and round in the live coals.

At the back of the room, under a kind of blue canopy, very faded and decorated with fleurs-de-lis, a judge sat in his long black robes and his curled wig. He was deep in conversation with one of the merchants, the one who had knocked Angélique out.

They were talking quietly and did not even bother to interrupt their conversation when the armed guards thrust Angélique into the room, threw her down on her knees in front of the executioner and began to take off her coat and open the top of her dress.

Angélique began to fight and shout like one possessed. But the strong hands held her still and she heard the back of her dress rip. A red glow seemed to be trembling before her eyes as it came nearer and nearer.
. . .

She let out a shriek like all the devils in hell.

Her nostrils were filled with the stench of burnt flesh. She was so determined to escape from the restraining hands that she had felt nothing. It was only after they had let go of her that she became aware of the terrible wound on her shoulder.

"There's one for you!" growled one of the men to his companion. "It'd take a whole regiment to keep her still! Talk about a fury!"

The burn sent waves of pain into Angélique's head and down her left arm to the very tips of her fingers. She was still on her knees moaning quietly. The executioner was putting away his instrument of torture. At the end of its long handle they had forged a fleur-de-lis, now blackened after much use.

The judge and the merchant went on talking. Their words echoed under the arched roof.

"I do not share your pessimism," the judge was saying. "We are still in a pretty good position and it is not true that the King wants to get rid of all the Protestants in his Kingdom. Indeed he approves of the honesty and thrift of our fellow-Protestants. Look, even here in the Sables, there are so few Catholics that out of four judges three are Protestants. And since the only Catholic judge is always off duck-shooting, more often than not it is we who are called upon to settle differences between Catholics."

"But what about Poitou? I assure you that I have seen a thing or two that has set me thinking. . . ."

"The troubles in Poitou! Straightforward and deplorable provocation, I know. Once again our brothers allowed themselves to be carried away by the ambitions of powerful noblemen like the La Morinières."

The judge walked down the steps leading from his platform and went up to Angélique who remained kneeling.

"Well, my girl, I hope you will have learnt a lesson from what has just happened to you. A woman will soon lose her reputation if she spends her time running about the woods with thieves and smugglers. From now on, wherever you go, you will bear the mark of the King's justice. You have been branded with the fleur-de-lis. Everyone will know that you have been in the hands of the executioner and that you are not to be trusted. I hope that this will make you a little more careful and discerning in the use you make of your charms. . . ."

She resolutely kept her eyes on the ground. Since she had not been recognized she did not wish to give them the opportunity of looking too closely at her. She had not heard a single word that the judge had spoken except when he had said: "You have been branded with the fleur-de-lis."

She felt the burn deep in her flesh, this infamous brand that marked her for ever as a criminal. She had joined the ranks of doubtful women: the prostitutes, the criminals, the thieves. . . .

For the time being she did not worry unduly about this. Nothing mattered except her need to get out of this prison and to find out what had happened to Honorine.

She let the judge ramble on in a kind of pastoral sermon and only pricked up her ears as he reached his conclusion.

"In consideration of the indulgence I owe you since you are a member of the Reformed Church, I shall not detain you within these walls. But I must hold myself responsible for the future of your soul and place you where you are unable to return to your evil ways. I could do no better than to hand you over to a family whose edifying example will draw you back into the paths of righteousness and remind you of your duty towards God. Maître Gabriel Berne, whom you see here, has told me that he is looking for a servant-girl to

245

look after his home and his children. He is willing to take you into service, thus putting into practice what Christ taught us about forgiving your enemies. Stand up, get dressed and go with him."

Angélique did not need a second bidding.

Out in the narrow street bustling with fishermen, women selling seashells and workers from the salt-flats, coming home from the shore with their huge rakes over their shoulders, she was watching for an opportunity to escape from the merchant, to whom she owed her freedom, but whom she had no intention of following quietly as the judge had told her to do. Maître Gabriel must have guessed her thoughts for he held on tight to her arm. She remembered that he had a powerful wrist and that he knew how to wield a stick. His manner was both calm and uncompromising.

When they reached the Inn of the Good Salt, he showed her to her room.

"We leave tomorrow at dawn. I live in La Rochelle, but I have customers to see on the way. So we shall only get home in the evening. I must ask you whether you are willing to be a servant in my household for I have given the judge an undertaking that you will not attempt to escape from my house to return to your previous disorderly life."

He awaited her reply. She should have given her assurance. But faced with his open, honest eyes, she found she could not. Her evil genius urged her on and, instead of agreeing, she burst out:

"Don't count on that. Nothing will make me stay with you."

"Not even this?"

He pointed to the bed which, like a peasant's bed, was set high above several drawers. She did not understand.

"Go and look," he said.

He seemed to be making fun of her.

She took two steps forward, then stayed rooted to the ground. On the pillow she had just seen a brilliant splash of red hair. Honorine lay there, snuggled up to her neck beneath the sheets, one thumb in her mouth, fast asleep.

Angélique thought she was dreaming, and that this last vision was just one more piece of madness added to the nightmare in which she seemed caught up. She threw an incredulous look at Maître Gabriel. Then she dropped her eyes and looked at the merchant's shoes.

"So it was you!" she breathed.

"Yes, it was me. I was passing by the other evening, walking through the prison courtyard after going to see the judge, when a voice stopped me. A woman's voice begged me to save her child. I got on my horse and, although I had no particular wish to revisit the place where we had been attacked, I did go there. Luckily I got there before nightfall. I found the child under the tree. She must have fallen asleep after much weeping and howling. But she had not been too cold. I wrapped her in my coat and brought her back here. I gave her to a servant-girl and asked her to care for her."

It seemed to Angélique that she had never known a more wonderful sense of deliverance. From that moment life seemed quite easy, now that this terrible burden had been lifted from her heart. Every miracle was possible since this miracle had occurred. Men were good, the world was a lovely place. . . .

"May God bless you," she said, her voice broken with emotion. "Maître Gabriel, I shall never forget what you have done for me and for my daughter. You can count on my devotion. I am at your service."

PART THREE

The Protestants of La Rochelle

CHAPTER 29

NIGHT WAS falling as Maître Gabriel Berne's light cart entered La Rochelle. The deep blue of the sky, still retaining some of the day's brilliance, lay behind the open-work steeples and the half-dismantled ramparts that stood as a reminder of the proud fortifications that Richelieu had battered down.

There were lamps burning at every crossroad. The town gave an impression of cleanliness and order. There were no drunks, no hang-dog faces. In spite of the late hour, people were still strolling about the streets.

Maître Gabriel made a first stop in front of an open porchway.

"These are my warehouses. They back on to the docks. But I prefer to unload my wheat-stacks at the back, away from prying eyes."

He let the mules and the two carts go inside, and, after giving his orders to his assistants who had come running up, he got back into the shandrydan. It bounced about on the round cobbles that paved the little side-streets, and several times the horse slipped and sent sparks flying from his hoofs.

"It is very peaceful where we live, under the ramparts," he went on to explain. He seemed pleased to be home. "And yet we are only a few steps from the quay-side, and ..." He was about to explain something else that no doubt emphasized how desirable it was to be both so near the port and yet away from the general hubbub, when, as they turned a corner, his words were belied by bright lights and noisy voices.

They could see soldiers coming and going with halberds and torches in their hands. The flames threw a crude glare on the tall white façade of a house with a carriage entrance standing open in the middle.

"Archers in my courtyard," grunted Maître Gabriel. "What is going on?"

Nevertheless he got down from the little cart without any display of emotion.

"Follow me, you and your daughter. There's no reason for you to stay outside," he said, seeing that Angélique was hesitating to show herself. She had, in fact, many very good reasons for not following him into this den of constables. But in order not to draw attention to herself, she was forced to follow her new master.

The archers crossed halberds.

"No callers. We have been told to disperse any crowds that form."

"I am not a caller, I am the master of this household."

"Oh, I see. Go ahead then."

After crossing the courtyard, Maître Gabriel went up a few steps and entered a long, low-ceilinged passage dark with heavy tapestries and pictures. A candelabrum with six branches was burning on a console-table.

A young boy ran down the stone staircase, jumping the stairs two at a time in his hurry.

"Quick, Father, come up. The Papists are trying to take Uncle to Mass."

"He's eighty-six and cannot walk. It's a joke," said Maître Gabriel reassuringly.

At the top of the stairs a man appeared, impeccably dressed in brown velvet. His cuffs, his cravat, and his carefully groomed wig showed his high rank, and he walked towards them, putting his heels down with an air of affected distress.

"My dear Berne, I am very pleased indeed to see you home again. I was terribly upset at having to break into your house in your absence, but the circumstances were exceptional. . . ."

"Lieutenant, I am indeed honoured by your visit," said the merchant, bowing low, "but may I ask for an explanation?"

"You know that it has recently been decreed, and we

252

must conform, you know, that any dying man or woman who is a member of the Reformed Church must be visited by a Catholic priest, so that wherever possible he may leave this world cleansed from the heresies that would deprive him of eternal life. A zealous Capuchin monk, Father Germain, who had heard that your uncle, Monsieur Lazarus Berne, was at death's door, thought it his absolute duty to fetch the priest from the nearest parish, along with the bailiff, according to the letter of the law.

"These gentlemen were given a most unfriendly reception by the women of your household—ah, we know what women are like, my good friend!—and were unable to fulfil their mision. Knowing how friendly I have always been towards you, they sent for me to calm the ladies, and I pride myself on having done so, for your poor uncle, before dying . . ."

"He's dead?"

"He has only a few moments more. Your uncle, as I was saying, seeing eternity before him, has at last been touched by grace and has asked to receive the sacraments."

All of a sudden a little girl's shrill voice began to shriek hysterically:

"Not that! Not that in the home of our ancestors. . . ."

The King's Lieutenant himself caught the thin little figure round the waist as it rushed towards him, and put his hand, heavy with rings, across her mouth.

"Maître Berne, is this your daughter?" he asked icily. At the same instant he let out a bellow. "She's bitten me, the little hussy!"

There was a great rumpus going on downstairs.

"Shoo! Shoo! Get out. . . ."

A little old woman, who had sprung out of a passage like a witch, began throwing things, Angélique realized they were onions: anything the old Huguenot woman could lay her hands on. . . . The menservants were stamping their heavy shoes on the stone floor of the vestibule.

Maître Gabriel alone was unperturbed. He told his daughter in a very curt voice to hold her tongue.

Meanwhile the Lieutenant had waved out of the window. Soldiers poured up the stairs. Their arrival calmed down the excitement, and curiosity made everybody crowd around the entrance to one of the bedrooms.

Angèlique could vaguely make out an old man's head on the pillow; he seemed at his last gasp, if not already dead.

"My son, I bring you Our Lord Jesus Christ," said the priest coming forward.

The words had a magical effect.

The old man jerked open one extremely acute and lively eye, and raised his hand on his long skinny neck.

"I do not believe that lies in your power."

"But a moment ago you agreed . . . "

"I have no recollection of that."

"We were unable to put any other interpretation upon the movements of your lips."

"I was thirsty, that's all. But don't forget, Monsieur le Curé, that I lived on boiled leather and thistle soup during the siege of La Rochelle. I didn't do that to deny, fifty years later, the beliefs for which twenty-three thousand inhabitants of my city out of twenty-eight thousand died."

"You're raving!"

"That's as may be, but I'm not going to rave to suit you."

"You're dying."

"Not by a long chalk."

He shouted out in a voice which was cracked but still had a gay ring to it.

"Bring me a glass of Borderies wine."

The servants roared with laughter. Uncle was reviving. The outraged Capuchin called for silence. These insolent heretics must be taught a lesson. A taste of prison would teach them to show at least outward deference. In any case, special regulations had been drafted to deal with those whose external behaviour was an incitement to scandal and disorder.

At that moment, Angélique sniffed a smell of burning which put it into her head that it would be a good idea to absent herself from such arguments, which boded no

254

good for her or for anyone else, and to take herself off to the kitchen.

It was a huge, warm, well-furnished room, which at once took her fancy. She laid Honorine hastily in an armchair by the fireside and, lifting the lid of one of the pots, discovered some artichokes which were beginning to catch. She was just in time to save them from going up in smoke.

She tipped a ladleful of water into the pot, quenched the flames, then glanced about her and decided to lay the places for the meal on the long central table.

Sooner or later the argument would die down and then it would be up to her as a servant to have the meal ready.

She was still bewildered and distressed by the fantastic spectacle that had accompanied their arrival. A Protestant house was not perhaps the ideal place of refuge, but the merchant had treated her kindly. He did not appear to suspect her identity. Her pursuers would lose track of her. Who would think of expecting to find her as the servant of a Huguenot merchant in La Rochelle? She pushed open the door of a dark, cool larder and found what she was looking for, a store of food supplies carefully arranged and labelled.

"Is this your sevant?" asked the Lieutenant-General.

"Yes, my lord."

"Is she a member of the Reformed Church?"

"Yes, indeed."

"And what about the child? Her daughter, is she? Probably a bastard. In that case, she must be brought up in the Catholic faith. Has she been baptized?"

Angélique was carefully keeping her back turned and busying herself with putting apples into store. Her heart was pounding. She heard Maître Gabriel answer that he had just recently engaged this serving-woman, but that he would make a point of inquiring into her own situation and her child's and seeing to it that she was made aware of the law.

"And what about your daughter, Monsieur Berne, how old would she be?"

"Twelve."

"Ah, yes indeed. A recent decree stipulates that girls brought up in the Reformed religion are to have the right at the age of twelve to choose the religion to which they wish to belong."

"I think my daughter has already made her choice," murmured Maître Gabriel. "You had the opportunity to see that for yourself a moment ago."

"My dear good friend," said the King's Lieutenant dryly, "I am very sorry to see you taking my instructions—how shall I say?—a trifle caustically, I might even say carpingly. I regret to have to insist. All this is an extremely serious matter. I have just one piece of advice to give you: abjure, abjure. Believe now, before it's too late. You'll be saving yourself a great deal of trouble and misfortune."

Angélique could have wished that Monsieur de Bardagne would betake himself elsewhere to enjoy the pleasure of listening to the sound of his own voice. She was tired of having to keep her back turned and of poking the fire to keep herself in countenance. At last the voice died away on the stairs. Shortly afterwards, first the outside gate, then the gate leading into the courtyard banged, to the accompaniment of a stamping of knee-boots and a clatter of hooves, and the members of the family appeared one after the other in the kitchen and stood in line around the table. The old serving-woman—the one who had thrown the onions—pattered over to the fireplace like a mouse and uttered a sigh of relief on discovering that the meal she had so utterly forgotten in the excitement of the preceding events had come to no harm.

"Thank you, dearie," she whispered to Angélique. "If it hadn't been for you, the master would have given it to me good and proper."

The old serving-woman, Rebecca, laid down the main dish and stood at the head of the table while Pastor Beaucaire delivered a short address. Then they all sat down. Angélique remained standing awkwardly by the fireplace. Maître Gabriel called to her:

"Dame Angélique, come here and sit down. Our servants have always been treated as members of the

256

family. Your child, too, honours us by her presence. Innocence draws down upon a house the blessing of God. We'll have to find her a chair of the right size."

The young boy, Martial, jumped up and came back a moment later with a high chair that must have been stored away in the loft since the youngest child, the little seven-year-old boy, had put on his first pair of breeches. Angélique sat Honorine in it, and she gazed over the assembled company with an Olympian stare.

In the white candlelight she seemed to be carefully examining all these townspeople's faces that shone in the darkness above their bands and immaculate collars. Their black clothes were swallowed up in the shadows. The white wings of the women's coifs turned towards her like timid birds. Then her eyes rested on Pastor Beaucaire, who was sitting at the other end of the table, and she smiled her sweetest smile at him, accompanied by a few meaningful gestures and a volley of words that nobody understood very well, but that undoubtedly spelt friendship. Everyone was enchanted at her tactful choice: her friend was the most revered member of the assembled company.

"Lord, how lovely she is!" exclaimed young Abigail, the Pastor's daughter.

"Isn't she sweet!" said Séverine.

"Her hair is like the copper saucepans," Martial remarked.

They laughed with delight, while Honorine went on examining the Pastor with a look of pious admiration. The old man seemed touched and even a trifle flattered that he had been able to fire this young lady with so exclusive a love. He asked them to serve her first.

"In this household we treat little children like kings. Our Lord loved to welcome them."

He spoke of the parable Jesus had told when he had taken a little child and stood it in the midst of a group of adults beset with the cares of this world, saying, "Except ye become as little children, ye shall not enter into the Kingdom of Heaven."

Their faces grew serious again as they listened to him,

and, as was the custom in bourgeois households, the oldest boy cleared the table.

"Father," said Séverine, the twelve-year-old girl, her voice quivering with indignation, "what would you have done if they'd forced Uncle Lazarus to take communion? What would you have done?"

"No one can be forced to take communion, my girl. Even the Papists consider it a sacrilege and worthless in the eyes of God."

"But if they had, all the same, what would you have done? Would you have killed them?"

Her eyes were black and intense, in her chalk-white face, and her white bonnet, rather like a peasant's coif, gave her the appearance of a little old woman.

"Violence, my child—" began Maître Gabriel.

She twisted the corners of her big, unattractive mouth in a grimace.

"Naturally, you would have let them. And our house would have been dishonoured."

"Children are no judges in these matters," thundered Maître Gabriel, in a burst of sudden anger.

He was a peaceable-looking man whom one could easily have thought rather pleasure-loving. But in spite of his somewhat portly figure and his mild blue eyes, this idea could not have been further from the truth. Angélique was to learn on closer acquaintance that people from La Rochelle were as hard as nails beneath their cloak of lukewarm materialism. Then she remembered in a flash the belabouring that he himself had given her on the road to Sables-d'Olonne. He was the sort of man who seemed to have been born to sit before a dish of ortolans and savour the succulent delicacy, whereas in fact he was quite happy to dine on a hunk of bread and a clove of garlic, as good King Henry had done during his long stay in La Rochelle before setting out to hear Mass in Paris.

When the family had gone off into another room to read the Bible, Angélique, left alone with the old serving-woman, was overcome by depression.

"I really do not know whether the meal was sufficient for you," she said, "but my child has not had enough to eat. Even in the depths of the forest she always used to have more to eat than she has had here. And yet this family seems wealthy enough. Have the famine and poverty from Poitou spread as far as this?"

"What nonsense is this you are talking?" exclaimed the old woman in great indignation. "We folk in La Rochelle are the wealthiest of all the townsfolk in the whole Kingdom. And yet we've had a long road to travel. After the siege, you wouldn't have found a single radish in the place. Just you go and take a look at the warehouse, and the quaysides. The place is running over with goods and wine and salt and foodstuffs."

"But then why this cheese-paring?"

"Oh, I can see you aren't from these parts! You know, when you've lived through a siege like that, it becomes second nature to cut herrings in four pieces and count your spuds. You should have seen Monsieur Gabriel's father! What a fine man he was! You could have offered him stones to eat and he would never have noticed! The only thing he was fussy about was his wine. We've got some of the best Charentes down there in our cellars," she added, striking the tiled kitchen floor with her clog.

As she talked she cleared the dishes from the table and began to wash them up in a bowl of boiling water. Angélique stood watching her, her arms hanging at her sides. She certainly made a poor servant. But she was hungry. She even felt shivery as if she were sickening for something. The burn on her shoulder was suppurating and her bodice was sticking to it. Every movement she made reminded her of that degrading episode, of her fear, of her torments of anxiety. All these things had occurred so recently that she felt their cold shadow still hanging over her.

She lifted Honorine up. Honorine was not complaining. She never complained. Provided her mother's arms were there as a refuge, that seemed to be all she needed. Perhaps she was like these Protestants who only ask the bare essentials of life and who seem to be able not to worry about the rest. How they had smiled at the child, earlier on! Accursed, was she? Should she stay on here,

259

beneath this roof, or should she go away? And what refuge would she be heading for?

"Here's some curds and bread for the wee thing," said the serving-woman, putting a huge dish of it down on a corner of the table."

"But what if your master—"

"They won't say nothing, especially not about her. I know them. Afterwards you can put her to bed there."

She showed Angélique a huge high bed covered with eiderdowns that stood in an alcove off the kitchen.

"Isn't that where you sleep yourself?"

"No, I've got a straw pallet down below, by the store-rooms. I sleep there to keep a look-out for thieves."

When Angélique had given the child as much as she could eat and put her to bed, she went back to the fireside. She was going to find it impossible to sleep. She would have infinitely preferred to keep old Rebecca with her there. She sensed that the old woman had plenty to say for herself and might well offer her some useful hints for her future life here. Rebecca was poking idly at the glowing fire.

"Sit down, my beauty," she said, pointing to a stool opposite her. "Let's have a bite of crab. And a bit of St-Martin-de-Ré to wash it down. That'll make you feel better."

The crab she pulled out of the tank in the larder was as big as a plate. It wriggled slightly and its violet colouring gradually changed to a reddish pink. Rebecca turned it over with a deft twist of the poker, then broke it cleverly in two and handed half to Angélique.

"Copy me, hold your knife like this. And don't leave a single scrap, only the shell. You can eat everything in a crab."

The steaming flesh that came from its claw tasted of the sea, so different from anything that grew on land that it seemed to carry with it a longing for distant horizons and the poetry of the sea-coast.

"Try that for wine," Rebecca urged her. "It has a tang of seaweed to it."

She listened anxiously for a moment. "If Dame Anna were to walk in! She wouldn't half say a thing or two!"

But the big house was quiet. After some psalm-singing they had all gone off to bed. An oil lamp burnt at the sick old man's bedside. In the basement Maître Gabriel was doing his accounts. The kitchen fire crackled, and behind the closed shutters you could hear a low whisper—the sea.

"No, you certainly aren't from these parts," the old woman went on. "With eyes like yours, perhaps you're from Brittany? . . ."

"No, I'm from Poitou," said Angélique, and immediately wished she had not spoken.

When would she learn to think of the world as a hostile place, set about with traps?

"It's been a nasty business over there," the other woman remarked with a knowing air. "Let's hear a bit about it."

Her eyes glittered with curiosity.

"Oh, I know what it is," she went on as Angélique remained silent, "you've seen too much to dare to talk about it. You're like Jeanne or Madeleine the baker's cousins, or fat old Sarah from the village of Vernon, who's just about gone off her head with it all. Don't look at me like that, I've said nothing. And get on with your food. Go on, you get used to everything in the end! We all think we've been harder hit than anyone else, but there's always somebody round the corner who could tell you a worse tale of woe. War, sieges and famines, what do you expect when they get going except misery? And why should they pass *you* by? They've no particular reason to. They say, 'When the troops are marching, girls lose their virtue.' I lived through the siege and my three children died of starvation. I'll tell you about it. . . ."

Angélique, slightly shocked at this over-simplified view of things, thought to herself:

"Yes, but I was the Marquise du Plessis-Belliére."

Beneath her tall broad head-dress old Rebecca's face peered out, all wizened, with laughing eyes half-hidden amongst its folds. Even when she was talking seriously about tragic matters, her eyes still kept their look of amusement.

Angélique spoke up, this time out loud, and she was surprised to hear her own voice:

"I've held my child in my arms after they had slit his throat."

She shook once again from head to foot.

"Yes, my dear, I know how you feel. When you've lost a child you move into another world. You're not like other people any more. I had to lay three of them, I say, *three* little innocents, in their graves during the siege. I went through the siege, I'm telling you, my girl. I was twenty-five at the time and I had three boys; the oldest was seven. He went first, I thought he was asleep, and I didn't like to waken him because I reckoned he'd be less hungry if he stayed asleep. But towards the evening when I hadn't seen him stir I began to feel uneasy. . . . And as I drew nearer to the bed I began to realize what had happened. He'd been dead since the morning. Dead of starvation! As I said, my lass, you can't expect happiness to come from wars and sieges."

"But why didn't you try to leave the city?" asked Angélique indignantly. Couldn't you have done that?"

"Outside the city there were Monsieur de Richelieu's soldiers. And it wasn't for me to decide whether the city had been beaten or not. Every day we hoped the English would arrive. They came, then they went away again, and Monsieur de Richelieu built his sea-wall. Every day we expected something to happen, no one knew quite what. The soldiers were dying of hunger on the ramparts. My man used to go off there, all gloomy. He hadn't the strength to hold up his halberd any more and I used to see him leaning against the walls as he went along. Then one evening he didn't come home, and I knew what had happened. He'd fallen asleep on the ramparts—dead he was—and they tipped him into the common grave. They didn't dare throw the bodies over the walls in case the King's men should see that soon there would be no one left in the garrison. Hunger, that's something you can't describe to anyone who hasn't suffered from it. You can't make them understand. Especially if it went on for a long time; every time you went out into the street, you had hopes. . . . There must be

262

something. . . . You'd look everywhere, behind every milestone, beneath every stair, you'd look at the walls as if there might be something you could eat growing between the stones . . . one blade of grass perhaps. . . . What a windfall the day I heard mice under the floorboards! I spent hours lying in wait for them, and my eldest boy was very clever at catching them. A Flemish merchant had some six- or seven-year-old skins for sale. They were wonderful. The city bought eight hundred of them and distributed them amongst the soldiers and those of the citizens who were capable of carrying arms. We used to make wonderful jellies by boiling them up . . . I was able to get hold of some for the two children I still had. . . . And still nothing happened except that we all felt a bit worse every day. . . . There was nothing to see in the streets but ashen skeletons, and dead bodies that people could hardly drag to the sepulchre. Husbands carrying their wives on their shoulders, like a side of bacon; two young girls on a stretcher, their old father . . . mothers carrying their sons in their arms as if they were taking them to be baptized. . . ."

"But could you not have left the city and escaped from the famine?"

"Outside the fortifications the King's soldiers were waiting for us. They used to hang the men, and do whatever they felt like with the women. And as for the children . . . How could we know what became of them once in the soldiers' hands? And in any case, you couldn't leave the town. That would have meant admitting it was beaten. There are some things you just can't do. Goodness knows why. You'd just got to die with the city, or . . . I can't remember when it was that my second child died. I only remember that when delegates were sent from the town and knelt in front of Louis XII to hand over the keys of La Rochelle to him on a cushion, only the baby was still alive. . . . Everyone shouted and rushed around: 'Get to the doors . . . take the cats . . . fetch bread.' And I ran with them all . . . I thought I was running but I must have been dragging myself along like the others. We all looked like ghosts and had to lean on the walls as we went.

"All ghosts, you'd have thought. I looked at my youngest, with his big black eyes in his tiny face, and I said: 'It's all over, the delegates have gone to make our submission to the King. He will enter the city, and so will the bread! It's all over, the city has been beaten. But you've still got this one. At least you've got this one. They gave in in time to save this little waif,' said I to myself. A few days more and you'd have been a mother with empty arms. God be praised! Well, you'll never guess what happened!"

"No, I can't," said Angélique, looking at her with horror in her eyes, having forgotten that the siege had taken place forty years earlier.

"Well!—drink up your wine instead of letting it get all warm: you've got to drink it good and cold, this Island of Ré wine. Well, there were the soldiers at the gates handing out large round loaves of bread. It was still hot, straight from the camp ovens. They had been given orders to treat the valiant people of La Rochelle properly. Well, soldiers, you know, when you don't get at them, they're human beings just like us after all. . . . I even saw some of them crying as they looked at us. . . . Well, I ate and ate and so did the wee boy, holding his loaf of bread in both his hands like a squirrel. Then suddenly he fell dead. . . . He'd eaten too much too quickly. His head fell on to his shoulders, and that was the end. All I could do then was to bury him like the others. . . . And what do you think I did after that? I went mad, well, more or less mad. Well, my girl, there's one lesson we can learn from all this, that is that no matter what happens to you, no matter what you go through, life is like a spider, it ties up all the broken threads again, sooner than you'd think, and you can do nothing about it. . . ."

She stopped for a moment, and there came the sound of her knife scraping busily at the crab's shell.

"What kept me going at first," she went on, "was the food. Seeing all the things we'd been deprived of, there right under our noses, that gave me a sort of satisfaction, and I would forget my troubles. And then there was the sea to console me. I'd go out on to the cliffs and would

264

stand there for a long time. I could hear the sound of pickaxes coming from where they were pulling down the ramparts and the towers of La Rochelle, our proud city. But the sea was there and no one could take that away. That's what consoled me, my girl. And then a man fell in love with me. He was a Papist. There were so many of them now in La Rochelle! You'd have thought they grew out of the flagstones. But this one knew how to talk to a woman, and that was all I asked of him. We could have been married, but what a lot of fuss! I'd have had to be converted. Well, I didn't fancy that. He went off in a ship to Saint-Malo, to his family and his property. I never saw him again. Pooh! He'd left me with a child, a boy. . . . Oh well, I had to start to live again, didn't I. . . . It's children that give you strength.'

When Rebecca had ended her tale, she stood up to shake the bits of shell from her pinafore. Then she listened again, straining her ears.

"No, it's the sea I'm hearing. It's getting angry, the trollop . . . I'd say. Let's have a look."

At the back of the alcove where the bed stood, there was a window. She opened the shutters and the casement with its leaded mullions. A sudden gust of wind burst in, bearing with it the strong smell of seaweed and salt; the waves beating on the ramparts made such a noise that you had to shout to be heard.

The clouds took on an unearthly hue like molten lead as they scudded across the face of the moon. They were like dark exhalations, fluttering ink-black scarves. The unmoving black mass of the ramparts stood out against the light and shade of the stormy night sky. On the left rose the silhouette of a tower topped with a tall gothic pyramid, at whose summit a lamp burned. It was a beacon to guide ships on their way through the currents running in the strait between the islands. They saw a soldier carrying a halberd silhouetted against the sky. He was facing into the wind, his back bent. After he had revived the flame that they could see dancing under the pointed arch of the tower, he went down the spiral staircase again to shelter in the guard-room.

There was only a narrow alley-way between Maître Gabriel's house and the ramparts. A nimble lad could have jumped from the window on to the parapet for a lark. Rebecca explained to Angélique that she knew all the soldiers who came on the day or night watch at the Lantern Tower. For she used to shell her peas by the open window, or sit there darning stockings for the family, while they walked by yawning, and they would stop for a chat. She was the first to know what was going on in the port because the sentries in the Lantern Tower had to signal the arrival of ships carrying wine or salt from Holland, Flanders, Spain, England or America, in fact every ship, be she warship or merchantman, from abroad or belonging to La Rochelle. As soon as a white sail was sighted on the horizon just below the islands of Oléron or Ré, the lookout raised his horn to his lips. Then as the ship entered the harbour a bell would ring out; and the brokers, the merchants and the shipowners would rush around excitedly. Life was never dull in La Rochelle with all these ships that tipped out little bits of the whole world each day on to the quayside.

In the old days they had signalled a ship's arrival from the St Nicholas Tower, but now that this lovely tower had been partly knocked down, the honour had fallen to the Lantern Tower.

It was a piece of luck for Maître Gabriel's household. Rebecca could give thanks to God for guiding her steps to this house in search of work.

She shut the window and drew the shutters to. The silence returned, all the deeper by contrast with the raging of the storm. Angélique ran her tongue over her lips. They tasted cool and salty.

She noticed that Honorine had been wakened. Sitting up in bed, with her glossy hair hanging about her bare shoulders, she looked like a baby mermaid listening to the call of the sea. Her eyes had a faraway look in them and seemed full of a strange dreaminess. Angélique laid her down again and tucked her in. She remembered that Honorine had the sign of Neptune on her. The small seven-year-old boy was sitting on the bottom step of the flight that led to the other floors. Hidden in the shadows, he must have been listening avidly to the old servant's tales.

The old woman walked past him and shook her head several times.

"That lad took his mother's life when he came into the world. He don't get much love. . . ."

She began to go down her steps, muttering to herself:

". . . Suffering orphans, weeping mothers, that's how it is. . . . And it'll not be stopping that soon, either, this hurdy-gurdy of tears, it's me that's telling you."

The white point of her coif was lost in the darkness.

"You must go off to bed," Angélique said to the little boy.

He got up meekly. He had a sickly face. His nose was running. His dead-straight hair made him look even more pitiful.

"What's your name?" she asked him.

He did not answer and began to climb the stairs, brushing against the wall as he went. He was like a fearful rat. She realized when he had already reached the next floor, that he had not asked for a light, and she ran after him.

"Wait, dear, you can't see, you might fall."

She took him by the hand, a little cold, thin hand, and her own heart gave a thud. It reminded her of an infinitely sweet gesture she had not made for so long.

He went on up and she followed him. He seemed like a little scarcely-embodied and mysterious shadow that was drawing her on. It was he, now, who seemed to have taken her by the hand.

"Is this where you sleep?"

He nodded, looking at her this time, as if he did not really believe she was there. A sort of bed had been fixed up for him in the loft, more like a pallet. The straw mattress obviously was not shaken out very often, the sheets were grubby and the blankets very scant for the time of the year. In winter it must have been icy up there. The moon shone fitfully through a round skylight, lighting up, with its pale face, the heterogeneous collection of chests and unwanted furniture that lay beneath the huge cross-beams.

267

Opposite the bed there was even a big cracked mirror.

"Do you like it up here?" she asked the child. "Aren't you cold, or afraid? Do you sometimes hear things moving about?"

She caught his frightened glance.

"Of course, there are rats," she told herself, "and he is frightened.

She began to undress him. These thin shoulders she felt beneath her hands, they were Florimond's delicate body when it was small; these closed lips were Cantor's, who spoke so little but would sing in secret; this nostalgic look was Charles-Henri's as he dreamt of his mother.

He seemed surprised that anyone should help him to undress. He wanted to take his own clothes off. He folded them and laid them on a stool with the greatest care. He seemed even thinner, standing in his white shirt.

"This child is dying of hunger."

She took him in her arms and clasped him to her. Tears were flowing from her eyes without her even being aware of the fact. She had never been anything but a perfunctory mother, she told herself. She had protected them from cold and hunger as animals do, because they were small, but she had never known and never sought the joy of hugging them to her, of feasting her eyes on them, of becoming absorbed in their lives. She had only become aware of the ties that bound them to her since they had been so cruelly torn from her. The open wound still bled, deepening her sense of loss at the things that might have been and that she had neglected.

"Oh, my sons, my sons!" They had been born too soon. They had been an encumbrance in her life. She had resented their existence at times because it had made her turn away from her own destiny to look after theirs. She had not been ripe for such subtle joys. A woman must fulfil herself as a woman before she can be a mother.

She tucked the little boy up in his bed and smiled at him in case her tears worried him. After kissing him good-night she went downstairs.

In the back kitchen, standing by the bed, she took off

her top bodice, then brushed her hair thoroughly. Now she no longer wanted to go away. The house under the ramparts, with the sea before it, spelt promise and protection to her.

CHAPTER 30

THE NEXT day, Madame Anna, not without a certain solemnity and a few appropriate words, handed her a Bible bound in black vellum.

"I noticed, my girl, that you do not join in the responses to our prayers. No doubt you have allowed your faith to grow cool. Here is the Book of Books wherein all women of faith may find that spirit of meekness, fidelity and devotion that their state demands."

When Angélique found herself alone again, she examined the Bible, then went off in search of Maître Gabriel. The clerk informed her that he was on the ground floor, in the store-rooms where he kept his books.

If you went through the courtyard and down a step, you came upon two or three big rooms where the merchant stored his most precious commodities, including his samples of Charentes wine and his brandy. He was one of the most important suppliers of brandy to Holland and England. As it happened, an English captain was just taking his leave after placing an order and, no doubt, sampling the wares. A smell of brandy hung in the air and flies were buzzing around the two glass goblets they had been drinking from.

The English captain passed stiffly by her, but nevertheless took the trouble to raise his faded hat to Angélique and to utter something complimentary about Maître Gabriel's charming wife. The latter, not even lifting his head from his book, said stiffly in English:

"Not my wife, my servant. . . ."

"Oh yes!" said the Englishman, greeting her again with a delighted look.

Angélique, who did not know any English, had not followed what had been said and had made no attempt

269

to understand. She was too preoccupied with the reactions that might follow her confession.

"Maître Gabriel," she said, summoning all her courage, "I must clear up a misunderstanding. I should have done it sooner. I am not a member of the Reformed Church, as you and your family seem to imagine. I ... I am a Catholic."

The merchant started and seemed very put out.

"But then why did you let them mark you with the fleur-de-lis?" he cried. "You should have told them you were a Catholic. You would have been spared that terrible fate. The law is quite clear on this point: any Protestant woman guilty of a misdemeanour must be branded with the fleur-de-lis and flogged. Thanks to the fact that the judge at Sables was a member of my Church, I was able to spare you the flogging. But he could not let you off the other part of your sentence because you had been caught in the company of dangerous thieves. Do you know that three of them have been hanged and the others sentenced to the galleys?"

"I didn't know that. Poor fellows!"

"Doesn't the news affect you more than that! They were, after all, your companions...."

"I scarcely knew them."

Maître Gabriel threw up his hands and spilt a great blot of ink over his calculations.

"Why on earth didn't you explain all this in time, you silly girl!"

He carefully blotted the spilt ink and wiped his pen.

"When a Catholic girl is marked with the fleur-de-lis it's a sign that she has committed some dreadful crime, that she is a murderer, or a prostitute, or a thief. If you are discovered you stand the risk of being sent to prison or to Canada as a 'settler's woman.' Why did you not say something before it was too late?"

He scrutinized her carefully, then said softly:

"Perhaps you did not want them to ask you too many questions?"

"Yes, you are right there, Maître Gabriel, I didn't. At that moment I could think of nothing but my daughter. I did not know at the time that you had rescued her. I let them do what they wanted with me, without fully realizing what was happening. ... And now it's too late, the brand will remain till the end of my life. But only you know about it, Maître Gabriel, and if you don't give me away ..."

"I have already taken you into my household. Nobody will attempt to harm you for as long as you remain beneath my roof. That is the ancient law of hospitality."

"So you are not going to send me away?"

"Why should I send you away?"

"I shall do my best not to fail you, Maître Gabriel, but ... I must say right now ..."

"I know what you are going to tell me," he growled; "that you have no intention of being converted. But there's nothing to stop you reading the Bible. Open it every day—any page will do. Every time you do, you will find an answer to your questions. As you read you will be reminded of a forgotten land and your heart will be uplifted."

He handed the book to her.

The sunshine—the sunshine of the south—was streaming into the courtyard. In the centre a palm-tree grew, its trunk all hairy and bearing the sharp wheels of its palms aloft against a clear and limpid blue sky. Against the wall, by a bench, stood a Spanish lilac and a bed of hollyhocks with flowers as big as cabbages, and there were some brown and yellow wallflowers growing in antique jars. In one corner there was a small pond with a fountain, nestling beneath a shell-shaped dome. The sound of its splashing waters created an exotic atmosphere in this courtyard that was half patio, half provincial garden. And the whole place was shut away from the dangers of the outside world by the tall carriage gates.

Angélique went back to fetch the glasses that had been left on the table so that she could rinse them out in the kitchen.

"Maître Gabriel, I'm sorry to bother you again, but is Madame Anna responsible for the running of the house? Shall I go to her for my orders?"

"My aunt has never been capable of telling a sauce-
271

pan from a hat," he growled. "Whenever she has anything to do with the running of the house, things go from bad to worse, and in any case she hates it."

"Then who is to organize everything?"

"Why not you?" he said peering at her over his glasses. "You seem to me to be a capable woman. All I expect is that there should be something to eat in the pot and no dust on the furniture. Come to me for money when you need to buy things. Here, here's some now."

He handed her a purse. Like most men, he was obviously irritated by these domestic matters. But he called her back all the same.

"Now be careful. I expect detailed accounts. Can you write and reckon up?"

"Yes, sir," Angélique replied.

The evening came, Angélique had fed the whole household, beneath Aunt Anna's puzzled gaze, on cabbage soup with bacon in it, grilled fish rubbed with herbs and dripping with butter, an apple cake and a salad. She had rubbed the copper pans in the kitchen till they shone, had polished the beautiful bedroom furniture, and had managed to get a smile out of little Laurier by telling him the story of Cinderella. Although she was worn out she felt calm and realized that she had once again come to terms with life. Such critical issues as knowing whether she would finally manage to evade the King's pursuit were forced into the background, and it seemed far more important to ensure that the small boy slept well that night.

She went up to see him several times in his attic. She cajoled him, told him stories and scolded him a little, but every time she crept stealthily up there, hoping to find him asleep, he was always sitting up on his mattress watching his own reflection in the mirror.

The fourth time she found him like this, she could bear it no longer. For far too long, perhaps for years, the little chap must have slept only by fits and starts from sheer exhaustion, waking up with a jump when he heard the scratching of rats, seeing the frightening shapes of the jumbled furniture looming about him, thinking about matters he ill understood, those gloomy psalms they

272

made him sing, and the words people said when they looked at him: "That child cost his mother her life. . . ."

Every night must be one long ordeal for him, lying there far from his familiar surroundings and the warmth of other people—a cold, sad journey that reached its end only when dawn peeped through the skylight. Only then, perhaps, would he slip into a quieter sleep. And that would not last long, for Aunt Anna woke everyone up at five at the latest.

Angélique opened a cupboard, took out a pair of sheets and went into a small room she had noticed. No one seemed to sleep here. Laurier could sleep happily in this room: the kitchen was close by, and the sound of Uncle Lazarus coughing in the night would serve to remind him that someone was near, and he would be able to hear the ticking of the big clock on the landing too. For the first few nights Angélique would give him a night-light.

With nimble hands she made up the bed and half opened its lovely silk brocade curtains. It was Dutch silk. Angélique could appreciate the value of everything in the house, perhaps even better than her hosts, who seemed both to seek and to despise such luxuries.

In the kitchen she took a warming-pan from the wall, opened it, and quickly threw in a handful of live coals. As she went back into the room, she noticed that the other door that led into it from Maître Berne's room was open.

He was standing on the threshold, with his finger in a prayer-book.

"Now what do you want in here, Dame Angélique? I must remind you that it is past midnight. The terms of your employment do not stipulate that you should stay up till so late an hour."

His courteous tone did not quite hide a certain annoyance. When Maître Berne had finished his accounts and gone to his room to meditate on the Holy Scriptures, he liked to feel that everyone in the house was asleep and not wandering about on domestic errands.

Angélique ran the warming-pan several times over the cool sheets.

"Forgive me, Maître Gabriel, I have taken note of what you say and shall try to abide by it. But I want to get this empty bed ready for little Laurier who is not at all comfortable up there in the attic."

She felt, rather than saw, for he had his back turned, the flash of anger that leapt to the merchant's grey eyes.

"This room is not to be disturbed. It belonged to my wife before she died."

Angélique faced him. He seemed considerably upset, furious in fact. She said gently:

"I quite understand. But I could find no other room to put him in."

Maître Gabriel seemed to be searching for an answer to a most difficult problem.

"Who?"

"Laurier."

"Why do you want to put him here?"

"His bed is up in the attic. He's frightened up there all on his own and can't get to sleep. I thought that if I were to put him down here, he'd be happier."

"What an idea! He must just get used to it. Do you want to turn him into a milksop? I had to sleep in that attic when I was a lad."

"And weren't you afraid of the rats?"

"Yes, I was. But I got used to them."

"Well, he's *not* getting used to them. Every night he sleeps badly, either very little or not at all. That's one of the reasons he is so thin and sickly-looking."

"He's never complained."

"Children hardly ever do complain, especially when they've no one to complain to," said Angélique dryly.

"A boy's got to be tough. You are talking like a woman."

"Not a woman, a mother . . ." she said looking at him earnestly. His eyes grew dim and heaved a deep sigh.

"I had sworn to myself that no one would ever sleep in that bed again: that was where my wife breathed her last."

"You should be greatly honoured for your faithfulness,
274

Maître Gabriel, but don't you think that she herself would have been pleased to see her child here?"

The merchant sighed again.

"Oh, I don't know ... You are turning the whole house upside down. I thought the boy slept with his elder brother. But it's true, that attic ... I must say my memories of it are none too happy. Go on then, do as you think best."

Angélique knew her way to the loft all too well to need a candle. She went up the stairs four at a time.

"I've come to fetch you," she said to Laurier, who was still sitting up and as wide awake as a small owl.

"Where are you taking me?"

"Where you'll be comfortable. Near your father. ..."

She carried him carefully down the stairs. Laurier was entranced by the warm room and by his father's presence. He sniffed at the familiar smells of the lower floors. From his bed he could just see, on the opposite side of the landing, the glow of the fire in the big kitchen. He was so astonished that he could not stop talking.

"Am I going to sleep here? Every night?"

"Yes, your father thinks that now you are such a big boy you need a larger bed."

"Oh, thank you, Father."

Angélique went off to get the night-light. When she returned carrying the red glass bowl, Laurier was fast asleep. His tiny head stood out against the pillow. He seemed to be lost in the vast bed, but his face was transformed by an expression of innocent well-being.

Maître Gabriel stood at the head of the bed and watched him, deep in thought. Angélique bent down and gently stroked the child's pale brow.

"Little man!" she said tenderly.

She looked up at the merchant.

"Don't hold this against me. I couldn't bear to see him unhappy."

"Don't worry, Dame Angélique. I think that things are well as they are."

He added, after a moment's hesitation:

"And yet, they aren't really. This evening, as I was

275

studying the Scriptures, I took myself to task for not having treated your fairly. I should have given you some of your wages in advance."

"You are not obliged to, Maître Gabriel. I know that a servant must give satisfaction for a month before receiving her salary."

"But you arrived her with absolutely nothing. And it is written in the Bible: 'Thou shalt not oppress an hired servant that is poor and needy, whether he be of thy brethren, or of the strangers that are in thy land within thy gates: at his day thou shalt give him his hire, neither shall the sun go down upon it; for he is poor and setteth his heart upon it.' So here is what I have decided to give you."

He handed her a purse that he had taken from amongst the folds of his clothes.

"Although it's a bit after sundown," he added.

A touch of humour occasionally belied his solemnity. Angélique thought that had he been born into another religion, in another city, he might well have become a witty epicure like the Chevalier de Méré.

"I am not oppressed in your household, Maître Gabriel," she said with a smile. "Have no fear, I shall not cry against you unto the Lord. I shall never forget your kindness."

As she went off, Angélique began to understand why a kind of familiarity, a mutual understanding, had immediately sprung up between herself and the merchant, as it does between people who have known one another before in different circumstances. Now she became certain that she must have met him somewhere before. Where? When? When was it that he had leaned towards her with that quiet open smile that sometimes lit up his cold, reserved face?

CHAPTER 31

FOR A LONG time she was troubled by the thought that she had met Maître Gabriel before, then she forgot about it.

In the evenings when Aunt Anna and the guests had gone off to their rooms after prayers, Maître Gabriel would occasionally indulge in a simple pleasure. He would go to his room and take down one of his many long Dutch pipes from the wall. He would fill it carefully with tobacco, then would come back into the kitchen for an ember to light it.

After that he would lean against the door-frame smoking and would watch with half-closed eyes through the smoke, the big family room, the servants coming and going, the children and the two household cats. On these evenings the children knew he was in an excellent mood, and they would ask him questions and tell him about their doings. For some time now Laurier had also joined in. He was transformed, was developing a sharp, bolder look, and stood up for himself when Martial saw fit to make sarcastic comments.

One evening as Angélique had him on her knees and was gently stroking his hair, she noticed the merchant looking at them pensively through the trails of blue smoke. She decided to forestall the reproach she read in his look.

"You think I spoil him too much for a boy, don't you? . . . But look how much stronger he is growing. His cheeks are pinker. Children need affection if they are to grow properly, Maître Gabriel, just as flowers need water. . . ."

"I would not deny what you say, Dame Angélique, I realize that your loving care is making a fine child out of the little stunted wretch that I admit I hated to set eyes on. I have sinned by my injustice, and by my ignorance too. I'm better at judging a good brandy or a Canadian fur than at knowing what a child might need. What intrigues me is that you are so loving to him, and yet show so little affection to your own child. Oh, of course you look after her all right, but I have never seen you kiss her, or smile at her or even give her a hug."

"What! Is that true?" Angélique exclaimed, going red to the roots of her hair.

And she looked in utter dismay at Honorine who was sitting in front of her plate of gruel.

They had left her sitting alone at the table because she was a slow eater. For some time now she had been taking hours over her meals, sitting there staring into space, her spoon in her hand. Angélique had attributed this loss of appetite to a dislike of being cooped up, for the child had always lived out of doors. Could it be that Honorine was suffering from a sense of neglect? What comparisons was she making behind those bright, wise little eyes? She often flew into violent rages that upset Angélique, who was astonished and indignant to find herself pitted against this little will. She would lose her temper, and Honorine, incensed, would say: "Nasty Mummy!" Then Angélique would put her to bed or hand her over to Rebecca for whom she had a soft spot. Angélique had let herself become absorbed by Laurier, for in him she saw her little boys, her real children. Honorine had not yet become a real child of hers.

"Maître Gabriel is right," she said to herself. "My daughter . . . I have accepted her existence in my life, but I cannot admit to loving her. He just doesn't know! That's an impossible thing to ask of me. If he knew, he'd understand. . . ."

"You have taken a fancy to my son, and I to your daughter," said Maître Gabriel, half smiling. "I shall never forget that little thing, all alone there asleep beneath the tree, who held out her hands to me when I woke her up, and babbled out all her sad story in my ear."

Angélique winced. She seemed so upset that Maître Gabriel cursed himself for having spoken. He became shy, like all men who feel embarrassed by emotion, cleared his throat and went off, apparently suddenly remembering something he had to do. Laurier went after him. Every evening Maître Gabriel allowed him to wander around amongst the stocks in the store-rooms.

Angélique was left alone with Honorine. She had a feeling that the next minutes were going to be crucial, and that the whole future course of her life would be decided by what she said and did. It was strange that the cause of all this commotion and anxiety was this "little thing," as Maître Gabriel had called her, sitting there with a look of dreamy haughtiness about her. Angélique thought she was looking at her shrewish sister Hortense. Although she had been ugly and nasty, she had always behaved as if she were a princess. Honorine, sitting here in her high chair, straight-backed and uncomplaining, brought back that forgotten image to her mind. She had the same way of holding her neck and her head, haughtily aloft. Hortense, even as a baby, had been small and thin, whereas Honorine appeared chubby, broad-backed and sturdy. But you could see the family resemblance, without a shadow of doubt, in her movements and in her black, penetrating eyes. Angélique found that the memory did not annoy her, in fact she felt relieved. She held out her arms to Honorine.

"Come here."

Honorine, snatched from her dreams, looked at her thoughtfully, then she broke into a smile that stretched from ear to ear.

"No!" she said, hiding under the table.

"Come on, do!"

"No!"

Angélique had to go after her and draw her out of her hiding-place, which proved quite difficult.

"My word, she's as heavy as lead...."

She stared anxiously into her daughter's face.

"You are a red-head, but you are lovely ... my child! Whether I like it or not, I did bring you into this world. And above all, you are here! You are tied to me by the very horror I felt at knowing you were inside me, by that complicity between the two of us, both helpless, both struggling to tear ourselves from our monstrous fates, from that implacable destiny, that blind destiny that would have it that we should be mother and daughter. Oh, my love!"

Angélique put her lips to the cool cheek. The smell of baby brought back to her the smell of the forest, during those extraordinary years of the Poitou revolt. She had transfused herself into the child to melt the dry hatred that inhabited her heart. Through all the massacres and the ambushes, Honorine had been there: Honorine who used to open her innocent eyes as she lay in Father de Lesdiguière's arms; Honorine who had called Angélique across the wintry forest and torn her away from the horrible fascination of that clearing full of hanged men.

Angélique shuddered and looked around, as if she had been dreaming. She was in Maître Gabriel's kitchen, in La Rochelle, and was sitting by the dying fire with Honorine on her knee. And she was clutching the child desperately to her.

"My life!"

The flood of love, so long dammed up, almost unnoticed, gushed out with the strength of a spring that has at last forced its way out into the clear air from the darkness of the earth.

"I never knew I loved you so much. And why shouldn't I love you?"

Why not? Her mind sought a reason, but failed to find one any more. Nothing, in fact, remained of her past life. The whole fabric of it had collapsed into a shadowy void. Honorine's innocent charm, the vitality that shone from her round face, her happy smile when she saw her mother—she who was her whole world—bending over her to kiss her, the sensation of physical possession that Angélique felt for her—all these things had conspired to blot out, as if behind an impenetrable curtain, any reasons she had once had for hating this little life.

How quickly the mind forgets!

The body takes longer. Sometimes still Angélique would hear Isaac de Rambourg's horn in a nightmare, and occasionally she felt her wrists and ankles shackled again beneath those brutal hands that had held her to the ground.

But when she woke, she could see the light from the flame that burned at the top of the Lantern Tower to guide the ships, dancing on the wall opposite. Honorine was asleep at her side. Angélique would look long at her and feel calm again, marvelling at this one treasure that she still had and which made her poor smashed and hunted existence worth while.

"Sleep, dear heart, sleep, my child, my very life . . .
your mother is here. Don't be frightened any more."

Since she had learnt that Angélique was a Papist,
Séverine regarded her with pious horror.

"That girl has been sent here by the Company of the
Blessed Sacrament to spy on us, I'm sure!" she would
declare in a stage whisper. Aunt Anna agreed.

"You are quite possibly right, my poor child. Let us
pray to the Lord to save us from her machinations!"

"What a couple of sour-pusses!" Angélique thought.
Her patience was sorely tried.

Séverine watched her wherever she went, trying to
catch her out. She held herself very stiff all the time,
imitating her aunt's deportment, and sometimes would
burst out in a mocking tone:

> "The sinful man, the wicked man,
> Walks with lies upon his lips.
> He winks his eye, speaks with his foot
> And talks to people with his hands. . . .

Isn't that right, Aunt?"

This was the way Angélique discovered that the
ladies thought some exuberance on her part misplaced.
. . .

"If you had been to Court, Séverine," she commented
one day, "you'd know that no well-educated person
stands the way you do, as straight as a pikestaff, making
stiff little movements like a puppet; you must learn how
to move gracefully."

"The Court is a place of perdition," said Séverine,
put out.

It was Angélique's turn to roar with laughter. The
big girl went off red with anger.

But she had her vulnerable points. Like all girls of her
age, she was very fond of babies, and longed to be in
Honorine's good books. Rather awkwardly she would try
to pick her up, would follow her about everywhere and
try to feed her and help her to get dressed.

"Leave me alone! Leave me alone!" Honorine would shout with the furious look of an outraged empress.

Angélique felt sorry for Séverine who would walk away humbly. It was hard to persuade her irascible offspring to be nicer to the girl.

Honorine had very decided likes and dislikes. By and large all members of the male sex found favour in her eyes. She was sweetly deferential towards Laurier. Maître Gabriel was an object of respectful admiration. Pastor Beaucaire continued to receive all the favours, whenever he put in an appearance. But her idol was Martial. He had carved a little box for her with his knife, to keep all her treasures in: her buttons, glass beads, stones and chicken feathers. . . . The little girl had a strong streak of the mother about her. When Angélique saw her toddling off with her little box under one arm and her kitten under the other, she would think of the small coffer inlaid with mother-of-pearl in which she used once to keep the souvenirs she had collected during her stormy career.

Honorine's relationships with the female of the species were more complicated. Once beyond the safe age, a woman inspired her with the greatest tenderness; Rebecca and all other grandmothers were entitled to her smiles. With middle-aged women, the baby observed a strict neutrality. Things began to go wrong when it came to young girls, and, as for her contemporaries, since they were rivals, Honorine could not stand them. Maître Carrère the lawyer's youngest daughter Ruth, who was three, very nearly had her eyes scratched out. Taken all in all, this plump little doll Honorine, reeling about in her skirts with a purposeful look, kept the household on its toes.

Often she would give a peculiar cry which Angélique had come to recognize. It meant that Honorine felt shut in and wanted to see the sea. Once on the beach, the world ceased to exist except for the waves, the seaweed and the marvellous seashells. She looked like a pumpkin with her skirts all rolled up as she paddled about delightedly. Angélique would follow her and exchange a few words with the mussel-gatherers.

Beneath the ramparts the sea uncovered huge rocky areas, all bristling with seaweed, with pools of clear water beneath them where crabs hid. A horde of boys frolicked there, along with the seagulls. Martial could often be found amongst them, more often than necessary, having deserted his school desk. Martial was causing his father a great deal of anxiety. He was good at his work but preferred to go off on raids with his gang of friends, amongst whom could be found most of the rowdiest lads of the district: Carrère the lawyer's two oldest boys, Jean and Thomas, and Joseph, the doctor's son.

Maître Gabriel was very sorry that the lad could not be under the strict discipline of a boarding-school. So he had decided to send his oldest son to Holland. There at least he would learn how to run a business properly.

Angélique was saddened by the thought of this inevitable departure. Martial reminded her in many ways of her son Florimond. She could detect, hidden beneath his smiling offhandedness, the uneasiness of an adolescent walking across the quicksands, who, after discovering what sort of a world he is going to have to live in, finds that he does not belong there any more. It was this terrible discovery that had made Florimond leave his mother and take flight in an attempt to find some corner of the earth where he could be himself without the double curse of his parents hanging over him.

Martial would also, one day, run off, and so would these young boys who were tied to the condemned shores by the incredible blindness of their parents.

They were sitting that day on the top of the rock, leaning towards one another and so absorbed that they did not hear her coming towards them. The wind was blowing their long hair about, and their open shirts showed their young chests. She was seized with anguish at the thought of the machine that was set up already, cowering like a monster in the very heart of the city, ready to crush them.

Martial was reading in a carefully modulated voice:
" '... It is never cold in the American Islands. Ice is
283

unknown there, and it would be like a miracle to see any there. There are not four seasons equal in length but all different from one another, as in Europe; there are only two. During one of them, from April to November, rain is very common, and the other is the season of droughts. Nevertheless the earth is always pleasantly green and is almost always decked with flowers and fruit. . . .' "

"Do they have vines over there?" a lad with straw-colored hair broke in, "because my father is a refugee from Charentes. He is a vine-grower. And what good would it be our going off to a country where there were no vines?"

"Yes, there are vines," Martial affirmed triumphantly. "Listen to what comes next. 'Vines grow very well in these islands and apart from a sort of wild vine, which grows unaided in the woods and bears fine big grapes, in many places there are cultivated vines like those in France, but they bear twice a year and sometimes even more frequently. . . .' "

The geography lesson continued with descriptions of bread-fruit trees, paw-paw trees whose branches bear a kind of melon, and the coconut with its delicious vegetable milk. " '. . . The soapberry tree produces a liquid soap for washing and bleaching linen, the calabash tree provides pots and utensils ready-made for use . . .' "

"And what colour are the inhabitants of these warm islands? Are they red-skinned and do they wear feathers, the way they do in New France?"

Martial flipped through the pages of the little book, and said that he could not find any information on that subject. With one accord they turned towards Angélique who was sitting near by with Honorine on her knees.

"Do you know what colour the people are in those islands, Dame Angélique?"

"I think they are black," she said, "because they've been taking slaves from Africa there for a long time now."

"But the Caribbees, they're not black," young Thomas

Carrère volunteered. He was a great one for listening to the tales of the sailors in the port.

Martial cut the discussion short:

"We've only got to ask Pastor Rochefort when we see him."

"Did you say Pastor Rochefort?"

Angélique was startled.

"Do you mean the famous explorer who wrote a book about the American Islands?"

"The one I'm reading to my friends. Look!"

He showed her the recently published newly-bound copy and added, lowering his voice:

"You run the risk of being fined fifty pounds and being sent to prison if you are found with this story of his travels, because it seems that the book is making the Protestants want to emigrate. We must be very careful. . . ."

Angélique thumbed through the book with its naïve illustrations of the trees and animals found in those distant lands.

From the void of her past a forgotten vision came back to her, a vision that had always seemed inexplicable and yet stamped with the seal of destiny: Pastor Rochefort's visit to Monteloup when she had been about ten years old.

This dark and solitary horseman had turned up during a storm that felt like the end of the world and had spoken of unknown and strange things, of red-skinned men with feathers for hair, of virgin lands inhabited by prehistoric monsters.

But at the time—and that had been over twenty years earlier—the odd feeling she had had about his visit had not been caused by his strangely sudden appearance nor by the exotic things he had spoken of. No. He had come as a Messenger of Fate, formidable and ill-understood, calling from afar.

Her older brother Josselin had heard the call as it came to him from the far ends of the earth, and he had answered it there and then. He had left his family and his native land, and no one had ever known what had become of him.

"But surely Pastor Rochefort must be dead by now?" she said in a voice that sounded to her weak and unsteady.

"Oh no! He's very old, but he still travels."

The young boy went on more quietly:

"He's in La Rochelle at the present moment. No one must know who is hiding him, or he'd be arrested straight away. Would you be interested to see him and hear him speak, Dame Angélique?"

And as she nodded, he thrust something into her hand.

It was a roughly-made lead disc, on which could be made out a cross with a dove over it.

"With this tag you'll be able to get into the meeting that's going to take place near the hamlet of Jouvex," Martial explained to her. "There you'll be able to see and hear Pastor Rochefort. He'll be speaking, because that's what the meeting's for. There'll be more than ten thousand of us there. . . ."

CHAPTER 32

THE YOUNG LAD had exaggerated when he said that ten thousand of the faithful would be present at the "Assembly in the Desert" to which Angélique was going.

Many had stayed at home through fear, and the dried-up salt-pan surrounded with dykes upon which large heaps of salt still stood, could only have held a few thousand people at the outside.

They had chosen the disused salt-workings because they formed an isolated gorge, bounded by two rocky spurs which hid the undulation from people crossing the marshy plain around La Rochelle. The sea was near by and its rumble mingled with the buzz of voices. Greetings were exchanged as people arrived and remarks passed back and forth as they found somewhere to sit.

A semi-circle of limestone blocks made a crude amphitheatre around a small table where the preacher was to speak.

"That's the pulpit, and the other one they're carrying is the communion table," Martial explained.

He had insisted on accompanying her, proud of having "recruited" her. She had come with him in the local baker's cart, his son and apprentice. Anastasius, being another friend of the Berne boy. Aunt Anna and Séverine, who had come in another cart with the paper-merchant and his wife and daughter, gave a sudden start when they noticed "that Papist woman." They could be seen from afar, conferring with Maître Gabriel, who was escorting them on horseback, no doubt pointing out to him how dangerous her presence was here. The merchant shrugged his shoulders. The crowd moved and they disappeared from sight. A pewter dish was carried in, covered with a white cloth beneath which there seemed to be a round loaf, and next, two pewter cups. At the end of the table someone placed a stone jug which was likewise covered with a cloth.

Angélique had been very hesitant about going to this meeting. She ran the risk of the direst penalties if such a thing should ever get about. But almost everyone there was running some risk, some of ruinous fines, some of imprisonment, and some even of death, like the "converts" who slipped sadly in, ashamed to meet their erstwhile co-religionists, but unable to overcome the anguish of mind that had assailed them since their abjuration.

All these hunted people wore black or dark colours. One of La Rochelle's most powerful shipowners, Manigault, on the other hand, looked very dignified in a plum-coloured velvet costume, with black stockings and silver-buckled shoes. Everyone thought he looked very smart, with his Negro servant Siriki following behind. He was holding his son Jeremy by the hand. He was very proud of this charming cherub with the long golden curls whom his four sisters and his mother worshipped like a young king.

Monsieur Carrère the lawyer was there with his family in full strength. Madame Carrère's ample curves betokened her eleventh pregnancy. A few noblemen

287

could be recognized by their swords. They stood about in groups deep in conversation.

"Make way! Make way for Madame de Rohan!"

Some valets carried an upholstered armchair to the front row, and an old lady, somewhat overbearing in manner, took her place in it, her hand like an owl's claws, resting on her silver-topped stick.

The place was quite full now, but everything went on in an orderly manner. Young men passed round cloth bags into which people put the contribution they were expected to make towards the ministers' upkeep. Most of the people were sitting on the ground amidst the sticky salt deposits. The wealthiest amongst them and those who had thought to do so had brought cushions or sacks, and some had charcoal-burning foot-warmers, for it was very cold and windy. Out on the heath stood the participants' horses, donkeys and mules, tethered to the sparse tamarisks or watched by boys anxious to make themselves useful. These boys were also acting as look-outs to warn the people if the King's dragoons should appear.

A hymn rose into the air and was taken up by the dull booming voices of the crowd.

Three figures dressed in black, wearing colossal round hats, also black, walked towards the centre where the tables stood.

One of them was Pastor Beaucaire. But Angélique eagerly examined the tallest and oldest of the group. In spite of the white hair that encircled his tanned, wrinkled face, she recognized the "Man in Black," that legendary traveller of her childhood. His wandering life and the dangers he had faced during his many journeys appeared to have kept his body very upright.

The third pastor was a thick-set red-faced character, with a sharp, authoritative look. It was he who spoke first in a powerful voice that carried well.

"My brothers, the Lord has seen fit to loose my bonds, and it is with a deep sense of joy that I am able once again to lift up my voice amongst you. My person is of no importance. I am only God's servant, but I am burdened by an immense task: that of caring for my little flock, and that means all of you, Protestants of La Rochelle, who seek the path of salvation amidst the pitfalls that grow more dangerous with each day that passes. ..."

From what he said Angélique realized that this must be Pastor Tavenez, who was in charge of the Colloquy of La Rochelle, the union of all the Protestant churches in the city. He himself had just been released from prison, where he had been held for six months.

"Some of you have come to me saying: 'Should we take up arms, as once our forefathers did?' This is a question which perhaps many of you have asked yourselves secretly, yielding to the dangerous temptation of hatred which is not always as wise a counsellor as prudence. I shall begin, therefore, by telling you my opinion: I am not in favour of violence. Far be it from me to minimize the heroism of our fathers who faced the horrors of the siege in 1628, but did our faith rise from that immense and proud rebellion any the stronger? Alas! Not at all! At the end there was hardly a single Huguenot left in La Rochelle, and our faith almost departed for ever from within these walls!"

Pastor Tavenez spoke in this vein for a long while. He called to mind the national synod that had been summoned to meet at Montélimar in the following year, during which a report would be drawn up listing the administrative and other types of interference to which French Huguenots were subjected. This report was to be handed to the King himself. He closed with a final appeal for confidence and calm, citing himself and Pastor Beaucaire as examples.

The old Duchesse de Rohan had several times manifested her impatience during this long discourse. She had tossed her head and banged on the ground with her stick. Such bourgeois counsel was not at all to her liking. But she must have realized that she was too old to play the rebel, so she breathed a deep sigh and held her peace.

A murmur of approval rose from the crowd. Only one man stood up, a peasant with a low-cut fringe, clasping his hat in both hands across his white shirt.

"I'm from the region of Jarans in the Gâtine. The King's dragoons came to our hamlet. They set our church on fire. Then they took my hams, my bread, my two cows, my donkey and my wife. So, sometimes, I feel that if I could only take an axe and kill the lot of them, I'd feel a bit better! ..."

A few laughs, soon stifled, had greeted the unfortunate man's enumeration of his losses.

The unhappy peasant looked about him in an attempt to understand.

"My wife, they dragged her into the road by her hair ... the things they did to her, I shan't forget them in a hurry. ... Afterwards, they threw her down the well."

His voice trailed away, drowned by the first outpourings of a psalm that rose, taken up in chorus by thousands of voices.

It was Pastor Rochefort's turn to speak. He reminded the faithful of the story from Exodus in which the Jews, pursued by the Egyptians, had gone to Moses, saying to him: "Rather let us serve the Egyptians than perish in the desert. ..." But the Almighty had made manifest His power by drowning Pharaoh's armies and the Jews finally reached the land of Canaan. They would have reached it sooner, had they not doubted the goodness of the Almighty, who was leading them into the desert only in order to tear them from a vile state of slavery in which they ran the risk of forgetting the beliefs of their forefathers.

Pastor Rochefort valiantly struck up the song Moses had sung:

> "I will sing unto the Lord, for
> He hath triumphed gloriously:
> The horse and his rider hath
> He thrown into the sea.
> The Lord is my strength and song,
> And He is become my salvation. ..."

His voice, slightly broken with age, remained powerful nevertheless. But he was singing almost on his own. The people were tired, and numb with cold, and only joined half-heartedly in the psalm which they seemed not to know too well.

The old man stopped, abashed, and cast an amazed glance at the assembled company. Then he went on with a note of urgency in his voice:

"My brothers, have you not understood the meaning of this tale? A candle hidden under a bushel will go out. Had the Jews continued to live as slaves, they would have ended up worshipping the Egyptians' gods. This is the danger that threatens us all. You were asked a while ago whether you wished to take up arms in your defence or else to resign yourselves to the persecutions you are called upon to suffer. In my turn, I am suggesting a third possibility to you: to get away! New and vast territories are holding out to you the refuge of a virgin land that you could make to prosper to the glory of the Lord, where your souls could grow freely as you practised your faith in honour. . . ."

His words were lost in the general hubbub that accompanies the end of a meeting. Around Angélique people had begun to talk softly to one another:

"Well now, what about that madder business of yours in the Languedoc?"

"If only we could salt the catch, the way they do in Portugal, we'd sell twice as much fish as we do, that's certain! But, there you are, the salt-tax won't let us."

"You might have worn your best things to come to a big meeting like this, Josias Merlut."

"What! In all this mud!"

Pastor Rochefort's suggestions were apparently of interest to no one.

The sound of a rattle, shaken by a young servant-girl, restored silence again. Pastor Tavenez, casting a glance at his colleague that said, "I told you so," spoke again.

The assembly could not be concluded until a show of hands had been called for to determine clearly what line of conduct the people of La Rochelle should adopt in future.

How many were there who wanted to see armed resistance? No one stirred.

Who wanted to leave?

"I do! . . . I do! . . ." shouted a group of about ten lads sitting in the front row.

"I do!" yelled Martial, getting to his feet next to Angélique.

Indignant protests from the boys' parents drowned their voices and the lawyer, Maître Carrére, slapped the face of his son sitting nearest to him.

Monsieur Manigault stood up, stretching out his powerful frame against the backcloth of the grey ocean, and held out his hand to still the eddy of unrest.

"Monsieur le Pasteur," he said, turning towards the celebrated old traveller, "you have honoured us greatly by coming to speak to us all, but you must not be surprised if so few people in La Rochelle feel inclined to emigrate. . . ."

He laid his hand upon his heart.

". . . The fact remains," he said with fervour, "that La Rochelle is our citadel, a city founded by our forefathers and one for which they died. None of us can desert it."

"Is it better than to desert your faith?" cried the old Pastor in a trembling voice.

"There's no quesion of that. La Rochelle belongs to the Huguenots. It will always belong to the Huguenots. Her soul sprang from the Reformation. You cannot alter the soul of a city."

There was clapping. Manigault had spoken sense, the kind of sense that went straight to the hearts of the men of La Rochelle.

"What can they do to us?" people were heard to mutter. "We've got the money!"

"Yes, it's obvious that without us the whole place would collapse."

"I hear that Monsieur Colbert has asked for Protestants to start up factories."

Angélique remained pensive, her gaze riveted on the strip of grey ocean, speckled with white, where it showed between the sand dunes.

A few yards away Pastor Rochefort was also looking at the sea. She heard him murmur:

"They have eyes and they see not. They have ears and they hear not. . . ."

What did he see, with his enlightened gaze? Was he already counting the martyrs and the renegades amongst his departing flock? They were all condemned!

Fear, which had left Angélique's heart alone for a while, was creeping back. "I must go." The shore was not safe; the tide would go on rising, and one day it would reach her and Honorine. Had she been alone, she might have let it come, from sheer weariness. But she had to save Honorine. A sweat broke out over her brow at the mere thought that the King's dragoons might one day get hold of Honorine, torment her with their coarse laughter, and throw her out of a window on to their pikestaffs. . . .

She set off at a brisk walk, back to her daughter.

Rain was falling. The puddles along the path reflected the whitish sky. A man on horseback overtook her and half turned round in his saddle. It was Maître Gabriel.

"Will you ride pillion with me, Dame Angélique?"

A sudden weird feeling swept over her. She saw herself walking along a bumpy road under similar circumstances; a horseman turned towards her and his smile was the smile of Maître Gabriel.

"No," she heard herself answer after a longish pause. "I am only your servant-girl, Maître Gabriel. People would talk. . . ."

"It's true that we are not on the outskirts of Paris here, on the Charenton road."

The veil was torn aside. La Polak was beside her. Her feet were frozen as they were now.

Just like today, her heart had been full of anguish for a child in danger: Cantor had been kidnapped by gipsies. Some men on horseback had drawn up beside them and she had ridden pillion with one of them into Paris. He was a young Protestant lad whose father was a merchant in La Rochelle.

"Do you recognize me now?" asked the merchant.

"Yes, you were the horseman who came to my assistance one winter's evening years ago."

She stood there stock-still beneath the rain. Twelve years had evaporated. The two scenes were side by side, twin situations. Totally forsaken as she had been, she had been momentarily comforted by the stranger's compassionate smile.

What struck her above all in her discovery was this fact. The two situations had been so alike, and between them lay the giddy heights of honour and wealth at the French Court.

"So," she told herself, "you had to go twice round the infernal ring before you understood! Before you realized that you had no place in this land, that you must get away ... get away across the seas. ..."

With a mixture of relief and humiliation as she thought about Maître Gabriel, the thought struck her: "Luckily he's only known me in my times of trouble. ..."

He must have remembered her as a poor wretch from the suburbs, and he had found her again in the role of a highway robber. His two encounters with her were hardly calculated to reassure him. The warm-heartedness he had shown her in welcoming her beneath his roof was all the more admirable. It did not fit in at all neatly with his prudent attitude to life.

"Why did you do this?" she burst out, "I mean—how could you have had enough confidence in me to have opened your doors to me?"

He had followed her reasoning, unspoken as it was, without any difficulty, and had understood the purport of her question.

"I believe in the significance of certain details," he replied. "That face I caught a glimpse of one winter's night—like the ravishing and heartbreaking symbol of the great cruel city—that face haunted me, and as the years went by, I finally realized that it must mean more than a mere memory, that the meeting had been a sort of warning—a bell tolling somewhere in the eternity of fate, its echo dying away. But then something happens and you remember the warning. When I recognized you in the thick of that battle, I was not all that taken aback. Fate had ordained it so. I could not do otherwise than concern myself with you and your child. I felt that it was my duty to do all I could to get you out of that prison before it was too late. I took advantage of the absence of the Catholic judge."

He remarked thoughtfully:

"Why did I say those words: 'before it was too late?' It is true that I was convinced that matters were very urgent, that for you it was only a question of hours. I was haunted by the passage in the Bible that says: 'Deliver them that are drawn unto death, and those that are ready to be slain. . . .' I feel that your presence amongst us has tremendous implications, but what are they?"

"I think I know," said Angélique, also carried away by these confidences made in the unaccustomed atmosphere of the desolate, windswept heath that now lay deserted about them. "One day I shall save you, you and yours, as you have saved me. . . ."

CHAPTER 33

SOMEONE OVERTOOK her and said:

"The French girl."

Angélique turned round. A man had stopped and was looking at her open-mouthed. He was dressed in a suit covered in tarnished gold embroidery, and was wearing red-heeled shoes whose leather was beginning to flake off, and a hat with a crumpled feather. He blinked like an owl in the sunshine.

"The French girl!" he repeated. "The French girl with the green eyes."

Angélique felt like running away and at the same time she wanted to know more. Impulsively she stepped closer. The man started like a frightened squirrel.

"Now there's no mistaking you. It's you all right. I'd know that look anywhere! But. . . ."

He took in her modest apparel and her bonnet that hid her hair completely.

"But ... weren't you a Marquise? And yet in Candia everyone said you were ... and I thought you were ... I saw your identity papers, come to think of it. What the devil! What are you doing here, got up like that?"

Now she recognized him, especially by his stubbly chin.

"Monsieur Rochat. Could it be you? So you managed to leave the Levantine colonies as you had hoped to do?"

"And you managed to escape after all from Mulai Ismail? I heard it rumoured that he had you tortured to death. ..."

"No, I'm here, aren't I?"

"I'm very glad of that."

"So am I! Oh, dear Monsieur Rochat, what a pleasure it is to see you again."

"A pleasure I entirely share, my dear Madame."

They shook hands effusively. Never could Angélique have dreamed that she would have been so delighted to see this droll little colonial official again. It was as if they were the sole survivors from an enchanted land, meeting again in Limbo.

Rochat, giving voice to their mutual feelings, exclaimed:

"Ah! At last! Someone from 'over there' to talk to in this northern port with no soul and no colour. What a relief! I'm absolutely delighted!"

Once again he shook her hand, so tightly that he almost crushed it; then his face clouded over.

"But . . . you weren't a Marquise, then? . . ."

"Sh!" she said, looking around. "Let's find a spot where we can talk and I'll explain," whispered Angélique.

Rochat grimaced scornfully and remarked that unfortunately he knew nowhere in La Rochelle where you could get real Turkish coffee. There was, of course, the Tavern of New France where they served a beverage that went by that name, but it was "their" coffee, from the islands. It had nothing in common with the beans from the Ethiopian plateaux, grilled according to the due rites, which went into the heavenly extract they drank "out there," in the East. They nevertheless went along to the pitiable tavern in question, which was fortunately empty at that hour of the day, and sat in a corner by a window. Rochat refused the proffered coffee.

"Quite honestly, I don't recommend it. It's a tincture of liquorice mixed with a decoction of acorns; that's what they call 'coffee' here. . . ."

They fell back on a local Charentes wine, an easy favourite in these parts. The landlord sent in a vast plate of seafood, and shell-fish to go with it.

"This is the only decent thing about this miserable place," said Rochat; "the shell-fish, the sea-urchins and the oysters. I make a regular pig of myself with them. . . ." He glanced towards the trellis-work of yards and rigging that darkened the brilliance of the sky, with a look of disenchantment.

"How dreary it all is! Where are the galleys from Malta with their banners, the oriflammes of the Christian pirates, the little donkeys with their baskets of oranges . . . and Simon Dansat with his red beard!"

Angélique was tempted to point out that this port was neither so northerly nor so devoid of colour as he seemed inclined to think.

"Didn't you use to complain once that you were being buried alive in the Orient? You could think of nothing but getting back to the Old Country."

"That's true. I moved heaven and earth to get back to France, and now I'm moving heaven and earth go out there again. . . . Paris! What a bore! There was a little dive near the Old Temple, where you could get real coffee, and where you could meet a few Knights of Malta, and a few Turks. I've been sent here to break the monopoly the Protestants have in the insurance business. I've taken the opportunity while here to sound some of the merchants; these people in La Rochelle have contacts everywhere. One of them is sending me off to Crete again. I'm off on Tuesday," he concluded, beaming.

"And what about the King's service?"

Rochat's gesture was fatalistic.

"Well, what can you do! There comes a time when a man of intelligence begins to realize that by serving
297

others, that is the State, he's being done down. I've always been something of a trader and it's time I took advantage of the fact. When I have made some money, I shall bring my family out. . . ."

Angélique was much reassured to learn that he was about to leave. She could speak more openly.

"Monsieur, you must promise me that you will never reveal what I am about to tell you."

She confirmed that she was indeed the Marquise du Plessis-Bellière. When she had returned to France, she had crossed swords with the King, who was angry with her for defying his order to stay in Paris. She had fallen into disgrace, had found herself penniless and had been forced to lead an extremely simple life.

"What a shame! What a shame!" Rochat said. "In the East they would not have allowed such dazzling qualities as you possess to fall so low. . . ."

All of a sudden, he leaned forward.

"You know, *he's* left the Mediterranean!"

"Who has?"

"Is there any need to ask, when one has knocked about the way you have out there? Rescator, of course! . . ."

And as she was staring somewhat fixedly at him, and showed no reaction, he repeated with a certain irritation.

"Rescator! The masked pirate who bought you for thirty-five thousand piastres at the slave market in Crete; the man you played the dirtiest trick on that ever a slave had played within living memory. Anyone would think you had forgotten everything that had happened to you!"

Her colour was coming back. How stupid to be so affected by a mere name!

"He's left the Mediterranean?" she asked. "And yet he was the most powerful man there. Did anyone ever find out why?"

"They said it was because of you."

"Because of me?"

She felt covered in confusion once more and her heart was pounding irregularly.

"Did he consider he had been made to look such a

298

fool by my escape that he could no longer face the sarcastic comments of his fellow-pirates?"

"No, it wasn't that. Although, from the moment he learnt of your escape, his Moroccan guards had a damned rough time of it. He came jolly near to hanging them all. But that wasn't his way: in the end he merely sent them back to Mulai Ismail, pointing out that they were a lot of incompetent dogs. I'll bet the poor devils would rather have been hanged. You can be proud of the amount of blood and tears you have made flow in the Mediterranean, Madame. And you end up here, in La Rochelle! Well!"

"But why because of me?" Angélique asked again.

"It was something to do with Mezzo-Morte, his worst enemy. Do you at least remember Mezzo-Morte, the Admiral of Algiers?"

"I could scarcely have forgotten him since he also captured me."

"Well now, Mezzo-Morte boasted that through you he could rid the Mediterranean of Rescator for ever. As soon as he had you in his clutches, he sent a messenger to Crete. But before going on I must tell you about something else. A short while after your escape, two or three days later, I think, Rescator sent for me."

"You?"

"Yes, me. Am I so pitiful a creature that I may not rub shoulders with the great pirate princes? I had already had occasion to meet his Highness, saving your ladyship. He was one of the merriest fellows you could ever have come across, but I must admit that on this occasion his state of mind seemed to match his gloomy looks pretty well. It's bad enough for a person he's speaking to to have to face that mask, but when a piercing and furious pair of eyes look out at you through those two slits in the leather, you would rather be somewhere else. He had taken refuge in his palace at Mylos. What a wonderful house; it's full of rare curios! His xebec had been too damaged by the fire for him to have been able to consider giving chase. And in any case, if I remember rightly, there was a violent storm raging at the time. No ship could leave the roadstead. Rescator had heard that I knew you. He asked me a lot of questions about you. . . ."

"About me?"

"Who else? When a man has paid thirty-five thousand piastres for a slave-girl he doesn't think it funny when she runs out on him! I told him all I knew about you, how you were a French lady of noble birth, a favourite of Louis XIV, vastly wealthy, since you actually owned the consulship of Crete. And about how I had found you in d'Escrainville's hands, who had been a fellow-student of mine at the School of Oriental Languages in Constantinople. In the end I even told how I'd moved heaven and earth to get you bought by the Knights of Malta. You must agree that I did my best, dear Madame! What's more, I did in fact receive the five hundred *livres* you sent me from Malta. That's how we knew in Crete that you had not died in the storm as everyone had imagined."

Rochat took a mouthful of wine.

"Hm! I suppose by now you won't hold it against me when I tell you that I thought it only right to go and inform Monsieur le Rescator of this. He's a man to whom I had certain obligations, after all. . . . He's very generous, isn't he? Money is nothing to him. And after all he was your owner, and it's only right to help a property owner to get his property back. Why do you smile? Because you think I'm more oriental than the real thing? Anyway I told him. But just as he was about to set sail for Malta, a messenger arrived from Mezzo-Morte. . . . Why do you seem so upset all of a sudden?"

"If you knew Mezzo-Morte's reputation you might guess that I have no reason to remember him with pleasure," Angélique answered, dismayed to feel how she was losing her self-possession.

"So Rescator went off to Algiers. We never found out what happened there. When I say 'we,' I mean all those engaged in coastal and general trade, the people of the Mediterranean in fact. Very few details ever came out. It would appear that Mezzo-Morte engaged in a kind of blackmail: either Rescator would for ever remain in ignorance of what had become of you, or else Mezzo-Morte would reveal where you were hidden away in exchange for Rescator's solemn promise never to set sail again on the Mediterranean, so that he, the Admiral of Algiers, could reign supreme there. Many said that it was idiotic to imagine that Rescator would think of weighing his colossal power, his even vaster fortune, his impregnable position as a trafficker in money, against a mere slave, however beautiful she was. But Mezzo-Morte obviously knew what he was about, because Rescator, that proud and invincible man, passed beneath the Caudine Forks."

"He agreed?" Angélique breathed.

"Yes!"

The erstwhile colonial official's slightly short-sighted eyes took on a dreamy look.

"Utter madness. No one understood it. We could only guess that you had fired him with something more than desire—with love perhaps. Who knows?"

Angélique listened with bated breath.

"And then?"

"Then? What more is there to say? No doubt Mezzo-Morte informed him that he had sold you to the Sultan of Morocco and Rescator learnt that he had had you put to death. Others said you had escaped but had died somewhere along the road. I see now that neither of those rumours is correct, since you are alive all right, here in the Kingdom of France."

His eyes sparkled.

"What a wonderful tale I shall have to tell when I get to Candia. No one could have guessed the tale would end like that. A woman getting out of Mulai Ismail's harem; a slave-girl reaching Christian shores after escaping. I shall be the only man to have witnessed all this ... I have seen you!"

"But, Monsieur, didn't I swear you to secrecy?"

"So you did!" said Rochat, very disappointed.

He reflected darkly for a moment as he emptied his glass. He would manage to find a way to tell his story without mentioning La Rochelle or naming any names.

"So," he concluded, "Rescator left the Mediterranean. Although he could not get you back, he had to keep his solemn promise to Mezzo-Morte, for he had kept his.

301

There's honour even among thieves. But before he went, he challenged Mezzo-Morte to a duel. The Admiral of Algiers took refuge deep in an oasis in the middle of the Sahara to escape from him and wait until his enemy had left. And Rescator went off through the Straits of Gibraltar. He went out into the Atlantic, and no one knows what has become of him since then," Rochat ended in a dismal voice. "What a gloomy story! Enough to make you despair!"

Angélique stood up.

"Monsieur, I must leave you. May I have your assurance that you will not betray me nor speak of our meeting to anyone, at least not as long as you are in France and in La Rochelle?"

"I give you my word," he promised. "In any case, who would I talk to here? The people hereabouts are as cold as marble. . . ."

On the threshold he kissed her hand. He was no longer the civil servant. A new life was opening up for him. And you could just catch a glimpse now of his mildly poetic and adventurous nature which hitherto he had always kept carefully buttoned up.

"Lovely captive with the green eyes, may the god of winds bear your barque far from the sad fate that you suffer at present. Although your charms, that once blinded Crete, are closely hidden away, one can nevertheless still see that they do not deserve to be lost to the world. Do you know what I wish for you? I wish Rescator would drop anchor off La Rochelle and take you off once again."

She could have kissed him for these words. But she protested feebly:

"Heaven forbid! I fear he might make me pay too high a price for the trouble I have already caused him. He must still be cursing me to this day."

She took a short cut home along the ramparts. They would be surprised how long she had been out. The soup would not be ready for the evening meal. The sun had just gone down and her thinly-clad arms were half-frozen by the bitter wind, for she had gone out

302

without a coat into the warm autumn afternoon. Beneath the pale yellow sky, the sea had a grey, dull look. It was calm and the waves were rolling up the seaweed-strewn beach. From time to time a bigger wave would strike the base of the walls and the wind would send the spray flying.

Angélique kept her eyes glued to the horizon. She thought she saw a ship appear, amongst so many others that had come that way. "He went off into the Atlantic. . . ."

Was she mad to be dreaming like a young girl whose heart stirred at the thought of having been chosen by a mysterious prince of the sea, who would give up everything he possessed for her sake!

She reminded herself that she was a disillusioned woman who had reason to know what life was like. She had been hurt beyond recovery by the coarse violence of men.

But a woman's imagination never stops running wild until her dying day. Her love of all that is wondrous and strange, her dreams of the unattainable must die only when she herself dies.

"It's the magic in the story which fascinates me," she thought.

How could she ever forget the softness of that great black velvet cloak, that low, slightly broken voice?

"There are roses on my island . . . there you will sleep. . . ."

She was so absorbed that she bumped into a soldier who turned out to be Anselm Camisot, blocking her way with his halberd.

"Now you're on my territory, pretty lady, you must give me a kiss."

"Please, Monsieur Camisot," implored Angélique kindly but firmly.

"When the queen says please, what can a poor sentry like me do but give way?"

He stepped aside to let her pass. Leaning on his halberd he gazed after her. His sad dog-like eyes took in her regal bearing and feasted on her rounded waist under

her cheap dress, on the line of her full shoulders, on her
straight neck and the curve of her white face turned
sideways towards the sea.

CHAPTER 34

ONE MORNING Uncle Lazarus was found dead in
bed with a peaceful expression on his face. Madame
Anna and Abigail laid him out and placed him between
fine white sheets. Pastor Beaucaire had already arrived
with his nephew. The paper merchant came shortly afterwards and neighbours began to flock in in increasing
numbers. Towards mid-morning there was a ring at the
gate. Angélique went down to the courtyard and let in
a man whose stern demeanour, black coat and white
bands made her feel uneasy, and who introduced himself as Monsieur Baumier, President of the Royal Com-
mittee on Religious Matters, and deputy to Monsieur
Nicholas de Bardagne.

Angélique had heard of the gentleman. She bit her
lips and was not surprised to see him accompanied by
four men-at-arms, who sauntered in, and a sinister-
looking individual whose coat was blazoned with the
arms of the town—a ship with two sails bedizened with
three fleurs-de-lis.

With a thoroughly funereal air, judged appropriate to
the occasion, Baumier made for the stairs followed by
his clerk and his sinister acolytes.

On observing their arrival the kneeling assembly stood
up and tension rose sharply.

Monsieur Baumier unrolled a parchment scroll and
began to read in a grating voice:

"Whereas Monsieur Berne, Lazarus, after undergoing
conversion on the sixteenth of May, fell back into his
culpable errors and neglected his eternal salvation, setting thereby a dangerous example, etc. . . ." He was declared under attainder of the crime of relapse into here-
sy, the punishment whereof was that his body would be
dragged on a hurdle by the public executioner throughout all the wards and crossroads of the town and thrown

into the public sewers. His estate was moreover subject to a fine of three thousand *livres* payable to the King and a hundred *livres* to be distributed as alms to necessitous prisoners of the Palace Conciergerie. . . .

Maître Gabriel interrupted the reading. He was very pale. He had taken up his station between Baumier and the bed on which the dead man, alone of all the company, retained a peaceful and faintly ironical expression.

"Monsieur de Bardagne cannot have taken such a decision in our regard. He himself witnessed my uncle's refusal, and I propose to go and fetch him."

Baumier rolled up his parchment with a grimace.

"As you wish," he said, very sure of himself. "Go and fetch him, but I will stay here. I have all the time in the world. He is carrying out a holy mission which will eventually rid the town of dangerous conspirators. For there is a conspiracy of the wicked angels against the good, just as there is a conspiracy of the wicked against the King's faithful subjects, and in La Rochelle the two things often go together."

"Are you by any chance suggesting that we are traitors to our country?" asked Legoult the Alderman, stepping forward with pinched nostrils and lowering eyebrows.

Maître Gabriel interrupted them.

"Who will go to fetch Monsieur de Bardagne?" he inquired.

"I shall stay here and so will my men," Baumier shouted with a sardonic smile.

"Then I shall go," said Angélique.

She already had her cloak over her shoulders, and she ran down the stairs.

"Well go then, and much good may it do you!' Baumier sniggered.

Angélique made her way across the town in such haste that she did not even have time to twist her ankles on the rounded cobblestones. When she got to Monsieur de Bardagne's house, she was told that he was at the Law Courts. She went there and after many fruitless inquiries at last succeeded in finding out from a clerk that Monsieur de Bardagne was visiting the wealthy shipowner Jean Manigault.

Angélique sped off on the wings of the wind. She could not help wondering what was going on in her absence in that house by the ramparts. When she had left it had been more highly charged with murderous passions than a powder magazine. What with Baumier's sarcasms, the boorish ways of the soldiers and the Protestants' indignation and anger, there would certainly be sparks flying! And she had left Honorine there! What a risk to have taken! She could just see herself standing outside an empty house with seals on the doors, and everyone in prison, goodness knows where. . . .

She was half dead with anxiety when she reached the Manigaults' stately residence.

Monsieur de Bardagne was taking refreshment with the Manigault family, seated beneath the watchful portraits of a whole dynasty of La Rochelle shipowners. The room was impregnated with an appetizing smell of spiced chocolate that Siriki the slave was pouring from a silver jug. A mountain of exotic fruits, pineapples and grapefruit mixed with the finest bunches of local grapes, stood in the middle of the table in a porcelain bowl. Angélique did not spare a glance for all this finery, but rushed breathless up to the King's Lieutenant.

"Monsieur, I beg you to come quickly. Maître Gabriel Berne wants you to come to his rescue. You are his only hope."

Monsieur de Bardagne stood up courteously, impressed by this apparition. Angélique's colour had been heightened by running, her eyes were sparkling and her chest heaved beneath her black bodice. All unbeknown to herself she radiated an atmosphere of feverish excitement which made her appear highly desirable. Her alarm, her imploring expression, allied to the most beautiful eyes imaginable, could hardly have failed to move any man with a weakness for the fair sex. And Nicholas de Bardagne undoubtedly fell into that category.

"Madame, calm yourself down and explain everything to me. Don't be afraid." As he spoke the look in his grey eyes grew gentler and his voice more caressing. "I do not know you, but I shall nevertheless listen to your tale with the greatest possible good will."

Angélique, realizing how impolite she had been towards Monsieur Manigault and his fat wife, dropped them a hasty curtsy. Then in a series of jerky phrases she described what had taken place in Maître Gabriel Berne's house: dreadful things were about to occur, might even have occurred already. . . . She caught her breath in a sob.

"But come, come! Calm yourself!" Monsieur de Bardagne repeated. "Why is this woman getting into such a state?" he said, calling the Manigaults to witness. "There's nothing to make such a fuss about!"

"It's just like Monsieur Berne to get himself into a mess," Madame Manigault remarked in an acid tone.

"But come, come, my dear Sarah, he can't very well allow them to drag his uncle around on a hurdle," the shipowner protested.

"All I know is that these things only seem to happen to him . . ." the fat woman said sententiously.

She clapped her hands together.

"Girls, go and put on your black velvet hoods and dress Jeremy in his cloth suit. We must go round to poor Lazarus's bedside to speed him on his way to his eternal home with our prayers."

"Yes, you're right. No one had told me he had died," said Manigault loking quite upset all of a sudden.

"I shall go ahead," Monsieur de Bardagne informed them in jovial tones; "this lady is in too much of a hurry to get me there for me to delay longer."

He helped Angélique into his private coach which was standing waiting for him with two archers as escorts.

"Oh, dear, I hope we won't be too late," Angélique whispered. "Monsieur, make them go faster."

"My dear child, how excitable you are! I would not hesitate to wager that you do not come from La Rochelle."

"No, as a matter of fact, I don't. Why?"

"Because you would be used to this sort of thing, which, in spite of what Dame Sarah just said, happens

307

quite a bit in our town. Alas! I sometimes do have to deal severely with people. Those who are too set in their evil ways must needs be punished. But I do admit that in the present case although Lazarus Berne stuck pigheadedly to his deplorable beliefs for eighty years he did not crown it all by the unpardonable sin of eventually denying the true faith. . . ."

"You won't allow that ghastly little runt to drag him through the mud, then?"

The King's Lieutenant began to laugh, showing a row of strong, very white teeth under his chestnut moustache.

"Are you referring to Baumier? That description fits him very well."

His face clouded over a little.

". . . I don't always agree with him on what methods to employ. . . . But, forgive me, it's very strange but I keep feeling, one, that I've just discovered you, and, two, that I've seen you before. If I have, how could I have forgotten so charming a lady's name?"

"I am Maître Gabriel's servant-woman."

Suddenly he remembered.

"Yes, that's it! I did in fact see you at Maître Berne's that evening when the Capuchins from the Convent of the Minims came and dragged me along by my coattails to convert poor Lazarus as he lay apparently at death's door. Maître Gabriel had just arrived home after being away and you were with him. . . ."

He added severely:

"You have a child who, according to law, must be brought up in the Catholic faith."

"I remember your saying that my daughter was probably illegitimate," Angélique said. She had decided inwardly that in order to avoid any general inquiries being made about her, she had better put her cards on the table. She continued: "Well, you were right, she is."

Monsieur de Bardagne jumped to hear such frankness.

"Forgive me if I have offended you, but it is my difficult job in this town to record the religion of every inhabitant down to the very last. . . ."

"That's the way it is," Angélique said with a shrug.

"When a woman is as beautiful as you," the King's official said, smiling indulgently, "I can understand that love ..."

Angélique cut him short.

"I only wanted to inform you that you need not concern yourself about her baptism nor about her instruction in the catechism, because she is already a Catholic, since I myself am one!"

Monsieur de Bardagne had just been telling himself that this young woman must be a convert or at least have been brought up in a Catholic convent. He congratulated himself on his perspicacity.

"That explains everything—I suspected as much. But whatever made you risk taking a job with people of this faith? It's a very serious matter."

Angélique had already thought out her answer. An idea had occurred to her, indirectly suggested by Séverine's hostile comments.

"Monsieur," she said, casting her eyes down, "my life has not always been an exemplary one, as you may well realize after what I have just admitted to you. But I did have the good fortune to come across a very pious lady, whom I may not mention by name, although she lives here, and she made me realize that I must make amends for my sins, and suggested to me how best I might do this. That's how I came to work for the Berne family, whom all ardent Catholics hope to see converted one day."

"You can rely on me, of course."

He cast about in his mind trying to guess which of the ladies of the Company of the Blessed Sacrament could have placed this girl as a pious spy in the Berne household. Could it have been Madame de Berteville? Or Madame d'Armentières? Never mind, he would control his inquisitiveness. The Company's rules insisted on the utmost secrecy: he knew that since he himself was a member.

Angélique was looking out of the window. The sight of the ramparts rekindled her fears.

"Monsieur, what an appalling thought that during our

309

absence these people may have been killing one another. And I left my little girl there. . . ."

"Come, come, don't go dramatizing things!"

She was quite delightful when she went white like that, and took on a wild look that gave her pale wide-open eyes a pathetic, heart-rending expression. A man wanted to take her in his arms and swear he would protect her always. He handed her down courteously from the coach. Louis XIV had instructed his peers to show deference towards humble chambermaids, and it was easy enough to forget this one's humble station.

Monsieur de Bardagne was inwardly jubilant. Now he knew she was a servant-girl he could hardly contain his delight. She could not fail to be flattered by the attentions of so influential a man as the Lieutenant, the King's personal representative in La Rochelle. And what was more, he would not meet with the prudishness which seemed bred in the women of the Reformed Protestant religion, whose reserve he had attempted in vain to break down. He had lost all hope of ever doing so, even where Monsieur Manigault's eldest daughter, the sharp-tongued but lively Jenny, was concerned.

One glance at this splendid creature suggested that the sins of which she was repenting were of the kind that he, Nicholas de Bardagne, was the most ready to forgive, especially if they were committed for his sake.

And the very fact that she had a bastard child put her into a position of inferiority which he could exploit to his advantage.

What a splendid business it all was and what an auspicious day for him!

As they entered the courtyard, he took her arm. Angélique scarcely noticed. In any case, she needed support, for her legs could hardly carry her any more.

"There you are!" said Monsieur de Bardagne reassuringly, "everything's in order."

In the hall on the ground floor the four soldiers, the executioner and Monsieur Baumier were drinking wine served by old Rebecca. Baumier was standing somewhat apart from the others: a gentleman of his quality did not want to compromise himself by associating with a common hangman.

He got up when he saw his superior and bowed low, but did not show any other signs of embarrassment.

"Listen to that!" he said casting a wearied glance up the stairs.

A slow sad psalm that sang of death and the soul's torment issued from Lazarus Berne's room. The Protestants were keeping the wake around his threatened remains, drawing solace from their prayers.

"There!" Monsieur de Bardagne repeated to Angélique, "what did I tell you? We're all well-bred folk here in La Rochelle. Things always sort themselves out."

She could not suppress a shudder as she listened to the distant singing. She would never get those sounds out of her head as she had heard them on the lips of her servants and the Rambourg children clustered around their mother, as the dragoons burst into the château, sword in hand. . . .

The King's Lieutenant was speaking softly to the President of the Royal Commission on Religious Affairs.

"I'm very much afraid that there has been a misunderstanding in this operation, Monsieur Baumier. We can hardly accuse Lazarus Berne of having relapsed when he never was converted."

"You told me that I was free to deal with all these matters as I thought fit," Baumier protested, stiffening.

"Yes, I did, but I was relying on you to see to it that the reports you filed were accurate in every detail. The slightest mistake made in these delicate matters could land us in a very tricky situation. The Protestants are very touchy and are all too ready to accuse us of acting in bad faith. . . ."

The Religious Commissioner made a gesture that implied that he thought going in for all these psychological niceties was taking things much too far.

"Monsieur, you worry far too much about these wretches who are in fact nothing more than deserters from the true faith. They should be treated with the same severity that is shown to soldiers who have been guilty of similar crimes on the battlefield."

Monsieur Manigault arrived in the midst of all this, holding his young son Jeremy by the hand and followed by his whole band of womenfolk.

The King's Lieutenant accompanied him upstairs, followed by Baumier, whose tight-pursed lips wore the smile of a martyr who still sticks to his view of how things should be done. He was used to pocketing affronts, and was helped in putting up with passing humiliations by the certain knowledge that he was on the right road, both from a spiritual and an administrative point of view. He never batted an eyelid while Nicholas de Bardagne spoke with compunction to the assembled company of the misunderstanding and even gave Maître Gabriel his assurance that nothing would be done to prevent the city gates being opened for the funeral.

The incident was closed.

But it nearly all started up again when a small round figure in an apple-green bonnet rushed up to Monsieur Baumier wielding a stick and shouting:

"You're nasty ... you're very nasty. I'm going to kill you!"

It was Honorine whom everyone had completely forgotten and who had decided to intervene. She had gone straight up to the man who had caused all the disturbance in the family. He was the evil genius, he was the man who had cast evil spells upon the troubled gathering. He must be got rid of. It had taken her some time to pull her stick out from amongst the logs in the woodstore. Baumier only just managed to parry the blows that fell on him from those valiant little two-year-old arms. Monsieur de Bardagne recognized Angélique's small daughter and merely laughed.

"Ah, there's that delightful child."

"That's how you describe her, is it?" the Commissioner grated out. "And will you allow this heretic brat to insult me?"

"Wrong again, my dear fellow. This child has been properly baptized into our Holy Mother the Church."

He gave him a knowing wink.

"Come, Maître Baumier, I must tell you all about the things that your short-sighted eyes have missed. . . ."

Angélique had already grabbed her daughter in one arm and Laurier in the other, and had escaped to the kitchen. Honorine was puce in the face and was having a terrible tantrum. She thought she had been patient too long throughout this day when the grown-ups hadn't taken any more notice of her than of the kittens around the house. She had been able to mess about with a whole bucket of water without anyone saying anything; she had spilt a whole basin of milk in an attempt to feed her hungry cat; she had wolfed half a pot of jam. The grown-ups had gone on looking at one another with unsmiling faces and talking solemnly to one another; every now and then they sang. Her mother had disappeared, and Honrine had begun to feel very uneasy. So she had gone to see the grown-ups to get a closer look at them. She had taken an instant dislike to Baumier after seeing him take a snuff-box from the folds of his suit, shove two or three pinches up his nose, and then sneeze violently. That funny way of behaving had struck her as the nastiest thing she'd seen so she had made up her mind to destroy the offender.

"I want to kill him," she repeated forcefully.

Angélique realized, as she tried to hold her, that her daughter was plastered up to the ears with jam. At that instant Laurier began to vomit from over-excitement. He had been frightened for his father without really being aware of the precise nature of the threat that hung over him. Fear brought back the pitiable look he had had in the early days. Angélique filled the big cast-iron cauldron with fresh water and hung it on the pot-hook. Then she made up the fire. Everyone was going to need a wash.

Séverine came in with Madame Anna. She was saying excitedly:

"So what then, Aunt Anna? They'd have dragged him round all the crossroads in the town. . . ."

"Yes, my girl, the rabble would have been allowed to insult him and spit on him and cover him with filth. . . ."

"Do you think it helps to describe the scene since it never took place?" Angélique asked sharply.

Suddenly Séverine grew whiter still and slid off her chair. Angélique only just had time to catch the little girl in her arms and carry her to her room.

She took her shoes off and laid her down. Séverine's hands were like ice.

Angélique went back into the kitchen and took down a container which she filled with some of the water that by now was almost boiling. She also heated the warming-pan.

Aunt Anna said somewhat primly that she was surprised at Séverine's lack of fortitude. She had always been spirited and robust, and had never been stupidly mawkish.

"And I'm surprised at your astonishment," Angélique replied. "You are a woman, after all, and you should realize that Séverine is twelve and that a girl needs to be taken care of at that age."

Madame Anna seemed shocked at the reference. There was no doubt about it, these Papist women lacked the most elementary sense of decency.

Angélique propped Séverine up with another pillow and told her to hold her hands in the good hot water until she felt better. She went back to fetch the warming-pan, then a small bottle of perfume and some white velvet ribbons she had bought.

She sat on the edge of the bed and with nimble fingers parted the child's long hair down the middle and made two brown plaits of it, mingled with the ribbons.

"There, you'll be able to rest better like that."

She shook a few drops of the perfume into the bowl of water and rubbed Séverine's forehead and temples with the palm of her hand. Séverine did not prevent her; she was torn between a feeling of remorse for having been so weak and a feeling of well-being now that she was getting over her indisposition.

"Aunt Anna won't be pleased," she whispered.

"Why not?"

"She's never ill. She says we must mortify the flesh."

"Go on with you! Our flesh takes care to mortify us, without our having to encourage it!" Angélique replied, laughing.

Séverine's face as it lay on the pillow suddenly looked different. Her bluish eyelids gave her a languishing look and beneath her unattractive childish features you could glimpse the face of a woman. Her eyes would be dark like the night and one could guess that her over-large mouth would later acquire an expressive sensuality.

Séverine was hard and unyielding, much harder than her brothers, but she would not escape the lot of her sex. She too, one day, would lie in a man's arms with the same vanquished look on her face. She, too, would yield to love.

Angélique spoke gently and reassuringly to her as her mother had once done. But the colour was beginning to come back to Séverine's cheeks, and her eyes began to shoot daggers. She had always hated being a girl between her two brothers, Martial, whom she admired, and Laurier, whom she envied because he was a boy.

"I don't want to be a woman," she announced passionately. "It's a horrible, humiliating condition."

"What an idea! I'm a woman too, and do I look miserable?"

"Oh, it's not the same for you," Séverine said. "To begin with, you're always laughing. ... And you're beautiful too."

"But you're going to be very pretty, too."

"Oh no, I'd rather not be. Aunt Anna says that women's beauty leads men into temptation and makes them commit sins that are an abomination to the Lord."

Once again Angélique had to laugh.

"Believe me, men commit the sins they want to. Why should a woman's beauty be a trap rather than a tribute to the Creator?"

"You speak dangerous words," Séverine said, and her voice had a ring of Madame Anna in it.

But she was yawning and her eyes were closing.

315

Angélique tucked her in and went away. She was pleased to see the girl smiling like a happy child just as Laurier had of late in his sleep.

CHAPTER 35

A FEW DAYS later Martial embarked in the dead of night on a Dutch ship. But the ship was stopped and examined by vessels of the royal navy off the Island of Ré, and the young passenger was arrested and brought back to land where he was locked up in Fort Louis.

The news had a shattering effect.

Maître Berne's son in prison. One of the foremost families in the whole of La Rochelle! Fancy their being humiliated like that!

Maître Berne went off immediately to request an interview with Monsieur de Bardagne, who was unable to see him that morning. But he did manage to see the sniggering and obdurate Baumier, after which he went and had a talk with Manigault. The day was spent in seeing this person and that, always in the hope that the next interview would be conclusive. Gabriel Berne came home in the evening, worn out and pale. Angélique did not dare to tell him that she had spent part of the afternoon arguing with the assessor for the Charentes farmlands who had come to collect the second tax instalment due from Berne as a Protestant trader. It never rains but it pours!

Maître Berne said that he had seen Nicholas de Bardagne but that he had been most disappointed to find him very reluctant to do anything. De Bardagne had assured him that the crime of fleeing the Kingdom was punishable by draconian measures, citing the case of Protestants strung up on the spot when caught heading for Geneva. Going off to Holland was just about as bad. Monsieur de Bardagne would need time to consider the matter in view of the boy's high social position. He had said that the whole situation was most awkward.

The Protestants spent a terrible evening.

Fear followed upon their indignation and shame. Monsieur Carrère reminded them gloomily that Protestant children arrested under similar circumstances had been sent to an unknown destination, and that rumour had it that they had been used as galley-slaves on the King's ships. The toughest amongst them never lasted more than a year. . . .

For two whole days Maître Gabriel completely neglected his business and ran hither and thither in an attempt to get his son set free, or at very least, to be allowed to see him.

On the third day Séverine, who had gone to an old spinster's house in the neighbourhood for her lute lesson, which should have lasted an hour, had not arrived home by lunchtime. They came to inform Monsieur Berne that his daughter had been arrested "for acts of sacrilege" and taken to the Ursuline Convent. The atmosphere in the house became nightmarish.

Angélique never slept a wink all night. Next morning she decided to hand Laurier and Honorine over to old Rebecca and she went off to the Law Courts where she asked in a very firm voice to see the King's Lieutenant, the Comte de Bardagne.

His face lit up when he saw her coming in. He had been secretly hoping she might come, and he told her so.

"Did your master send you here? Because I must tell you that it's a very serious matter, and that nothing can be done."

"No, he certainly did not. I came of my own accord."

"I'm delighted. I expected someone of your intelligence to do just that. In view of the fact that things are moving fast, it was vital that you should make your report to me. Do you consider that Maître Berne is about to give in?"

"To give in?"

"I mean, to be converted. I must admit that I find the whole idea most exciting. I've got a list of a few names here, ten at the outside, that I've chosen after a whole year of patient observation. I know that as soon as I've

317

brought these people to heel, the pillars of Huguenot La Rochelle will crumble *ipso facto.* . . ."

The room was very hot. The chimney-piece, flanked by carvings of gryphons and sailing ships, was filled with a roaring fire that the wind, which was blowing at gale force that morning, fanned into a fine blaze. Angélique's cheeks rapidly took on the hue of ripening peaches and Monsieur de Bardagne's thoughts likewise quickly took a more gallant turn.

"But do take your cloak off. We're out of the weather here."

He himself slipped Angélique's heavy cloth cloak from her shoulders. She accepted his help automatically: her mind was entirely taken up with working out a new line of approach. She had had her speech ready in her head: she had come as a suppliant, determined to fall on her knees if it came to that, at the Lieutenant's feet. She now realized that this would have been the worst possible line to take, for he had received her as a collaborator and accomplice to the forced conversions.

"Do sit down, please," said the King's representative.

She obeyed, and sat very straight with all the ease of one who has spent much time in society. She was still thinking and had not noticed that Bardagne was devouring her with his eyes. "She certainly is very lovely," he told himself. When she had first come in, when he had first set eyes on her in her austere clothes and white bonnet, he had taken her for what she was: a servant-girl. But after a moment or two he had not been able to help treating her like a lady. She radiated such a calm self-assurance, her movements and her speech were so easy, genuine discretion mixed with simplicity in such a manner as to put everyone she spoke to at their ease. She really had a fascinating charm, due no doubt to her exceptional beauty, or else . . .

There was something mysterious about this woman! The Comte stood before her, where he could just see, thanks to the fairly low cut of her white cotton kerchief, the beginning of her marble breasts, whose curves were

318

not completely hidden even beneath her coarse fustian bodice.

Her bosom and her firm, full, slightly golden neck gave her a healthy look, a peasant robustness that contrasted with the delicacy of her features with their noble relief that bordered on the tragic when she was deep in thought. Monsieur de Bardagne was irresistibly attracted by that satiny neck and by the hollow of her shoulder that promised soft smoothness. He was burning to place his lips there. His throat was dry and his hands clammy.

Angélique suddenly became aware of the lengthy silence and looked up at him. She hastily looked down again when she saw the undisguised admiration in the man's eyes staring down at her.

"No, I beseech you, don't lower your eyes," he begged her. "They are so rare a colour, such a luminous green that one could only compare them with the emerald! It is a crime to hide them!"

"I would gladly change their colour for another," Angélique said testily. "They have done nothing but make trouble for me. . . ."

"Don't you like compliments? Anyone would think you were frightened of having homage paid to you. And yet all women enjoy it."

"Not me, to be frank. And I am grateful to you, Monsieur de Bardagne, for having guessed it."

The King's Lieutenant took the rebuff, champing at the bit. He would get nowhere by trying to rush things, so he went back to his desk, sat down and tried a little banter.

"Could it be that those Protestants have so contaminated you that you are upset when I tell you how sincerely I admire your beauty? Isn't it normal to pause, entranced, in front of a flower, that masterpiece of nature, whose glowing colours have been created for the delight of our eyes?"

"We don't know what the flowers think about it," Angélique replied with a trace of a smile. "We do not know whether perhaps our admiration does not occasionally embarrass them. Monsieur le Comte, what are you going to do for Maître Berne's children? . . ."

319

"Oh yes! That's true, where was I?" said Bardagne, drawing his hand across his brow.

The case of the Berne children, that had kept him sleepless for three days, had seemed to have suddenly gone right out of his mind. It was extraordinary. Never, no, never had a woman had the power to make him desire her so violently. In fact she had got him so worked up that he felt somewhat embarrassed by it himself. He had felt something akin to it the other day when he drove her home in his coach. Then the memory of it had faded. He had gone on thinking about her in a happy, indulgent way. One day soon, he must do something about that beautiful servant-girl. But no sooner had she reappeared than he had felt all afire and excited in a way hardly appropriate to the occasion. It was disturbing, worrying and almost humiliating for him. . . . At all events it was terribly exciting. This time Monsieur de Bardagne would make the most of his advantage! He had learnt that a man never gets a second opportunity to meet the sort of woman who is capable of attracting him so strongly. Unfortunately he was deep in work, he had these tough Protestants to subjugate, jealous colleagues who were constantly accusing him of weakness, and all the Church dignitaries who never considered his lists of converts long enough. How on earth was he going to find time in the midst of all these tactics to sacrifice to Venus! Ah! People didn't know how to live any more! He was a conscientious man who wanted to succeed, so he made an effort to pull himself together.

"Where were we?" he repeated.

"Do you regard my master as one of the pillars of Huguenot resistance?"

"Do I indeed!" cried Bardagne in indignation, lifting his arms heavenward. "He's one of the worst! He works in the shadows, but what he does is more harmful than if he got up and preached in the public square. He helps pastors placed under interdict, refugees, and goodness knows who else. You must have noticed his suspicious comings and goings."

"I see Maître Gabriel doing his accounts and reading

his Bible," Angélique said. "There's nothing conspiratorial about him."

And yet, as she spoke, she saw in her mind's eye a whole series of impressions: unknown furtive faces, only half glimpsed, passing between Maître Berne's house and the paper-merchant's or Pastor Beaucaire's, whispered conferences and footsteps in the night. Luckily the King's representative seemed to have been impressed by her assurance.

"You surprise me. Or perhaps it's because you aren't keeping a sufficiently close eye on them."

He banged his hand down on a thick file.

"Because here I have reports that leave no doubt whatsoever about his dangerous and reprehensible activities. I have cautioned him on many occasions, and he seemed to understand and listened to me in a friendly way. He seemed sincere but I have been cruelly disappointed by his son's flight."

"Young Martial was going to Holland to study the rope trade."

"How naïve you are! His father was sending him away because he realized the lad was about to become converted, and he wanted to help him to stick to his faith."

"Yes, I did hear that," said Angélique feeling that things were going against her. "But I think you are allowing appearances to deceive you. I've been living in this family for many a long month now and I can assure you that Maître Berne only wanted his son to complete his education. You must not forget that Protestants are keen travellers."

"Much too keen," replied Monsieur de Bardagne dryly. "That's a habit they would do better to lose. In any case, the law is perfectly clear on that point."

"I had thought that you were a nicer sort of person."

The King's official seemed alarmed.

"What do you mean? I disapprove of violence and . . ."

"I mean that this inquisitor's job seems to me to be ill suited to your nature, which seemed to me to be especially accessible to worldly pleasures."

He laughed readily, feeling flattered in his heart of

hearts. She was not so unconcerned and dreamy as she tried to make out.

"Let there be no misunderstanding," he went on. "Like any good Christian, I want to work my way to heaven, but I will admit that the work in question attracts me above all on account of its worldly side. At the present moment the quickest way to get on in the King's service is to concern oneself with religious matters.

"On the other hand I admire Monsieur Berne greatly, and would like to help him. But he is digging his toes in and will not be reasonable. . . ."

"In what way?"

"He won't get it into his head that we can entrust only a Catholic family with the education of his two children. Too much harm has been done already to their young souls."

"Why has his daughter Séverine been arrested?"

"Because the time had come for her to decide which religion she wishes to follow."

"These decisions sap a father's authority in his own family which forms the very basis of this country's society."

"What does that matter, if it's a harmful authority? I've got a report here. . . ."

He took hold of another file but stopped as he was about to open it.

"But . . . you are standing up for them," he said, looking suspiciously at her.

Angélique was very angry with herself. She had committed a blunder in allowing her personal views to become too apparent. She now felt incapable of bluffing her way through the situation as she would once have been able to do. Once she could have used cunning and lies much more easily. Perhaps the fact was that she had never taken things too much to heart.

She must at all costs retrieve the situation.

"I am not standing up for them, but I am stressing these points just to prove to you that I *am* aware of what goes on in this family. And I find you acting upon the tittle-tattle carried to you by your myrmidons, which they pompously call 'reports', whereas nobody even asks *me* anything."

"That's because you never have anything to say! I had hoped to obtain much information precisely from you, but I hoped in vain."

"There was nothing of interest to inform you about."

"And yet you let Martial Berne fly the country without warning me of their plans which you could not have failed to be aware of."

"He wasn't flying the country. He was travelling."

"They've pulled the wool over your eyes."

"Why don't you tell me straight out that I'm a fool?" Monsieur de Bardagne, seeing her standing up and about to walk out of the room, was overcome. He walked swiftly round his desk to stop her.

"Now let's not get all upset about a thing like that! You misunderstood what I meant. I'm terribly sorry. . . ."

Under the pretext of holding her back he put his hands on her shoulders. He could feel her firm yet soft flesh beneath her sleeves. Her delicate wholesome scent made him quite intoxicated. Angélique could scarcely have any illusions about the nature of her hold over him. It made her feel very ill at ease, but she told herself that it was her duty to take advantage of it, and she disengaged herself as diplomatically as she could.

"Yes, you have hurt me."

"I am so ashamed," he said repentantly.

"Because I honestly believe that you will never get what you want from Maître Berne by going about matters the way you are. I am beginning to know him well and I know that he will only dig his toes in and become more intransigent than ever. Whereas he would be much more likely to listen to your arguments if he felt moved by your indulgence and the help you have given him."

"Do you really think so?"

"Perhaps!"

The King's Lieutenant weakened again. He could hardly feel otherwise, standing near her with his eyes wandering over that fascinating neck. He wanted nothing better than to believe her and trust blindly in her.

"But I still can't give him his children back," he groaned, "that's out of the question. In any case, I might as well tell you, it's that blasted Baumier who started up all that business. But now proceedings have been started and the fact that he tried to fly the country is known, and the girl has been arrested, I can hardly call it all off."

"What are you going to do with them?"

"The boy will be handed over to the Jesuits, and the girl will go to the nuns. . . ."

"So we'll never see them again," Angélique thought, quite shattered.

"I came to see you, Monsieur le Comte, precisely to suggest another scheme. Maître Berne could hardly object to it. He has a sister who is a convert. She is married to an officer in the royal navy and lives on the Island of Ré."

"You are quite right, that is Madame Demuris."

"So the children could go to her. I've been assured that this is often done. When a Protestant child has to be removed from his parents' care, they look for his closest Catholic relatives and make them responsible for his education. Incidentally it is a humane as well as a sensible thing to do."

"But how on earth was it that I never thought of that myself!" the King's Lieutenant exclaimed delightedly. "As you say, it is the perfect answer. Even Baumier won't be able to object and Maître Berne on his side will, I feel, be grateful to me. You are wonderful. You are as intelligent as you are beautiful."

"And yet, it would seem, you have your doubts about that."

"What can I do to make you forgive me?"

Bardagne, overcome with relief as he was, and enchanted by the treasures that this extraordinary creature kept on revealing to him, was carried away on impulse. He grasped Angélique around the waist and laid his lips upon her smooth neck, whose gentle curves and graceful movements had never ceased to intoxicate him during the whole time they had been talking.

Angélique leapt into the air as if she had been

burned. She tore herself so suddenly from his embrace that the unfortunate man looked at her aghast.

He stammered:

"You really find me as distasteful as all that?"

He felt heavy-eyed and his lips were trembling. Although it had been so brief, this contact had been enough to confirm all he had hoped. He had never known a more exciting woman. "Damn it," he thought, "is she going to turn out to be as prudish as all the other heretics? Just my luck!"

CHAPTER 36

ANGÉLIQUE LEANT against the inlaid desk, wondering what sort of attitude to adopt. After all he was not unattractive. He was charming. He was good-looking, his hands were delicate and his lips experienced. Who knows whether once—that once that seemed extraordinarily far away now—she might not have let herself be tempted? She could not forget that she was a humble serving-girl and he represented the King himself in La Rochelle, which meant that, from the point of view of status, he was the most powerful man in the town.

Fortunately he was not conceited. For the moment he seemed to be taking his rejection by Angélique less as an insult than a painful blow of fate. She sensed that he needed to be cheered up.

"I don't find you at all unattractive," she said. "On the contrary, I must admit that I find you most charming. But . . . how can I put it? . . . I promised my patroness . . . the lady whose name I must not mention . . . that I would behave myself, to atone for my past sins."

"A plague on these sanctimonious old hags!" cried Nicholas de Bardagne. "I bet she is uglier than the seven deadly sins. She doesn't realize that a woman as lovely as you can't lead the life of a nun."

"And suppose I wanted to remain virtuous of my own free will, Monsieur le Comte. Is it your business to lead me into temptation?"

Monsieur de Bardagne gave a deep sigh. The affair

325

seemed to be more awkward to handle than he had at first reckoned. He decided to be a good loser.

"In my opinion it's the business of any normal man who finds himself in your company," he said cheerfully. "You've enough sense and experience, I am sure, to understand and forgive me."

He held out both his hands to her.

"Let us forget all about it, Dame Angélique, and be friends again."

She would have been most ungracious not to have accepted his attempt at reconciliation. He kissed the tips of her fingers very softly, and she felt a truly feminine pang of dismay at the thought that her hands had been spoilt and roughened by housework.

She allowed him to slip her cloak over her shoulders and he saw her to the door where he bowed with respectful tenderness.

"Dame Angélique, please remember that I am your friend and that I shall always be ready to help you, no matter what happens. . . ."

His charm enfolded her. It had been such a long time since she had been so treated, that she indulged herself a moment with her sensual caressing memories. So many men had bowed before her with this same eager look in their eyes. She knew their approach: it was always the same, humble yet imperious.

How well she knew those thrilling, veiled glances, those broken tones, that gentle courtesy cloaking the cruel weapons of possession, ready when the moment comes to transform the suppliant into a master and the inaccessible goddess into a vanquished woman.

Angélique would never have thought that she could still be affected by the subtleties of the eternal game. It was torture to her and yet it held her, like the memory of a once familiar land.

Her cheeks were burning and her voice almost shaking with agitation as she took her leave of the King's Lieutenant, who was both delighted and disconcerted by her attitude.

She rushed off, her mind in a whirl, not even noticing the murderous looks she got from other petitioners who had been kept waiting. The benches were almost empty, for some of them had tired of waiting and had gone off to lunch. It was past noon. Out in the street Angélique was caught up in the wind, and had a struggle to keep her cloak on. She had difficulty in making any progress against it. The sky was incredibly blue. The tempestuous wind was twisting the winter light into fine-spun pennants which seemed to rise up snorting from the hollow of the narrow alleyways.

Angélique walked on heedless of her fight against the raging elements, so absorbed was she by the recollection of the interview that had just taken place. What she felt above all was an acute sense of embarrassment at how clumsy she had been and how she had bungled things.

The time had long since gone when she had neatly seduced the Persian ambassador Bachtiari Bey and brought him like a lap-dog on a leash to the feet of Louis XIV. That had been a piece of high feminine strategy. And all without sacrificing one iota of her virtue! Whereas today she had been . . . lamentable. There was no other word for it. This man, from whom she hoped to get so much, had been all worked up and bleating like a billy-goat within five minutes, and yet, instead of being delighted, she had gone all tense. She had almost lost his goodwill once and for all by taking his rather cavalier advances like a prim miss fresh from a convent-school. At her age it was positively ridiculous! In the old days she would have put him in his place with a smile or with a sharp word. . . .

Angélique the unknown servant-girl, dressed in serge and fustian, lost in the streets of La Rochelle, thought for a moment with great respect of the glamorous woman she had been a few years earlier when she had been so adept at handling the weapons of her sex. But between then and now lay the night at Plessis. Little by little she had taken up the threads and had started all over again. Life had burgeoned in her. But, she thought, there was one thing she would never get over. There was no man on earth who could ever work that miracle for her. No man would rekindle her former delight in love, nor make her feel the thrilling attraction of one body for another. She would never feel the strange blossoming of sensual pleasure, nor delight in her own weakness any more.

"It would take a magician," she thought suddenly. And her eyes turned automatically towards the black and turbulent sea where not a sail was to be seen.

CHAPTER 37

MONSIEUR DE BARDAGNE kept his word. And Angélique's mortified spirit drew great solace from the fact that, in spite of her blunders, he had hastened to follow her advice and grant her plea. The very next day Martial and Séverine were transferred to their aunt's home on the Island of Ré.

Angélique was never short of work with all the youngsters around. Her household chores left her no time for meditation. She used to go to rinse the washing in a public fountain, which was bigger than the one in the courtyard, taking Honorine along with her. One morning when she had finished the washing and had just piled it into her wicker basket, she was surprised to see her daughter playing with a glistening object.

"Let me have a look," she said.

Honorine, whom experience had taught to be wary, put the toy behind her back, but Angélique had just had time to glimpse a very lovely rattle, of chased gold with an ivory handle. It was a real gem.

"Where did you find that rattle? Honorine, you must not keep things that don't belong to you."

The little girl hung on to it.

"It was that nice man who gave it to me."

"Which nice man?"

"Over there," said Honorine, pointing vaguely towards the far end of the square.

Angélique wanted to avoid the sort of scene that would have ended in the shrieking child being surrounded by a chorus of town gossips, so she dropped the matter, saying to herself that she would sort it all out

328

when they got home. She put her basket under one arm, took her daughter by the hand and set off homeward.

In a quiet, narrow street a man came up to her and drew back the fold of his cloak that hid his face. She let out a little cry, but was reassured when she recognized the King's Lieutenant, Nicholas de Bardagne.

"Oh! You frightened me!"

"I'm terribly sorry."

He seemed very excited by his amorous escapade.

"I have ventured out into this hostile area without an escort, and it would be better from every point of view for me not to be recognized."

"That's the nice man," Honorine said.

"Yes, I wanted to let you know I was somewhere in the offing by giving your delightful child a gift."

Honorine looked at him. Her eyes were brimming with admiration. What a little woman she was already, to be won with a golden rattle!

"I cannot accept it," Angélique said, "it is far too valuable a gift. I must give it back to you."

"Oh dear, how relentless you are!" he sighed. "I have been dreaming about you by day and by night, trying to visualize you with a sweet expression of surrender on your face. But no sooner do I appear than down comes the curtain between your eyes and mine. . . . May I walk along with you? I have left my horse tied to a tethering ring not far from here."

They began to walk on slowly. Once again, Monsieur de Bardagne told himself despairingly, this woman had fettered him with her strange charm. So long as he continued to dream about her at a distance, he remained the patient lover, but as soon as he found himself face to face with her, he lost all self-control. Perhaps this was not quite normal, but it was a fact which he recognized and accepted. He was yielding. . . . He felt he would be capable of going down on his knees to her.

She had the attractive arms of a servant-girl, all reddened by the cold water they had just been plunged in, the eyelashes of a child, and the mouth of a queen, at present puckered with mild anxiety and trembling.

"Forgive me, Monsieur le Comte. You are a great man

and I only a poor, lonely, defenceless woman. Do not be offended by what I am about to say, but you must expect *nothing* from me. I ... it's out of the question."

"But why?" he moaned. "You led me to believe that I was not altogether displeasing to you. Do you doubt my generosity? You would, of course, leave your present lowly existence. If you so desired, you could have a comfortable home of your own in which you alone would be mistress; you could have servants and your own carriage and horses. All your needs and those of your child would be met."

"Stop!" she ordered brusquely. "It's all quite out of the question."

He forced her into a doorway so that he could look her in the eyes.

"Maybe you think I'm mad, but I must tell you the truth. Never has any woman inspired me with so consuming a passion as you. I am thirty-eight and my life, I admit, has not been one of exemplary virtue; in fact it has been full of amorous adventures I am not in the least proud of. But since I met you I have come to realize that something has happened to me that all men both fear and desire: to meet a woman able to captivate them utterly, to make them suffer torments when she says no, to delight them with her favours, a woman whose domination they are prepared to accept, whose whims they are willing to gratify rather than lose her ... I do not know where this particular power you have over me comes from, but I have begun to think that before I knew you I knew nothing. All my pleasures were shoddy and insipid. Through you alone can I know love. ..."

"If he only knew what other lips had spoken almost identical words to me before him," she thought. "The King ..."

He went on: "How could you refuse me all this? You would be refusing me life itself."

His expression, normally pleasant and agreeable as befitted a ladies' man, hardened, and his eyes darkened as he examined her avidly. He wondered what colour her hair was that she kept hidden away beneath her severe cotton bonnet. Was it blonde, auburn or perhaps red like her daughter's, or even brown as her warm complexion seemed to suggest?

Her lips were glistening with a smooth sheen like mother-of-pearl.

He was in such a state that, had Honorine not been standing there watching them both with her nose in the air, he would have forcibly taken her in his arms and tried to rouse her.

"Let's go on," she said, pushing him politely aside. "Indeed you must be mad, and I don't believe a single word you have uttered. You must have known women far more attractive than me, and I think you are trying to take advantage of my simplicity, Monsieur."

Nicholas de Bardagne followed her with death in his heart, only too well aware of how mad his declaration had been. He could not get over it himself, but told himself yet again that that was how things were. His love for her was enough to drive him out of his mind, to make him compromise himself, to wreck his career. As he glanced at the little girl toddling along holding her mother's hand, another thought struck him.

"I swear that if you ever had a child by me, I would recognize it and make every provision for its upbringing."

Angélique jumped. He could scarcely have thought of any promise that could have made her feel less aglow with passion. He realized his mistake.

"I'm a clumsy dolt," he sighed.

As they had reached the Bernes' house, Angélique put her basket down and took the key to the side door from her belt.

The King's Lieutenant followed her every movement with a fierce sensation of pain and delight. She was grace personified, she would adorn any house.

"Your modesty is driving me mad. If it were only feigned, I would gladly take on the task of curing you of it. But I sense, alas, that it is only too genuine. Listen, I believe . . . Yes, I believe I would even marry you."

She exclaimed:

"But . . . surely you are married already!"

331

"As a matter of fact, no, I'm not. That's just where you are wrong. I will make no secret of the fact that since I've been fifteen I've had every possible heiress hurled into my arms, but I have always managed to escape in time and I had fully intended to live a bachelor till the end of my days. But for you I think I could take on the bonds of marriage. If the only obstacle that stands between us is the thought of a life lived outside the divine laws, I shall remove that obstacle."

He bowed deeply to her.

"Dame Angélique, will you do me the honour of taking me as your husband?"

He certainly was disarming.

She could not treat his offer lightly, without running the risk of gravely offending him. She said she felt quite bowled over, that she had never hoped for so signal an honour, but that she felt quite sure that no sooner had he reached his stately home than he would regret his mad offer, which she herself was unable to accept. The barrier that kept them apart was not one that could easily be removed, even at a price.

"You must understand, Monsieur de Bardagne. . . . It is very hard for me to explain the reason for what you call my indifference. I have suffered greatly during the course of my life at the hands of men. Their brutality has wounded me and made me for ever shun the pleasures of love. . . . I am frightened of them and can no longer find them pleasurable. . . ."

"Is that all it is?" he cried happily. "But, you silly little thing, what do you need to fear from me? I am used to women and I treat them with courtesy. I'm no dock labourer, I'm a gentleman, my lovely lady, and I'm asking you to love me. . . . Trust me and I will give you back your confidence and make you think differently about love and its delights. . . ."

Angélique had managed to get the door open; Honorine had gone in and she had put her basket down in the courtyard. She wished the conversation would come to an end.

"Promise me that you will consider my offers," said the King's Lieutenant, holding her back. "I will uphold them all and you can chose whichever one would suit you best."

"Thank you, Monsieur le Comte, I shall think about it."

"Might I just ask what colour your hair is?" he begged.

"White," she said, shutting the door in his face.

Maître Berne had given Angélique a message to take to the shipowner, Jean Manigault. She was walking home along a narrow alley under the ramparts when she noticed two men following her.

Up till that moment she had been deep in thought and had not taken any notice of them. But in the deserted alley she now became aware of the sounds of footsteps behind her: they always seemed to keep the same distance.

She cast a glance over her shoulder and saw two fellows she did not like the look of at all. These were no sailors on the prowl, nor even watermen from the docks. They were wearing quite elegant bourgeois clothes which nevertheless contrasted sharply with their sly ill-shaven faces. It was as if they were in disguise.

"The police," she thought, sensing danger. She began to walk faster. Straightaway the sound of heels drew nearer and one of the men called out:

"Hi, pretty girl, don't run away!"

She pressed on even faster, but they had already caught up with her and were walking one on either side. One of them grabbed her by the arm.

"Gentlemen, would you kindly leave me alone," she said as she disengaged her arm.

"But why? You don't look very cheerful. Surely we can keep you company for a bit!"

Their sly smiles made her fear the worst. If she was forced to slap these impudent fellows in the face she ran the risk of drawing attention to herself. If they were young rips from wealthy families, perhaps they would accept the fact that they were not in luck. But somehow, she did not quite know why, she was frightened that their fine clothes might be a cover for something much more formidable.

Her eyes wandered over the closed house-fronts looking for help. But it was just after lunch-time and La Rochelle followed the southern custom of closing the shutters for an hour after the meal. The sun was dazzling and hot for the time of year, and it was not a day for people to feel like missing their siesta. There was no one about, either at the windows or on the doorsteps. Luckily Angélique realized she was not far from Maître Berne's warehouses.

Rather than attempt to reach the house, which was still a long way off, and have to put up with her unpleasant escorts, she would take refuge there. She knew Maître Gabriel would be there and that the merchant would know how to put these troublesome wretches in their place.

They went on spouting trite compliments. After all, perhaps they were only fellows who had been drinking and had got a bit tight.

She took an alley that slanted off to the right and was relieved to recognize, at the far end of the long blank wall, the porch where Maître Gabriel had first halted to deposit his cartloads of wheat on her first night in La Rochelle. She was only a few steps away when the taller of the two men, who seemed pretty hefty beneath the sheen of his duck-egg-blue coat, seized her by the hand and slipped his arm round her waist.

"That's enough of that, my pretty one! You're surely not going to sulk at a couple of nice lads like us. We're only asking for a smile and a little peck provided you put your heart in it. We were told that the La Rochelle girls were a lively lot and had a warm welcome for strangers. Let's see whether they're right!"

As he spoke he bent over her and tried to reach her lips.

She jumped back and slapped him resoundingly across the face as hard as she could. He let go of her and clutched at his cheek. She took one leap forward but the other man had already grabbed her. A nasty, triumphant smile was playing about the lips of the man she had struck.

"Go on, Johnny," he shouted. "hang on to her. We'll

soon have her skirts around her ears, the pretty heretic!
What a bit of all right! It's our lucky day. . . ."

Between them they overpowered her. With one brutal
kick behind her knees they had her over. She yelled,
and they hit her across the mouth. Hands tore at the
lacing of her bodice. She thought she was going to faint
but pulled herself together and fought back desperately,
scratching and biting.

She managed to get free and ran frantically towards
the porch. She tripped on a stone, fell to her knees, and
dragged herself along shrieking:

"Help! Help! Maître Gabriel! . . . Help!"

They were on top of her again. Then began a nightmare struggle, like the struggle against Montadour's
dragoons, filled with the same sensation of helplessness
and terror.

All of a sudden her assailants seemed to take wing.
One of them reeled against the wall, propelled there by
an irresistible force. His eyes looked glazed. He staggered
and collapsed on top of Angélique, as limp as a rag
doll. Blood was gushing in red spurts from his temples.
Horrified, she tried to push the gory burden away. The
blood was spurting out of him. Angélique could not
manage to disentangle herself from this body that
pinned her down with all the force of a dead weight.
She fought against it frantically, and finally succeeded in
throwing it to one side. Before her the man in the blue
coat confronted Maître Gabriel. The merchant was far
bigger and stronger than his opponent and his fists were
hammering blows home. The man was already begging
for mercy; he had gone down twice, his clothes were
crumpled and covered in dust, and his face was becoming haggard. His wig had been ripped off and was lying
in the gutter, while his filthy greasy hair kept on falling
into his eyes.

"Enough! . . . Stop!" he panted.

A violent blow to the stomach made him grunt. He
leant against the wall with his head flopping this way
and that.

"Stop, I said. . . . Leave me alone. . . ."

Maître Gabriel went up to him. The man must have

read something terrible in his expression, for his eyes suddenly bulged wide open.

"No . . ." he said in a strangled voice, "no, have mercy!" Another blow knocked him to his knees.

"No, you can't do that. . . . Have mercy!"

The merchant was leaning over him inexorably. He hit him again, then seized him round the throat.

"No . . ." the man croaked.

He tried to raise his pallid, weak hands to pull away the two knotty arms, as tough as iron bars, that held him fast. He made a few convulsive movements with them, then they fell to his sides. Inarticulate noises were coming from his wide-open mouth.

Maître Gabriel's thumbs were sinking into the yellow flesh as into a lump of clay. It seemed as if they would never manage to free themselves again.

Angélique, frozen with horror, saw the muscles in the merchants two hands begin to stand out, as he slowly tightened his grip. A sinister rattle made itself heard in the nightmare silence of the street.

Angélique bit her lips to stop herself screaming. This must end, it must end quickly. The man's face took on a deep purple tinge. And still it went on.

At last the gurgle came to an end. The wretch lay dead, his eyes bulging from his head which had fallen across the cobblestones. Maître Berne examined him carefully before letting go and rising slowly to his feet.

His pale eyes looked strangely transparent in his face flushed with the effort he had made. He walked over to the other fellow, turned him over, shook him and let him fall back into the pool of blood, muttering to himself.

"He's dead! He struck his head on that ringbolt in the wall. Well, so much the better. I shan't have to finish him off. . . . Dame Angélique. . . ."

He looked up and stopped short in the movement that was carrying him towards her. He felt a strangely indefinable stirring of desire. Although she could scarcely stand, Angélique had got up and was leaning against the wall in the same flinching attitude that the man in the blue coat had adopted just before, when he had realized in a flash that the merchant was going to kill him. He no longer recognized her. . . .

Or at least not quite. . . .

Angélique's eyes looked in horror from one lifeless body to the other. Faced with the tragedy that had just occurred because of her, the panic of a hunted animal seized and overwhelmed her, transforming the lines of her face, normally so serene and proud. She looked like a mortally frightened child.

Absorbed as she was with her own fear, she had not noticed the state the two wretches had left her in. Her bodice was all unlaced and her blouse ripped open. Her bonnet had been torn and her hair had cascaded down over her shoulders and her half-uncovered breasts. Caught in a shaft of sunlight, the long pale gold strands glistened like a precious metal, standing out in even greater contrast against her white skin on which there were traces of blood. There was blood, too, now beginning to turn black, on her fustian skirt.

"Are you hurt?"

The merchant spoke softly, as if his thoughts were far away. It was not only bloodstains he saw on her. Obscene fingers had left their imprint on that pearly skin so suddenly exposed. Perhaps they had pressed their vile lips on her. At this thought the merchant felt a new wave of murderous passion sweep over him. This body that he forbade himself to think about as she came and went about the house, this woman with the easy and graceful movements, this body which moved beneath the heavy folds of its skirt and held its sweet delights imprisoned in a stiff bodice, these were the things those swine had tried to besmirch.

They had done the things which he would never have dared to do, even in his thoughts. They had stripped her, they had uncovered those legs, so delicate and curving that they looked as if they must belong to a statue or a goddess.

Never would he forget the picture that had met his eyes as he came out on to the porch. In one glance he had taken in the scene of violence and lust: he had seen

337

a woman pinned on her back by two thugs, and it had been her!

"Are you hurt?"

His voice sounded so hard that Angélique suddenly came to her senses. Monsieur Berne's massive black silhouette stood between her and the blinding sunshine, between her and the scene of horror.

She ran to him and hid her face in his shoulder in her desperate need to feel protected and to forget.

"Oh, Maître Gabriel! You have killed ... you have killed two men ... because of me. What's going to happen? What will become of us? ..."

He folded his arms about her and nearly crushed her.

"Don't cry, Dame Angélique. Not you ..."

"I'm not crying . . . I'm much too frightened to cry. . . ."

But tears were pouring unheeded from her eyes and were soaking the bands at her comforter's neck. Her fingers clung to him, her nails dug into him. He repeated:

"You never answered my question ... you didn't tell me whether you were hurt or not. . . ."

"No ... I don't think so. . . ."

"What about that blood?"

"That's not mine. . . . It's . . . his."

The merchant began to stroke her soft hair with its golden-bronze lights.

"There, there! Gently now! . . . my sweet, my dearest. . . ."

He was soothing her as if she were a child, and she became aware of the note of patience in his voice and the forgotten and delightful sensation of male protection.

Someone had come and stood between her and danger, someone had defended her, had committed a murder for her. She let herself go and cried her heart out against this inviolable rampart that reminded her somehow—she could not think why—of Desgrez the police officer's shoulder. The feeling of horror she had had a little earlier was beginning to grow blurred. Her starts of disgust and fear were becoming less marked. No longer

338

did she feel almost choked by her own panting breath; it was returning to normal. All of a sudden she thought to herself:

"Here I am in a man's arms and I'm not afraid," It was like the revelation of a cure she had ceased to hope for.

At the same time she felt ashamed. She felt hot hands on her bare flesh and became aware of the dreadful state her clothes were in.

She furtively raised her tear-filled eyes and met Maître Gabriel's glance. The expression on his face made her blush and she drew away.

"Oh, forgive me!" she whispered. "I am out of my mind." He released her gently.

Angélique struggled feverishly to cover her breasts and shoulders with the tattered remains of her bodice. Her embarrassment made her clumsy, and her efforts were fruitless. He had to come to her assistance by finding the strap that had slipped or the lace that had been torn. She blushed more and more.

"Don't get all worked up. Those brutes have knocked you about terribly. We'll never be able to make anything decent out of these rags, you'd do just as well to throw this bodice away. Now we must get a move on. . ."

His voice froze and Angélique, following the line of his gaze, saw Anselm the soldier, the Keeper of the Lantern Tower, watching them from the top of the ramparts.

A long expectant silence hung over the alley for what seemed interminable minutes. Then the soldier seemed to come to a decision. He started heavily down the stone steps.

He came towards them with his wild boar's tousled head nodding beneath his steel helmet. The hammering of his boots and his halberd on the stones made a tremendous clatter. The merchant looked down at his bare hands as if he were wondering whether they still had enough strength in them to destroy this new and armed enemy.

"Nice bit of work, mate," the soldier growled in his hoarse voice. "I saw the last bit of it from up there.

339

You've got some grip there, and I'm not saying that just to be polite, Maître Berne. . . ."

He touched one of the corpses with the end of his pikestaff.

"I know these two, they're scum. Baumier pays them to provoke the wives and daughters of Protestants. Then the husband or father steps in, there's a fight, and there's your opportunity to chuck a few more Huguenots into gaol. . . . Me, I'm not playing that game."

He leaned chattily on his halberd:

"When you've been strappadoed and been made to run the gauntlet like I have, what else can you do but abjure? I'm a poor soldier and I must eat. But that's no reason for betraying the folk who were once my brothers. Go on, get rid of those swine. . . . I've seen nothing."

He turned his back on them and walked slowly back to his post on the ramparts.

"Go and look in the yard," Maître Gabriel told Angélique, "I don't want my assistants to know anything about this. If there's no one around, go and open up the storeroom on the left."

Fortunately, the yard was deserted. Angélique pulled open the door of the shed he had indicated, and the smell of pickling brine almost choked her.

She came back to where Maître Gabriel still stood. He had taken the coat off the man he had throttled and had tied it round the other one's head to mop up the blood. In spite of these precautions, as they dragged the body along, they saw to their horror that their shoes, which had become stained with blood, were leaving a red trail of footprints across the courtyard flagstones. They left the body in the shed and went back to fetch the other.

"We'll put them in the salt," whispered the merchant. "It won't be the first time it's been done. It's a good hiding-place; the salt will preserve the bodies and it will give us time to wait for the best opportunity for getting rid of them."

He took off his black cloth coat, took a shovel and set about digging into the snowy mountain that glistened in the dim light.

Angélique helped him, shovelling with her hands. She was so keen to see those two grimacing faces with their hideous expressions disappear that she never felt the salt crystals biting into her torn hands.

They buried the two bodies as deep as they would go beneath the piles of salt and covered them over carefully. Angélique and the merchant worked on in silence. While the merchant put the warehouse in order until it looked quite normal again, Angélique took a bucket and filled it from the fountain. Then, brush in hand, she began to scrub the stains off the flagstones. A couple of assistants who had just come back from the docks with a consignment of casks came in by the other door. They saw her from a distance but did not think anything of seeing Maître Berne's servant scrubbing out the court-yard. She often came to the warehouses and, although it was chiefly to deal with the accounts, she did some-times do more menial work as well. Luckily the two lads knew that their master was around and so they did not come over. They might well have been astonished to see her with her clothes all torn and her hair falling about her shoulders.

They disappeared into the shed where the wines and spirits were kept.

Angélique went back into the alley. Flies were be-ginning to buzz around the pool of blood. The water in the gutter was red right down to the culvert that opened at the end of the road, straight into the sea.

Luckily no one had come that way yet. She went down on her knees and washed the spot over and over again. Her hair kept falling into her eyes, but she only relaxed when the last swill of water showed only a faint pinkish tinge which could not have aroused anyone's suspicions.

Then she carefully closed the porch doors which, one hour earlier, Maître Gabriel had more or less wrenched off their hinges as he rushed out to help her.

"Come into my office," said the merchant. "Everything is tidy now. We must do something to make you feel better."

Angélique was reeling. He put one arm round her

341

waist and held her up until they reached the shady room where, side by side, with all the account books and scales of all shapes and sizes, there lay piles of precious Canadian furs, cutlery from England and samples of Charentes brandy.

As a precaution, he slid the bolt.

Angélique had slumped on to a bench, and she leant on the table with her head on her arms.

Maître Gabriel pushed a glass of spirits over towards her.

"Dame Angélique, drink this up ... you must."

And as she made no move, he sat down by her, lifted up her head, and forcibly put the glass to her lips. She took a few gulps and stopped. The colour began to come back into her cheeks.

"But why did all this happen?" she asked, looking around her distraught. "I was on my way home ... they began to walk along with me ... I thought I would come in here to ask you to help me ... they became more and more bold ... and then all of a sudden ..."

"Forget all that," he said. "You have nothing more to fear, they are dead."

She shuddered violently.

"Dead? Isn't that ghastly? Everywhere I go people are left lying dead."

"People have to die," Berne said roughly. His eyes still had that extraordinary glint in them. "One death calls for another, one crime calls for another. It is written in the Bible, 'A life for a life, an eye for an eye, a tooth for a tooth, a hand for a hand, a foot for a foot, a burn for a burn, a wound for a wound, and a bruise for a bruise.'"

Angélique moved away from him along the bench. She got up and stepped back as if she had just discovered an enemy at her side.

"I hate men," she said, in a muffled voice, "I hate them all and I hate myself. I would rather not be here at all. You look at me as if I were mad. Perhaps you would like me to remain calm but I've had enough—I will *not* remain calm!"

"How young and childish you look all of a sudden. You

are not talking at all like the woman of discernment that you have accustomed me to see in you."

"But don't you understand, Maître Berne. Those devils got into my château, they set it on fire, they massacred my servants and cut my youngest son's throat, and as for me—Honorine was born as a result of that night, do you understand? She is the fruit of crime and rape, and you are surprised that I am unable to love her. . . ."

At first he seemed to think that she was delirious, then suddenly realized that she was referring to events in the past.

"But you must leave your memories. You have forgotten all that."

It was his turn to get up and leap over the bench. She watched him, full of fear, as he came towards her. And yet at the same time she wished that he were near her, very near her to sustain her. She also wanted to know whether the miracle had really come to pass, and whether she could again be happy in a man's arms.

"Just now you forgot all about them," he repeated softly. "Just now . . . when I was holding you."

He was just touching her. His hands were resting on her waist and, as she made no attempt to escape, he drew her to him. They were both tense and trembling but Angélique did not resist him.

She was as cold and insensitive as a virgin, but the curiosity she felt about her reactions had the upper hand. "Just now I wasn't frightened," she told herself. "That's true and, if he wants to kiss me now, I wonder what will happen?"

She was not put off by the wild look in the face that bent towards her. She submitted to having her own body held tight against this huge strong frame racked with desire and did not find it unbearable. The very personality of the man who touched her thus was wiped out. She forgot his name, she forgot who he was, it was only a man who held her in his arms and whose passionate appeal to her she recognized without taking fright.

She became aware of the sensation of inexpressible

343

relief and she began to breathe long and deep against his broad chest, like someone rescued from drowning beginning to breathe again. So she was still alive!

Her head fell back languorously.

His lips, thirsting for her but not yet daring to brush her, buried themselves in her hair. She began to notice that his trembling hand was caressing her bare skin. Her whole attention was riveted by her new discoveries and she was quite unaware of anything else.

It only took one word, a word which only they could see the dangerous significance of, to bring her back to herself again.

"Salt . . . Salt . . ." an assistant outside was shouting, as he banged on the closed door.

Angélique, torn from her torpor, stiffened.

"Listen," she said. "They are talking about the salt. They must have discovered something! . . ."

They stood stock-still, listening.

"Shall we load the salt, sir?" the assistant's voice repeated behind the door.

"What salt?" roared Maître Gabriel, galvanized.

He composed himself fairly quickly, glanced rapidly over his clothes and his bands to make sure they were all straight.

The assistant explained:

"It's for the tax. They've come to fetch the wine and the salt."

"I warrant this is one of Baumiers' tricks," growled the merchant.

He opened the door. A tax-collector, accompanied by two clerks and four armed constables, was standing on the doorstep behind the terrified assistant. They had two carts with them for loading this tax in kind.

"But I have already paid all my taxes," Maître Gabriel declared. "I can show you the receipts."

"Are you a member of the Reformed Protestant religion?"

"I am."

"Well then, according to the new decrees, you owe a further tax of the same value as the one you have

344

already paid. But have a look for yourself, it's all down there," he added handing him a piece of parchment.

"This is just another piece of injustice. There is no reason whatsoever for it."

"What do you expect, Maître Berne? Converts from your religion are exempted from paying income tax for a whole year and they don't have to pay the *taille* for three years. We've got to make up for those losses somewhere. So the pigheaded ones like you have to pay for the others. In any case it's only going to cost you twelve barrels of wine, a hundred and fifty pounds of salt bacon and twelve bushels of salt. That's not much for a rich merchant like you."

Every time she heard the word "salt" Angélique grew pale.

The royal tax-collector looked her up and down insolently.

"Your wife . . . ?" he asked Maître Gabriel.

But he was studying the writ the men had given him and did not bother to reply.

"This way, gentlemen," he said as he walked from his office towards the sheds.

Angélique heard the tax-man snigger and say in an offstage whisper to his clerks:

"These Huguenots are always preaching to us, but it doesn't stop them having fancy women like the rest of us."

CHAPTER 38

SEVERAL HOURS of horror followed during which Angélique expected disaster to strike at any moment. She listened to every noise from the courtyard. She felt sure that there would be shouts and that she would see Maître Gabriel escorted out under an armed guard. Suddenly she made up her mind that she must get away, all dishevelled as she was. She must run and fetch Honorine, then go, looking neither to right nor left, as far away as possible, on and on, until she fell exhausted somewhere in the open country.

345

She was saved from her mad impulse by the departure of the tax-collector. The carts rolled by loaded with their booty and the doors closed behind them.

The saffron-coloured evening air was full of dust. Maître Berne crossed the courtyard to rejoin Angélique; he looked worried but was quite composed. Nevertheless he poured himself another glass of brandy. It had been no easy matter to keep a constant eye on the snooping clerks, to make the labourers understand that they could take the salt from only one side of the pile and not from the other, and to escape the suspicious looks of the tax-man.

"I could not have helped you," said Angélique. "I would have given myself away."

The merchant made a weary gesture.

"This was one of Baumier's tricks," he said again. "Now I am quite sure that he was the man who sent those two miserable wretches after you. The tax-collector's visit was supposed to come right after they had reported the matter of the fight and our resistance to royal authority. In a few hours' time they are going to begin to wonder what we have done with their minions. So I have sent my assistants and porters home and shut up shop. We can't wait any longer now to get rid of the bodies."

He glanced towards the doorway, all golden in the sunshine.

"Soon it will be dark, then we can take action."

They waited silently in the dusk and did not attempt to move towards one another.

Their imminent danger kept them on the alert and occupied all their thoughts. They stood there rooted to the ground like hunted beasts trembling deep inside their lair.

The sky, which they could see through the doorway, took on the colours of a seashell and they could hear the rhythmic rumble of the sea mixed with distant sounds from the port.

Night came on, cold, blue and soft.

"Come on, we can go now," said the merchant.

They reached the shed where the salt was kept. Maître Berne fetched a wooden sledge from a small shed.

Once again they hacked away together at the bitter snow that tore their hands. When they had got the bodies out they lifted them on to the sledge, and covered them with sacks of wheat and piles of furs.

The merchant hitched himself to the shafts. When they had left through the back way, he turned the key several times in the lock.

"I don't want anybody to be able to get in here before I get back myself and have a good look round."

He picked up one of the shafts of the sledge again and Angélique took hold of the other. The wooden runners slid easily and noiselessly over the little round Canadian cobblestones with which every street and alley in the town was paved. They had been forced to use the sledge because of these special cobblestones, which were a legacy of a thrifty mayor who had discovered this way of using up the gravel from the St. Lawrence in New France which had been used as ballast in underladen ships. A car with iron-rimmed wheels would have made an infernal noise. Angélique and her companion dragged their sinister load along as fast as they could, like furtive shadows.

"This is the best possible moment," Maître Gabriel whispered. "They haven't lighted the lamps yet, and in this area where all we awkward Huguenots live, they make us wait for our punishment longer than the other folk on purpose. Persecution sometimes has its brighter side. . . ."

Nobody they passed in the street could possibly have asked what Maître Berne and his servant were doing or what they were trundling along, because the whole place was pitch-dark.

The merchant seemed to know where he was going. He kept on going off at a tangent down narrow alleys, following a very complicated circuit, which was presumably calculated to keep them off the bigger and more frequented streets.

Angélique had the impression that their expedition had gone on for hours and she was very surprised to find herself back not far from their own house, standing before the big gates of one of their neighbours, the paper-merchant, Jonas Mercelot.

Her master let the bronze knocker fall three times on to the door. It was the paper-merchant himself who came and opened it.

He was a white-haired, amiable man, very erudite, who once upon a time had owned practically all the paper-mills in the Angoumois. A law had been introduced forbidding Protestants to employ skilled artisans of their own religion, and this law, coupled with ruinous taxation, had left him only his beautiful house in La Rochelle and a very small business in art paper, which he alone knew how to manufacture.

"I've got something here to put down your well-shaft," Berne said to him.

"Splendid! Come along in, my dear friends."

He helped them most courteously to push the sledge and its gruesome load into a cellar that smelt sweetly of apples. He held his lamp high to light their way.

The merchant unloaded the furs and wheat. He uncovered the leering bodies, thick with salt and blood, and the gentle paper-merchant looked at them without any trace of surprise.

"Would Dame Angélique be so kind as to hold the lamp? Then I could help you to move them." This was all he had to say, and he said it with his habitual courtesy.

Berne shook his head.

"No, it would be better if you led the way. She doesn't know where to go."

"You're quite right."

Once again Angélique had to take hold of two stiff feet which weighed like lead. Her arms were stiff and aching. The paper-merchant went ahead lighting the way, and they descended three stone steps which led into a workroom all cluttered up with reams of paper piled on top of one another, bales of old rags, and huge demijohns of acid. Somewhere near the back Maître Mercelot, not without some difficulty, pushed aside an old-fashioned hand-press which had been hiding a little worm-eaten door. The key to it was tucked away in a
348

small hole in the wall. The door gave on to a spiral staircase, which luckily was fairly short.

Now they were in a vast underground room with a very low ceiling upheld by broad Romanesque pillars. In the middle there was a shaft. Jonas Mercelot lifted up its padlocked lid, and the room was filled with the sound of the rise and fall of splashing waves.

"This shaft leads straight into the sea," Maître Gabriel explained to Angélique.

He had to raise his voice to be heard.

"Anything you throw down there is smashed on the rocks and washed right away by currents," he shouted.

The ocean clamoured as if freed from its prison; its long-drawn-out roar re-echoed, again and again.

In all this din their actions took on the semblance of a nightmare. They never heard the bodies fall after they had tipped them into the sombre abyss. They seemed to be sucked in, and disappeared from their sight.

The lid was put back on again and the noise stopped. Then Angélique leant on the rim and closed her eyes. Maître Gabriel had said, "It isn't the first time, alas!"

That distant rumble she could still hear, that was the secret La Rochelle, haunted by her accomplice the sea, and by the sound of psalms that had risen in the sixteenth century from these underground caves where the first Calvinists had met together. It was the echo of that fight to the death which had taken place within these walls beween the two antagonists, and which in these present days of persecution was beginning again with the same harshess and the same crimes, equally justified on either side.

How could she escape from the blood and the fear?

She found Honorine lying on her stomach with her arms outstretched and her forehead resting on the cold stone floor, just like a small animal hopelessly waiting for death.

"She's been looking for you all day," Abigail explained. "She seemed to be abnormally anxious. She looked under every piece of furniture, she wanted us to open all the windows and the doors; she didn't call you but sometimes she would let out a scream that really hurt us."

"We offered her all sorts of goodies, but she refused them all."

"I lent her my wooden horse," Laurier explained. "But she didn't want it."

"Perhaps she's ill?"

They were all standing with worried expressions around the little prostrate bundle. They were even more concerned when they saw the state Angélique was in when she arrived home.

"But what on earth has happened to you?" cried Aunt Anna.

"Nothing serious."

She picked up her daughter and clasped her frantically to her.

"Here I am, my little love, here I am."

"Honorine must have felt I was in danger," she thought. "That's why she was worried."

Honorine had been born into danger; her instinct made her aware of the approach of the huge dark beast with the velvet tread. She must feel it there all the time, crouching behind the window-panes.

As she clung round her mother's neck, she demanded in no uncertain tones that they should put up the wooden shutters to hide the night. Everybody rushed to do as she bade, and only then would she slacken her grip on her mother and smile. Her mother was there and she could no longer see the black cruel face of doom in the reflections on the glass.

They put her into her chair and brought her a bowl of gruel. Angélique went off to change her dress; she put on a well-starched cotton dickey and hid her straggling hair under a new bonnet.

Maître Gabriel was talking in a very low voice to Pastor Beaucaire and his nephew, who was also a pastor and a refugee from the Cévennes. He had turned up one day holding the little boy of four, Nathaniel.

The child was with him tonight as well and so were the twin girls of the Carrère family. This completed the household; for neighbours had shared out the poor lawyer's ten children among them while the eleventh was being born.

Honorine was delighted to find herself the centre of attention of such a numerous gathering, and she grew talkative.

"Mamma," she said to Angélique, when she came back, "where is that pretty man who gave me the gold rattle?"

"What pretty man?" Maître Gabriel asked.

"What gold rattle?" Aunt Anna said suspiciously.

Angélique would have thought it ridiculous to pretend.

"Monsieur de Bardagne was kind enough to give the child a present."

There was an icy silence, during which Honorine busily patted her gruel carefully with her spoon. She was deep in thought.

"I would like a daddy like that so much," she said at last with an enthusiastic smile.

For some time now she had been desperately trying to find a father. First she had chosen Pastor Beaucaire, but he had disappointed her terribly.

"My dear little child, I love you as a spiritual daughter, but in all truth, I must tell you that I am not your father."

She was fond of the man who fetched the water, but he also was unwilling to accept such a responsibility.

She was obviously trying to discover how matters stood with Monsieur de Bardagne now, but she had chosen her moment badly.

Angélique thought it as well to take her off into the back kitchen and put her to bed. But Honorine's thoughts were still running on the same lines.

"He's not my father?"

"No, my love."

"Where is my daddy then?"

"A long, long way away."

"Over the sea?"

"Yes, over the sea."

"I'll get on a ship then," said Honorine.

Her eyes closed on a vision of a fabulous voyage and she fell asleep, worn out by the stress and excitement of the day.

Angélique set about preparing the evening meal. She had to keep busy with her daily tasks in order to keep her anxiety in check. She had not seen Monsieur de Bardagne again since he had proposed to her and had only sent him a letter in the hope that it would help him be patient.

They all sat down around the table and were just going to tackle the steaming mussel soup, when there was a ring at the outside bell.

They looked at one another, their faces tense in the candlelight. The bell rang again impatiently and Maître Gabriel got up.

"I'll go," he said. "If we don't answer it will look odd."

"No, I'll go," Angélique interposed.

"Let's send the valet."

But the valet was frightened without quite knowing why.

"Let me go," Angélique insisted laying her hand on the merchant's arm. "The most normal thing would be for your servant to go. I'll find out first what it's all about through the spy-hole, and I shall come and tell you."

Through the spy-hole a voice asked:

"Is that you, Dame Angélique? I want to talk to you."

"Who's that?"

"Don't you recognize me? I am Nicholas de Bardagne, the King's Lieutenant."

"You?"

Angélique nearly collapsed.

"What have you come for? To arrest me?"

"To arrest you?" the voice repeated, almost choking. The unfortunate man took a while to pull himself together again.

"So you think I'm only good for that sort of thing? To go around arresting people indiscriminately? Many thanks for your opinion of me. I know that the pighead-

352

ed people you mix with would gladly put it about that I am a werewolf, but all the same . . ."

"Monsieur, I have hurt you, do please forgive me. Are you alone?"

"Am I alone! Of course I am, my dear child. And I've got a mask on. And I'm wrapped about in a cloak the same colour as the walls. When a man in my position is stupid enough to go in for amorous escapades he prefers to be alone and not attract attention. If I were discovered, I'd never live it down. But I absolutely had to talk to you. It's very serious."

"What's happened?"

"Are you going to let me talk on without even offering me the shelter of a corner of your courtyard, or coming out to join me in this very quiet and discreetly dark street. Damn it all, Dame Angélique, what are you made of? When the King's Lieutenant, the Governor of La Rochelle, comes along secretly to give you a pleasant change from your ovens and to offer you his homage, you make him about as welcome as a dog in a skittle-alley."

"I'm terribly sorry but, King's Lieutenant or no King's Lieutenant, your secret visit is making me run the risk of losing my reputation.

"You certainly are intractable; you will drive me mad. The truth is you don't want to see me at all."

"Under the circumstances I must admit I don't feel at all happy about it. You do not realize how delicate my position is amongst these people that I have to serve. If they had an inkling . . ."

"I have come precisely to snatch you out of this nest of heretics where you are running the gravest risks."

"What do you mean?"

"Open this door and you will know."

Angélique hesitated.

"Let me warn Maître Berne."

"You must be mad!"

"I won't mention you by name, but I must find some sort of explanation to justify my absence, however short."

"You're absolutely right, but hurry—I feel a different

353

man after merely hearing the sound of your voice and breathing your sweet-scented breath."

Angélique got back to the house at the very moment when Maître Berne was leaving it anxiously.

"Who was it?"

She quickly explained Monsieur de Bardagne's presence and his request. The merchant's eyes began to glint dangerously, as dangerously as when he was getting ready to strangle Baumier's thugs.

"That whippersnapper of a Papist! I'll have a word or two to say to him. I'll teach him to come and seduce my servants under my very roof."

"No, don't interfere. It seems that he's got some serious news to give me."

"And what sort of news do you think he'll have? Your innocent little girl has made a few revealing remarks. Everyone knows that he is after you and would like to install you in town as his mistress. It's common knowledge all over La Rochelle!"

Angélique was holding Maître Gabriel back with all her strength, although he could have pushed her aside like a wisp of straw.

"For goodness' sake keep calm," she insisted severely. "Monsieur de Bardagne has all the power on his side. This is not the moment for us to sniff at his help just when we have made matters much worse—and they were bad enough already—and when you are running the risk of being hanged."

Gabriel Berne's anger was calmed less by her words than by the pressure of her delicate hand on his wrist.

"Who knows what you may already have granted him!" he growled. "Up to now I have always trusted you...."

He broke off because he was reliving that moment when his trust had been shaken. In a confused way he had remembered the months of domestic peace that had just gone by under the aegis of a first-rate servant who never by a single gesture or expression had given him the slightest reason to suspect her of coquettishness. God knows, he would have been very hard on her if she had!

But his suspicion, which had been keen at the beginning, had been allayed.

And then there had been that wounded Eve who had thrown herself into his arms weeping, that inert and, as it were, fascinated woman whom he had slowly drawn towards him. If she had pushed him away then, he would have been able to have controlled himself in time. He was sure of that. But Angélique's weakness had let loose in him that devil of the flesh that he had been overpowering, not without difficulty, since his tormented youth. He had lost his head; he had buried his face in her silky hair and had put his hand on her almost naked breast. He felt as if he could still feel its voluptuous warmth in the hollow of his hand.

His look changed.

Angélique smiled sadly.

"You trusted me before, did you say? And now ... now you think I am capable of every kind of wickedness, because in a moment when I was distraught, I allowed my senses to be stirred—by you! Isn't that unfair?"

He had never noticed before just how sensual and soft her voice could be. It was because she was talking very softly to him and was very close to him in the shadows; he could see her shining eyes and lips.

How painful and yet thrilling it was to discover, in such a familiar face, the mysteries of voluptuousness. Was this the way she talked at night when she made love? He began to hate all the men whom she had ever loved.

"And should I suspect you of the blackest of sins, Maître Gabriel, because you too lost a little of your self-control?"

He bowed his head guiltily, and he was glad to be guilty.

"Let's forget all that, shall we?" he said gently. "Indeed we must forget it. We were neither of us quite ourselves, neither I nor you. We had just been through a terrible experience. Now everything must be the way it was before."

But she knew quite well that this would be impossible. Between them would always stand the double complicity of a crime and of a moment of surrender. Nevertheless she insisted:

"We must save all our strength to struggle to save ourselves. Let me talk to Monsieur de Bardagne. I can give you my assurance that I have never allowed him to take the slightest liberty with me."

He thought he heard her add somewhat mockingly:

"Less than you."

"All right," he said. "Go on then. But be quick."

So Angélique came back to the little doorway where Monsieur de Bardagne, the King's representative, was fuming with impatience.

She opened the door and two possessive hands grabbed her by the wrists.

"Ah, there you are at last! You're making fun of me. What on earth were you saying to him?"

"My master is suspicious and—"

"He's your lover, isn't he? There's no doubt about that. Every night you give him what you're refusing to give me."

"Sir, that is an insult."

"And who do you think would believe anything else? He's a widower, and you've been living for months under his roof. He sees you constantly, coming and going, laughing, talking and singing ... and goodness knows what else! It would be impossible for him not to have fallen madly in love with you. It's intolerable, completely immoral, in fact it's quite scandalous."

"Do you reckon that it's anything short of scandalous for you to come and court me on a moonless night?"

"That's not the same thing at all. I am in love with you."

He drew her close to him in a dark recess. The night was so dark that Angélique could not make out his features, but she did notice the smell of the lilac-scented powder that he used in his hair. His whole being exuded an impression of refinement and comfort. He was on the right side; he had nothing to fear. He was stand-
356

ing on the other side of the wall behind which the outcasts suffered.

Did not the folds of Angélique's clothes still reek of salt and of blood?

Her chapped hands hurt her but she dared not remove them from the grip of the hands that were clasping them.

"Your nearness drives me mad," Monsieur de Bardagne murmured. "I have a feeling that if only I dared you might perhaps be less hard on me in this darkness. Wouldn't you perhaps give me one kiss?"

His voice was humble, and Angélique thought that it was up to her to make an effort. You could not make a royal official humble himself as much as this, without occasionally attempting to boost his self-esteem.

This had been a day of experiments. After taking away her most powerful weapon, had nature at last decided to give them partly back to her?

"All right then, you may kiss me," she said in a resigned voice which could scarcely have been very flattering.

But Nicholas de Bardagne was none the less quite overcome with joy.

"My darling," he stammered, "at last you are mine."

"Sir, I only said a kiss."

"What bliss! I promise I shall be very respectful."

He found it hard to keep his promise. This victory had given her lips all their sweetness, and he could have wished that they were less tightly shut. But he was tactful enough to be satisfied with things as they were.

"Oh! If only I had you at my mercy," he sighed, as she stepped back, "I'd thaw you."

"Monsieur, was that all you wished to say? I think I must go in now."

"No, I haven't finished. I'm afraid, alas, that I must come back to more unpleasant matters. My sweet, what brought me here to see you tonight, as well as my urgent desire to be near you again, was the fact that I simply had to come and warn you about a plot that is being hatched against you. I am very worried indeed about your fate. Oh! Why should I have fallen in love with you

357

like this? At first I knew hope, then anxiety, and now I am full of grief, because you have lied to me, you have knowingly deceived me."

"I have? But I haven't."

"You told me that you were sent here by the Company. But that isn't true. Baumier has been making inquiries about you, and he has established without a shadow of doubt that not one of the Ladies of the Blessed Sacrament has ever had anything to do with you or even knows you."

"That only proves that Monsieur Baumier has got his information wrong...."

"No!"

The Lieutenant's voice was ominous.

"It only proves that you have been lying. Because, as it happens, that rat Baumier is always very well informed about everything. He has a very high position in the Secret Company, in fact a much higher one than mine. That's why I often find I have to humour him. I dislike seeing him trying to find anything out about you but I am powerless to stop him. I heard through one of my spies that he is moving heaven and earth to find out exactly who you are."

He came closer and whispered:

"Tell me, who *are* you?"

He tried to take her in his arms again, but she stiffened. She was upset.

"Who am I? What a pointless question! I am only a simple—"

"Oh no. You are still lying. Do you take me for a fool? Let me tell you that, in the whole of the French Kingdom, there never could be a *simple* servant like you, capable of writing such well-composed letters, in such a swift hand as the one you wrote to me recently. I was both dismayed and delighted by it, but it also confirmed my impression that you were hiding your real identity under a borrowed name and clothes.

"As soon as Baumier ever set eyes on you he was suspicious. I can hear your heart pounding. You are frightened. If he were to find out anything, could it harm you? Come, you're saying nothing. Why don't you

358

trust me, my angel? I am prepared to do anything to save you. First of all you must leave the miserable Huguenots whose presence can only do you harm. One day they will be arrested, and, if you are found in their midst, you will not escape police inquiries. So when that happens, you must be far away in a place of safety. I could take you off, you and your daughter, to one of my estates, in the Berry. Later on, when all this religious trouble has settled down, and when Baumier is busy with some other matter, I would bring you back to La Rochelle. You would be my wife, of course."

He repeated nobly, frightened lest she should not have been fully aware of the depths of his devotion: "I don't know who you are, but I will marry you all the same!"

Angélique was incapable of uttering a single word. These revelations, crowning such a day, had thrown her into the most terrible confusion. She began to walk away, without a word, and he held her back.

"Where are you off to? You certainly are an extraordinary woman. You haven't even answered me. Will you consider my suggestion?"

"Oh yes, most certainly I will."

"You already promised you would once before. But make up your mind soon. Tomorrow I have to go to Paris for a few days; I have to attend the King's Council. If only you had agreed to come with me I could have dropped you in Berry."

"I can't make up my mind as quickly as that."

"Well, can I be sure, at least, that you will give me an answer when I get back?"

"I shall try to."

"You must say 'yes'! Baumier is a clever and tenacious man, and I am frightened for you."

He tried to kiss her once more, but she slipped from his grasp and shut the door.

She stood quite still for a moment in the dark courtyard, then ran like a mad thing towards the house.

She bumped into Maître Gabriel who took her by the elbows.

"What did he say to you? Why were you so long? He has persuaded you to go with him, hasn't he?"

She wrenched herself free and tried to run up the stairs. But he grabbed hold of her again in exasperation.

"Answer me!"

"What do you expect me to say? Oh, you're all mad! You men have got less sense than a lot of children. And yet death is here, waiting for you, maybe even for tomorrow. Your enemies are setting their traps and you fall into them, you're up to your knees in crime and surrounded by informers. And what do you think about? All you can think about is being jealous about a rival, and kissing a woman...."

"Did he kiss you?"

"And what on earth would it matter if he did? Tomorrow we shall all be in prison, tomorrow we shall be less than bodies beneath a gravestone with their names carved on it. We shall be walled up alive in prison. You don't know what it's like in prison.... I do."

She tried to get away again and he had to clutch at her, and put his two strong arms around her to hold her back.

There was an old lamp burning on the landing above them and in its dim light Angélique's face, with its wild expression that transfigured her beauty, seemed to have come from another world. He was holding a wandering ghost in his arms, whom the sorcery of an evil night had made visible to human eyes. Even now she did not seem real any more.

"Where are you running to? You will have everyone terrified."

"I've got to get my daughter and Laurier and take them away. We must get away."

He did not ask her where. He was looking at her as if he did not really see her properly. With her tense expression, and her eyes wide with fear, she looked like the woman he had battered with his stick on the road to Sables-d'Olonne, whose green eyes had looked at him so unhappily before they clouded over. Today she looked like that wretched woman who rose up through a curtain of rain on the muddy road to Charenton, the very symbol of all the wounded beauty, perplexed innocence and condemned weakness in the world. This was the woman who, over the years, had so often appeared to him in his dreams, whom he had finally come to call "the woman of destiny." He had asked himself in anguish what she would actually say one day, when he eventually heard her voice. For in his dreams she moved her lips, but he could never hear what she was trying to say to him.

And here she was, this evening, talking. He had heard the words of doom which for years had been destined to reach his ears: "We must get away."

"What, now, in the depths of the night? It's you who are mad."

"Do you think I'm going to wait for the King's dragoons to come here and murder us all? Do you think I'm going to wait for Baumier to come and arrest me and deliver me up to the King's justice? Do you think I'm going to wait and see Laurier go off crying in one of those carts which leave the town every day full of Protestant children, taking them goodness knows where? I've seen enough children crying and screaming and shouting for help; I've known enough prisons and guards and long waits and injustice. You can know them too if you want to. But I'm going off with the children. . . . I'm going to put to sea."

"To sea?"

"Across the sea there are new lands, aren't there? The King's men won't be able to get me there. Only there shall I ever be able to look at the sunshine and the flowers growing again. Even if nothing else is left to me, at least I shall have that. . . ."

"Your mind is wandering, my poor soul."

Because he did not lose his temper and his voice was full of tenderness, Angélique felt her tension ease.

She felt infinitely weary and utterly empty.

"This day has been too much for you," he went on. "You're at the end of your tether."

"I certainly am," she whispered. "And if only you realized how lucid it makes one, Maître Gabriel! I am not mad, I can simply see where I stand now: at the end of my tether. A pack of wild dogs is behind me, and they're getting closer. In front of me there's the sea. I must go, I must save the children, I must save my daughter. I can't bear the thought of her being torn from me and handed over to a lot of indifferent strangers, crying and calling me in her loneliness, a bastard, whom nobody wants. Can't you see why I haven't got the right to let myself be caught. I haven't even the right to die."

She added, struggling again:

"Let me go, you must let me go. I must run to the harbour."

"To the harbour? What for?"

"To set sail."

"Do you think it's as easy as that? Who would take you? And how would you pay for your passage?"

"If it came to that I'd sell myself to the captain of one of the ships."

He shook her furiously.

"How can you dare to say such a scandalous thing?"

"Would you rather I sold myself to Monsieur de Bardagne? If I have to sell myself to some man, I would rather it were to the one who would take me as far away as possible."

"I forbid you to do it, do you hear me, I forbid it!"

"I don't care what I have to do, but I'm going."

She was shouting, and her voice echoed through the old house where, above the hanging tapestries, the pale or red faces of shipowners and merchants looked down from their wooden frames. Never had these many generations of La Rochelle men heard shouting like this, nor such scandalous words. The Pastor with Abigail and Madame Anna were all drawing near, and were leaning over the banisters with their candles in their hands.

"Right you are," Maître Gabriel said. "You shall go ... but so shall we all."

"All?" Angélique repeated, unable to believe her ears.

The merchants face was tense but resolute.

"Yes, we shall all go. We shall leave the house of our ancestors, the fruit of all our work, and our city. We shall go away and earn the right to live on some distant shores. Don't tremble any more, Dame Angélique, my dear one . . . my lovely one. You are the one who is

362

right. The earth is slipping away from beneath our feet and we in our cowardice are letting our children slide into the abyss too, our children who have only just begun to live. It is useless to attempt to blind ourselves to it any more. Today I saw the cavern yawning wide, and I knew that I did not want to lose you. We shall go."

CHAPTER 39

SHE WOULD look at the sea twenty times a day; she could see its dancing greyness, stretching far away above the ramparts.

"Take me away! Take me away!" she would say to it softly.

But they had to wait. She had realized that they must. Two days had gone by since Angélique and Maître Berne had tipped the two disfigured corpses down Mercelot the paper-merchant's shaft.

Life appeared to have gone back to normal. There had been no policemen ringing at the bell, neither had any come to the warehouses. One might almost have believed that nothing was going to happen, and that all they had to do was to convince themselves that nothing had happened. They only needed to tell themselves that life was peaceful, that there was nothing better to do than to hook the pot over the fire and to iron the dry marjoram-scented washing on this lovely sunny afternoon.

But it was no use Honorine asking them every evening to fix the wooden shutters on the window; a threat hung over the house none the less. It was marked by an invisible seal, it and its occupants. The city encircled them like a trap. For the harbour, the gateway to freedom, was constantly patrolled by officious police, and every ship was carefully examined. Before they could breathe freely they would have to do more than spread canvas and sail between the chain tower and the St Nicholas Tower, round Richelieu's dyke, and pass out beyond the semi-circle of white cliffs. There were royal naval ships cruising up and down off the coast of the Island of Ré for the purpose of stopping people getting away.

The children were dancing around the palm-tree. Their shrill voices came to Angélique with the rhythmic tapping of their little wooden clogs on the paving stones of the courtyard.

> A la pêche aux moules
> Je ne veux plus aller, maman,
> Les garçons de Marennes
> Me prennent mon panier, maman. . . .

There was a whole horde of little people from the neighbourhood there whose parents had brought them along, after being summoned to a Council of Elders. The little girls' embroidered bonnets and their brightly-coloured pinafores on top of their big full skirts, looked like flowers dotted amongst the dark serge suits worn by the boys.

Every shoulder was adorned with bouncing curls, blond, brown or red; their cheeks were pink, and, when they looked up, their eyes looked like stars.

Angélique kept on putting her iron down to lean out of the window and watch them. At any moment, she thought, the doors might open, men in black might come in, or armed soldiers, who would seize these children by the hand and take them away for good.

The members of the Consistory came out on to the landing. Their wives, whom Aunt Anna had been entertaining, joined them. They began to come down in small groups, talking softly and whispering as if someone was dead in the house.

Soon afterwards Maître Gabriel came into the kitchen. He drew up a chair and sat down, but he did not reach, in his usual way, for his long Dutch pipe, as he did when everything was peaceful.

He spoke without looking at Angélique.

"We have decided that we shall go to Santo Domingo," he said. "Our group will consist of about ten families accompanied by two pastors, Beaucaire and his nephew. Everyone concerned is determined to make a go of it and to begin all over again in a new land. For some of them things are not going to be easy. The paper-merchant Mercelot, and Carrère, the lawyer, want to come with us with all their brood. How are we going to give them work on the islands? I don't even know whether the master-fishermen like Gasserton and Malire will be able to eastablish any sort of fishing business out there. People make their living mainly from the plantations of sugar-canes, tobacco, and cocoa."

"I'm interested in cocoa," Angélique said eagerly. "Once I had something to do with the manufacture of chocolate and I know how to choose top quality beans."

She was already dreaming. She could see herself free, with a huge straw hat on her head, like the one her mother used to wear, walking about an emerald-green plantation with Laurier and Honorine somewhere behind her, trying to catch the sapphire and golden butterflies.

Her green eyes were filled with light, as if they were already full of the magical reflections of the Caribbean sea with its palm-trees.

Maître Gabriel surreptitiously cast a sad glance at her. It had taken him only a few days to learn to appreciate all the subtleties of her beauty which, up to then, he had denied himself the pleasure of contemplating. He reproached himself violently for it, but he would constantly return to her face which showed traces of an intense and yet most secret life. "She came into our lives like a torch," he would tell himslef. She cast her light upon all of them, and yet not one of them knew anything about her. Today, she was carefully ironing the starched coifs. Her cheeks were pink with the scalding steam which rose from the damp clothes. She went about her task in an alert and capable manner, but her big eyes revealed bottomless depths, and, when he sat and watched her fixedly like this, it was less on account of his desire than because he was fascinated by her mysterious past. The odd word would escape her from time to time, and the merchant would store them all in his mind, and attempt to piece together the very varied

365

pictures. Had she not just said that she had had something to do with cocoa? He wondered when and where. He had not failed to notice her business acumen, particularly where the sea was concerned. But what connection could there be between the woman he had seen rise up like an unhappy angel in the grey mud of the Charenton road, and the one who had cried in that distraught voice: "They entered *my* château, they murdered *my* servants . . ."?

"She's an adventuress!" Madame Manigault would say categorically, putting her finger on the end of her nose. "I can smell her out, and I have never been proved wrong yet!"

Angélique's eyes met her protector's shrewd gaze, and she smiled with a trace of embarrassment. They had mutually agreed to "forget" and to preserve an appearance of normal friendly relations until the departure. She was very grateful to him for managing to do so. A tough Huguenot education had accustomed Maître Gabriel to overcome his feelings. He was a sensual and choleric man, and had managed to transform himself by prayer and his own will-power into this prudent, calm man, capable of leading the life of an ascetic whom everybody looked up to and some feared a little in La Rochelle. This moulding of his character had produced a man of great strength and goodness. In this hour of danger he would not be the one to impose upon others the consequences of his own inner upheavals. He had enough common sense to see that, if things were to continue along certain lines, they would all go quite mad and would be caught up in disaster like sheep in a panic.

Thanks to him and to his icy expression a semblance of peace once more filled the house. Angélique's nerves were growing calmer again, for the merchant's moral strength gave her enough courage to withstand her own anguish. Nevertheless, when they were alone, there were often long silences between them.

"How are we going to get away?" she asked.

The merchant's face lighted up.

"As you Papists say, it's like a miracle. Jean Manigault, the shipowner, who was one of the people who most strongly opposed our leaving, has suddenly decided to come with us. A most unfortunate thing happened to him recently and it has made him change his mind: his young son Jeremy was taken away from him. The little lad had been stupid enough to stop and watch a religious procession going by. 'They' saw in this a wish to be converted and, since the youngster is over seven, they took him off to the Minim Brothers. It cost Manigault a fortune to get him back, and he has only been temporarily released. Now in spite of all his wealth, Manigault is terrified about his child. So he's leaving too. Things are going to be a lot easier with him as one of the party. He already owns many warehouses in Santo Domingo and so we shall be able to sail in one of his own ships.

"This is what he has in mind, and it seems a good plan to me. One of his slave-trading ships is due here from Africa soon. The slaves will be kept in the warehouses on the quayside while waiting to set off on the next leg of their journey to the islands. Manigault will make a list of them all, which he has to submit to the authorities, but at the last minute, we shall take their places. Provided nobody else comes on board the examine the ship between the time that we have left the quayside and the moment when we have crossed the Straits of Antioch we shall be safe."

"But what about the slaves?"

"They will have been left on land, in the padlocked warehouses, and we shall have taken care to drug them so that they are not discovered until as late as possible."

"So Monsieur Manigault's great courage consists in jettisoning the profits he would have made on his precious cargo," Angélique said, her practical side getting the upper hand again.

"There are going to be many other things that we shall have to abandon," Berne answered thoughtfully. "But Manigault is not going to be the worst off amongst us; he expects to be able to start trading with his successor here. In fact his business will be just the same, except that he will be in Santo Domingo instead of

367

being in La Rochelle. He has done everything necessary to make sure that nothing goes wrong. As far as I'm concerned, I have a little money in Holland and some in England. In addition we shall make the most of the days that remain by transferring the best part of our wealth into gold. That won't take up very much room on the ship."

"Don't you think that there is a possibility of people becoming suspicious if they know we are selling up?"

"We are being very careful about it. The Catholics with whom we deal know quite well that Protestants are being forced to sell in order to pay these double taxes."

Angélique came out with the question she had been aching to ask.

"When is it to be, when are we going to embark?"

"In two or three weeks' time."

"In three weeks!" she exclaimed. "Heavens, what a long time!"

He shuddered and seemed to be full of resentment towards her.

"It seems a very short time when it means tearing yourself from the land of your fathers," he growled.

He brought his fist down hard on the table.

"May those who are forcing us to do this be damned!"

She would have liked to have said she was sorry, but she said nothing, for fear of annoying him still more.

Angélique, who had already lost all she had, found it hard to understand what kept the Protestants clinging to their painful restricted life here.

But the Protestants continued to clutch at the tenuous thread of their existence, like the peasant who clings to the barren piece of earth he tills and looks without envy on the fertile valley which is a stranger to him. They became sad at the mere thought of these American islands, with their sunshine and promise of freedom. They had always been used to rowing across a tempestuous sea, and so overcoming one obstacle only to see a new one rise up before them, and in this way they had bred a race of men who clung desperately to their roots, resisting every assault. For two hundred years now they had lived under persecution; and now it seemed more unbearable to leave their town and their province than to continue the secret battle they had always been used to.

To think that they would no longer live beneath the bright blue sky of La Rochelle! To think that their children would no longer breathe the familiar air heavy with the scent of the sea and would no longer tread where their fathers had trod.

Generations of La Rochelle youngsters had run along the beach, with their bare feet pattering on the sand: they had prised shells off the rocks with their knives, and had opened oysters to drink their cool bitter water in the shade of the Lantern Tower, as the russet tide began to fill the harbour and make the tall white sails of the huge merchantmen bob up and down.

To leave all that . . .

"Three weeks is a very short time," the La Rochelle merchant said, "yet at the same time I know that danger looms large. But we must try to have the chances as far as possible on our side, and that is why it is well worth the risk of waiting these three weeks. For in three weeks at the outside the Dutch merchant fleet will be leaving La Rochelle. You know as well as I do that these people don't like to travel alone, the way the French do; twice a year they leave Amsterdam or Antwerp all together. They form regular armadas of merchantmen protected by warships. Now Manigault's insurance is taken out in Holland; this gives him certain advantages, including the privilege of membership of these convoys with the advantages of the protection they offer. So we must wait until they arrive. They will not only create activity in the port, but some confusion as well, which will be helpful to our plans; then, when we do set sail in the midst of this whole fleet, we will be bound to escape the royal naval check, for they would really have far too much to do if they had to tackle every ship. That's how we shall avoid any last-minute prying by the authorities. Once we have left the quayside—and I bet that will be one of the days when the civil administrators of the Admiralty won't be particularly punctilious—no one will come near us any more!"

Angélique nodded. The plan seemed to her to be not only sensible but very clever. And yet she was still frightened: the weeks of waiting seemed longer than a whole year to her. What plots was Baumier hatching in the shadows? He was not the sort of man to let go of his prey; might he not take advantage of Nicholas de Bardagne's visit to Paris to make decisions which his superior might not necessarily approve of?

Angélique's heart was held tight as in a vice, but she bravely raised her head.

"May God hearken to you, Maître Gabriel."

CHAPTER 40

THE PATH along the cliff-top meandered through the dry, salty grass, following the winding coastline which, from La Rochelle, led through a maze of creeks, bays, and jagged headlands to the little hamlet of La Palice opposite the Island of Ré. The grey sand made walking difficult, and Angélique was making slow progress.

She was not worried; she had plenty of time, and, although she would have preferred to have completed her appointed task, she was beginning to enjoy this impromptu walk.

Honorine was trotting along gamely at her side. Since the day the two police agents had been killed, Angélique would never leave her behind when she went out. In any case she herself only left the house rarely, for she was very loath to risk herself outside. She saw suspicious shapes everywhere, and thought she could read an enigmatic look of condemnation in the eyes of people she passed in the street. She was quite certain that the net was being drawn tighter.

The hours went by peacefully enough, and so did the days, but Angélique felt as if the sand was crumbling away beneath the solid foundations of her life. More and more sand would disappear, then suddenly the whole structure would cave in!

All around her there was tremendous activity, as swift as it was carefully hidden, amongst those who were planning their escape. Not a soul could have been accused of packing anything, and yet somehow, each night, mysterious bales would find their way to the docks. The most heterogeneous collection of treasures was being stowed away in the hold of the *Sainte-Marie*, the slave ship that had recently arrived from the African coast. Whether they were poor or rich, each one was taking away the things that meant most to him. They were quite willing to go, but could not face the idea of sleeping without that yellow satin counterpane, nor of cooking in any other cast-iron pot than the very one which had been used to prepare so many delicious cauldronfuls.

Manigault the shipowner had lengthy arguments with his wife, who wanted them to take their superb dinner service, the pride of her dressers, which had been made by a famous Huguenot, Bernard Palissy, once a refugee in La Rochelle. The shipowner ranted and stormed but eventually allowed her to pack a dish from here or a tureen from there; he himself was unwilling to part with his chequered gold snuffboxes.

In the dockside warehouses the musky smell of the black slaves from the Guinea coast mingled with the aroma of vanilla, pepper and ginger; the men drew consolation for the hardships of their exile from singing nostalgic laments. Down in the bowels of the *Saint-Marie* blacksmiths were busy checking the chains which would be used for the slaves as they were being shipped to the islands. There was not the slightest hint anywhere that the passengers who were actually going to embark would be so very different from those they were preparing for.

Aunt Anna found the thought of travelling in the slaves' hold extremely unpleasant.

"The air will be unfit to breathe," she said. "And the children will all die of scurvy."

Several times a day she would make a pile of the books she wanted to take with her: there was her Bible, a book on mathematics, and one on astronomy. The pile was always too tall, and the old maid would sigh.

Angélique had bought a whole supply of figs and

371

raisins from the little shop run by a Levantine; she had obtained these for the children, for Savary had once told her that these fruits would prevent scurvy, the fatal disease that made your whole body swell, and your gums begin to bleed.

They were all busy getting their things ready, and they all wanted to believe that everything would go well. In fact it looked as if it would, and Angélique wavered between peaceful reassurance and anxiety. Her instincts never betrayed her and already she was aware of hidden threats in the air. But how was she to tell what they were? Should she consider the fact that Monsieur de Bardagne had not returned from his trip to the capital as an evil omen, or, stranger still, that the disappearance of the two police agents had called forth no comment or inquiries at the time? The Police Provost had recently ordered that the city gates were to be kept shut by day as well as by night, and that anyone wishing to enter or leave the city was to be screened with the greatest care. To justify this measure he had said that there were pirates prowling along the coast. Should they take his excuse at its face value or should they rather interpret it as a decision to watch the Huguenots much more closely? Of course here the people had no reason to fear armed attacks as they did on the Mediterranean coast, but the worthy mechants knew well where their fears lay. The pirates would anchor somewhere near by, would mingle with the local people inside the town, and would sell their booty at cut-throat prices, for they had not had to pay the pretty stiff entry and sales taxes. They could always find shopkeepers willing to enter into some sort of agreement with them for an appreciable and tax-free profit. Was it really true that some of these men, with their gallows-bird faces, had been discovered within the last few days offering Canadian furs for sale? Was it only because of them that an entire regiment of dragoons had been quartered within the city walls? For whatever reason, the gates now remained shut and guarded.

That was why Angélique had been detailed to fetch

Martial and Séverine from the Island of Ré. Earlier it had been decided that Maître Gabriel should go for his two elder children, as the time drew near, but now it had become extremely hard for Protestants to leave the city. Their names were checked on a list, they were questioned at great length, and an eye was also kept on whether they returned, and how many did so.

On the other hand time was getting short. Their secret departure was imminent, for the arrival of the Dutch fleet had been announced. Angélique often leant out of the window that looked onto the ramparts to call out to Anselm Camisot:

"Any sign of the Dutch yet?"

The keeper of the Lantern Tower would shake his head.

"Not yet; but why all this impatience, Dame Angélique? Have you got a young man on board one of the ships?"

Now it was rumoured that they had put into Brest. They would be in La Rochelle in two or three days' time. Sails would bob up all over the horizon, and within a few hours the sea would be white and dancing like a bird-strewn shore, and tough-looking men with ham-coloured faces and rough accents would pour out into the town.

Then their time would come, and in the black of night a handful of hunted men, women and children would go on board; there would be whispering and the wails of babies rocked in soothing arms.

They would be there, those furtive shadows, escaping from the city, their city, the city of their forefathers, and during that night proud Protestant La Rochelle would reap the harvest of its defeat.

There they would be, deep in the hold, anxiously awaiting their departure, each one of them on the alert for distant orders and the sound of footsteps over their heads. The ship would creak, and they would feel her get under way while the swell rose along her sides. Later the time would come when they could come out of the evil-smelling 'tween-decks without risk. The sea would lie deserted all around them and on this bare horizon they would be able to see the image of their freedom.

Angélique drew a deep breath. The air was heavy with the smell of salt and of bitter wormwood. Tiny dark-yellow flowers grew in the hollows between the dunes. Honorine was gathering some with great care.

"Hurry up, my love," Angélique said.

"I'm tired."

"Well, I'll carry you then."

And she knelt down so that the child could climb on to her back.

She found it very pleasant to walk into the wind with this light bundle on her back. Honorine's silky locks, which had been blown about all over the place, kept stroking her cheek. She heard the little girl laugh. They both enjoyed the silence of the open countryside, a silence that was made up of a thousand sounds: the sound of the surf on the shingle at the foot of the cliff, and of a bird's call as it flew up out of the gorse. Angélique realized—and she was quite sure that Honorine felt the same way—that neither of them had been born to live in a town. Once outside the ramparts they had all of a sudden discovered that they preferred the open country with its far-away horizon and the lure of what lies like a promise behind it. This region was flat and bare, with no trees, and today it lay beneath an impalpable veil of greenish mist, which made the plain of sand-dunes, swamp and poor fields appear to stretch for ever into the distance.

On their right, far away, they could see a group of wretched hovels which made up the hamlet of St Maurice. Looking towards the sea, you could still see the central pier of Richelieu's dyke rising, thick with limpets, out of the water. On either side its broken beams lay higgledy-piggledy and mouldering in the tideway. Angélique only glanced at it. The Straits lay before her, running between the islands of Oléron and of Ré, but even in this narrow channel she could sense the call of the open sea.

374

Honorine tightened her little arms around her mother's neck.

"Are you happy?" she asked her mother with that gentle indulgence that is the prerogative of well-loved children.

"Yes, I am happy," Angélique answered.

And she was. The time of their deliverance was at hand. As she looked at the landscape, still wild and independent of men and their passions, she became quite certain that the sea would not betray her. A new stage in her life was opening out before her.

However difficult it proved to be, she would live that new life with new courage, and for she would be delivered from an oppression which had weighed on her entire existence. Her only regret in leaving this ancient land was that she must needs leave behind that little grave at the edge of the forest of Nieul, near the ruins of a white château. The only treasure she was taking with her would be her daughter, her precious child, her friend. Only a few more hours to go and she would be at peace like a bird resting, worn out by the storm, carried intoxicatingly along on gentle currents. Happiness lay at hand.

"Well then, if you're happy, sing me a song!" Honorine said.

Angélique began to laugh. Her daughter would always know how to seize her opportunities on the wing.

She began to hum Florimond's favourite song, "The Green Windmill." It was all about a windmill covered with emeralds, about a devil who wanted it for himself and the owner who was trying to prevent his getting it. It was a very long story.

As she went on singing, Angélique moved away from the edge of the cliff. At this point she must cut across the heath to join up with the road that would take her to the little port of La Palice, the first shanties of which she could already make out.

"Look over there," Honorine said, "I can see the Devil of the Green Windmill."

Her mother turned automatically to look in the direc-
375

tion in which the small finger was pointing, and she caught her breath.

Almost exactly at the point they would have reached if they had gone on following the coastal path, a silhouette had appeared. By now Angélique was too far away to be able to make out the features of this apparition, but she could see that he was a very tall man, dressed in dark clothes, with a vast black cloak on, which billowed in the wind.

It was Mephistopheles in person!

At the very same moment the sea wafted a veil of wandering mist towards the shore, and Angélique found herself standing in the middle of an unearthly dream, in which the only living, moving thing seemed to be the black wing of the huge cloak.

She thought that she could no longer be alive, or, at least, that her mind had leapt from her and been carried off into the land where vague imaginings become realities, or where dreams become palpable while the real world becomes blurred.

This was the kind of thing that must happen when your mind became unhinged.

She had so often called to mind Monsieur Rochat's quip: "I could wish that Rescator would come and anchor off La Rochelle." And here it was, actually *happening*. Here she was living in the very heart of the dream she had dreamed in all its details. She thought that she must have just gone out of her mind, and she became frightened.

Then the wave of damp fog passed over and the sea took on its brilliant, clear hues once more. Everything became bright again, sharp and incisive as it had been before, and she could see La Rochelle itself in the distance, white and chiselled like a pure silver crown. The strange man raised his arms and put a spy-glass to his eye to look at the town. Now he had taken on the solidity of human flesh, and his black inky presence on the shining edge of the cliff, though still worrying, nevertheless no longer seemed ghostly or diabolical.

He continued his examination, standing firmly on his leather-booted legs. Then he lowered his glass and seemed to be signalling to some other people on the shore whom she could not see.

Angélique collected herself: he was going to turn round and see a woman standing there. Why did she suddenly become convinced that this man and those who accompanied him had no desire to be recognized nor even be seen?

She looked about her, then hurried behind a tamarisk bush where she and her daughter hid themselves. Because she was stretched out in the sandy hollow, it was difficult to make out what was happening farther away, but she saw two men come up to the first and the three of them stand conferring together.

Then they disappeared. She might have thought that it had all been a dream if she had not put her ear to the ground and heard the stifled sound of voices and of irregular hammer-blows such as might have come from a carpenter's mallet.

A squall of wind brought her the bitter and unmistakable smell of molten pitch, and a plume of smoke rose up over the cliff-top, which at this point curved deeply inwards to form a sort of cove.

"Don't move," Angélique said to Honorine.

But Honorine had no intention of moving. Her wild nature enjoyed crouching in this small hollow like a young rabbit on the look-out, and it must have reminded her of the early days of her childhood.

Angélique crawled flat on her stomach through the grass until she reached the cliff-top.

There she saw, moored in the middle of the cove, a three-masted ship carrying neither colurs nor oriflamme. She rode fairly low in the water and was relatively broad in the beam, and could equally well have been Dutch or English, but certainly not French. She undoubtedly did not belong to the cod-fishing fleet based on La Rochelle, for they were ships of under 180 tons and this one must have drawn 250 tons or more.

What was a merchantman doing in this cove only a league from La Rochelle? It was quite unsuitable as a mooring place. It was well-known that the steep but low cliffs gave only poor shelter, and that the bottom was shallow and muddy. Only fishing vessels ever sheltered in these creeks.

And in any case was it really a merchantman? When she was in the Mediterranean, Angélique had become accustomed to recognizing certain tricks of camouflage. Now she became certain that the ship must have two decks, and that a battery of cannons lay behind the set-in ports, which, though almost invisible even from close up, must open when necessary, to reveal the black muzzles of about fifteen guns.

On the deck, by a particularly tall and heavy poop-rail, some inoffensive-looking tarpaulins were strewn, no doubt hiding the culverins. The presence of a sentry close by made this almost certain.

The other bits of canvas no doubt hid heaps of long wooden poles, boathooks and ladders which were used at sea to ward off assaults from other ships . . . or to assist in boarding them.

A caïque left the ship, and headed for the beach; then, as it reached the shore, Angélique lost sight of it.

She moved still further forward very quietly, and carefully raised her head.

She could hear the ring of voices now, but could not make out what language they were speaking. Below her she could see a huge pot hanging over a fire that had been lit on the shingle; it contained shimmering Swedish pitch, or tar, which was used to repair ships. Small barrels were lined up all round. The sailors were dipping pieces of oakum into the tar then placing them in baskets for the caïque to carry them back again. All Angélique could see of the men was their backs and heads; some had thick mops of hair and others were covered with woollen caps.

The ship's crew was, to say the least of it, strange. It looked as if each of the four men who made it up was of a different race, and that they had come together at some nautical festivity to present a ballet describing the four corners of the earth. One of them was lean and nimble, with a tanned face and the big eyes commonly seen in the Mediterranean peoples: perhaps he was from Sicily, or Greece or even Malta. The second was as thick-set as a bear beneath his fur cap, and seemed to find it hard to move in his stiff coat and sealskin boots. The third was a regular gingerbread man with his slit eyes; the muscles of his hefty, bare arms stood out as he lifted a fair-sized barrel of oakum containing pieces of pitch on to his head. He must be Turkish. The last one, a haughty and gigantic Moor, was keeping carefully away from the rough work the other members of the crew were doing, and seemed content to keep an eye on their neighbourhood, his musket in his hands.

"The pirates! . . ."

So the Provost's pretext for closing the city gates had not been trumped-up! Pirates really had been spotted, and here they were, unbelievably bold, for only a few cables lay between them and the St Louis fortress of La Rochelle, and it was not much further to St-Martin-de-Ré where the royal naval squadron lay!

The sails had been furled so that they could be set very quickly; an indication that the ship was on the alert and ready to get under way again at the first suggestion of danger. It seemed strange that they should be caulking her under those conditions. Perhaps it would make their presence there more plausible to any casual observer from the land or from a passing ship.

Close by the sound of rolling stones made her flatten herself even closer to the ground. She heard surprising and unexpected grunts, followed by piercing shrieks, which could well have spelled tragedy had they not come from a pair of hefty pigs whom their owners, peasants from the village of St Maurice, were attempting to drive down to the beach. The sailor in the fur hat went up to them and began to bargain. It seemed as if the peasants were getting on well with the boatload of pirates who had dropped anchor in their vicinity, but this did not make them any less of a parcel of adventurers ready for anything. They were real, all right, these pirates: she could see them, hear them, and almost touch them. It was the man in the black cloak who was not real. It was quite inconceivable that *he* should have come in flesh and blood and cast anchor in front of La

379

Rochelle. Especially him . . . Why him? . . . She must have dreamt it, and in any case she could no longer see him. And the ship, save for the motionless sentries, seemed quite abandoned. It rose and fell gently and the light shone on the gilded mouldings of its strikingly large and ornate poop. These carvings would hardly have disgraced a royal vessel, and Angélique managed to decipher its strange name written in golden lettering: the *Gouldsboro*.

The pressure of a small hand on her arm brought her back to earth. Honorine, who must have found the time dragging, had crept up to her as stealthily as a kitten.

Seeing her there, Angélique realized that they could not stay where they were. These tough seamen were not exactly renowned for their gentle dealings. They became less and less easy to cope with in proportion to the dangers they ran. And if their captain really was the Rescator she thought she had seen earlier, what was to be gained by falling into his hands again?

She slid from sand-dune to sand-dune, taking infinite precautions, and eventually managed to get a bit inland. When at last they reached the road, she took Honorine on her back again and walked as fast as her legs could carry her into La Palice. She almost ran into the inn where the fishermen came for a glass of wine after drawing in their nets.

"You look as if you'd just seen the Devil himself!" the landlady said to her, placing the inevitable jug of Island of Ré wine on the table before her.

"Yes, we did see him," Honorine agreed.

"She's cute, that little one!" the woman remarked, laughing.

Angélique asked for some milk and a slice of bread and butter for her daughter, and some hot broth for herself. In spite of much urging from the landlady, she would not touch the wine, which would have deprived her of what little strength her legs still had left. She must not lose sight of the fact that what she had to do was to fetch Martial and Séverine from the Island of Ré.

A couple of hours later she was in the little capital, St

Martin, all a-glitter with the gold-braided red and blue coats of the King's officers.

She inquired where Madame Demuris—Maître Berne's sister—lived, and found the house easily. Angelique looked pale and a trifle distracted; in fact she fitted the part she had to play perfectly. Maître Gabriel had been taken ill suddenly: he was dying, and wanted to see his children before he passed on.

His sister would never have the heart to prevent their going, and indeed she was the one who seemed most upset at the news. She was not a bad woman, but she had become a convert because she was ambitious and intelligent enough to see that as a Protestant girl her life was going to be an endless succession of misfortunes and blighted hopes. She was younger than Maître Gabriel and had been very upset at the rift that had come between herself and her brother, whom she greatly admired. She wept bitterly and, thinking only about her brother's imminent death and quite forgetting the Lieutenant's orders that the two children should never leave her house without special authorization, she let her two charges go.

The owner of the small boat that rowed them back to the mainland watched the sky as it clouded over. A storm was brewing, and the boat began to bob up and down on the great white-crested black waves. As they reached the shore, fine squalls of rain began to lash at them. Angélique found a covered wagon to take them back; in any case she would not have dared to walk back over the heath. The driver was a Huguenot and was glad to do a good turn for Maître Berne's children.

It was a short drive and soon they stood beneath the ramparts by the St Nicholas gateway. It was guarded by a sentry sheltering beneath an oilcloth cape. He scarcely bothered with them and allowed the peasant to go through with his cart. Angélique was already congratulating herself on their good fortune in meeting a storm when two archers stepped out of the guard-room.

They stepped in front of the horse to stop it and glanced into the wagon.

"Here she is," said one of them.

Angélique recognized the man who had asked her her name and occupation that morning as she had left the town.

"Are you Dame Angélique, a servant in Maître Gabriel Berne's house, which stands on the corner of the Rue Sousles-Murs and the Place de la Marque au Beurre?"

"Yes, I am."

The two men took counsel, then one of them climbed up beside the driver.

"We have been instructed to await your return and escort you to the Law Courts."

CHAPTER 41

THE HUGUENOT who was driving the wagon went pale. It was not a good thing for a member of the Reformed Church to find himself in the company of people who were to be escorted to the Law Courts.

But he was given no option about where he was to go. As Angélique stepped out in front of the long medieval wall, whose gargoyles were spouting great jets of water, she still thought, for some inexplicable reason, that they wanted to see her about the pirates. Then she told herself that Nicholas de Bardagne must have returned and wished to see her again.

But they did not take her up the familiar main staircase, with its gilded, panelled ceiling, at the end of the courtyard.

She and the three children were hustled towards the offices that stood beneath the shadow of an arcade. Inside they had already lighted the candles, and clerks were busy amongst a welter of papers, ink-wells, and goose quills. Others were sitting around in the corners on stools, and appeared to have nothing better to do than bite their nails.

The place was heavy with the bleak smell of tallow and dust, allied to the more military one of tobacco and bootleather, which aroused unpleasant memories in Angélique. It was a smell that characterized police stations. A man got up, looked the young woman up and down with an air of insolent resignation characteristic of a policeman, then opened a door behind him.

"Get in there," he said, pushing her in.

As he did so, he took her hand and loosed Honorine's hold on it.

"You children, you stay where you are."

"But they can stay with me, can't they?" Angélique protested.

"No, they can't! Monsieur Baumier's got a few things he wants to ask you."

Angélique exchanged glances with Martial and Séverine; they were breathing rapidly through half-open lips. Their hearts must have been pounding, for they had already been here on the occasion of their arrest. She felt like shouting: "Above all, keep your mouths shut," for she had made the mistake of whispering something to them about their departure for the American islands, while they were crossing from the Island of Ré to La Palice.

All she could say was:

"Hang on to Honorine. Try and make her understand that she must be good and *not talk*."

Her final words were swallowed up by Honorine's yells, for she was furious at being taken from her mother. They shut the door, and Angélique stood there anxiously in the middle of the room she had just entered. She was listening to her daughter's howls rising above rough but no doubt well-intentioned men's voices that were trying to pacify her. The noise grew quieter as they took the child away somewhere. She heard the sound of more doors closing, then all was still once more.

"Come forward and sit down."

Angélique jumped. She had not noticed Monsieur Baumier sitting there behind his desk. He pointed to a stool in front of it.

"Sit down, Dame Angélique."

She had the impression that he had stressed her name in an indefinable manner. He pretended not to be watching her as she sat down, and thumbed through a file as

383

he scratched his head with one finger, through his thinning hair.

Little bits of snuff were sticking out of his nostrils. Several times he growled, "Yes, indeed ... Yes, indeed," then he shut the file and leant back against the threadbare upholstery of his chair.

Baumier's eyes were very close-set and he had that rather shifty, converging and sharply pentrating look that seemed to be the hallmark of all inquisitors. Nicholas de Bardagne was as much out of place in the job that had fallen to his lot as this man was suited to his.

Angélique was aware of all this, and she realized that she would have to fight. The silence went on and on. It was part of Baumier's tactics to impress the people he was about to question in this manner, but, as it happened, Angélique was able to use this respite to muster her forces. She did not know which of her vulnerable points he would first attack. Perhaps Baumier did not know either. Sitting there deep in thought, he ran his tongue over his thin lips, and it made him look like a cruel fox.

At last he made up his mind and leant towards her with a sugary expression.

"Now tell me, my dear, what did you do with the bodies?"

"The bodies?" Angélique repeated in astonishment.

"Now don't start to play Miss Innocence. You wouldn't be looking so upset if you didn't know what I was talking about. It isn't a very nice thing to think about, is it, those bodies you had to carry away and hide, is it now?"

Angélique managed to maintain her expression of polite bewilderment.

Baumier was becoming irritable.

"Let's not waste any more time. Whatever you say now, you'll confess in the end. Now, the bodies, those men ... You remember. . . . One of them was wearing a bright blue coat."

He brought the flat of his hand down on his desk.

"Are you telling me that no man in a bright blue coat

accosted you in the street last month and tried to make up to you?"

"Do forgive me, Monsieur,"—and she managed a somewhat puzzled smile—"but I don't understand a word of what you are saying. Please don't be angry. . . ."

The Commissioner for Religious Affairs grew red and his mouth twisted nastily.

"Don't you remember the two men? On the third of April last, at exactly one in the afternoon, you were coming back from the Manigault warehouses on the quayside. The men followed you along the Rue de la Perche and down the Rue de la Soura. Surely, don't you remember anything?"

He turned on his persuasive manner, lacing it with irony. She did not know just how far she could lead him on, so she muttered:

"Perhaps."

"Ah! Now we're getting somewhere," he said with satisfaction.

He leant back once again in his chair, and scrutinized her as if she were his prey, no longer able to escape him.

"Well, now, tell me all about it."

Angélique pulled herself together. She realized that, if she allowed her questioner's diabolical assurance to intimidate her, she would slide from one admission to the next and become hopelessly entangled. Then she would be finished.

"Tell you all about what?" she asked, simulating a kind of rough vulgarity. "Do you think I'm not accosted by hundreds of men in the streets? And, while we are on the subject, La Rochelle's reputation is growing worse and worse. And do you think I've nothing better to do than to keep a count of all these sorry characters, and to worry about whether they are wearing red or blue coats?"

Baumier silenced her, ignoring her protest.

"But I'm quite certain that you remember these two perfectly well. Come on now, try hard. They followed you then . . ."

"Well," she said bitingly, "since you insist that they did follow me, I suppose I sent them packing."

"Then you went on?"

"I suppose so."

"On the third of April, as you were coming back from Monsieur Manigault's, did you go straight home to Maître Berne's house in the Rue Sous-les-Murs?"

She sensed the trap and pretended to be considering the matter with great care.

"On the third of April, you said? I might well not have gone straight home that day. I could well have gone first to my master's warehouses as I often do when there is any message for him from Monsieur Manigault."

This reply seemed to satisfy Baumier and he bared his yellow teeth in a grin.

"It was a lucky thing for you that you finally remembered your peregrinations of that day. For, if you had told me anything else, I should have known that you were lying. Let me now tell you that I sent the two men we are talking about after you, and I saw them start to follow you from a tavern on the quayside where I was sitting when you left Manigault's. Another of my men with two soldiers was waiting near Maître Berne's house in the Rue-Sous-les-Murs. Now this man assures me that you never came back all day, neither did the two pseudo-gallants whom they were supposed to meet there. And as for them, they have never been seen since that day."

"Oh!" said Angélique as if she was unaware that the Superintendent, whose voice had dropped lugubriously by about a tone, had said anything at all sinister.

"Now don't start to play the little innocent again," he shouted, banging the table once more.

He was grinding his teeth in anger.

"You know very well why they have never been seen since. It's because they were murdered, and I know who did it. I shall tell you exactly what happened, since your memory of it seems to be so poor. You arrived at your so-called master's warehouses and there my men did what they had been instructed to do—oh, I know they were perfectly willing—and they tried to get their little

386

reward from you. Then Maître Berne and his assistants stepped in and there was a fight. My men were outnumbered, and they were both killed in the scuffle. Now, what I want to know is, how you got rid of them."

Angélique managed to open her eyes wider and wider in utter amazement as he told her this story. But there was something wrong with Baumier's account, the bit about the assistants, which proved that he had not got his facts quite right.

"Heavens above!" she cried in somewhat exaggerated, naïve tones, "but this is absolutely ghastly. I can hardly believe my ears! Are you accusing my master of being a murderer?"

"Yes, a murderer!" Baumier hammered out.

"But that's quite impossible, Monsieur. He's a very pious man, he reads his Bible every day of the week."

"That proves absolutely nothing. In fact these heretics are capable of anything. And, believe me, I'm being paid to find out, so I should know."

But Angélique's outbursts of indignation and her apparent frankness nevertheless seemed to have left him a bit shaken.

She went on:

"He would not hurt a fly, he's a very quiet and gentle person."

The inquisitor smiled unpleasantly.

"I have no shadow of doubt that you would be capable of appreciating such qualities, my pretty one."

"My master never . . ."

"Your master! your master!" he growled. "Let's not get the names the wrong way round here. He is far less your master than you are his mistress."

Angélique sat there for a moment with a look of outrage on her face, then threw her last card on the table, the one she had held in reserve from the start. It could well turn out to be her last hope in this very nasty situation. Baumier's coarse reference had given her her opportunity.

"Monsieur," she said in a very dignified manner, with eyes downcast, "you are no doubt aware that the Monsieur de Bardagne has done me the honour of noticing me, in spite of my humble position. I do not think that he would be at all pleased to hear the dubious and insulting accusations you have just made against me."

He was not the slightest moved. In fact he merely smiled his sugary smile, and he began to do something that filled Angélique with secret dread. He took a goose quill from a writing stand and began to roll it dreamily between his fingers. This gesture brought back the almost sickening fear of the questioning which that formidable Police Officer François Desgrez had made her undergo. While he was making secret preparations to pillory her, he too had had this habit of fiddling with a goose-quill pen.

Angélique found she was unable to take her eyes off the unconscious movement of his fat, tobacco-stained thumb.

"It so happens," Baumier said with studied sweetness, "that Monsieur de Bardagne will not be coming back to La Rochelle. His superiors feel that he has shown a certain lack of drive in his appointed task."

He stuck his lip out disdainfully.

"What they wanted was figures, not promises. During his over-indulgent rule here the Huguenot's arrogance has only gone on growing, and it must be admitted that the only conversions we can claim during this period were due entirely to my zeal, which, I must say, I have not really been given credit for."

He spread his hands out before him, and suddenly became intimate, almost pleasant.

"So, you see, young lady, the situation is quite clear. There is no Monsieur de Bardagne to come to your assistance, and to get caught on your hook. From now on you will be dealing with me, and I reckon, yes, I reckon we shall get somewhere."

Angélique felt her lips trembling in spite of herself.

"He's not coming back . . ." she whispered, genuinely dumbfounded.

"No . . . but, well . . . If his attentions were genuinely advantageous to you, and I admit that they were, you've nevertheless got a reliable asset and a safe investment in
388

Maître Berne. How wise you were to get that wealthy widower into your clutches. . . ."

"Monsieur, I will not allow you . . ."

"And I won't have you making fun of me any longer, you dirty little hypocrite," bellowed Baumier, feigning self-righteous anger. "You aren't his mistress, indeed! And what might you have been up to in Maître Berne's office on the famous third of April, when Grommaire the bailiff turned up to collect the taxes? He saw you! You had your bodice hanging half off you and all your hair tumbled over your shoulders. And they had to hammer on the door for goodness knows how long before that depraved heretic would make up his mind to come and open up. And you've got the nerve to tell me to my face that you are not his mistress! You are just a liar and an intriguer, that's what you are."

He came to a halt, quite breathless, but pleased to see that her cheeks had become a fiery red. Angélique could have kicked herself for not having been able to control her blushes. How could she deny what he had said? At least the bailiff, thanks to the fact that it was so dark inside the office, had not noticed that her clothes were torn and spattered with blood. All was not lost if he had only attributed the state she was in to amorous play. But one could hardly have expected the most indulgent of men to condone her conduct.

"Ah! Now you look less proud!" her tormentor hurled at her.

He congratulated himself on having made her lower her eyes. These women were bolder than you could ever have imagined; they could all too easily make you almost believe that it was you who were raving.

"Well, what have you got to say for yourself?"

"Monsieur, everyone is weak on occasion. . . ."

Baumier screwed up his eyes and his features took on a sugary and evil look.

"Oh yes, indeed! A woman like you, who is well aware that every man that passes stops to look at her, of course she can have her little moments of weakness. In fact, I might say, it is only part of your job. I'd be very surprised if you were to suggest anything else. And after all

389

it's entirely your affair if you have chosen to throw your cap at this man Berne. But you lied brazenly to me about this matter, and had I not exposed your lies, you would have gone on indignantly defending your outraged virtue. If you can lie like this about one thing, you can lie about all the rest. I've got the measure of you now, my beauty, I've got you summed up. You're a pretty tough customer, but I'm going to be even tougher."

Angélique began to realize that she was caught in the toils of an extremely nasty business. This little man, steeped as he was in incense and red tape, seemed to be a particularly sly dog, unless it was that she had lost her capacity to react appropriately to people. He frightened her even more than Desgrez. Where Desgrez was concerned, even on the occasion when he had bent her fingers back upon themselves in order to make her admit her complicity in some housebreaking case, there had always been something between them—a physical attraction—which made even their most ferocious battles exciting.

Angélique was overcome with disgust at the mere thought of having to use her charms to neutralize the nastiness of this evil-smelling rodent. That would have been more than flesh could bear and, in any case, where Baumier was concerned, any such attempts ran the risk of being doomed to failure from the start. Although of an even lower breed, he was the same type of man as de Solignac. All his pleasure lay in the satisfaction of fulfilling his uncompromising task, in the sight of the man he had beaten grovelling before him begging for mercy, in beseeching looks and in the feeling of power which stemmed from the fact that with one stroke of his pen he could bring the whole structure of a man's life toppling about his ears.

He had clasped his hands across his skinny belly with that beatific gesture more commonly seen in the obese. When he did it it only accentuated the skinniness of his body and made him look like an old maid.

"Come now, my dear, let's be good friends. Why on earth did you ever go and get yourself involved with these heretics? I don't deny that once old Berne and his moneybags could have come in handy, but you're quite sharp enough to have realized that these days a Protestant's fortune is worth about as much as the wind. Unless of course he becomes a convert. That would be quite a different matter. If you had been cunning, you would have had Gabriel Berne and his family converted a long time ago, and you would have been the winner all along the line, whereas now you are in a pretty ghastly mess: you are an accomplice to a murderer and you are involved in the Huguenots' plans, in fact you are losing all the advantages you had in being a Catholic. You might even find yourself being accused of wanting to join their guilty sect, and that would be a most serious matter."

He glanced again at a small piece of paper.

"The priest from your nearest parish church of St. Marceau says that he has never seen you at Mass, neither has he ever heard your confession. What does this mean? Could it be that you are letting your faith slide?"

"No, indeed I am not!" Angélique said with a start which had the precious advantage of being quite sincere.

Baumier felt this and seemed rather taken aback. Things were not going as well as he would have wished. He took a pinch of snuff, sniffed it up, sneezed noisily without thinking of apologizing, then cleaned his nose at great length with repulsive care.

Angélique could not help calling to mind that moment when Honorine had rushed in, her face puce beneath her green bonnet, her eyes glinting with hatred, and had begun to belabour Baumier with her stick, shouting: "I want to kill him."

Love welled up in her heart for that small indomitable creature who already like herself stood out against everything low and hateful.

She must get out of here and fetch Honorine and make the most of the few hours which lay between them and their flight.

"And what about this?" Baumier said. "What have you to say about this?"

He handed her some sheets of paper with a list of

names written on them. Gabriel Berne's was on it, and
those of all his family, the Mercelots, the Carrères, the
Manigaults, all of them were there with many others.
Angélique read it over twice. At first she was intrigued,
then began to feel disquieted. She looked inquiringly at
her interrogator.

"Every one of the people on that list is going to be
arrested tomorrow," he said with a beaming smile, then
suddenly he hammered out:

"Because they are planning to escape."

It was then that Angélique recognized the list; it was
a copy of the one Manigault had drawn up of all the
clandestine passengers going aboard the Sainte-Marie;
they were all there right down to the Carrères newest
baby, little Raphael, the one who had been declared a
"bastard in the eyes of the law" because pastors were no
longer recognized, as they had once been, as official
registrars for births.

Her name was on the list too, after the Berne family. It
read: "Dame Angélique, servant-girl."

"The Saint-Marie will not be sailing," Baumier went
on, "from this moment on, it will be under the closest
guard."

Angélique's mind was assailed by a bewildering succession of ideas about what to do and say as a way out
of the situation, but she had to rule them out one by one.
She had reached such a pitch of nervous excitement
that she could see immediately just how Baumier would
twist each one into a weapon to be used against her. He
knew a great deal, in fact he knew everything. But she
was not going to let him have it his own way. Anything
was better than this silence that would begin to look like
an admission if it went on much longer.

"Escape," she said, "but why?"

"All these Huguenots are trying to salvage their fortunes by escaping to countries that are enemies of
France rather than by obeying the King."

"But I have never heard a word about all this, and
why would I be on their list? I haven't been converted
to their religion so I don't need to run away, nor have I
any fortune to salvage."

392

"But you might be afraid to remain in La Rochelle. After all, you are accessory to a murder."

"I beg you, Monsieur," Angélique cried out, pretending to be horribly afraid, "I beg you not to repeat such a terrible accusation. I give you my word that you are wrong, and I can prove to you that you are."

"So you know something, do you?"

"Yes, I do."

Angélique buried her face in her handkerchief.

"Monsieur, I will tell you the whole truth."

"Good, that's fine," Baumier said, his face lighting up in triumph.

"Go on, my child, I'm listening."

"The men ... the men you said you sent after me on the third of April ... I ... it's quite true I remember them very well."

"I thought as much."

"Especially the lad in the blue coat. I don't know how to explain things to you. I feel so ashamed. But the truth is that in spite of what you thought, my master is a most austere man and life in his house is not much fun. I'm only a poor girl with a child to care for, and I agreed to work for these Huguenots because he offered me good wages. But he is very strict. My life consists of nothing but work, more work, and Bible reading. So when the nice young man came up to me in the Rue de la Perche, I rather enjoyed listening to him. Monsieur, please don't be angry."

"I'm not angry," growled Baumier, "it proves that he was doing the job that he was being paid to do in a satisfactory manner. And then?"

"Then we walked along chatting pleasantly until we reached Maître Berne's warehouses where I had to call; I think that I had managed to convey to him that I would very much like to meet him again later in somewhat greater privacy. I remember him saying something to his pal and the other chap answering something a bit like: 'The lousy old thing has filled our pockets so that we can get on with this affair—'"

"The lousy old fellow?" Baumier yelled, leaping into the air.

"I don't know who he was referring to, Monsieur, but I suppose it must have been . . . you."

"Go on," he said, furious.

"Yes, they seemed to be saying that they had plenty of money to play about with."

She was sticking her neck out, for this was one of the details that she knew nothing about, but she did hazard a guess that, when the President of a Royal Commission sent out a couple of his hired seducers on to the streets of La Rochelle, he would see to it that they had enough money in their pockets to dazzle the girls they were after. Her deduction had been right, for he did not bat an eyelid. Angélique grew bolder:

"Then he said: 'We've hit on an easy one at last who doesn't try to slap us across the face, so we mustn't spoil our chances. Go and wait for me at the Nicholas Tavern and order yourself a pot of wine at the old so-and-so's. expense! Afterwards we can have a chat about what we are going to do.' "

"What did he mean by that?" Baumier asked, seething inwardly.

"I've no idea, Monsieur. I must admit that my mind was on other matters. He was such a pleasant lad; I must say you chose well. He was very bold, not that I minded, of course, for, as I already explained to you, my life is so terribly dull in the Huguenots' household that it was a long time since I'd had any . . . as you might say . . . fun. There was nobody about in the street . . ."

She hated having to fabricate this unpleasant story, but for the time being at any rate Baumier seemed to be falling for it. He looked so thoroughly shaken that Angélique was stirred to further flights of fancy.

"Then, of course, Monsieur Berne my master came out and found us and that spoilt everything. He is a man of very violent temper, and he got into a furious rage. He is extremely strong as well and my new-found friend was in no fit state to begin a fight with him. So he ran off, which I reckon was the best thing he could have done, don't you think?"

"Damn these whipper-snappers. Why didn't they stay

together? If I send them off in twos, there are good reasons for doing so!"

"And as for me, my master dragged me off to his office to give me a good talking-to. As I said, he was absolutely furious. . . ."

"He was jealous."

"It could be," Angélique said somewhat coquettishly, "but the fact is that he was just about to give me a beating when Grommaire the bailiff interrupted us and prevented my being punished."

Baumier's agitation was growing: it was becoming obvious that he was quite taken aback by this new picture of what had occurred.

"Is that all?"

"No, it isn't," Angélique murmured, bowing her head again.

"What else happened?"

"I . . . did see the boy in the blue coat again."

"Where? When?"

"The same evening. We had just had time to fix a rendezvous by the ramparts. And I saw him the following day, too. . . ."

She was feeling her way all the time. As she tried to lend authenticity to her tale, was she not running the risk of making the entire fragile structure of lies collapse to the ground?

"After that, I never saw him again. I imagined he must have left the town. . . . He had mentioned the possibility . . . I was awfully disappointed."

Baumier shrugged his shoulders with a look of bitter disillusionment.

"They're all the same! You slave away to teach them the job, you try to make them realize how vital their work is, you send them out on a job of the utmost importance, then they go and do a midnight flit on you to try their luck somewhere else. But, you know, I'm nevertheless surprised that Justin Médard would have done a thing like that. Whom can one trust?"

Angélique did not give him time to puzzle for too long over the unfortunate Justin Médard's inexplicable conduct. That wretch had paid for his devotion to a just cause and his zealous professional conscience by becoming food for the crabs. She said beseechingly:

"Monsieur, now that I have confessed everything to you, please don't be too hard on me. I give you my word that I shall leave the Huguenots tomorrow. Since I have been there I have had nothing but troubles. I don't yet know where I can go, but, never mind, I'm leaving them, I promise."

"Oh, but you're not," he protested. "On the contrary, you must stay with them and keep me informed about everything that's going on. For instance, you know all about this proposed flight on the *Sainte-Marie*, don't you? Your name was on the list."

"That's nothing to do with me! I don't know anything about it, Monsieur. I would have thought that if my master had been about to leave, he would have let me know, or at least I would have seen him getting his things ready."

"And have you noticed nothing?"

"No."

She tried to look naïve. Baumier was fiddling with the tell-tale list.

"And yet the information I have received seems accurate enough."

"If the people who gave you that information earn their pay as well as Justin Médard did . . ."

Angélique laughed.

"You shut up, you," Baumier bellowed. "Just because I listened patiently to what you had to say, here you are already rearing your head again. You insolent and shameless creature! You deserve to be locked up in the Institution for Women of Disorderly Life; you're nothing but a whore, and of the very lowest breed at that. But, if that is what you really are, you can be of greater use to me in the outside world than locked up."

He was calm again, and looked at her very thoughtfully.

"If that is what you really are," he repeated softly.

He stood up and walked round the table. Angélique wondered rather apprehensively what he was about to do. She hoped he would not expect her to obtain her freedom by kissing him, but he toddled off towards the door.

"Monsieur, Monsieur," she begged, clasping her hands together, "tell me I may go free, and give me back my daughter. I have done nothing wrong."

"Yes, I think I shall let you go," he decided with olympian condescension, "there's just something I would like to check up on ... then you can go."

He went out.

Had she not been so wrought up, she would have noticed the somewhat disquieting way he had said "just something I would like to check up on." But she was overcome with relief at the promise he had made: "I shall let you go." At one time things had begun to look desperate. She hoped to goodness they would give her back the Berne children as well as Honorine!

Her shoulders crumpled, she closed her eyes, and two tears of weakness trickled down her cheeks.

Then the door opened again and someone walked in.

It was the Police Officer François Desgrez.

CHAPTER 42

THERE HE stood with his square jaw and his brown eyes that looked straight at you. His shoulders were massive, and his dark-brown cloth coat, with a touch of gold braid around the buttonholes, fitted him closely. His tie, his high heels, in fact everything about him smacked of the capital, Paris, with its carriages and its blue nights. Angélique was so surprised that at first she did not realize the implications of this apparition from her past.

It would now be revealed that she was the Marquise du Plessis-Bellière, the Rebel of Poitou, and as such she would be arrested in the name of the King, thrown into prison and tried; Honorine would be cast into everlasting nothingness, and she would lose her as she had lost Florimond; she would never be able to escape to the islands. . . .

Her mind became paralysed and she found herself

incapable of thinking of anything beyond her present amazement. She recognized him and realized that she was even somewhat pleased to see him once more. Fancy Desgrez! It all seemed so far off and yet so near!

He bowed, as if he had only taken leave of her the day before.

"How do you do, Madame. How are you?"

She shuddered at the sound of his voice, for it reminded her of the fights they had had, of the hate and fear she had felt on his account and of those moments of passionate and brutal love-making he had inflicted upon her.

She watched him cross the room and sit down at Baumier's desk. He was not wearing a wig. It reminded her all the more of how he had once looked, and although his features had grown harder still he now looked like the roistering penniless student she had known before he had joined the police force. But, on the other hand, she was not familiar with the studied elegance of his attire and his self-assured movements, and the way in which he settled into his chair like a man accustomed to bearing heavy responsibilities.

His features had become more sharply chiselled than before. The ironical lines, now deeply set in the corners of his eyes, would now never disappear, and, even when he was not smiling, his mouth had a half-bitter, half-tender fold at each corner. But as soon as he saw her, he beamed amiably at her, showing his cruel flashing white teeth.

"Well now, my dear Marquise of the Angels, so we were destined to meet again in spite of the haste with which you fled from me the last time we met. Now let me see, when was that? It must have been a long time ago ... four, no, five years ago! As long as that! How time flies! Of course, a great deal happens to some people in a short time, you for example. It has always been your hallmark, not to be able to keep still. And what about me? . . . Oh well! Of course life is undoubtedly more tranquil when you are not constantly bursting in. I deal with everyday matters as they come along. I've just recently arrested one of your neighbours,

398

the Marquise de Brinvilliers. I don't know whether you remember her; she used to live just a few streets from your place at Beautreillis. She poisoned her entire family as well as a whole bunch of other people. For years and years now I've been after her, and it was you who helped me to make the arrest. Yes, you did. That precious information that I managed to get out of you so gently about that burglary some of your good friends from the Court of Miracles had done. . . . Don't you remember it any more? . . . No, obviously too much has happened to you since then. My dear, there is a great deal of poisoning going on in Paris at the moment. It's keeping me frantically busy. And at Versailles, too, they are all poisoning one another, though that is somewhat more tricky. . . . Ah well! I see that all these bits of gossip are not of great interest to you. Let's talk about something else.

"I was given the job of finding you and laying hands on you. They always give me the nastiest jobs to do. Just imagine, catching the Rebel of Poitou! Not all that easy! And it's not exactly my forte to go wandering about in a province like yours. Poor province," he muttered, "bled to death, devastated, full of men like wild animals whose mouths button up as soon as your name is mentioned. I had to give up and just trust to luck. That old ferret Baumier had a share in it all. He had come up to Paris to report on these everlasting religious matters, and a the same time he was trying to find out something about a woman who ... a woman that ... I wonder what it was that made me feel that it could be you; I don't know. But any doubts I had ever had were completely dispelled after a chat I had recently with Monsieur de Bardagne, the charming Governor of La Rochelle. So I came post-haste to see you, my dear. It *was* you, so my job is done.

"Do you know that you look younger than ever? Yes, you do; I was struck by the fact as soon as I set eyes on you. Maybe it's that modest little bonnet you are wearing, which reminds me of Maître Bourjus's servant-girl, in the days when I used to go and drink a glass of white Suresnes wine at the Red Mask. Later on, I was disappointed by your new face. It was the face of a King's favourite, all rigged out with jewels. Believe me, I was beginning to see the hallmarks of my poisoners in your face. Their faces are full of greed, ambition, fear, and a desire for vengeance. Now all that has gone. I can see those candid young girl's eyes once again; there is something more too. I can see a weight of experience in them. What was it that cleansed you of all that? What gave you back your pure, smooth cheeks again, and your huge, devouring eyes that are crying out for help?

"Just then when I came in, I said to myself: 'Good God! How young she is! And I must admit it was a pleasant surprise after not having seen you for five years. Perhaps it was because of the tears on your cheeks. . . .

"Was it that old rat Baumier who made you cry, my love? Why did he? What have you done now to be back in the black-clawed clutches of the police? When are you going to learn to be more careful? And when are you going to answer me? Your eyes speak volumes as they always did, but that is not enough. I want to hear the sound of your voice."

He leant forward, looking very earnestly at her, straight in the eyes. She said nothing, for she was incapable of uttering a single sound. From the depths of her despair there came a cry:

"Desgrez, Desgrez my friend, please help me!"

But not a sound could pass her lips.

Desgrez said nothing, and sat looking at her for a long time. He needed to become familiar once more with the features and details of this face and figure which had all too often haunted his dreams.

He had been ready for anything. He might have found her blighted, old, arrogant, bitter or full of hate, but he had not expected such serenity in her distress, such a dumb and heart-rending appeal in her green eyes, which seemed even brighter and more limpid than before.

"You were lovely when I knew you' before," he thought, "but now you are still lovelier. What miracle has done this?"

He was overcome by a genuine respect for this woman who had performed such a feat. In spite of those terrible years of war and defeat, in spite of having led an existence that could have been no better than that of a hunted animal for ever in danger, she had managed to keep her spiritual integrity.

He leant forward, looking earnest.

"Madame, what can I do to help you?"

Angélique gave a violent start as if she had just come out of a hypnotic trance.

"To help me? Are you willing to help me, Desgrez?"

"What else have I done but help you ever since I first knew you? You know, even when I tried to arrest you in Marseilles, that was only to help you. What would I not have given to have been able to prevent you from embarking on that disastrous escapade for which you paid so dear!"

"But you have been instructed to arrest me, haven't you?"

"Yes, I have, not once, but twice. But I'm not going to."

He shook his head.

"Because, this time, it would be the end of you. You would never escape again. I should be obliged to hand you over hand and foot, my lamb, and I don't even know to what extent your life might not be in the balance. Of course, you would never go free again; you would never again see the light of day."

"You are risking your whole career, Desgrez."

"It's not very bright of you to remind me of the fact just when I am offering to help you. I just cannot bear to think of you shut up till the end of your days, for you were born to live beneath an open sky. By the way, is it true that you were about to set sail for the West Indies with about thirty Protestants?"

He thumbed casually through the *Sainte-Marie's* passenger list. She could see the names of Manigault, Berne, Carrère, and Mercelot dancing before her eyes. There were the Christian names too: Martial, Séverine, Laurier, Rebecca, Jeremy, Abigail, Raphael. For one last second she remained hesitant.

The police have hundreds of ways of getting at the truth. Was not Desgrez's alert voice with its trenchant phrases and sudden bursts of tenderness calculated to calm her suspicions and to win her round? She had only to say one word and she might be betraying the friends whom at all costs she wished to protect. Her lips trembled; she staked her all.

"Yes, I was," she said.

Desgrez leant back with a strange little sigh.

"Thank goodness you trusted me," he said. "Had you not done so, I might well have arrested you. It's strange, this job of ours, as you get older you become tougher, and at the same time more sentimental; you grow more cruel and yet more tender. You give up everything except for one or two small things that are worth their weight in gold; and the more time passes, the more precious they seem. Your friendship was one of those things. Although I am not in the habit of so doing, I am allowing myself to confide in you like this, my sweet, because I know that if I let you go this time, I shall never see you again."

"Are you going to let me go?"

"Yes. But it doesn't seem to me that just letting you go will keep you safe for very long, for once again you are in an awful pickle. Why didn't you leave sooner for the islands? That would have been the best solution; then I should never have seen you again and would have been greatly relieved. Now I don't know what on earth I am going to do about you. Baumier has stolen a march on you; all your accomplices are just about to be arrested. Their ship is under constant watch, so it's no good your trying that one. What a stupid idea to have gone and got yourself mixed up with all these heretics, my pet, when you have a hundred good reasons to avoid people finding out who you really are. Nowadays these people are far too much in the public eye for their homes to have offered you proper cover. Not to mention the fact that they are not exactly a particularly attractive crowd. A lot of straightlaced bastards who don't even know how to make love. You do disappoint me!"

"Did you say they are going to be arrested?"

402

This was the only thing Angélique had heard him say. "When?" she asked.

"Tomorrow morning."

"Tomorrow morning," she repeated, going pale.

Nobody had the slightest inkling that this was going to happen. Tomorrow morning men dressed in black would come with the militia and would enter the courtyard where the Spanish lilac and the wall-flowers were in bloom. The children would be dancing around the palm-tree; they would take these children by the hand and carry them off for ever. They would put chains on Maître Berne's wrists; they would hustle old Rebecca out with the worthy Aunt Anna, protesting loudly with her Bible and her mathematics books clutched to her hands and hurled into the gutter. . . .

And women would come from all the houses that lay beneath the ramparts, in their white head-dresses, carrying hastily tied bundles, and men in chains and little bewildered children would run down the alleyways behind the great-booted soldiers, who were taking them away.

"Desgrez, you said you were going to help me. . . ."

"And I suppose you will make the most of it to help these folk. We'll have none of that, my sweet. No more nonsense from you! I shall just give you enough time to collect your goods and chattels, and I shall keep an eye on you while you do so, then I'm going to get you out of this mess you have so stupidly got yourself into. You seem to forget all too easily that you too are wanted for the gallows, and the fact that you are a Papist won't save you when anyone else but me decides to investigate you."

"Listen to me, Desgrez."

"No."

"Give me twenty-four hours. I am only asking for a stay of twenty-four hours. Please use your power to make them wait till the day after tomorrow, or at least until tomorrow evening before making the arrests."

"Hell's bells, you must be mad," Desgrez shouted, well and truly angry. "You are becoming more and more demanding. It's already going to be hard enough to save you with a price of five hundred pounds on your head. And even that is not enough."

"Give me twenty-four hours, Desgrez, and I promise I shall get away with them all."

"Are you trying to tell me that by tomorrow night you will have managed to conjure away about fifty people who are wanted by the police, and to get them far enough away not to be caught again?"

"Yes, I'll manage it."

Desgrez considered her in silence for a moment.

"What star do I see flickering in your eyes?" he said with sudden tenderness. "Ah, I know it of old! You will never change, Marquise of the Angels. Oh well, all right. You shall all have the respite you seek; because of the way you smiled when you said 'I'll manage it'."

She was already standing up and he held her back with a gesture.

"Careful now. Twenty-four hours, no more. Even if I wanted to I couldn't extend it beyond that. I am respected here because I am Monsieur de La Reynie's right-hand man, and he is the head of the whole State police force. But I came here to deal with one thing only, and that was you, and it is not my business to meddle in provincial matters. Baumier is certainly not going to like my interfering in the arrest of 'his' Protestants. But I shall try to find a pretext for delaying it till tomorrow night. Anything later than that would be out of the question. He's cunning; he knows that the Dutch fleet is about to put into La Rochelle, and the fuss they all make would give these people he's been after for so long far too good an opportunity. They've all got to be under lock and key before the fleet arrives."

"I understand."

"Come through this way," he said, putting his hand on her elbow to guide her towards another door that stood behind the desk. "I'd rather nobody saw you leaving. Then I shan't be asked any awkward questions."

Angélique stopped.

"What about the children? I can't go without them."

"I sent them back home ages ago," he growled. "That

little red-headed termagant, who it seems is your daughter, was nearly deafening us with her roars. So I said to the eldest boy: 'Clear off back to your father, don't speak to anyone, and wait for Dame Angélique to come back.' That was when Baumier was questioning you. But I knew that my turn was coming."

"Oh, Desgrez," she whispered, "how kind you are!"

He had led her down a narrow dark corridor and at the end of it he pulled a door open. It was already quite dark outside. Close by a gargoyle was spewing out torrents of water, and yet it was no longer raining. But the moist wind was blowing in great drunken gusts along the alleyway.

Desgrez stopped on the threshold. He took Angélique in his arms in that off-handed and irresistible manner he had, which made all resistance impossible.

"I love you," he said. "I can tell you so now since it doesn't matter any more."

Her head was tipped back imprisoned against his strong arm, and she began to feel a trifle weak, not because of his embrace, but because she no longer saw or felt him, for the night and the wind had taken hold of her. He was becoming unreal again. She felt only one thing now deep inside her, the haste of a captive bird to get free once and for all.

He realized that his arms were only clutching a body that was no longer really with him, a spirit that had already taken its leave. He, who stood there alive, a man of flesh and blood, or who thought he was, was to this hunted woman no more than a ghost from the past who sought to draw her into its grave. She was flying towards a future where he had no place.

"She was made for boundless horizons," he thought, "she was made to be free. . . ."

He bent over her lips but did not even brush them.

"Farewell, Marquise of the Angels," he murmured.

Very gently, he let his arms fall to his sides. She broke loose, took a few steps, then seemed to have second thoughts. She must have turned round, but he had already lost sight of her. He heard her say:

"Farewell, Desgrez my friend. Thank you. Thank you."

Angélique ran through the dark town. The wind gave her lips a salty tang. This was how Lot's wife must have run when the deadly particles of fire and brimstone were massing over the city in preparation for its annihilation.

She was quite breathless when she reached home.

They were all there: the children, Maître Gabriel, old Rebecca and Aunt Anna, Abigail and the old Pastor, the young Pastor and his small orphaned child.

They threw themselves at her and surrounded her, plying her with questions. The merchant urged: "Tell us all about it. They arrested you. Why? What is happening?"

"Nothing serious."

Even Aunt Anna said in a quavering voice: "You gave us a dreadful fright. We feared they might have thrown you into prison."

"It was nothing."

She tried to force a smile to reassure them. Now that she had found them there all together, she was sure her scheme would succeed and that she would be able to save them. They led her to the kitchen where she had to sit down, and Rebecca brought her some wine. Which would she prefer? Rebecca suggested they might as well open several bottles, for in any event they would not be able to take their glorious stocks aboard with them.

"It was because of the ship, wasn't it?" Maître Gabriel said. "That was why they arrested you, they must have got wind of something."

"Nothing much."

"You keep on saying it was nothing much, but you are as white as a sheet. You must tell us what is wrong; should we warn Manigault?"

He was very hard to throw off the scent. He put his hand on Angélique's shoulder.

"I was just about to set off to the Law Courts at top speed."

"That would have been a bad error of judgment,

Maître Gabriel. I have come to the conclusion that these gentlemen do suspect something, but as yet they have no proof, and by the time they have, we shall be far away! I assume that Martial and Séverine said nothing.

"Nobody asked us anything, luckily,' Martial said. "As soon as you had left us a tall man came in. He picked Honorine up to stop her shrieking and then he said to us: 'Run along home. Dame Angélique will be along later.' The others didn't look any too pleased, but he took us down into the street himself."

"I think he must have been from Paris," Séverine remarked, her eyes shining. "The others all seemed to treat him with great respect."

Angélique agreed:

"Yes, that gentleman is a friend of mine and he has given me his word that we can all rely on him not to be bothered tonight."

"So you have friends amongst the Paris police, have you, Dame Angélique?" Maître Gabriel asked sharply. Angélique drew her hand across her brow.

"Yes. It so happens that I have. And, as you have seen, it can come in useful. I promise to tell you the whole story tomorrow, but tonight I am very tired and I think we should put the children to bed."

But as they were all going off, she asked Abigail to remain behind, saying: "I must have a word with you."

They waited until the big house fell silent again and Honorine was fast asleep. Angélique opened a chest that stood in one corner of the back kitchen and she took out her thickest cloak and a woollen headscarf which she tied tight under her chin to keep her coif in place.

"I didn't want to explain my scheme to Maître Berne," she said to Abigail, "because he would certainly have stopped me from carrying it out. I am the only person who can do anything now, but I must tell you about it."

And out came the whole story, pell-mell. They had been betrayed, but by whom? Possibly by one of Manigault's assistants, perhaps by one of their own people. But what did it really matter who had done it!

407

What mattered was that Baumier knew all about everything. He knew their names. Spies and constables had an eye on them, and on the warehouses and on the *Sainte-Marie*. All their houses were marked. The black angel of disaster had placed his invisible hand on the façades of these beautiful homes and on the humble workshops of the part of the city that lay beneath the walls. Tomorrow they would come and arrest them all.

Abigail listened without flinching. She looked more than ever like a Flemish Madonna with her long, gentle face with its pale eyebrows beneath her white coif. She remained quite calm. She had sufficient strength in adversity to resign herself to what was to come, but, Angélique thought, it was easy for her because Abigail did not know what real misery was. She did not know what it was like to be in prison, or to be hunted like an animal, without a single stone to lay her head on, nor what it was like to call for help from your own people and find you called in vain.

"We have one chance left," she said. "I'm going to try it. That's why I have to go out again tonight."

Abigail shuddered.

"Tonight? In this storm? Listen. . . ."

The wind was rattling the shutters and the windows. It had begun to rain again and the noise of teeming water mingled with the dull roar of the sea.

"Every hour counts," Angélique said. "By tomorrow we must all be on board, otherwise we are lost."

"On board? How can we be? You yourself have said that the port is being watched, and no ship is going to sail in weather like this."

"Isn't one ship all we need?" said Angélique obstinately. "I must take the risk; it's our last chance. You get ready, Abigail. While I am away I want you to get everyone's things ready. Only bring a very little: one change of dress and a few underclothes."

"When will you be back?"

"I don't know. Perhaps by dawn. But be ready. I may well come back with the news that the ship is waiting for us to go aboard and that we must make haste."

408

She reached the door, then stopped as if a new idea had struck her.

"If I should not come back, Abigail . . . Whatever happens, try to look after my daughter Honorine. But how silly I am! I shall *have* to come back; it's the only possible way."

Abigail went up to her and put her arm about her shoulders.

"What are you going to do, Angélique?"

"Just something very simple. I am going to find a ship's captain I know and I am going to ask him to take us all away."

The young girl squeezed her tight and, when Angélique looked up, she was struck by the way her features seemed to shine with a strange radiance.

A childish vision she used to have once came back to her now and mingled with the comfort she felt in this newly-discovered friendship. When she had been a little girl and a storm had blown up and whistled across the marshes at Monteloup, she used to imagine that the Virgin Mary was holding her in her arms, and her fear would vanish. She let her forehead fall on to Abigail's shoulder, who said very softly:

"Why are you trying to take us all along too? It is only making things more difficult for you. I have a feeling that you could well have got away on your own, Angélique."

"No, I couldn't," Angélique said, shaking her head. "I would never have had the strength to do that. My gentle Abigail, you may not understand why, but I know that if I didn't help you to get away, you and your Protestant brethren, I should never have been able to redeem all the blood that has been spilt, nor the mistakes I have made in my life. . . ."

She finished on an almost gay note:

". . . So it's tonight or never. That is why I *must* succeed."

Abigail went with her as far as the main gateway. A sudden gust of wind blew the candle out. The two young women embraced one another in the darkness, and Angélique slipped away towards the ramparts, clinging close to the walls for greater protection against the squalls of wind. She did not hear the gate close.

While she was fighting for them all, Abigail would be watching like a lighted lamp. Angélique would not be alone. She almost had to crawl up the dripping wet steps that led to the top of the battlements where the sentries went their rounds. Up there she could hear nothing but the wild roar of the sea and the violent hammering of the waves as they beat against the dyke. Huge showers of spray kept on rising, drenching everything and settling in frothy pools on the stones. By the time she reached the guard-house of the Lantern Tower she was already soaked through.

For a moment she stood in the shelter of a buttress to get her breath back again. Then she stretched up on tiptoe to look in through a small slit window. She could see Anselm Camisot, the soldier on duty, sitting gloomily over his brazier whose red-hot coals cast a ruddy glow on his unshaven jowl.

Luckily Angélique knew just how shy her admirer was at heart, for no sight could have seemed less reassuring to her than the sight of this solitary soldier seen between two bars, sitting beneath the vaulted roof of the medieval guardhouse. And in any case she had no choice in the matter. She rapped at the window.

Finally the soldier glanced up and she saw on his face a look of deep and utter astonishment as he noticed this apparition that the storm-gods had sent him this night. He rubbed his eyes several times and leapt up; he caught his feet in his halberd, tripped against his helmet which was lying on the floor, and the noise must have set all the echoes of the tower ringing. Finally he reached the door and unbolted it.

Angélique had already slipped through it. She came into the room and threw off her water-sodden hood with a sigh of relief.

"You, Dame Angélique," Anselm Camisot said, all puffing as if he had been running. "You! In my place! ..."

She found the way he said "my place" consisting as it

410

did of this gloomy round room, a straw pallet and humble meal of crayfish and black bread, rather touching.

"Maître Camisot, I have come to ask you a very special favour. I want you to open the little corner-door for me, because I have to get out of the town."

The guard considered her request and his disappointment made him stern.

". . . You expect me to . . . What! Is that all! But that's not allowed, my pretty one."

"That's exactly why I've come to you. This is the only way I can get out, and I know that you have the keys."

Poor Camisot knit his gorilla-like eyebrows even harder.

"If it's to go running after a lover, don't count on me. I have to keep an eye on people's morals as well as everything else."

Angélique shrugged. "Does this seem to you to be the sort of weather for a rendezvous with a lover out on the heath?"

The soldier listened to the splashing of the rain and the wind howling around the tower.

"No, I suppose not," he said. "Even in here it's better than outside. But then why do you want to leave the town?"

She had not thought of a lie to tell him beforehand, but she found one readily enough.

"I've got to get a message to someone in hiding in St Maurice. . . . It's a pastor. If he is found he will be killed."

"I see," growled Camisot, "but you know, Dame Angélique, if you go on sticking your nose into all these matters, you'll end up in prison. And as for me, I'll run the risk of being hanged this time, not just strappadoed."

"No one will be any the wiser. I have promised to take this message right away and I thought of you. I haven't told anyone what I am about to do, but, if you refuse to help me, who can I turn to with the same confidence?"

She laid her hand gently on his great hairy paw and looked up at him with imploring eyes. Poor Anselm

Camisot was quite bowled over. Even if, in the past, when he had seen her go by, he had made a few bantering remarks like any self-respecting fellow, never, never had he even dared to hope that she might one day look him straight in the eyes, and especially not the way she was doing now. He ran his hand over his chin, very much aware of his unshaven beard and his ugliness which had always called down the mirth of women upon him.

"I would be so grateful, Monsieur Camisot," Angélique went on, "so very grateful."

Not even his wildest flights of fancy let him suppose that she would do more than allow him to kiss her, but the mere thought that those wonderful lips might possibly show him a little kindness, to him, the garrison outcast, was enough to make him lose his head. His pals often used to talk about how cold the Bernes' beautiful servant-girl was. What if one day they were to learn that he, Anselm, the grotesque butt of the whole garrison, had managed to obtain what the most dandified of all of them had always thought of as an unimaginable stroke of luck. . . . Ah! That would be something he could even bring himself to light a candle for in one of the Papist churches! He felt almost frightened before the time.

His eyes clouded over and he stammered:

"Oh well, all right. After all, I'm not harming anyone! I'm the boss here on the ramparts, and if I can't put myself out a little for a woman like you, who *would* I do it for?"

He unhooked his bunch of keys.

"When you come back, you'll stop at my place for a moment, won't you?"

"Yes, I'll stay for a bit," she said, ready to agree to anything.

And she smiled at him because she felt that this great boorish lump of a man was really a nice lad, who did not expect her to pay in advance as so many others would have done. Anselm Camisot reckoned that he would have time to shave himself, using his breastplate as a mirror, and to go down to the secret dungeons beneath the tower to fetch the treasures that only he

412

knew about. There was a small barrel of white wine and a ham. This was going to be his great day!

Angélique was trembling with impatience as they went out and she followed him to the corner of the ramparts where a small postern had once, in the event of a siege, given shelter to a group of archers whose task it was to riddle the attackers with arrows. A wooden door opened on to a narrow stairway that led down to the dunes. Angélique stepped through it and began to climb down the slippery steps, almost breaking her neck at least twenty times as she did so. The guard lighted her way from above, but the wind blew out his lantern several times, and the young woman waited for the light to shine out again, clinging to the wall from which the fury of the tempest seemed to want to tear her and cast her down to the ground below.

At last she felt the soft wet sand beneath her feet. She was outside the city.

She found the path along the cliff-top by listening to the unleashed fury of the waves as they broke on the pebbles, and she set out along it. She could only tell where she was by the feel of the sand. Occasionally she would wander off into the grass or would bump into a tamarisk bush. Then she would feel around with one foot until she found the bare ground that was the path. She thought that she had never tried to find her way through such utter darkness.

There was not a single light, not a single glimmer to guide her in this black ocean. A cold and endless stream of rain poured down in her wake. Her eyelashes were soaking wet and sticking together. There were times when she went on with both eyes closed. On her left she sensed the sheer drop of the cliff-side. One false move could be the end of her; she would have fallen heavily to her death at the foot of the wall of limestone.

Little by little her fear grew on her so much that she did not dare to take a step more. She went ahead on all fours, testing the muddy path, which the rain was turning into a stream, with her hands and knees. She was getting nowhere. Finally she decided to remove the cause of her fear by climbing down to the bottom of the

413

cliff and walking along the beach. She would get there just the same and at least would not be running the risk of falling. She knew now where she was from a detail she had noticed when she had come that way with Honorine; she had just bumped into a wooden cross that stood at the edge of the path. Not far from there she knew there were some rocks lying heaped up where it was possible to clamber down on to the shore.

She found the spot and began to climb down. But a bit of earth gave way beneath her feet and she was caught up amongst a small avalanche of stones and slipped down, only to find herself, badly scratched but at least all in one piece, somewhat lower down. Her hands must have been bleeding, and her dress was torn about the knees. Luckily she had come out of it without even twisting her ankle, so she was able to get up and go on walking. She touched the cliff-side as she walked on, to guide herself.

It was then that the snarling sea intervened. Angélique's eyes, now accustomed to the darkness, could make out the white crests of the waves and the long stretches of foam as it rushed towards her. She was being assaulted by pale and menacing shapes that tried to reach her through the infernal din. Some of the waves broke a long way off, while others, apparently unaware of their own strength, slid towards her, fierce and supple like serpents, and came right up to her feet.

There was one moment when a wave rushing towards her seemed to be so high that Angélique, terrified, clung to the cliff-side as if she were trying to get inside it.

The wave broke only a few paces from where she stood, with a horrible gurgle, the cold water swirling around her ankles, then around her knees. The next time this happened, it would reach to her waist.

As the water ran back, it sucked at her so powerfully that she fell over. She clung on where she could.

Another wave might well wash her right out to sea.

"I shall have to go up higher again," she told herself.

But how was she going to find her way out of this trap? She began to run to escape the threat of the

414

pursuing waves as they raced after her. Her feet kept on twisting over on the stones. There were some places where the beach became dangerously narrow.

Now, she only had one idea: she must get back on to the heath. The tide must be coming in; if she remained down below she would surely be drowned. The young woman clutched at the cliff-side to try to find a hold, but at this part of the beach the rocks were almost overhanging. Nevertheless, by struggling on, she came upon a small bay where ships must have occasionally moored and there she found, towards the back, the precipitous path used by the fishermen. She clambered up it, tearing herself out of the infernal pit.

As soon as she reached the top of the cliff she fell, exhausted, full length on the ground, and lay there for quite a time with her cheek on the damp ground.

This journey through the depths of the night must be rather like what one felt after death. It was a slow and agonizing search through an unknown land.

Osman Faraji, the great black magician, would explain it thus: "You are not always aware of dying. Some people find themselves, without quite knowing why, deep in an unfamiliar darkness where they have to find their way, guided only by the light they have acquired during their earthly life. If they have gained nothing from life on earth, then they will again get lost in the world of the spirits. . . . That is what the wise men of the East say. . . ."

Osman Faraji! He was standing before her, as black as the night, and was saying:

"Why did you flee from that man? Your fate and his must cross time and time again."

Angélique raised herself on her hands and said between her teeth: "If his fate and mine are to cross again, that means that I shall be successful!"

It could not have been pure chance that had brought Rescator to these shores. It must surely signify something. It meant that Angélique was destined to link up with him again. She would reach him in spite of the wind and the sea and the night. A hoarse voice whis-

415

pered in her ear, fantastically near: "In my house you will be able to sleep. In my house there are roses growing." And once again the magic of Crete came back to her, and the curious power of that inexplicable moment when she had stood by the masked man who had just bought her, and had felt that this was where she wanted to stay forever.

Angélique stood up again.

She noticed that it had stopped raining. But the wind seemed to be blowing harder than ever. It seized her by the shoulders and hurled her forwards, then barred her way, and she had to fight to move forward foot by foot, as if a strong man were holding her back.

When she had gone a few steps she began to fear that she had set off in the wrong direction. She spun round again like a puppet, and this time found she could not tell where she was at all. But eventually the sky cleared, and suddenly she was able to see the red flame of the Lantern Tower shining towards the east. Looking the other way she could see a smaller light that came from the tip of the Island of Ré.

She was no longer in limbo. She saw the plain stretching around her, windswept but free from mist. She could walk faster now. When she got near the bay where she had seen the ship at anchor that same afternoon, she slowed her steps.

"Supposing it has sailed?" the thought suddenly occurred to her.

Then she felt reassured again. So many dramatic things had happened during the past few hours—she had fetched the children, they had all been arrested, Baumier had interrogated her, then Desgrez—that she had the impression that several days had passed. When she had last seen them, the pirates had been busy caulking the ship. This meant that it had needed some repairs, and they could hardly have decided to set sail in the middle of the night with that storm coming on.

And, in any case, there was a brighter light suspended above her like a huge star. She realized that it must be the *Gouldsboro*'s main masthead lantern.

In spite of their wish not to be noticed, the pirates

still preferred to be able to see, for the bay in which they had taken refuge was scarcely a sheltered one, and the ship, lying at anchor, tugged hard at its moorings. She could make out the silhouettes of the watch as they stood on deck trying to shelter from the weather as well as they could.

Angélique stood expectantly for a long while on the cliff edge.

No one could see her watching the ship as it lay, just visible through the shadows, a mere ghostly shape, with its sails furled close to the masts so as not to let the wind catch them. It lay there, bobbing up and down in the seething foam as if at the bottom of a witch's cauldron.

A short while back, when she had left La Rochelle, it had seemed an easy matter to set off and run here as if to a haven where her only possible salvation lay.

Now the madness of her action became apparent to her. She was voluntarily putting herself at the mercy of this lawless man, making her presence known to this dangerous pirate whom she had offended and flouted, and she was going to ask for his help in a difficult and thankless task! Just so many foolhardy actions that could only lead to disaster. On the other hand disaster lay behind her as well, and she had already gone too far to turn back.

Lower down she could see the flickering of another light; the sailors had lighted a fire in the shelter of one of the caves that riddled the cliff-side, and some of them were sitting by it on watch.

The same hand that had helped Angélique to her feet a while back—perhaps it was the hand of Osman Faraji—now urged her on. "Go on, go on! There is your destiny. . . ."

Hope and fear both filled her heart. But she did not hesitate a moment more, and when she had found the path along which she had seen the fishermen from St Maurice come with their animals that same afternoon, she began to clamber down it.

She reached the shore. Her feet sank into the silvery shingle that was made from millions of crushed shells. She stepped forward with great difficulty.

Hands seized her around the waist and grasped her wrists from behind, forcing her to stop. Someone held a dark-lantern in front of her face. The pirates were talking to one another in their strange tongue, standing around her. She could just make out their brown faces beneath their blood-red headscarves, their cruel teeth and the flashing gold ear-rings that some of them wore.

Then she called out, hurling the name before her as if it were a shield:

"Rescator! I want to see your captain, Monsieur le Rescator!"

CHAPTER 43

SHE STOOD there waiting, leaning on the wooden handrail, while the ship tossed violently up and down.

The watchers on the shore had made her get into a caïque which the waves threw about like a nutshell, and she did not know where she had found strength of will enough to manage to clamber up the rope ladder as it flapped about on the side of the ship, in the inky darkness of the night.

She had reached her objective. They had put her in a kind of glory-hole that must have been the cook's quarters, for it reeked of frying.

Two men guarded her. Another one came in, wearing a mask under a felt hat with sopping-wet feathers on it, and straightaway she recognized his squat form.

"Are you Captain Jason?"

In her mind's eye she could see him standing once again on the deck of the King's galley, *La Royale*. Captain Jason, the dread Rescator's first mate, had on that occasion been dictating his orders to the Duc de Vivonne, the Grand Admiral of Louis XIV's fleet. Today he was perhaps a little less grand, but he still had the air of assurance which is the hallmark of a man acting on behalf of a master who always has his way in the end.

"Where have you seen me before?" he asked her after a moment's surprise. From behind his mask he looked with puzzled eyes upon this soaking-wet, dishevelled, ragged, peasant-woman.

"I saw you in Candia," she replied. He looked astonished, and it seemed quite clear that he did not recognize her.

"Tell your chief, Monsieur le Rescator, that I am the woman he bought for thirty-five thousand piastres in Candia, four years ago, the night of the fire."

Captain Jason was literally dumbfounded. He looked at her again quite transfixed, then swore several times in English. He told the two sailors in their own language to keep a closer watch on the prisoner, showing an unaccustomed degree of agitation for a man of such an apparently placid disposition. Then he dashed off, and she heard him running along the deck.

The two men thought it necessary to hold Angélique's arms, and yet she would have found it extremely difficult to escape, for now she was right in the lion's den.

She was not exactly reassured by the effect her statement had had. To judge by what she had seen, they had not forgotten her. She was going to have to meet the master face to face. Memories thronged back to her. She could see Candia all lighted up by the brilliant blue rocket. She could see the whole place on fire, and the pirate d'Escrainville's ship, the *Hermes*, gleaming and incandescent like a solid gold monument, with her masts crumpling in a shower of sparks. She saw Rescator running through the clouds of smoke as they poured from his xebec, and the old wizard Savary dancing up and down on the prow of the Greek ship as he shouted: "It's Greek fire, it's Greek fire!"

She drew her sopping-wet cloak about her; it weighed like a ton of lead on her exhausted shoulders. In Crete, on the night of the fire, two destinies had crossed, then, like a flash, had parted again. Now, at a different point of the globe, contrary to all logic and in opposition to the will of the gods themselves, they were about to meet. Was this what Osman Faraji had read in the stars as he stood at the top of the Mozagreb Tower?

There were footsteps outside. Angélique straightened up in readiness to meet *him*, but it was Captain Jason.

He beckoned, and the men dragged Angélique off. She crossed a narrow gangway, and felt the wind tearing at her again and heard the near-by roar of the waters. They made her climb up a short wooden companion-way. There were red lights shining through the poop-castle windows; in their stillness they reminded one of the diabolical glow that shone from the retorts of that servant of the Devil, the alchemist. Why should such a thought have occurred to Angélique as they pushed her inside and the wind hit them in a final mighty squall? Perhaps she had remembered that the man who ruled this ship was known as the wizard of the Mediterranean.

At first she felt as if she were standing on a bed of moss and flowers, and as the door closed behind her she became aware of the pleasant warmth of the room. In fact the heat almost overcame her after her exposure to the icy rain and battering wind. She had to summon every vestige of her strength so as not to faint.

Then gradually she began to feel better. Her eyes were adjusting themselves to the unaccustomed brightness. A man stood before her and his presence seemed to fill the entire room.

It was the man she had seen on the heath, it was Rescator. She had forgotten how tall he was: his head touched the low ceiling. She had forgotten how strongly built he was. When she had known him before he had never seemed so hard, but that was probably because she had seen him walking nonchalant and cat-like amongst the eastern folk in Crete. He looked to her as if he had been hewn out of a kind of black rock; he was all angles, with his square shoulders, his waist drawn in by a broad leather and steel belt, from which hung the holsters of two elaborately worked pistols, and his long, taut thigh-muscles standing out beneath his close-fitting leather breeches. Standing there with his feet apart to counteract the ship's roll, with his hands clasped behind his back, he had the cold, observant and suspicious look of a judge.

420

He seemed to be waiting for something. How different he was from that Prince of the Mediterranean.

She only recognized his narrow head which was covered by a satin square, tied in the Spanish manner, and his inhuman leather mask with its shaped nose-piece, that almost covered his lips, the black curly beard, and the two diamonds of his eyes glittering through the slits in the mask, with their indefinable and unendurable gaze.

This was Rescator all right, but a harsher magic had taken hold of him now, the magic of the Atlantic. For many a long year now she had been dreaming of this enigmatic person as if he was a hero from *The Thousand and One Nights*; now she realized that the man who stood before her was no more than a pirate.

There was a Venetian lantern on either side of him, all red and gold, and these in no way helped to make him seem more reassuring.

The ship gave a heave and Angélique stumbled; she fell against the door and had to cling to it. It was then that the black statue came to life. His shoulders shook spasmodically, and he threw his head back.

She realized that Rescator was laughing in his usual stifled way that always ended in a fit of coughing.

"The French girl from Crete!" he exclaimed.

Angélique reacted exactly as she had before to his harsh yet muffled voice which sometimes seemed almost grating. It tore at her painfully. There was something unbearable about it, and yet she always felt she must hear it again!

She saw him walk towards her with measured tread, and glimpsed a row of white teeth gleaming through his black beard.

She was far more disconcerted by his laughter than she would have been if he had shouted at her.

"Why are you laughing?" she asked in a toneless voice.

"I am wondering what extraordinary set of circumstances could have turned you, the most beautiful captive of the Mediterranean, for whom I paid a fortune, into this woman I now see standing before me, for whom I would not give a hundred piastres!"

He could hardly have been more contemptuous or more insulting. Angélique realized just what she must look like: she was soaked to the skin, her plain working woman's clothes were torn, her face was all mottled beneath her black sopping-wet headsquare, and she probably had wisps of hair sticking to her forehead. She must have looked like a witch.

Instead of upsetting her, this new thrust suddenly stirred her to action.

"Oh, indeed," she said sarcastically. "Perhaps it's just as well. Now you won't feel bad any more, if you ever did, about the trick I played on you in Crete."

She leaned against the door, her head low and her eyes shining, and looked at the masked man; it was then that she realized she was not frightened of him. She had made up her mind that he must save them because he and his ship were their last chance. So she had to get round him, she had to touch him somehow. But he seemed to be out of all proportion to life, and quite inaccessible. He seemed far away and not quite real, an apparition that stood half-way between a nightmare and a waking dream. The impression she had was only reinforced by their silence.

She wished he would speak again. The sound of his voice helped her to escape his mesmerizing gaze.

"You're a pretty cool one to be reminding me of your exploits," he said at last. "How did you know where to find me?"

"I caught sight of you a while back, when I was walking across the heath. You were standing on the edge of the cliff, and taking a look at the town."

She saw him shudder as if he had been struck.

"There's no doubt that fate is making fun of us," he shouted. "So you went right by and I never saw you?"

"I hid straightaway in the bushes."

"I should have spotted you all the same," he said almost in anger. "What is this special power you have that makes you capable of appearing and disappearing like this, of slipping through my very fingers?"

He began to pace up and down and she found this preferable to his immobile hostility.

"I shall have a thing or two to say to my men about the way they keep watch," he went on. "Have you told anybody of what you saw, or about our being here?"

She shook her head.

"That's just as well for you. . . . So you caught sight of me, then you ran off again, and now here you are, almost on midnight, back again to see me. Why? What have you come for?"

"I've come to ask you to take some people on board who have got to get away from La Rochelle by tomorrow morning at the latest. I want you to take them to the American islands."

"Passengers?"

Rescator stood still again. In spite of the ceaseless rocking of the ship he moved about with an extraordinary grace. Angélique remembered his figure as lithe as a circus performer's as he stood on the bowsprit of his xebec, and cast the anchor which was to save the slaveship *Dauphine*. As she stood there in the ship's saloon, one part of her mind went on calling up visions torn from her past. It was like an underground search whose object was ever this black and enthralling man. Just as he had done before, when for the first time he had walked towards her in the slave market, straightaway he claimed her entire strength and attention.

Ellis, the young Greek slave-girl, had whispered her confidences into Angélique's ears; now they fluttered around in her memory like strange butterflies: "He seduces every woman . . . every woman. . . . Not one can escape his power, my friend. . . ." And yet there was her own voice, answering him clearly:

"Yes, passengers. They will pay you well."

"They must be very odd passengers indeed to need a pirate ship so badly! They must be trying to flee La Rochelle."

"Flee is the right word, my lord. They are families who belong to the Reformed religion. The French King

423

won't have any more heretics in his kingdom; so those who refuse to accept conversion have no alternative but to leave their country or go to prison. But the coastline is carefully guarded and it is very difficult to get out of the harbour without anyone knowing."

"Families, did you say? Will there be women too?"

"Yes, yes. . . ."

"And children?"

"Yes . . . mainly children," Angélique said in a tone-less voice.

She could see them dancing around the palm-tree, with their pink cheeks and starry eyes. It was as if she had heard the rhythmic beat of their little wooden shoes rising and falling behind the howling gale.

But she also knew that her admission would almost certainly mean that her request would be refused. No captain of a freighter would willingly take passengers at all, and, as for women and children, they only caused endless palavers. They fuss, they die, and the men on board fight over the women.

Angélique had lived long enough in a port to be aware of the enormity of her request. How could anyone dare mention Carrère the lawyer and his eleven children to a pirate? She felt her assurance ebbing away.

"The proposition gets more and more attractive!" was Rescator's summing up.

His tone was one of mocking irony.

"And how many are there in this dull consignment of psalm-singers, with which you propose to fill my holds?"

"Round about . . . forty people."

She had made at least ten of them vanish into thin air.

"Huh! . . . You're joking, my beauty. What's more, I reckon that this will be the last we hear of this particular little jest. But all the same, there is still something that intrigues me. How comes it that the Marquise du Plessis-Bellière—for that was indeed the name you bore when I bought you—how comes it that she is suddenly so interested in a handful of pasty-faced heretics? Could it be that you have relatives amongst them? Or a lover? Although I must admit it seems hardly likely for an erstwhile concubine. Or perhaps, who knows, possibly you have selected another husband from amongst the heretics, for I seem to remember you had the reputation of getting through them at an alarming rate."

His nasty irony seemed to her to be a cover for a deep-seated curiosity.

"Nothing like that," she said.

"Well what is it then?"

How could she explain to him that she just wanted to save her Protestant friends? It would be an indefensible action in the eyes of a pirate who must surely be an unbeliever, and who might even be Spanish, as she had heard tell. If he was, he would possess the double disadvantage of being not only irreligious but intolerant like the rest of his race.

There was something rather disquieting about the way he seemed to know everything about her life. Admittedly an astonishing amount of information is passed around the Mediterranean, and often very accurately too.

He refused to let the matter rest, and said in an ironical tone:

"So you've married one of the hertics, have you? You certainly have fallen pretty low."

Angélique shook her head. She was untouched by these sarcastic probing remarks, although they could scarcely have been said to have been uttered without malice. Her sole concern was at seeing her plan turning out so badly. What arguments could she bring to bear to convince him?

"There are shipowners amongst them who have got part of their fortune in the American islands. They will be able to make it up to you if you save their lives."

He brushed her proposal aside with a single gesture.

"They would be unable to offer me anything to make up for the nuisance of their presence on my ship. I've no room on board for forty extra people; I am not even sure whether I shall be able to leave the habour and cross the straits without being stopped by that damned royal fleet, and in any case the American islands are not on my route."

425

"If you don't take them, they will all be thrown into prison tomorrow."

"Ah well! That happens to a lot of people, I believe, in this charming kingdom.'

"You must not speak so lightly of these things, Monsieur," she said, clasping the hands together, quite carried away with despair. "If only you knew what it was like to be in prison!"

"And who ever said that I didn't?"

It occurred to her that he must indeed have known what it was to have been condemned and rejected by his own land, to be living as he was, outside the law. What could he have done to have deserved this?

"So many people go to prison nowadays. There are so many lives lost! What does it matter if there are a few more or a few less! You can still be free at sea and in a few of the virgin lands of America. But you have not answered the question I asked you. Why is the Marquise du Plessis concerning herself with these heretics?"

His tone brooked no argument.

"Because I don't want them to go to prison."

"So it's out of sheer high-mindedness, is it? I find it hard to believe of a woman of your character."

"Well believe what you like!" she said in exasperation. "I cannot give you any other reason. I just want you to save them!"

This day of all days she had taken stock of the gulf which divides women's hearts from men's. After Baumier, there had been Desgrez, then Rescator! There these men had stood, full of their own power, strong and indifferent to women's tears or the sobs of wounded children. Baumier would have delighted in it. Desgrez had only agreed to spare them because he was still in love with her. But now that Rescator no longer found her attractive, he was going to do absolutely nothing for her!

In any case he had turned away from her and had gone and sat down on a vast oriental divan. His posture revealed utter perplexity, not to say discouragement. He stretched out his long high-booted legs in front of him.

"I must admit that women can be pretty mad, but you undoubtedly have overstepped the expected limits by a

426

very long way. Let us take a look back: the last time I met you, you left me, by way of a reminder, with my xebec on fire and with a debt of thirty-five thousand piastres.

"Four years later, it seems perfectly natural to you to come and see me, without in the least fearing any reprisals, and ask me to take you on board my ship with forty fugitive friends of yours. You must admit that this is a somewhat outrageous demand."

With a flick of his finger he upturned an hour-glass that stood beside him on an occasional table. The instrument was held in place by its heavy bronze pedestal and did not rock about as the ship pitched and tossed. The sand began to run through it, and cascaded down in a thin, swift and shining trickle. Angélique stared at it. The hours were passing, the night would soon be gone.

"Well, that's enough of that," said Rescator. "This transport business of yours doesn't interest me. Neither do you for that matter. But since you have been imprudent enough to place yourself in the hands of a master who has a hundred times over sworn to make you pay dearly for all the trouble you have given him, I shall nevertheless keep you here on board. . . . In America women are less highly valued than on the Mediterranean shores, but perhaps if I sell you I might get something back of what I paid for you."

Although it was so hot in the room, Angélique felt an icy chill strike at her very heart. Her soaking clothes were sticking to her skin, but up to this moment the discussion had been so lively that she had not even noticed the fact.

Now she found she was shivering.

"I am not in the least impressed by your cynicism," she said, and her voice grew husky, "I know . . ."

She was shaken by a fit of coughing that cut short what she was about to say. It put the finishing touch to this picture of a defeated woman. She already looked ghastly enough, and now appeared to be sickly and out of breath into the bargain.

With this pitiable sight before his eyes, she certainly had not expected him to do what he did next. He walked

427

back towards her and put a hand beneath her chin to make her lift her head.

"That's what happens to you when you go running about the open countryside after a pirate on a stormy night," he murmured.

The mask came right up close to her face, and the contact with the hard, cold leather and those burning, paralysing eyes shining from it, was an astonishing sensation.

"What would you say to a cup of coffee, Madame?"

Angélique suddenly felt better.

"Coffee? Real Turkish coffee?"

"Yes, real Turkish coffee, like the coffee in Crete. . . . But first take off that sopping-wet cloak. You have drenched my carpets."

She looked down at the soft oriental carpeting which gave the impression of walking amid moss and flowers as you trod on it. It was in a pitiful condition all around where she had stood.

The pirate took her cloak off her, and hurled it into a corner as if it had been a bit of rag. He lifted his own cloak from the back of a chair.

"You already owe me one, the one you took away quite unscrupulously after I had put it over your shoulders on the night of the fire. Ah! Nobody has ever managed to make Rescator look as ridiculous as you did then. . . ."

And just as she had done on that eastern night, she felt the heat of two hands on her shoulders and the warm sweet-smelling folds of a sumptuous velvet cloak about her. He drew her towards the divan, still holding her up against him. When she was sitting down he walked over to one end of the room and she heard a bell ring outside. The storm must be easing now, for the ship was moving much less violently. The sand was still trickling through the handsome timer, and sparkled under the somewhat orange light cast by the Venetian lanterns.

Angélique was escaping from the real world about her. She was in the wizard's den.

A barefooted Moor, wearing a short burnous over his red sailor's trousers, came in answer to the bell. With the

428

supple gestures common to all his race, he knelt down and pushed a low table towards the divan, and laid upon it a Cordovan leather coffer glittering with silver. The two sides of the box let down to form two trays upon which everything necessary for the preparation and drinking of coffee was firmly fixed. There was a silver samovar, the heavy gold tray with two china cups on it, a small china jug filled with water with a chip of ice floating on it, and a saucer of candy sugar.

The Moor went out and returned almost immediately with a samovar full of boiling water. He prepared the beverage with great care and without spilling a single drop; Angélique was overwhelmed by its smell and felt herself filled with an almost childish pleasure. Her cheeks were suffused with colour once more as she held out her hand towards the silver goblet that surrounded the china cup. As he sat close by her with an enigmatic expression, Rescator watched her pick up the tiny cup between two fingers, according to the Moslem rite, and pour one drop of iced water into it to settle the grounds then raise it to her lips.

"It's obvious that you have been a guest in Mulai Ismail's harem," he said. "What mastery! Anyone would think you were a Moslem. Although you have fallen so low, you have still kept some good habits that make it possible to recognize you."

The Moor had vanished. Angélique put her cup down into the stand which prevented it from being tipped over, and the pirate leant over to pour her some more. As he did so he noticed smears of blood on the cup.

"Why is there blood on this cup? Are you hurt?"

Angélique showed him her lacerated palms.

"I never felt a thing. It happened some time ago on the cliff rocks. . . . Goodness, I've seen worse on the tracks of the Riff."

"When you escaped? Do you know that you are the only Christian slave ever to have managed that! For a long time I thought your bones must be whitening on some desert track."

With staring eyes Angélique was reliving that long, hard odyssey.

"Is it true that you went to Meknès to try to find me?"

"Yes, I did. And in any case it wasn't hard: you had left a trail of slaughter in your wake. . . ."

The young woman shut her sad eyes; horror was written in every line of her face.

With an ambiguous smile the masked man whispered:

"Wherever the French girl with the green eyes passes, nothing remains save wreckage and dead bodies."

"Did those words become a new proverb throughout the Mediterranean?"

"Yes, something like that."

Angélique looked down at the blood on her own hands.

"There were ten of you who got away from Meknès. How many reached Ceuta?"

"Two."

"Who was the other?"

"Colin Paturel, the king of the slaves."

Once again there seemed to be a feeling of tension around them, an indefinable sense of danger. In an attempt to dispel it, she forced herself to look once more into his eyes.

"You and I have many memories in common," she said very softly.

He gave his sudden hoarse laugh that frightened her.

"Far too many; more than you think."

Suddenly he handed her his handkerchief.

"Wipe your hands."

She obeyed him automatically. Hitherto her hands had felt numbed, but now she became aware of the pain, and the salt stung her wounds.

"I tried to walk along the beach so as not to get lost."

She told him about how once again she had thought her last hour was at hand as the tide rose around her. She wondered by what miracle she had been able to clamber up the steep cliff.

"I seemed to be struggling in the very throes of death. But I reached you in the end. . . ."

As Angélique uttered these last words, her voice took on a gentle dreamy note. She was quite unaware of how she sounded as she said: "I reached you in the end."

All she could see in the mysterious light was the black, still face, and there all her dreams ended.

430

For one instant Angélique thought that she was going to throw herself at the pirate's broad chest, and hide her face in the folds of his velvet jerkin.

It was not black velvet as she had thought, but a very dark green like the moss that grows on trees. She looked at it and thought: "How good it would feel!"

Rescator stretched out one hand. He touched her cheek, then her chin; it seemed strange that he, whose piercing eyes never missed anything, should have these gentle gestures like a blind man trying to make out features he could not see.

Then slowly, with one finger, he untied the wretched little headscarf which still held Angélique's hair imprisoned, and cast it aside. Her hair, sticky and darkened by the sea water, tumbled down over her shoulders. The wisps of white stood out in brilliant streaks. Angélique would have liked to hide them.

"Why were you so keen to see me again?" Rescator asked her.

"Because you are the only person on earth who can save us."

"Oh, so you are still thinking about those folk?" he cried, manifestly put out.

"How could I forget them?"

Once again her eyes strayed to the sand as it trickled through the hour-glass. At regular intervals the instrument would turn over, and Rescator would fix it with an automatic gesture.

Honorine was asleep back in the town, in the big kitchen bed, but her childish serenity, which Angélique had so often watched over with delight, was disturbed now. She was restless and cried out in her sleep. Once again threatening faces had loomed around her and she had sensed her mother's fear. Abigail was watching over her and praying for Angélique with clasped hands. Perhaps Laurier was awake too as he used to be when he slept in the garret. He was listening to his father's distraught footsteps as he paced around the next room.

"How could I forget them? Just now you told me that whenever I went I left nothing but desolation behind me. . . . You might at least help me to save these few."

431

"These men, these Huguenots, what do they do? I mean what are their professions?"

He questioned her sharply, fidgeting with his beard. She had seen this man master of himself under so many circumstances, that when she saw his perplexity now, she realized that for some inexplicable reason she had won. Her face lighted up.

"Don't you look so triumphant," he told her. "Even if it looks as if I am giving in to you, about all this, you are not the one who will come out on top."

"What do I care! If you agree to take them on board your ship and to help them escape from imprisonment and death, what does all the rest matter? I would pay for that a hundred times over!"

"What words! You are unaware of the price I intend to make you pay. You are almost naïve in your confidence in me. I am a buccaneer who sails on the high seas and it must surely occur to you that my job consists not in saving human lives but rather in ending them. Women like you shouldn't meddle in anything except love."

"But it is a question of love."

"Oh! don't start philosophizing," he shouted, "or I shall simply be taking you on board my vessel in order to drown you when we get out to sea! You were far less talkative in Crete and much more charming! Now answer my question. What sort of people are they that you are asking me to take on board, apart from the pious women—they are the worst sort—and the squalling brats?"

"There is one of the most important shipowners of La Rochelle amongst them, Monsieur Manigault, and traders who know all about the sea. Over in the islands they have got . . ."

"Are there any artisans among them?"

"There's a carpenter and his apprentice."

"Ah, that's better. . . ."

"There's a baker and two fishermen. They used to be seamen once and they organized a small fleet to keep the La Rochelle fish-market stocked. There is Monsieur Merlot as well; he is a paper-manufacturer, and Maître Jonas the clockmaker. . . ."

"All useless!"

432

"Maître Carrère the lawyer."

"Worse and worse."

"There's a doctor. . . ."

"Oh! That's enough. . . . Let's get them on board since you want to save them, *all of them*. I have never known a more overbearing woman. And now, my dear Marquise, are you able to submit a plan to me that will enable this whim of yours to succeed? I have no intention whatever of hanging around any longer in this crabhole where I have been silly enough to go and stick myself. I was reckoning on leaving at dawn. I can wait for the next tide, at the very latest, and that is at the end of the morning."

"We shall meet you on the cliff-top," she said as she stood up, looking radiant. "I'm off to fetch them."

CHAPTER 44

ANSELM CAMISOT, who had spent part of the night keeping himself warm with hope and visions of paradise, standing in the postern at the corner of the ramparts, jumped as he heard a soft scratching noise against the door leading down from the ramparts. His hopes were beginning to fade like the flame of a burnt-out candle, for the night was coming to an end and dawn was about to break.

He found it hard to stir his big body, stiff as it was with the cold.

"Is that you, Dame Angélique?" he whispered.

"It is."

He turned the creaking key and Angélique slipped in through the open doorway.

"You have been a long time," the soldier sighed.

As he spoke, the steely vice of a powerful arm gripped him round the throat, while someone pummelled him in the back, making him lose his balance. A violent blow, neatly applied just at the right spot on the back of his neck sent him off to the land of dreams to pursue his idyllic projects.

"Poor man," Angélique murmured looking at Anselm

Camisot's long bony body gagged and tied up just like a sausage.

"We couldn't have done anything else, Madame," said the sailor, who had come with her.

There were three of them whom Rescator had picked from his crew.

"I have told them that they are not to let you out of their sight for a single moment, and that they are to bring you back here dead or alive. . . ."

When they reached the Bernes' courtyard Maître Gabriel was standing there with a lantern that lit up Angélique in her night-coloured cloak all braided with silver, and the three villainous-looking sailors standing around her, who looked as though they should have had knives between their teeth. The men laid down a colossal package on the flagstones, which the merchant recognized as the watchman of the Lantern Tower well and properly tied up.

"Listen," said Angélique very rapidly, "I have found a ship's captain who has agreed to take us all away. He is sailing in a few hours' time. These men are to accompany me while I go to warn the others. We must lend them some clothes to make them less conspicuous. It's a foreign corsair vessel. . . ."

This was how she discreetly disguised the true identity of a pirate who was answerable to no sovereign nor to any flag other than the famous skull-and-crossbones.

"The ship is lying at anchor in a small bay near the hamlet of St Maurice. That's where we are all to meet. We must each make our own way there. As for you and your family, Maître Berne, I suggest that you leave the town by the little gate through the ramparts. It will be open for another three hours because they don't change the watch until seven in the morning. If we hurry about it, other families can get out that way too."

Maître Gabriel was sensible enough not to argue. Abigail had told him what was happening. He knew that, since all would be up if they did nothing, they now had to grasp at any opportunity to get out of the town and put to sea as soon as possible. The night was still dark and misty, but the new day, the day that would see their flight or their incarceration in His Majesty's prisons,

434

had already begun, and its hours were ticking away slowly but surely. He pointed towards the cellar where they were to lock up the tied soldier, then he went upstairs after Angélique saying that he must waken his children and his aunt.

He would worry later about this strange bodyguard of hers, with their tanned faces and scruffy fur hats, and he would wait until later to wonder what could have happened to her to transform her into this unfamiliar woman who was giving him orders.

He was obscurely aware of the fact that this was so grave a moment that Angélique could no longer feign a personality that was not her own. This dawn of crisis was showing her once again in her true colours: she had taken them all in hand with all the coolness and utter selflessness of the great nobles of olden times, and the only way that he could prevent her sacrifices from being in vain was to obey her promptly in all things.

Abigail had prepared a scanty parcel of things for each of them as she had been instructed. Pastor Beaucaire was there already with his nephew, and little Nathaniel was still asleep, lying beside Honorine.

"I shall get them up and dress them," Abigail said without further questions. "Meanwhile, Angélique, you go and get yourself warmed up in that tub of hot water that I got ready for you there, and then put on some dry clothes."

"You're a good fairy," Angélique said, and without wasting a single second she closed the kitchen door. The boiling hot water was standing ready in a small cubicle, and she slipped in beside the tub the young woman had prepared for her and let Rescator's cloak fall to the ground, followed by her soaking torn clothes. A shudder of well-being ran through her body as she plunged into the water. Had it not been for this respite she might well have collapsed in spite of the kind of exaltation that had been keeping her going. And she was not through yet.

She could hear Abigail gently waking the children and talking to them of a marvellous land full of flowers and good things, to which they were about to set forth. The girl was managing to draw them gently from their sleep without communicating any of the anxiety that hung over these last minutes, where every second weighed like lead.

"How I admire you, Abigail," Angélique said from behind the door. "You are so calm."

"That's the least I can do for you, Angélique," she replied, as tranquil and alert as when she was spinning her woollen thread of an evening. "But where have you come from? You seem quite transfigured."

"I do?"

All of a sudden Angélique caught sight of herself standing there naked in front of the tall polished-steel mirror that leant against the wall. Normally she only used to glance in it absentmindedly to arrange her hair and her head-dress.

In an instant she took in her white body, the very picture of healthy womanhood with its neat waist, high breasts, long back and graceful legs, "the most beautiful legs in Versailles" with the round red scar that Colin Paturel had had to make to save her from the snake in the Riff.

How she had forgotten her body!

She could hear that insulting voice in her ears again:

"A woman for whom I wouldn't give a hundred piastres today."

She gave a casual mocking shrug.

"What *does* he want? Ah, well, so much the worse for him!"

She slipped on the clean shift that Abigail had placed close by on a stool, shook out her hair defiantly, and once again it fell in a sunny halo about her head.

"How can I explain it? He's my worst enemy ... and my best friend. ..."

He had behaved both unkindly and cynically towards her. He had jeered at her; he had treated the unbearable anguish she felt as a hunted woman as if it did not matter. "And now, my dear Marquise, have you a plan for carrying out your little whim?" As if the wish to save several human lives was merely a somewhat misplaced fantasy! But he *had* agreed to take them on board. He, a pirate, was taking this risk which many a self-confident captain, even with a well-stocked ship and a guaranteed escort, would have refused to take upon himself.

436

So what did his cynical words add up to? Angélique had stopped being touchy about such things long ago. She had had to cringe often enough beneath the blows of fortune. Now she had come to realize that actions alone counted. Even he had been surprised at this, and, as she had left the ship, he had commented on it.

"My dear, I know you have a dreadfully bad temper, and yet you never took offence at the ungallant way I treated you."

"There are so many far more important things in life. If you save us all, you can treat me just as you like."

"I shall, don't worry."

Angélique had to overcome her temptation to laugh. Abigail would never have understood.

But the thing that was keeping her going was this complicity that two opponents in a battle feel when they realize that they are equally matched, and are confident that they can always fight back.

She came out from her little nook still tying up the aglets of her skirt, twisted her hair up to keep it in place beneath her clean bonnet and wrapped herself up in a cloak.

"I'm ready."

"We're all ready."

Angélique cast a glance at the fine old clock. Half an hour had not elapsed since she had got back to the house. Time seemed to have become elastic.

Honorine, all bundled up in her double skirts and hooded cloak, was asleep on her feet. Angélique picked her up all drowsy as she was and held her in her arms. Rebecca made a move to empty the water from the tub, but Angélique stopped her. Time was short. Then she wanted to tidy the house. All they had time to do was to put out the smouldering embers in the hearth. It was Maître Gabriel who trampled on them.

They went downstairs in complete silence with a single candle to light their way. Each one of them clasped a basket or a bundle in his hand. When they reached the courtyard Maître Gabriel asked what they should do with the soldier who still lay tied up in the cellar. They might well be abandoning him to a cruel fate if they left him alone in the house, since no one was ever going to come back to it. Besides, Anselm Camisot had helped them once. There was a moment's indecision. Angélique pointed out that even if no one became aware of their flight beforehand, the military would be coming that very evening to the Bernes' house to arrest the whole family. They would find the house deserted would search it and would set the poor soldier free, if he had not already managed to struggle out of his bonds.

"All right then. Let's be off," said Maître Berne.

The night was already less dark as they crossed the threshold and closed the heavy door behind them. They reached the foot of the ramparts through the thick mist and soon were standing by the little door. Angélique handed Honorine to Abigail.

"I can't come with you now, I must go and warn all the others. You go to the hamlet of St Maurice. As soon as we are all gathered together there we can set off for our place of embarkation. The fishermen in the hamlet must not be told a thing about our plans. Say you have come for the funeral of one of your brethren somewhere on the heath."

"You know the way, don't you, Martial?" Maître Gabriel said to his son. "You show the women the way to the hamlet. I must stay with Dame Angélique."

"No," she protested.

"Do you think I'm going to leave you alone with these foreign toughs?"

Angélique managed to persuade him to accompany his family. As for herself, she feared nothing; she felt as if nothing could harm her and she wanted to see as many of them as possible outside the city walls. That would be the first stage.

"We must have a man like you to reassure the people I am going to send to the hamlet. They will be leaving their homes without proper time to reflect, but it is quite possible that when they get to the meeting-place they may take fright."

When at last the group that consisted of the Berne family, the two pastors and Abigail carrying Honorine had vanished, Angélique quickly reverted to her role of the faithful sheep-dog once more and began to collect her flock together.

438

The Mercelot couple and their daughter Bertille were very calm and did not ask for any explanations. Angélique told them that they must either leave immediately or find themselves in prison before nightfall. They got dressed. Maître Mercelot tucked the book he had been working on for many a long year beneath his arm. It was written on paper bearing the King's arms as a watermark, and was called *The Annals of the Torments and Sacrifices inflicted upon the People of La Rochelle during these Years of Grace, 1663 to 1676.*

It was his life's work. . . .

Bertille asked what they were to do about the things they had already stowed away in the *Sainte-Marie.*

"We shall see to that later."

The Mercelot family walked off towards the ramparts while Angélique went to wake up the clockmaker.

A little later she rang the Carrère's bell. This briefless barrister, saddled with his eleven children, was the most useless of all those Rescator was taking on board, yet he was the one who made the greatest fuss.

They had to go away now? But why? Because they were going to be arrested? How did she know? She'd been told? Who had told her? Had she any proof? Angélique refused to discuss the matter and went from room to room waking everybody up. Luckily the children had been wonderfully well brought up by their mother and did not cause the slightest trouble. The older ones dressed their younger brothers and sisters and they each tidied up their own pesonal belongings. Within a few minutes everyone was ready, the rooms were tidy and the beds made. Maître Carrère was still standing in his nightshirt and nightcap, asking for proof that they were indeed to be arrested, while his brood stood in the hall completely ready to go.

"We want to leave, Father," said the oldest boy, a lad of sixteen. "We don't want to go to prison. The clockmaker's sons were taken off and they never came back."

"Come on, Matthew," his wife said. "Since we have already decided that we must go, let's go. It makes no difference whether we do it now or later!"

She handed the latest arrival to Angélique so that she could pass the husband's breeches to him. She

439

dressed him as if he had been a child, taking him to task the while, then pushed him outside without further ado.

"My snuff-box," he wailed.

"Here it is."

The mist was becoming more transparent, as the dawn flooded it with light. The city was beginning to wake up.

Angélique with the three sailors close on her heels helped the lawyer's family to find the little doorway.

As she watched them disappearing one after the other along the cliff path, hidden from sight in the mist, Angélique felt an inexpressible sense of relief.

There were still three or four other families to warn, and the Manigaults, who lived somewhat farther away.

The bells pealed out and almost at the same moment they heard the Angelus chime, muffled in the mist. You could feel a sudden stir in the place and craftsmen began to take down the shutters from their workshops.

As she made her way yet again towards the steps leading up to the ramparts with the baker's family, Angélique suddenly stood rooted to the spot.

There were people running about on top of the ramparts; men's voices could be heard shouting to one another. Then something scarlet bent over to look down into the alleyway.

The mist had not yet cleared sufficiently for the soldier to notice the fugitives, and they withdrew quietly and discussed what they should do, standing beneath a neighbouring porch.

"The other guard has come on duty and they have discovered Camisot's disappearance," Angélique explained. "They must think he has gone off through the postern gate. But in any case they will close it or post a guard at it now."

Visibility was constantly improving now and there seemed to be many red uniforms up there.

"Red jackets, that means dragoons," the baker muttered. "Why this show of force?"

"Perhaps it is because the Dutch fleet is just arriving. . . ."

The baker's wife began to cry.

"Just our luck! If only you had hurried a bit more,

Anthony, we'd have been able to go through there. Now how are we going to get out?"

"But you can go out through one of the city gates," Angélique reassured her. "They will just about be opening them now." She explained that they would not attract any more attention than all the other workmen and merchants who went each day at dawn to La Pallice or the Island of Ré.

"The town is not besieged and the police are giving us one day's respite. You can go through with your baskets of bread. If anyone asks you any questions, just give them your names."

She had managed to make them feel better and they went off, mingling with the first people on the streets. Maître Romain had provided himself with a good stock of bread from his last baking. At least they would have that to eat until they had to start eating ship's biscuits.

That morning, those who saw him go by must have thought of him as nothing more than one of La Rochelle's bakers walking amongst his fellow-citizens, and yet as he stepped towards the St Nicholas Gate with a heavy heart, he already felt an exile.

Their departure had been so hasty that it had helped to dull the pain, and he still felt that it was all not quite real.

Angélique found the Manigault family sitting round the table in their sumptuous dining-room, with Siriki busy pouring steaming hot chocolate into their cups. She was at least as breathless as she had been the day she had come to their house for the first time to fetch Monsieur de Bardagne.

For the sun was already high in the sky; it looked as if it was going to be a wonderful day after the stormy night. The last wisps of mist were vanishing, the town was seething with life, the night was no longer there to help them, and now they had to face danger in the full glare of the daylight.

Angélique explained the recent events to them as briefly as she could. Their plans had been discovered; their arrest was imminent; there was only one way out now: they must set sail there and then in a ship that had agreed to take them on board and which was lying at

441

anchor not far from La Rochelle. Their difficulty would be to get out of the town without being noticed. The Manigault family were very well known and almost certainly there would be orders out concerning them. They would have to leave the town in separate groups under false names. Once outside, they were all to meet in the hamlet of St Maurice.

Monsieur Manigault, his wife, his four daughters, his son-in-law and his young son sat there absolutely thunderstruck, their cups poised in mid-air.

"But the girl is quite mad!" Madame Manigault exclaimed. "What! Is she suggesting that we should leave for the American islands just as we are, and leave everything behind? . . ."

"What is the name of this ship you are talking about?" the shipowner asked, looking very serious.

"The . . . *Gouldsboro*."

"Never heard of it. Are these men with you part of her crew?"

"Yes."

"If their appearance is anything to go by, it can hardly be a very respectable ship and is in fact probably highly questionable."

"You are right there, but the captain has agreed to take us all aboard, and we could well be regarded as a questionable lot. So much the worse for you if you prefer the appearance of Baumier's guards to theirs, for they will be coming tonight to arrest you and throw you into prison."

"But one can get out of prison, and I have influence, you know."

"No, Monsieur Manigault, this time you won't get out."

One of the sailors who had accompanied her touched her arm.

"Madame," he said, speaking in French but with a heavy accent, "the boss told us not to hang around in the town after daybreak. We must hurry."

Angélique was enraged by this family, calmly seated before their expensive china, nibbling at delicacies as if unaware that their whole world was about to crash about their ears. If Manigault was left behind, they
442

would be without a skilled wholesale merchant who owned most of the wealth of the little community. She had promised Rescator that he would be paid. And above all there was Jeremy, the lovely golden-headed child who looked like Charles-Henri.

"Well, so much the worse for you and your son," she said, "but I wish I had not risked my life to come and warn you. If I had not had to run all the way here, I would already be in the hamlet of St Maurice. Our chances grow smaller with every minute that passes. The fact is that you had decided to go but you didn't want to. You were sitting there waiting for the miracle that would allow you to keep everything: your position, your money, your beliefs, and your city. You who spend so much time pondering the Scriptures, you should have remembered that the Jews, when they were prisoners in Egypt, were told to celebrate the Passover standing up, with girded loins and a stick in their hands, all ready to go, so that they could take flight as soon as the signal was given. . . . Before Pharaoh had time to change his mind."

Manigault stared at her. He went very red, then the colour drained from his face.

"Before Pharaoh has time to change his mind," he murmured. "I had a dream last night. All the threats that loom over us took shape. I knew that a colossal serpent was coming to strangle me and my family. It came closer and closer and its head was the head of . . ."

He broke off, stood up, still staring before him, and after carefully wiping his mouth with his table-napkin, laid it down beside his half-drunk cup of chocolate.

"Come on, Jeremy," he said, taking his son by the hand.

"Where are you going?" cried Madame Manigault.

"We are going to embark."

"You're surely not going to believe the mad tales this woman has told you?"

"I do believe them because I know they are true. For several days now I have suspected that someone has been betraying us." He turned to the old Negro. "Go and fetch a coat and hat for Jeremy and me."

"Bring some gold with you," Angélique whispered, "all you can get into your pockets.'

Madame Manigault began to wail:

"But he's out of his mind! What is to become of us, my daughters?"

The young girls looked from their mother to their father.

The young officer, the shipowner's son-in-law, was the next to rise.

"Come on, Jenny," he said taking hold of his young wife by the shoulders.

He looked at her gravely and tenderly.

"We must leave."

"Just as we are? Right now?" she stammered, all agog.

She had already been anxious about the proposed voyage on the *Saint-Marie*, for she was expecting a child.

"But you have a small bag of things ready for our departure. Bring that along now. The time has come."

"I have a bag of things too," Manigault said. "It is rather large but Siriki can carry it."

"Siriki must not come with us," Angélique warned in a low voice. "He is far too well known throughout the city as your Negro servant. They could get their hands on you just like that, for you are being very closely watched."

"But I can't possibly abandon Siriki!" the shipowner protested. "Who would look after him?"

"Your partner, Monsieur Thomas, who is going to look after your affairs after your departure and contact you when you have reached the islands."

"My partner ... he is the one who has betrayed us. Now I am sure of it. I suppose he hopes that everything will fall into his hands."

And he added darkly:

"The serpent whom I saw in my dream had his head."

Once in the hall he cast one bitter glance at the heavy carved ceiling, the glazed doors that opened on to paths running down the big garden. Others led to the courtyard with its inevitable palm-tree.

Manigault took Jeremy's hand again and crossed the

444

courtyard. One of the sailors walked behind him carrying his bag.

"But where are you going?" wailed Madame Manigault. "I'm not nearly ready. I've still got to wrap up two or three of the most precious of our dishes."

"Wrap up whatever you like, Sarah, and get there as soon as you can, but for once in your life, hurry," the shipowner replied philosophically.

The young couple came behind him, then one of his daughters caught him up at a run just as they reached the street.

"Father, I want to come with you too."

"Come on then, Deborah!"

She was his favourite after Jeremy.

He found the courage to cross the threshold and walk along the street without once turning his head.

As they neared the St Nicholas Gate, their group, consisting of the shipowner, his son, his daughter, his son-in-law with his young wife, Angélique and the three sailors from the *Gouldsboro,* decided to split up. The officer Joseph Garret with Jenny and Jeremy went through first, then Monsieur Manigault with the three sailors. Their spokesman from the pirate ship answered all the questions they were asked in English. It so happened that the guard did not know a single word of this language, but he did know that an English ship had come in the day before and was lying at anchor in the port. So with a knowing look he let them through taking them for strangers out on a walk. They seemed to have two pretty local girls with them, Angélique and Deborah. As soon as they had permission to go through they ran off gaily through the gate without bothering to give anyone their names and occupations, and the soldiers did not like to call them back.

The party wandered off, and the guards watched them go with friendly smiles.

"That was the most difficult bit," Angélique whispered to Monsieur Manigault. "They didn't recognize you."

They walked in single file for greater speed. The wind was keen. Clouds were scudding across the sky, dazzlingly white and teased out like feathers. The sea still looked dark after the stormy night.

"What about Mother? And my sisters?"

"Either they will come or they won't. . . ."

They could see far away across the plain, and already the huts in St Maurice were visible.

They were greeted by exclamations.

"You at last!"

The fugitives came out of the houses where they had been waiting, sitting by the fires. Maître Berne had found it hard to keep them all patient and confident. They had been told there was a ship. Where was it? Each one of them was beginning to discover that he had left behind some essential object.

"Raphael's shawl!"

"My purse! It had five *livres* in it! . . ."

Thanks to the influence that Gabriel Berne had over them all, they had nevertheless remained calm. The children had been given some cold milk to drink, then Pastor Beaucaire had begun to intone some prayers, and the inhabitants of the hamlet, looking as villainous as if they were all wreckers, had joined in with them, for in spite of the name their village bore, they were all Huguenots.

The roll was called, and the only people missing were Madame Manigault and her two elder daughters.

"We must go on nevertheless," said the sailor from the *Gouldsboro* who spoke such odd French and answered to the name of Nicholas Perrot, "the tide is beginning to come in. And we can always begin to embark some of the passengers. One of my pals can stay here to wait for the latecomers and show them where to go."

They gathered up all the children who by now were fully awake, absolutely delighted by this unexpected outing, and busy organizing games.

They were waiting in family groups, and were just going to set off along the path the French-speaking sailor indicated, when they were all transfixed by a shout from across the heath. A sort of orange flame was bounding from copse to copse at a giddy speed. It was the old Negro Siriki, running like an antelope in his amaranth satin livery with its gold braiding.

"My master! Where is my master?"

"Ah! My son!" Manigault cried, clasping the elderly slave to his heart. Siriki had removed his high-heeled shoes so that he could run faster. His woolly head bobbed this way and that and his golden ear-rings shook.

"You not go without me, Master! Or me die."

"What did the guards say when they let you through?" Angélique asked.

"The guards? ... Say nothing. Me run, me run!" And he burst out laughing, revealing a row of white teeth.

"We must hurry!" Angélique advised them, pushing them all towards the path the sailor was pointing to.

She was holding Honorine's hand again. The first groups of people were beginning to cross the heath. There was a broad, flat open space between them and the first of the sand-dunes. The plain seemed to stretch out vast and bare. You could still see La Rochelle with its towers and its ramparts very clearly. Angélique did not feel at all easy. Siriki the slave must have attracted attention, running like that after his master.

"Come on," she said to the Manigaults. "Now we mustn't lose a single moment."

But they were trailing behind. The shipowner was clearly torn between the temptation to free himself once and for all from this shrew who had led him such a dance for the last twenty-five years, and the worry of abandoning his wife and two of his daughters.

"She'll always get by," he told himself. "She would even be capable of dealing with my dishonest partner! But if they throw that unfortunate Sarah, who is so keen on good food, into prison, she would waste away."

A sound of wheels came to them, bumping along the path, and Madame Manigault appeared puffing and blowing and covered in sweat, harnessed like a donkey to the shafts of a small cart into which she had piled carpets, rolls of brocade, clothes, caskets and above all the famous Bernard Palissy china which seemed to mean more to her than anything else. Her two daughters and a servant-girl were walking by the wheels and pushing.

Exhaustion had not defeated her, far from it. For as

447

soon as she caught sight of her husband, she hurled abuse and reproaches at him.

"You take a turn now," she said, handing the shafts to her son-in-law. "And you, you lazy wretch," she shouted to Siriki, "couldn't you have waited for me instead of flying off like a swallow?"

"Do you mean to tell me you came through the St Nicholas Gate with all this paraphernalia?" Manigault asked her, red with anger.

"So what?"

"And nobody said anything?"

"Yes, they did. They certainly did. But I soon shut them up, the coarse brutes. It would have been a fine thing if they had stopped me coming through!"

"Well, since you are here now, get along and hurry up," Angélique said in exasperation.

The fat woman must have created a terrible stir as she went through the St Nicholas Gate. There she was, on foot, pulling a cart just like a gypsy woman! In her anger she would have been quite capable of shouting that she was going away, that she was putting to sea and never coming back again, that she had had enough of La Rochelle and all its inhabitants! For indeed this was one of her favourite themes, since she had come from Angoulême, and had never got used to living in a port.

Angélique was carrying Honorine along the cliff path. From time to time she would turn round and shout, "Hurry up!" to the Manigaults who were walking behind dragging their cart and arguing the while.

Then she would look towards the town. La Rochelle lay there, like a dazzling white crown with a thousand fleurons. But the thing that was worrying Angélique above all was a little speck of dust that seemed to spring from the foot of the ramparts near the St Nicholas gateway.

She walked on faster, and caught up with the baker and his family.

"Those Manigaults have got a cart, they have," the baker's wife said resentfully. "If I'd known that, I'd have filled my wheelbarrow, I would."

"The Manigaults could well be the end of us all with their cart," Angélique replied dryly.

448

She ran on ahead past the long line of fugitives until she reached Maître Berne.

"Look over there, what can you see?" she puffed. The merchant, who was walking very fast holding Laurier by the hand, looked the way she was pointing.

"I can see a cloud of dust thrown up by a band of men on horseback."

He watched them for a moment then added:

"Men in red uniforms. They are coming straight for us."

The sailor who was leading the way had also spotted them. He began to run, snatching up two children under each arm, calling to everyone to hurry and take cover behind the dunes.

Angélique turned back to call to the Manigaults:

"Hurry! Leave your cart. The dragoons are after us!"

They were all running now, stumbling along the sandy path. The women's skirts kept catching in the gorse bushes. Now they could hear the dull thudding of galloping hooves.

"Quick! Quick! For the love of God, leave that cart!"

Manigault tore his wife from the shafts which she tried to grab again. He pushed her along and she kept shouting and shrieking. Angélique had grasped Jeremy with one hand. He at least was as nimble as an elf, and was running, convulsed with fear, as fast as his little legs would carry him. Joseph was supporting Jenny, who was quite out of breath. She wailed: "I can't go on."

As soon as they spotted the fugitives, the dragoons let out a savage yell. They had been told that there were some Huguenots trying to escape in this direction. So far this had only been hearsay, but now they could see them scattering and running towards the sea like so many frantic hares. Hell! This brood of heretics was not going to escape from them, from the "Jackbooted Missionaries"! They had run their bayonets through plenty of others in Poitou and in the Cévennes.

They drew their swords and their Lieutenant sounded the charge.

As they went by, one of their swords struck the Manigaults' abandoned cart and tipped it over. Lengths

449

of material were sent flying, and the beautiful china was smashed into a thousand iridescent pieces.

Angélique heard the death charge.

"This time, we are well and truly done for," she told herself.

This mad race reminded her of her dash for safety with Colin Paturel beneath the walls of Ceuta. Jeremy stumbled, and she dragged him along by the arm, managing to get him on his feet again. Honorine was letting out deafening shrieks of laughter right into her ear. She was quite delighted by all the rushing about. Angélique reached the sand-dunes and threw herself down behind the first available cover.

What a precious shelter it was!

The dragoons were now only a few paces away, almost on top of the wailing groups of stragglers, the two Manigault couples.

All of a sudden, just as she thought the deadly swords were about to strike her and the children, Angélique heard the crackle of several musket shots. Her nose stung with the smell of gunpowder, and clouds of bitter smoke rose up around them.

She heard Nicholas Perrot saying to the fugitives:

"Don't stay there, move back carefully towards the edge of the cliff and we'll get you down on to the beach."

A hand lighted on her shoulder. It was the sunburnt sailor who had stayed close to her, bringing up the rear, no doubt having been ordered to do so by the French-speaking sailor. She had been wondering in vain since the previous day where he came from, and, strangely enough, it suddenly occurred to her at that moment.

"I've got it. He's a Maltese!"

What an incongruous thought for a time like this! He made signs to her to get back too, keeping close to the ground.

Angélique raised her head above the grass just high enough to see the horses, who were standing neighing in the smoke, and some of the men in their red uniforms who had been hit and were lying on the ground.

The dragoons had been brought up short by the running fire from the muskets, hidden behind the low dunes, and had retreated to regroup a bit further off.

Angélique's heart felt as if it would burst. So he had thought of that too, he had realized that they might well be followed! He had stationed an armed pirate behind every hillock to defend the beach where they were to embark. She began to move back, urging the children to do likewise. Now when she looked round, she could see the ship in the little bay, with its sails set. She was very close now to the path that led down to the beach.

"Dame Angélique, you aren't hurt, are you?"

Maître Berne slid down beside her. He was holding a pistol in his hand.

"Why did you stay behind?"

"Because of those gawks there," she replied with a somewhat bitter gesture towards the Manigaults.

They were crawling heavily along, slowed down by the slithering sands.

"I'm wounded! I'm wounded!" Madame Manigault wailed.

Perhaps she was. She collapsed completely, letting her full weight fall on her husband who dragged her along and tried to hold her up, swearing like a corsair.

"Where is Laurier?" Angélique asked.

"The sailors have begun to take the children on board in the longboat. But I was worried about you, so I climbed up again. God be praised, the captain of this ship thought about giving us armed protection! He's down there on the beach organizing the embarkation."

"He's there, is he?" Angélique repeated. "Isn't he an extraordinary man!"

"He is indeed! From what I could see he seemed to be wearing a mask and to be in charge of a crew of buccaneers. . . ."

There was another burst of gunfire. The newly-grouped dragoons had tried to charge them again, and once again they had been brought up short.

But some of them had leapt off their horses and were beginning to crawl towards the dunes to fight their adversaries hand to hand.

The sailors from the *Gouldsboro* who were acting as

lookouts on the cliff-top were trying to withdraw to rejoin their fellows.

As long as they remained on the top of the cliff, shielding the Protestant refugees as they embarked, the dragoons would find it hard to move any closer. But as soon as the last of the pirate musketeers had reached the shore, the King's soldiers would be able to massacre them all from the rocks above.

Some of them were already trying to creep round the sides, and the approaches to the beach were peopled with red uniforms. Fortunately the dragoons had very few muskets with them, being armed mainly with pistols and swords. Their Lieutenant gave an order and two of the most desperate-looking tried to leap straight down on to the beach. But they broke their legs as they landed, and any keenness to follow suit that their comrades might have felt was quickly chilled by their shrieks of pain.

The only way down the cliff was still being most carefully guarded and protected by the *Gouldsboro*'s crew. Other sailors were handing the women and children down, and piling them into the longboat, which was then rowed at top speed towards the ship as it lay at anchor. Sailors thronged the yards, hands on the shrouds, ready to let out the sails and to trim them in preparation for getting under way.

Maître Gabriel and Angélique, who was clutching Honorine, slowly made their way towards the edge. The Maltese had taken charge of Jeremy. The musketeers from the pirate ship were gradually moving back too, crawling like everyone else.

The Lieutenant's voice rang out again.

"Don't worry, dragoons; when these bandits get down to the bottom, we can pepper them to our heart's content. You, over there, fire on the longboat."

He was addressing the soldiers who had managed to reach the edge of the cliff away on the right. They were too far away to aim at the refugees or the pirates as long as they remained beneath the overhanging rocks. But as soon as the longboat came out from under cover and headed for the ship, in spite of the distance that separated them it became a possible target for their better shots.

Bullets began to ricochet around the small boat and shrieks of terror rose from the group of women and children huddled together in it. Pastor Beaucaire stood up in spite of the protests from the crew of pirates. His old, broken voice rang out above the hubbub as he began a psalm.

The sailors in the longboat were trying to get out of the danger zone as fast as they could. This time they managed it without anyone on board being wounded. But they still had to return to fetch those who remained on land.

The dragoons would have time to correct their range.

"We've got them! Keep going! We shan't miss next time," bawled the Lieutenant, "get everything ready now!"

They could hear the clicking of gun-hammers and the scraping of cleaning rods inside the barrels, then the sound of powder-horns tapping against the chains.

A few of the soldiers, emboldened by the thought of victory, rushed foward to try to stop those who were still standing at the top of the cliff.

Angélique had just begun to descend the steep path when the heavy moustachioed face of one of the dragoons, brandishing his sword above his head, loomed up in front of her. Gabriel Berne threw himself between her and the soldier and fired; the man fell to the ground. But he had struck Maître Gabriel in one last convulsive movement. The merchant staggered, badly cut about the shoulder and temple and would have fallen right over the edge of the cliff if Angélique had not clutched at him and held him back at the last moment. She was weighed down by the huge, almost lifeless body, and she herself began to slip towards the chasm, shouting for help. One of the sailors from the *Gouldsboro,* his face blackened with gunpowder, came to her rescue. He supported the wounded man and helped them both to get down the goat path as well as they could.

A voice from the beach shouted an order in English. It must have been to tell them to withdraw, for the last of
453

the pirates still in action behind the dunes leapt up like a band of monkeys and slipped down the cliff-side to join up again with their companions.

"It's all clear now; now it's our turn," the dragoons shouted, rallying once more.

Angélique reached the beach in a veritable landslide trying to support Maître Berne's bleeding head.

"He's dead! He's dead! Oh, my poor friend."

Two hands gripped her round the waist and forced her to turn round. It was Rescator.

"Ah! Here you are! Last, of course. You're quite mad, you know." She could have sworn that he was laughing beneath his mask. He seemed to be unaware that this was a moment of tragedy, that he himself and all his crew were in a desperate position there on the shore, with their longboat unable to come any closer, with the dragoons standing above them. He seemed oblivious of the fact that many of his men were lying on the beach wounded, staining the pebbles with their blood, and that their last hour was surely at hand. . . .

He laughed and clutched her to him. It was as if he was in love with the slave-girl he had bought in Crete, as if his passion had only become all the more demanding after the affronts and hardships it had already cost him.

But a new and terrible thought had taken hold of Angélique and she struggled and looked about her frantically.

"Honorine! Where is Honorine? I let go of her to support Maître Berne when he was wounded. I'm sure she must still be up there. . . ."

She wanted to dash up the path again, but he held her back in a vice-like grip.

"Where are you off to? Stay here, you idiot! They are just about to fire the cannons. You'd be blown to smithereens."

All along one side of the *Gouldsboro*, the fake port-holes were opening to reveal the black muzzles of ten cannons. Angélique let out a shrill cry like a wounded animal. She had just spotted Honorine's green bonnet up on top of the cliff. The little girl was dangerously near the edge. There was too much noise for them to hear her cries, but it was fairly clear that she was shrieking in fear, a tiny dot standing out against the blue sky, between the approaching dragoons and the precipice at the bottom of which she could see her mother.

"My daughter!" Angélique shouted, beside herself. "My child. Save her! They will kill her! She'll fall!"

The inexorable hand of steel stopped her from rushing up.

"Let go of me, that's my daughter, my child, Honorine! Honorine!"

"Stay where you are. Don't move. I'll get her."

Paralysed with fear, she saw Rescator rush forward, and clamber up the steep path with extraordinary agility. One of the King's soldiers had just reached the child. Rescator fired straight into his face, and snatched up the baby in his other hand as if she had been a mere parcel. The soldier reeled forward and fell, toppling on to the rocks a few paces from where Angélique stood, with a dull thud.

At the same moment the *Gouldsboro*'s cannons went off with a thunderous roar.

Angélique thought that Rescator and Honorine must have been buried completely and utterly beneath the shower of earth and stones that rained down. Then bit by bit she began to make out the pirate's silhouette as he stepped out of the cloud of dust and smoke.

"Here's your daughter! Now hang on to her."

"Is she hurt?"

"I don't think so. And now let's get aboard."

The longboat had made the most of the confusion caused amongst the dragoons by the hail of cannonballs, and had reached the shore once more. The last of the sailors from the *Gouldsboro* placed Maître Berne's inert body in the longboat along with one of their own men who had also been wounded. They bundled Angélique unceremoniously after them and she was advised to lie down on the bottom.

"We shall not be able to make another trip," she heard Rescator say. "We must get everyone in this time."

He himself was the last to embark, with a theatrical gesture towards the white walls of the Charentes cliffs.

"Farewell, inhospitable shores!" he said.

As he stood there at the very end of the longboat, he was a perfect target.

Fortunately the soldiers had been demoralized by this direct attack; many of them had been killed, and they no longer thought of firing. Their Lieutenant was seriously wounded. The Adjutant was yelling contradictory orders, which the fugitives could hear booming through the megaphone.

"One of you take a horse and gallop full speed to the fort of St Louis to ask them for help.

"We must warn the fleet in St-Martin-de-Ré and the Great Fortress at Sablonceaux Point. . . .

"We mustn't let that bandit get away. . . ."

The *Gouldsboro* was weighing anchor with a harsh grinding of chains. At the same moment the top-men released the sails and the wind filled them straightaway. Captain Jason, standing on the bridge, was shouting his orders as calmly as if they were setting sail peacefully from some quayside beneath the idle gaze of passers-by. The top-men were running nimbly along the yards and up and down the masts, tightening a rope here and a sheet there.

The ship was all atremble, ready to plunge forward.

Meanwhile the longboat, greatly overloaded with the remaining fugitives, had rowed round the ship. Now it was sheltered from any attack and they were able to proceed to the embarkation of its passengers without hindrance, as the *Gouldsboro* began to edge out of the bay on each wave.

A sailor took Honorine in his arms to carry her up the rope ladder. He had a black patch over one eye and reminded Angélique of the unprepossessing face of Coriano, d'Escrainville's mate. The mere sight of him was enough to subdue Honorine, who clasped him round the neck and never uttered a sound while he lifted her aloft up the rope ladder.

Getting the two wounded men on board proved to be a much more hazardous operation.

At last they were on deck, and, after a great deal of heaving on the block, the boat was raised and firmly lashed to the poop rail. All these different actions had been performed with exemplary calm and speed.

Angélique, feeling the firm deck beneath her feet, looked up.

The cliffs were already getting farther away, and all along the top they could see a red line of dragoons shaking their fists. The *Gouldsboro*, irresistibly driven on by the wind, was leaving her place of shelter and coming out into the Straits.

On their left lay La Rochelle. It looked very close, glittering in the sunshine above the water, with its broken but still majestic towers of St Nicholas, the Chain and the Lantern. The ship was heading towards the town.

CHAPTER 45

RESCATOR was the last to come up on the deck. In one glance he took in the whole situation. Nicholas Perrot, who was standing beside him, shook his head.

"There's a nor'-wester blowing. We're out of luck...."

"Yes, we are."

Even Angélique realized that the wind was driving them towards the town. Up on the bridge Captain Jason was roaring out orders to hoist some of the sails and to pay off others so as to turn the ship towards the La Palice channel.

A sailor came up to Rescator and handed him his telescope. The pirate looked for a moment as if he was going to remove his mask, then he thought better of it and cast a brief glance about him.

"Get the wounded and the passengers down into the hold! I don't want anyone on deck except the crew."

He raised his telescope and made a rapid assessment of the *Gouldsboro*'s position and the efforts she was making to get away in spite of the unfavourable wind.

"No, not you," he said without turning round.

He must have sensed Angélique's movement as she meekly made to follow the group of men and women going below.

Rescator lowered his telescope, turned and gazed at

Angélique. She was standing there, her face still convulsed with fear, clutching her daughter in her arms. Honorine's head looked as if it was on fire, as her hair blew about in the wind.

"She's your daughter," he said in a dull voice. "Yes, she looks like you. Which of these Huguenots on board is her father?"

Was this a time to be asking such questions?

Angélique had the impression the town was getting nearer. You could almost make out the inquisitive faces on the ramparts and at the windows, where people had gathered to watch the desperate manœuvres of the unknown vessel.

"Her father?" she said, staring at him as if he had gone quite mad. "Well, I'll tell you. I was told it was Neptune, believe it or not. And now, wouldn't it be just as well for you to take a look at where we are? We are just about to pass within range of the Fort Louis guns. If the garrison have been warned, it will be the end of us."

"My dear, that is indeed all too likely."

The *Gouldsboro* had not managed to round Chef de Baie Point. She was still in sight of La Rochelle and of the battlements of her fortress where they could make out a suspicious amount of activity.

"You, come here!" Rescator suddenly decided, signalling to Angélique to follow him.

He strode along the deck, climbed the quarter-deck companion-way, then went up to the poop-deck.

"Madame, you must take shelter," said the man in the fur hat, Nicholas Perrot, and pointed to the door leading into Rescator's suite beneath the poop-deck.

He added with a smile:

"The boss is going to take the helm. We'll get out of this mess all right now."

His confidence in their leader's skill seemed to be shared by the entire crew. The men were completely calm, and some of the lascars, perched up amongst the topping lifts or in the rigging, were even joking, imitating the bantering manner of the man who had taught them to look philosophically on danger with a smile on their lips.

458

"But they are going to fire on us from Fort Louis," Angélique said in a toneless voice.

"They might well at that," Perrot answered in his quaint accent. No doubt he had been detailed to keep an eye on her, for he remained with her.

All of a sudden a volley of orders to the top-men rang out over their heads through Captain Jason's megaphone. Immediately there was a burst of activity in the forest of shrouds, masts and canvas above their heads, where human forms moved about with ape-like agility.

Just as the smoke began to rise from the lighted wicks above Fort Louis, every sail on the *Gouldsboro* was altered, and they turned into the wind. The ship came almost to a halt and seemed to be stopping right in line with the fortress and its cannons trained upon her.

"Cast anchor!"

Almost instantly they heard the noise of a chain being paid out and of the splash of the anchor as it hit the water.

Angélique looked with anxious incomprehension at her companion.

"Surely Rescator doesn't intend to parley?" she asked wildly.

He shook his heavy bear-like head.

"That's not in his line," he growled. "Reckon he probably thinks he's in the St Lawrence estuary, catching sperm-whales."

The anchor had reached the bottom. The ship lay motionless, turning very slightly with the wind.

As the order came to fire, all the guns of the fortress went off together with a thunderous roar. But at the same moment, the ship, pivoting on the fixed point of its anchor with a powerful wrench of the helm, went about gracefully.

A hail of cannon-balls fell a few inches from where she now lay, sweeping across the stretch of foaming water where three seconds earlier the *Gouldsboro* had lain broadside on.

The ship had dodged the blow like a skilful duellist.

But the danger had only been postponed. There would never be time to weigh anchor before a second round was fired.

No sooner had Angélique become aware of this than the megaphone boomed out:

"Jettison the anchor."

An anvil appeared as if by magic on the forecastle, and three powerful blows from the sledge-hammer severed the chain.

"Full sail ahead! Course north-east!"

The ship, freed from constraint, responded to the pull of the sails. They had proved too quick for the Fort Louis gunners, whose attempts to catch them in their sights were now a failure. Another broadside almost grazed the ship, which was violently shaken and splashed, but nevertheless continued on its way.

"Hip, hip, hurray!" shouted Nicholas Perrot.

The crew took up the shout as one man. Perrot remarked:

"Those swine would have had ten balls at least in our vitals if the boss had not been the finest helmsman alive on the ocean. We'd have been at the bottom by now, my oath! Did you see how he brought the helm hard over? But, Madame, do go into the saloon, for I'm afraid we are nothing like out of this hornets' nest yet. . . ."

"No, I want to stay out here till it's over, until I see the open sea before us."

"Well, just as you like, Madame. There are some people who prefer to look death straight in the face, and after all it may not be such a bad idea, because sometimes you frighten it away."

Angélique began to feel a certain fellow-feeling growing up between herself and this trapper from the distant St Lawrence. He did not seem to be so much of a godless and lawless buccaneer as his fur cap and blue-tattooed arms suggested.

After the acrobatic turn which had enabled the *Gouldsboro* to escape from the broadside from the fortress of St Louis, she seemed to give a snort like a horse in battle. The wind had veered very slightly towards the west and the ship was able to make good way. She put on full sail in order to make the most of this passing clemency of her enemy, the nor'-wester, and drew swiftly away from La Rochelle, even managing to get beyond Chef de Baie Point.

To reach the open sea they had still to cross the straits between the two islands. They could not go through the straits of Antioch which lay to the south between the islands of Ré, Aix and Oléron, because of the strong north-west wind. But to reach the Breton straits which were narrower and more sheltered and lay between the mainland and the northern side of the Island of Ré, they still had to traverse a narrow channel between La Palice and Sablonceaux Point.

This was what Rescator appeared to have decided to do. Captain Jason called out through his megaphone:

"Hi there, aloft! Take in the topsails. Let out the spritsail, the spanker, and the staysail."

With all but her lower sails furled, the *Gouldsboro* entered the channel between the two promontories. Angélique could hardly breathe. She knew how treacherous this shallow, rocky, hidden channel was which the sailors in the port always referred to with considerable respect. The strong wind was throwing choppy waves violently against the side of the ship, and could at any minute force them to swerve out of the narrow channel, beyond whose confines any big ship would run into disaster.

"Have you ever come through this channel before?" she asked her guard.

"No, we came in from the south."

"Then we should have a pilot. There is a fisherman called Le Gall amongst my friends who knows all the dangers of this strait."

"That's a good idea," exclaimed the man in the fur hat.

He ran off to hand on this information to the two captains.

Soon after Le Gall appeared on deck accompanied by one of the sailors. Angélique could not resist following them on to the poop-deck.

Rescator was at the helm and still had his mask on. His whole body seemed to be tensed, as if he were trying to feel where the difficult channel lay from the slightest tremors of the ship. He exchanged a few words with the navigator from La Rochelle, then handed the helm to him. Angélique stood as still as she could and so did Honorine. The little girl seemed to understand that the bridge was no place for a woman and a child when the ship was in danger, but she would not for the world have been anywhere else.

The *Gouldsboro* was progressing more smoothly now.

"And what if the Grand Sablonceaux fort fires on us," Le Gall said, looking towards the farthest headland of the Island of Ré where they could just make out the fortress.

"We shall just have to chance that!" Rescator answered. The atmosphere was growing hazier. A golden mist was rising with the heat of the day. A voice came from aloft.

"Warship on the bow. Coming towards us."

Captain Jason swore; he seemed very despondent.

"We're caught like rats in a trap."

"Well, we ought to have expected as much," Rescator said as if it were the most natural thing in the world. "Give orders to slow down."

"Why?"

"So that I have more time to think."

The warship, which they had not yet seen themselves, hove into view around Sablonceaux Point, and her billowing sails stood out white as chalk against the misty skyline. They had the wind on their stern and were moving swiftly towards the *Gouldsboro*. Rescator laid a hand on Florentin Le Gall's shoulder.

"Tell me, Monsieur, the tide is going out, isn't it? If these straits are difficult enough for us to navigate, won't they be even more dangerous for a bigger ship coming towards us?"

Angélique's eyes lighted on the hand that gripped the sailor's shoulder. It was muscular and yet aristocratic, with a heavy tooled-silver ring on the fourth finger of the left hand. She felt herself grow pale.

She knew this bare hand with its inflexible yet gentle grip. Where had she seen it before? Possibly it had been in Crete when he had taken off his gloves to lead her towards the sofa. But there was more to it than that. She felt as if it were infinitely familiar. She thought that

462

no doubt, as their last hour was approaching, her mind was becoming confused. She must be becoming aware of the destiny that Osman Faraji had read in the stars, now that death was near.

And yet at the same moment she also knew that they would not die, for it was Rescator who held their fates in his hands. This enigmatic man seemed to be in some way immune like the heroes of old. She trusted naïvely and wildly in him, and so far he had succeeded in his incredible endeavour, and she had not been proved wrong.

The pilot's face had brightened.

"Yes indeed!" he exclaimed. "You're quite right! They must be pretty keen to catch us to have thought of sailing down this fairway at this time of the day. They certainly must have one of our best pilots on board. But their position is somewhat . . . delicate."

"And we shall make it even more so. And we'll crown it all by using them as a shield in case the fortress decides to intervene. I'm going to force them to sail between the guns and us. . . . Full sail! Clear the decks for action!"

And as the top-men hurried about amongst the yards, the rest of the crew who had been waiting in the forecastle poured out of the hatches; boarding swords and hatchets were handed out to each man and they removed the canvas covers that hid the culverins against the forecastle rail.

Each man took up his position.

The buccaneers climbed up to the look-outs on the four masts clutching their muskets, and heaved up barrels of grenades after them, to throw on the enemy's decks when the moment came.

"Shall we sprinkle sand on the decks?" asked the mate.

"I don't think it will come to that," Rescator answered, his glass held to his eye. And he repeated ironically, smiling under his mask:

"Sand on the decks! Pooh!"

Angélique remembered this last resort in the Mediterranean. They would strew sand on the decks before a battle to stop the survivor's bare feet from slipping in the pools of blood.

"They will come to grief before they have even managed to cast a single grappling-iron in our direction," the pirate added with a shrug.

He seemed so sure of himself that the tension of these last moments in which the two ships moved inexorably closer was eased. Besides, it soon became obvious that the warship was in a bad way. She was finding it difficult to keep on course, what with the weight of her forty cannons and the fact that she had been unwise enough to hoist full sail. The waves were driving her towards the shore.

"And what if she fires at us?" Le Gall asked.

"What, in the position she's in! She's far too badly placed to line herself up to fire. And our bowsprit is facing her; she'd find the target too narrow."

So the *Gouldsboro* went on boldly. The warship was struggling harder and harder to keep afloat. Then suddenly she was irresistibly driven on to the rocks, where they saw her keel over and heard a dull crunching sound.

"She's aground!" Everyone on the *Gouldsboro's* poopdeck shouted with one accord.

The crew were waving their caps in the air for sheer joy.

"We must take care the same thing doesn't happen to us" Rescator warned them. "The sea has become dangerously shallow."

And he sent the depth-finders with their long poles down on to the forecastle.

As she went by, the pirate ship gave her helpless opponent a wide berth, and the crew of the warship hurled abuse at them.

"Shall we fire a broadside at them?" Captain Jason asked. "We are ideally placed."

"No! There's no point in leaving too many unpleasant memories behind. In any case, we're not through yet."

It occurred to Angélique also that other ships might well still appear and prevent them getting through. But they got out of the narrow waterway into the Breton Straits without further mishap.

Le Gall straightened up, his hands still on the helm.

"We're through the worst now, Monsieur, and I suggest that we should crowd on all sails and follow the northern coastline until we get to Grouin du Gou Point."

"Agreed."

The ship was handling more easily now. The straits formed a sheltered roadstead where the wind, now blowing less violently and from a better direction, became the fugitive's ally. Through the light mist they could just make out the curve of the mainland with its snowy line of salt-pans.

But St-Martin-de-Ré lay on their other side, and soon they perceived ships of the royal navy leaving the shore one by one like dream-shapes, and scudding towards them. The whole pack was after them.

They watched them coming towards them in a tense silence.

"So nearly there," Le Gall muttered. "We've just passed Arçay Point."

"Full speed ahead! The wind has veered slightly and is helping us."

"It's helping them too."

"But we've got a start."

With those few words he had taken the ship's bearings, weighed up their chances, and made it clear that they must seize every opportunity. The first ships of the fleet had appeared at first to be growing bigger with alarming rapidity, but now the distance separating them seemed to be keeping constant. The *Gouldsboro* was still out of range of their cannons.

Once again Rescator laid his hand on the man's shoulder.

"You get us out to sea, then on my oath, we shall get under the lee and not one of His Majesty's ships will ever be able to catch us up."

"We'll manage it, Monsieur," the pilot answered as if transfused with new life.

He kept his eyes firmly fixed on the route, seeking the slightest currents, the slightest of breezes, to give the greatest possible speed to the ship he was steering. How well he knew this area where he had so often cast his nets and drawn up his lobster-pots, singing as he worked

465

and looking lovingly about him at the clear golden lines of water, mainland and islands, which made up the familiar landscape of his life. His family had originally come from Brittany, but had lived in La Rochelle for the past three generations, which explained why he was a Huguenot and why he was as stubborn in his faith as a Catholic Breton is in his. He thought of how he was sailing over the places where he had always been so happy, trying to escape from them, and that his wife and children were in the hold of this pursued ship; and he thought what a terrible thing it would be to die here, sunk by the King of France's cannon-balls just beyond his own islands and his own city!

He was less frightened of death, which he had faced many a time during his life at sea, than of such a betrayal.

"Oh, Lord, see what we have to suffer in Your name! Why, oh why? ..."

Angélique glanced round. The pursuing sails were growing larger once more. The *Gouldsboro* seemed to be nearing the open sea, for the swell was increasing and the crests of the waves were topped with white foam. The coastline was broadening out and dwindling. The wind was now more biting and had a bitter taste to it. And the misty horizon seemed to stretch out endlessly before them. They were out at sea, but were they not too late?

She looked at Rescator and noticed that he was staring at her though the slits of his mask.

She thought he was going to tell her to go away, to tell her that she had no right to be up here on the poop-deck. She thought he was going to send her away with all the irony he knew so well how to use against her.

But he said nothing. She had the feeling that he was looking at her in this way because things were going badly and because he was upset. And she, who up to now had felt confident, began to feel frightened.

"Are we too late?" she asked.

Just then Honorine straightened up in her arms and said, joyously, pointing towards the horizon:

"Look at all the birds over there."

They were not birds. They were ships.

There they were, bobbing up one by one over the horizon, blocking the way out of the bay. Within a few moments they had become too numerous to count. The *Gouldsboro* was caught between them and the approaching royal fleet, like a wild animal at bay, surrounded, unable even to turn and face her adversaries assembled to finish her off.

The crew, gathered together prepared for battle, let out the same incredulous gasp of consternation. This was too much. They could fight, but they would never win, and every escape route was blocked. Almost immediately Rescator let out a shout and began to laugh. He laughed so much, nearly choking himself with coughing, that he was quite unable to speak.

"He's gone mad," Angélique told herself, petrified.

But eventually the pirate managed to get out:

"It's the Dutch!"

Immediately everyone's consternation was transformed into delirious joy.

"Hoist the English merchant flag on the main masthead," Captain Jason bellowed in English through his megaphone.

He repeated the order in French.

Up went the colours, flapping in the wind: the red cross over the white cross of St Andrew on a blue ground were hoisted on the mainmast, and the red ensign with the three-coloured flag similar to the one on the mainmast in one corner.

The heavy merchant fleet which had been battered in the recent storm entered the Breton Straits at a slow and solemn pace. First came two powerful five-masted three-decked men-of-war, with seventy-two cannons on board. Behind them were about four hundred merchant vessels of varying tonnage, but the smallest must have been over three hundred tons—a pot-bellied fleet, hedged about by twenty warships, smaller than the great three-deckers.

The *Gouldsboro* wove in and out between these ships with the agility of a hare in a dense forest. Within a few moments there were at least ten ships of the huge oncoming fleet lying between the *Gouldsboro* and her pursuers. His Majesty's officers were unable to fire a single shot from their cannons without running the serious risk of hitting one of the worthy merchants as they came in to dock in French waters.

So they simply had to give up any attempt to punish this audacious pirate who had had such a good laugh at their expense.

The fugitives, shut in between decks, realized from the new feel of the swell that they had reached the open sea. For many a long hour they had listened to every noise, they had followed the ship's creaking struggle against the contrary wind. They had all been hurled on top of one another when the ship had performed its manœuvre opposite Fort Louis, and had thought their last hour was at hand when they heard the dull explosions from the cannons. Then they had felt the ship sail haltingly along the narrow waterway. They had heard orders being shouted, and the decks being cleared for action, and bare feet running about over their heads. Then they had waited. For long hours they had prayed, or spoken the occasional words to break the terrible tension or to calm the children's anxiety.

And, as in the Ark, there was no window, and they could not know what was going on outside.

Then the ship had begun to pitch and toss with smooth regularity as if it was now at peace, and they felt the tension of the sails, now set without constraint, filled and stretched by the wind; and as it bounded freely along, the wooden hull trembled with joy like a thoroughbred whose reins have been loosed.

Then Le Gall appeared on the threshold, exhausted, and with a look in his blue Celtic eyes of both triumph and despair.

"We've given them the slip," he said. "We are out at sea, we are safe!"

It was then that all their hearts were torn.

"Farewell, city of La Rochelle, our city! Farewell, our kingdom! Farewell, our King!"

They fell to their knees, their eyes brimming with tears.

"We are still within sight of land," Rescator said, stepping towards Angélique and looking at her with a hard expression through the slits in his mask. "Aren't you going to look back once at the shore you are leaving for ever?"

Angélique shook her head.

"No," she replied.

"You don't show very much feeling for a woman, I must say. I'd do just as well not to get into your bad books. Is there nothing you regret back there? No memories, no one you love?"

"A dead child," she thought, "a small grave on the fringe of Nieul Forest, that's all."

"I've got my only precious possession here with me," she said, clasping Honorine to her heart. "She's my only treasure."

She had the impression, and indeed she felt the same every time Rescator's ingratiating curiosity manifested itself, taking her unawares, that she was being watched, and that the interest he showed in her in some way constituted a threat.

An immeasurable weariness came over her. She felt the oppressiveness of the hours she had just lived through, the oppressiveness of her whole life, at this moment when destiny was closing a door behind her that would never again be opened. Her stiff arms which for a very long time now had never let go of Honorine now suddenly began to hurt her.

"I'm tired," she said faintly. "Oh, so tired. I want to sleep. . . ."

Angélique was quite unaware of what had happened between the moment she spoke these words and the moment she woke up in the red glow of the sunset. All she could see was a ruby-red sun standing out against the dull silvery backcloth of the sea and sky like a huge lantern. It reached the horizon and dropped into the sea with disconcerting speed. For a brief moment it left a pink glow behind, more dazzling than the glow of dawn, then little by little this began to pale.

Angélique felt the ship's movements, that rhythmic, incessant rocking which carried her back several years to her Mediterranean days. In those days, even as a captive on board the *Hermes,* a feeling of immensity had made her heart swell and had overwhelmed her passionate, unsatisfied soul. There were the things she remembered after a voyage in which she had died a thousand deaths. It had been a time of enchantment, and she thought of it nostalgically.

Tonight she was discovering the sea again. Through the glass panes of the poop-castle the twilight was giving its brief fiery display, then came the solemn mystery of dusk before night fell.

She heard the splash of the waves off the hull, and, at intervals, the sharp smack of the sails and the singing of the wind in the shrouds.

She half sat up on the oriental divan where she had been laid and propped herself up on one arm, her head empty of all thought but keenly aware of an overwhelming sense of happiness. She was free.

Honorine slept in an attitude of surrender beside her, all pink and beaming. The colour in her full cheeks was further heightened by the setting sun.

Angélique leant over her with a gesture of infinite tenderness.

"You're coming with me, my love," she murmured. "Flesh of my flesh, heart of my heart. . . ."

The superhuman joy she felt was becoming almost painful. An old dream had long haunted her life, and now it was coming true.

She was putting to sea.

She filled her lungs with the salty air; her eyes clouded over, her head swam, and she threw it back in her nameless intoxication. An ecstatic smile played about her lips.

There, alone in the evening light, Angélique offered up to the Atlantic, as if to a long-lost sweetheart, the tense, ecstatic face of a woman in love. . . .